and has worked in the safari industry in Zimbabwe
for many years. She took up writing in 2010.
Sibanda and the Black Sparrow Hawk is her third novel.

Also by C. M. Elliott

Sibanda and the Rainbird
Sibanda and the Death's Head Moth

SIBANDA AND THE BLACK SPARROW HAWK

C. M. Elliott

First published in South Africa in 2017 by Jacana Media (PTY) Ltd
First published in the UK in 2021 by Constable

This edition published in 2021 by Constable

1 3 5 7 9 10 8 6 4 2

A CIP catalogue record for this book is available from the British Library.

ISBN: 978-1-47213-054-9

Typeset in Berkeley by Initial Typesetting Services, Edinburgh
Printed and bound in Great Britain by Clays Ltd, Elcograf S.p.A.

Papers used by Constable are from well-managed forests and other responsible sources.

Constable
An imprint of
Little, Brown Book Group
Carmelite House
50 Victoria Embankment
London EC4Y 0DZ

An Hachette UK Company
www.hachette.co.uk

www.littlebrown.co.uk

For Josh

Chapter 1

Detective Jabulani Sibanda stared through his office window. A coiled, sun-faded hose pipe attached to a dripping tap was delivering a spray to the winter yellow couch. All other self-respecting, broad-leafed species of grass had long since withered and dispersed their future generations to the biting winds. The earth was rock hard, the remaining roots doomed and the pools of water puddling on the bare patches would have been a waste of the precious commodity if not for the birds they attracted. Winter was a dry, unkind season in Matabeleland North and Gubu Police Station yard the very example underlining the gruelling adversity.

Sibanda watched as tiny sprays of water fountained from the hosepipe's cracks and punctures, much to the delight of flocks of thirsty waxbills, mannikins and finches – seedeaters who bathed and fluffed in the late morning sun. The detective kept a list of birds spotted through his window. Pen in hand, a scatter of papers was camouflage for the official paperwork he neglected. His rules were strict and there were only two: no craning of the neck allowed and the birds had to be seen from his desk within the frame of the window. So far, he'd identified forty-seven species. He was pretty certain number forty-eight, a blackcheeked waxbill, was about to be ticked off, he just needed another minute to identify the chestnut breast, belly and flanks and the white markings on the wings, when the phone rang.

'Detective Sibanda?'

'Yes.'

'It's Warden Edison Bango.'

'How is everything in the park? Poaching under control?'

'It's a tough battle. Cyanide poisoning has kept us busy. A hundred and forty-eight elephants dead so far and there'll be more,' he hesitated, 'I've got a patrol out along the railway line. The driver of the overnight goods train thought he'd hit an elephant. We were lucky he even noticed. The powerful diesels they're running nowadays swat the elephants without so much as a stutter, as though they're mosquitoes. We can pick up the tusks from a carcass months later on a random patrol.'

'How can I help?' Sibanda hated elephants being killed, even accidentally; wildlife was his passion.

'You can't help the elephant, it's dead; my guys have already radioed to say they found the remains, but they think they have found a body nearby.'

Sibanda turned away from the window and ferreted on his desk for a notepad. 'What do they mean "*think* they have found a body"?'

'That's what I asked. They recognise the shape, but the corpse is in a bad state.'

'Decayed?'

'No, fresh, from what they are saying.'

'Was it hit by a train or have scavengers been at it?'

'Neither, as far as I can make out, nothing has touched it.'

'So what's the problem?'

'It's got no skin on it.'

As soon as the phone call ended, Sibanda was on his feet. He grabbed his jacket – the sun might be out but it was powerless, subdued by icy gusts sweeping in from the south. Last night had been well below zero, the water in his birdbath had frozen.

He hurried down the narrow, grubby corridor leading to reception and strode into the assistant detective inspector's office. He wanted the keys to the most reliable vehicle on station, hard to prise from Chanza's grip, but he wasn't there. Sibanda cursed. What was the man up to? He had hardly pitched up at all this week. Technically, Chanza was Sibanda's subordinate, but he was also the nephew of the Officer-in-Charge, Stalin Mfumu, and enjoyed both his protection and the custodianship of the keys. Gubu station politics were a tangle of both blood and tribal loyalties; Sibanda kept his distance where he could.

'Sergeant Ncube,' he bellowed down the corridor with little

expectation of a response. The rotund sergeant would either have his well-fed face stuck in a pie or be tinkering with the wreck of a Land Rover, the station's only other means of transport.

The pair met in the station reception, although Sibanda barely recognised the sergeant; a school-green, hand-knitted balaclava covered most of his face leaving only watery eyes and a dripping nose exposed. A scarf and a bulky jacket took care of the rest of his large body.

'Is that you under all the padding, sergeant?'

'Yes, sir, I've been seeing to Miss Daisy. She doesn't do well in this cold weather.'

'Doesn't like the rain, expires in the heat and now battling with the cold, still as rubbish as ever.'

The sergeant began muttering in defence of the old Land Rover that had seen them capture several criminals. Without her the district would be mired in murderers, but as usual he kept those thoughts to himself. The detective was a man who understood neither women nor vehicles, in that order. Ncube's suggestions so far on both topics failed to educate him.

'Concentrate on the task in hand, Ncube. There's been a report of a body along the railway line, a few kilometres from Mpindo siding. Let's get going. We'll take Miss Daisy.'

'A long way on a rough road, sir, should I drive?' The detective was also well known as a reckless driver. Miss Daisy suffered agonies as a result of his insensitivity and the sergeant spent long hours rebuilding, re-tightening, applying rekin bandages, strips of cut inner tube, and generally placating the old Land Rover after an outing with Sibanda. Ncube preferred to drive when he could.

Sibanda gave the sergeant a look that brooked no dispute. Ncube was glad he had spent time this morning warming Miss Daisy. Her heater plugs had never been the best and she didn't like a cold start. She gna-gna-gnaed a few times as though she was chewing gum with her mouth open, spluttered and spat but at least she did get going and would avoid the detective's sharp tongue for now.

The Land Rover left a trail of vapours in her wake as she hopped, skipped and stuttered through the village, the icy air keeping the fumes afloat, visible like a jet stream and reeking of unburnt diesel long after she passed. Ncube fretted, Miss Daisy really needed her injectors seen to.

Detective Sibanda was normally a bloodhound when he got on a case, never stopped for anyone or anything and kept his foot flat to the boards, so Ncube was surprised when the detective pulled up abruptly outside Barghees general dealers in the middle of the village. 'Won't be a minute,' he said, over his disappearing shoulder. He returned moments later with a can of cold drink in his hand, the orange fizzy stuff Ncube seemed addicted to. He tossed it into the sergeant's lap.

'Sir?' Ncube queried, wondering what he had done to earn the treat.

'It's the body, Ncube; it isn't in the best of condition.' Ncube's stomach was delicate, unreliable and given to inappropriate outbursts, a can of the day-glo orange stuff settled it, the detective was only looking after himself.

They came across the elephant first. Sibanda left Ncube in the vehicle, sparing him the grisly sight. The scene wasn't different to any other butchered animal except for its magnitude, turning the tableau into one of a bloody massacre. The tusker died ten metres from the track, probably from a broken back. Some elephants survived a train impact with internal injuries or broken legs, leaving them suffering for days or sometimes weeks. This old boy had been lucky; his death had been instant. The crew had already skinned the beast and hacked out the tusks. Most of the men had stripped off despite the cold and were inside the cavity excavating and harvesting the internal organs and intestines.

One man appeared from the cavernous rib cage with the liver. He was dripping from head to toe in gore like an extra from a vampire movie. He heaved the mass of dark red tissue onto a waiting tarpaulin already laden with great chunks of flesh, where it splattered and wobbled like a large port wine jelly. Despite the cold, flies were buzzing and landing in plague proportions. Overhead, in the trees, vultures were awaiting the leftovers. The man broke off a switch, swatted the pests, dislodging them briefly from their egg-laying frenzy and then threw the branch across the new meat. Sibanda waylaid him before he could step back inside the bloody crater.

'Where's the body?'

The man kept his mouth firmly shut; elephant blood was dripping down his cheeks. He pointed with his axe handle further down the track to a park ranger standing guard with a weapon.

Since the road was blocked by the makeshift butchery, the detective drove through the bush and around the carcass back towards the line. He parked under a large Zimbabwe teak. 'Come, Ncube, time to see what we're dealing with, and bring that can with you.'

It was all Sibanda had expected and worse. The victim lay sprawled face down like a discarded marionette with strings cut and limbs at impossible angles. The warden was right, the body had been skinned. The raw flesh had deepened to the colour of cooked meat. He swatted away a swarm of hovering flies and took a few photos with his phone. Gubu station didn't run to crime scene cameras.

'I have tried to keep the flies away, but …' the young ranger left guarding the body was deathly pale with signs of dried vomit around his mouth.

'You've done well, thanks. Go back to your patrol now, we will take over from here.' Sibanda felt sorry for the ranger and the nightmares to come. The armed man stumbled away toward the rapidly disappearing bulk of the elephant.

'Was that wise, sir?'

'I'm sure he thought it was.'

'But he had a weapon and could have defended us from the lions and hyenas surely circling.' The railway line served as the national park's eastern boundary. Ncube swigged a mouthful of drink. In truth, the corpse was a hideous sight and he wouldn't sleep well tonight with visions of twisted limbs and the body naked of even the covering it was born with, but he was less worried by the surprisingly bloodless scene and more anxious about what lay in wait in the thick bush a few metres from the track.

Sibanda pointed to the noisy chopping and excited chatter of the rangers fifty metres away. One of them started a chant and there was a singing response as large haunches of meat were rhythmically swung into the back of a five tonner. There is nothing like a windfall to lift spirits and lubricate an Ndebele vocal cord.

'Have I taught you nothing, Ncube? No self-respecting predator is coming anywhere near us with that lot signalling our presence,' the irritation in Sibanda's voice was palpable.

A late-clinging teak pod cracked in the cold, dense air like a gunshot, Ncube jumped and spilt some of his precious orange antacid. Sibanda didn't notice. He was bending over the corpse, trying to make sense of what happened.

'This is a lonely place to die, sir. Remote and wild.' Ncube could think of nothing worse. He hoped his end would come in a bed surrounded by people and noise.

'She didn't die here, Ncube.' Sibanda was irritated by the remark, as though the conclusion was obvious. 'A black woman,' he added.

'How can you tell?' Ncube asked, hoping this wasn't a stupid question. Everyone was the same colour under the skin.

'Look at the hands, Ncube, the skin is still on them, dark, and still relatively youthful,' Sibanda pointed with a stick, 'and the nails are long, with red polish. She's not a rural woman, check her feet.'

Ncube glanced down. The feet still had their covering and the soles were soft and unmarked. This was no shoeless, wood-gathering, water-hauling, wash-wringing village woman, the detective was right.

Sibanda held her left hand. 'Look at this, the killer wrapped something tightly around her ring finger, some sort of wire viciously twisted with pliers. The finger is swollen and engorged with blood. He must have done this to her before she died, but why? Torture? What have you noticed, Ncube?'

The sergeant was staring at the corpse. He swallowed a belch and nipped in his buttocks just in case of an accidental escaping squeak. This was the worst bit – Sibanda's questioning. How was he, Thadeus Ncube, supposed to know if the grass was trodden by a murderer, or there was a weapon hidden under the body? He didn't have the detective's X-ray vision or an ancestral spirit to whisper in his ear. Everyone knew Sibanda had some kind of mystical phone connection when it came to crime scenes, and if the detective asked him to move this victim, even one centimetre, he would absolutely refuse. The sergeant scrabbled in his brain for a reasonable answer, one that wouldn't embarrass him.

'A good knife man, sir.'

'What makes you say that?' Sibanda looked up with interest from his crouch position over the body.

What made him say that? Ncube was digging himself a deep, dark, humiliating hole for the detective's sarcasm to fill. He gazed searchingly at the body. 'The, er, cuts around the wrist and ankles are very neat and there are, um, no bits of hide left on the meat. The skin came off cleanly, in one piece ...'

Sibanda looked at his sergeant with renewed interest. 'Go on,' he encouraged.

Sergeant Ncube began to prickle under his barrage of clothing. All of a sudden the double-knitted, padded insulation was an oven. He unzipped his jacked, unknotted his scarf and rolled up the face covering of his balaclava.

'Well, let me see ...' he began, buying time with slow and careful enunciation. He was saved from further discomfort by a series of short sharp whistles; a train was heading towards them from the north. The engine was moving slowly and almost stopped as it came parallel to the elephant carcass. A much used, plastic taxi bag full of meat was slung onto the footplate, blood flinging in droplets like red rain as it arced to its destination; the driver waved and responded with a fair rendition of the opening bars of Shosholoza on his whistle, the rousing song that had gone viral at the 1995 Rugby World Cup in South Africa. The coal wagons lumbered by, gaining speed on the long straight, making conversation difficult as each displaced a blast of Antarctic air as they passed. Ncube reassembled his winter wadding and listened to the music of the powerful diesel engine as it gained traction and sang its way down the track towards Bulawayo. He watched the marvel of engineering until the last wagon passed. Boyhood dreams of being an engine driver still lingered, no bodies and no terrifying wild animals to deal with, a satisfying career. He sighed and turned back to the crime scene.

Sibanda continued to stare at the slender body. At one point he prodded it experimentally with a stick, and once it became possible to make himself heard over the train's passing, he said, 'Biltong.'

'Where, sir?' for a moment Ncube thought the detective was offering him some of his favourite snack, the addictive, air-dried, salted and spiced meat his wives made for him and tucked away in his lunch box. His digestive discomfort faded briefly in anticipation.

'The body, Ncube,' Sibanda poked it again, harder, the stick didn't penetrate. Ncube winced.

'A skin has formed on the outside of the meat. The wind and this cold weather have preserved the flesh. This new skin is quite deep and leathery, which means the body wasn't dumped last night. It's been here for some time; a few days at least.'

'How can you tell, sir?'

'Rigor mortis has left the body,' Sibanda picked up her wrist and let it drop to demonstrate flexibility. 'It only lasts up to two days. Forensics will have to look at recent temperatures and insect activity to get a more accurate timing. Unlikely, but let's hope they've got an entomologist on staff.'

'There are no, er, car tracks, sir.' Ncube wanted to divert attention from the big 'ologist' word, but why did he open his mouth? He hadn't even looked. Tyre marks could be hidden in the long dry grass along with numerous biting and poisonous creatures. He waited for the mocking comments and some tedious explanation about the behaviour of grass in winter. Sibanda could be worse than Mr Ndlovu, his grade six teacher, at times. He instinctively rubbed his backside in memory of the regular stripes he received.

'There are no signs of struggle or blood loss and no car tracks this time, Sergeant, so we can discount the revered governor.'

Ncube was pleased he had been right about the tracks, but he still heard the irony. Detective Sibanda had no fear of authority, in fact, no fear of anything. It made him a severe risk to work with in these difficult times and wild places. All clues had pointed to the governor in that previous murder and Ncube had been right to want to tread cautiously.

'No footprints either,' Sibanda continued, 'just the boots of the patrol as far as I can make out.'

'So how …?'

'… I'm betting the train. She was thrown from it, slung out like rubbish.'

Ncube winced at the picture, 'I wonder who she is and how she died.'

'Hard to tell. I can't see any signs of violence on the back of the torso. We have to turn her over. If the murderer is handy with a knife, there could be stab wounds. Take a swig, Ncube, it won't be pleasant.'

Ncube wanted to shout out that he absolutely refused to move the body, but all that exited was a loud, echoing belch, briefly surprising the singing butchers down the track in mid a cappella.

The front side of the torso was much worse. The back had somehow been impersonal, could have been a dead animal, but the front defined the body as a person. The flesh hadn't dried as much, it seemed to scream and ooze with pain. One look at the skinned face sent him heading for a bush. His fizzy dyspeptic ended up on the roots.

Sibanda turned away. He spat bile before he turned back. The girl's eye balls were still in her head; lidless, they protruded from the skull like bulging white grapes. Their prominence made him wonder what might have been her last vision – a jealous husband, a mad stranger, an angry lover? And why would they want her skin? Was he dealing with someone deranged? He gave the rest of the body a cursory glance. There were no entry wounds he could make out. He looked closely at the neck and couldn't be sure but he could detect the bruising of a ligature. Had she been strangled? Or could it just be where the neck folded on itself after death. Forensics would have to sort that out.

'Ncube, toss the tarpaulin from the back of Miss Daisy. I've finished here. We'll cover the body.'

Sibanda looked down the track. 'I'm going to walk this way, further down the line towards the south to check if her clothes were dumped or any other personal items. You stay with the body until Forensics gets here.'

'Sir …' Ncube felt the heat rising again, beads of sweat dribbling. He didn't want to be abandoned with this mutilated creature or looking over his shoulder for danger lurking in the tangled bush beyond the cleared railway firebreak. He rolled back his knitted visor.

'Okay, Ncube, sit in the vehicle. You'll be safe in Miss Daisy. The guys from Detaba should be here soon with the body box. Keep an eye out for them.' He wondered if the woman lying not far from the tracks had been alert, kept her eyes out. They were certainly peeled now.

Overhead the winter sky was as clear and blue as Berry's remarkable eyes, not a cloud to be seen. He didn't think so much about her anymore. She didn't consume his every waking moment, but she still brought a smile to his face. When she stood him up, not pitched up for a housewarming drink as she promised, without even a phone call of apology, he had had to move on. It was hard but he could be disciplined if he put his mind to it. Angel Better, the district nurse, was helping him over his obsession; they'd had a few casual dates.

There should have been a team of police on hands and knees scouring the scene but Gubu Police Station didn't run to teams and he was probably on a wild goose chase anyway. The girl had been murdered elsewhere and her body thrown out of the train at this remote spot. The wind and leaf litter would have camouflaged her in a few days. She might not have been found for years if the elephant hadn't strayed across the track.

Maybe the murderer tossed out her bag and clothes at the same time. Why did he not believe that for a minute? A scenario was forming in his mind, something he never thought to encounter in Matabeleland North. Sibanda walked along the cleared firebreak trying to concentrate on anything out of place. He noted where a herd of zebra had dug their hooves into the dry sand and ran for cover, startled by a passing train or a whistle. A troop of baboons had foraged for bulbs and seeds, their winter fare, along the cleared firebreak. He could see evidence of their picking fingers and cracking incisors. Some of the clan rested on the rails warming their backsides, the heat absorbed by the steel offering underfloor heating for a chilly evening. Overhead, vultures, bored and stiff from perching and staring, took off in relay and completed a circuit before landing again and taking up their watch. The roosting scavengers led his eyes to a tawny eagle's nest in the canopy of an acacia. The couple should be returning soon, starting repairs in time for spring pairing when the pods were over and the herds finished shaking the trees to dislodge the protein-rich food. The tawniess wouldn't want their eggs addled by an overzealous elephant. If he hadn't spotted the nest and spent a few moments speculating about the inhabitants and their comings and goings, his eyes would have been scouring the ground and he would have missed it. The scrap of lacy cream material clung to a high branch like a creamy baobab flower freshly blossomed. In a few days the fabric would have turned grey from the wind and the abrasive Kalahari sand swirling high in dust devils on winter days. Sibanda looked back to the crime scene a hundred metres away. A detail had already arrived to take the body. Was this lace a clue or just some random train jetsam tossed into the trees by racing carriages? He threw off his jacket and shinned up the trunk. The prize was high up and on the end of a slender branch. Sibanda made the climb with ease and edged along the limb as far as was safe until it began to bend under his weight. He broke the branch and let it fall to the ground. He walked back to the crime scene.

'Did you find anything, sir?

'These, let's bag them, Ncube.'

'What is it?'

'Lady's panties, newish, no weathering, only been here a couple of days. Ripped at the side, traces of blood and look at these stains, semen.'

'She was raped?' Ncube shuddered; he had three wives and three daughters. He fretted about them constantly.

'And violently, I'd say, given their state. We can safely say our murderer was a man.'

'No other clothing?'

'Nothing, this guy is a careful worker. He didn't want to leave any trace of his victim. He wanted to obliterate her from the face of the earth. These panties are light, Ncube, the murderer let them go by mistake. They must have flown out of the carriage and been swept up into the tree by the train's passing.'

'But he left the victim's fingerprints.'

'He doesn't care if *we* find out who she is. His desire to destroy her is probably a personal fetish like stamping on a spider.'

Ncube shuddered again. He did not like spiders, in fact, he hated them, particularly those large ginger things skittering around at night as fast as Usain Bolt, only at least the Olympian ran in a straight line. Ncube splattered the long-legged monsters until they were pulp.

'Overkill.'

'What, sir?'

'Arachnophobia. Some people, terrified of spiders, stamp on them over and over again even though they are killed by the first heel twist. Terror leads to a desire for obliteration. Our murderer is frightened of women. He needs them, but he fears them and fear brings hatred. We're looking for a psychopath, Ncube, someone with a dark and twisted past.'

Ncube shuddered for a third time. There were too many big words he didn't understand and none of them sounded pleasant. He needed to get back to the station and his mid-morning snack of Nomatter's deep-fried maize balls filled with Suko's homemade peanut butter, and Blessing's bottle of emergency stomach relief distilled from the bark of the mukwa tree. It was red and bitter and caused his saliva to dry and his eyes to wrinkle and water, but it worked. Something about this murder was making him very uncomfortable. He didn't like it one bit.

Chapter 2

Sibanda was first through the Gubu Police Station door, letting it slam, forcing a blast of icy air around the nipped ears, suffering kidneys and frozen toes of the few complainants waiting their turn on a cement bench. Sergeant Ncube, despite his own trials, felt he should see to Miss Daisy. The detective had driven her hard along the punishing firebreak road, bouncing her ancient gubbins like one of those crazed rubber balls Beauty and Basil, his young twins, liked to play with. The Land Rover was steaming despite the chill and he wanted to take a few minutes to check her over.

Police Constable Zanele Khumalo was perched on a high stool behind the counter like a well-fed giant eagle owl, ponderous and watchful. Off duty, she often wore bright pink eyeshadow, which made the comparison very apt, but in uniform make-up was frowned upon. As usual, she was dealing with issues in the thorough and careful manner that was her way. Time was the only commodity she had to spend, wallow in like a spa bath full of bubbles. Not that she'd ever been lucky enough to have one of those, but she'd seen the pictures. Time was like money in the bank that never involved an overdraft. Why do today what can be put off until tomorrow was her life's philosophy. She glanced up from her paperwork as Detective Inspector Sibanda strode through the outer office. Now there was a man always in a rush. His handsome face was bleak with frown lines, his jaw set and those hard, pale lips harder. He was a man on a mission and his demeanour spelt more work than she cared to consider.

'Zee, my office, now.'

PC Khumalo dropped what she was doing and waddled down the corridor, her thick crepe soles squeaking on the recently polished floor. Why did she only hurry for Detective Sibanda? Why did she drop everything and race to his beck and call? She knew why, of course – the man could cast a spell over a snail and get it sprinting.

'Another murder, Zee, and we may be dealing with an *uhlanya*.'

'A mad man, a nutter?'

'It looks that way, but he might not even be from around here, so keep it under your hat for now, we don't want to alarm people. There's a body dumped by the railway line. She could have come from anywhere between Bulawayo and Victoria Falls. Check out missing persons for a black woman, impossible to tell age, maybe under forty, slim, but not a villager. She looks as though she leads a town life.'

'How long has she been missing? It might narrow down the search if I know.'

'Given the cold and windy weather we've been having it could be four or five days, hard to tell, maybe even a week.'

'What was she wearing? Any jewellery?

'Nothing.'

'Nothing at all?'

'Not a stitch, not even her own skin, but keep that to yourself for now.'

'No skin? Lord help us, poor woman, what a thought,' she shivered. 'The search might take a while, sir. These days everyone's going astray. It's hard enough to find the ones with something on to identify them.'

Sibanda raised an eyebrow.

'Lots of people ducking and diving because they can't pay their bills, men abandoning their families, women crossing borders to trade or work, times are hard. We're getting queries about the missing almost daily. But I'll do my best,' she said.

'Start with anyone expected to arrive by train, heading north.'

PC Khumalo didn't query how he knew which way the victim was travelling. Everyone at the station believed the detective had 'visions' about the crimes he investigated. How else did he come up with his theories?

'Is that all, sir?'

'No, where's Chanza? I haven't seen him all week.'

'Nobody knows and nobody is asking. Cold War is scurrying around like a genet in a chicken run, a big smile on his face; something is going on.'

Sibanda rubbed his troublesome jaw. The very mention of the Officer-in-Charge, Stalin Mfumu, aka Cold War, and office politics made him irritable. 'Okay, thanks, Zee and tell Sergeant Ncube to get into my office. He's fiddling around with that wreck of a Land Rover and he'll be there all day if you don't pull him off it.'

'I doubt it, sir, even Miss Daisy takes second place when it comes to lunchtime,' she glanced at her watch.

'Just get him here now, his stomach can wait. And Zee, not sure if this will help, but the only distinguishing features we have to go on are long painted fingernails and manicured feet.'

The constable glanced down at her own stubby, short-nailed, hardworking hands, imagined the broken toe nails inside her chunky man-like shoes and thought again about a spa and all the treatments they offered. She sighed. 'It's some detail at least.'

Sergeant Ncube put his head around Sibanda's door. 'You called me, sir?'

'Yes, Ncube, come in and sit down. There are problems with this murder: we can't identify our victim and we don't know exactly where she was murdered, it could be anywhere between Bulawayo and Vic Falls.' He stroked his chin, massaging last night's stubble. 'But we do know a bit about the man who killed her. Until we understand more about the victim, we can work on the murderer's profile.'

Ncube looked at the chair he was expected to occupy. Not so long ago, Sibanda's office had been cleaned out and the chair had been visible for at least a week, but once again it lay hidden beneath dust, curling papers that would never be filed and a family of paperclips that linked themselves together for safety and strayed in a chain from the torn box. Everyone at the station now knew the willing cleaner of the legendary chaos was another of Mfumu's relatives, PC Tshuma, snooping around under the guise of organising the office. Had they known of this strategy, they could have advised Tshuma he was wasting his time and energy; Detective Inspector Sibanda didn't make notes or use fancy charts with arrows and pictures. He shared little and kept all leads in that remarkable head. His memory was better than any chart.

Ncube moved what he could onto the floor and sat down. He had no idea what Sibanda meant by a *murderer's profile* but he was about to find out.

'Do you know what a profile is?'

'Not exactly, sir.' 'Exactly' was a word he had recently learned to mitigate his confusion at the detective's complicated language.

'It's an investigative tool to help us build up a picture of the murderer. We're going to put together everything we know about his behaviour and modus operandi – his MO – a social and psychological assessment of the man.' Sibanda could see the blank look on his sergeant's face; this was going to be more difficult than he thought. He should have been working with that weasel Chanza, the assistant detective at the station. At least he would have some idea of the terminology. He sighed and decided to take another tack. Patience was not a virtue and his was wearing thin.

'You've heard of Adolph Hitler, Ncube?'

'Of course, sir.'

'Well, he was "profiled" in the middle of WWII by Dr Walter Langer who read his speeches, and his book, *Mein Kampf*, and managed to talk to people who actually met him. Did you know, for instance, Hitler was very superstitious and always crossed a room diagonally, whistling a marching tune, had a mother fixation, and feared germs?'

'No, sir, I only read he was an *uhlanya* that gassed six million people.'

'He also had some pretty disgusting sexual habits to do with shit and urine, but was prudish about his own body. He couldn't form close relationships and loved the operas of a man called Richard Wagner.'

'So did this profiling help?' the sergeant was a little uncomfortable. Some people, the detective included, said he, Ncube, was highly superstitious and he did like to whistle, particularly to get his children to listen. Could he be like Hitler? No, surely not, he always walked in a straight line, didn't know what an 'opera' was and couldn't imagine what sex had to do with body waste. He wouldn't even talk to his wives about that.

'It was too late to save the millions who died, but the doctor predicted he would commit suicide rather than surrender. He was able to accurately predict the end of one of the world's most notorious mass murderers.'

This profiling was an unpleasant task. The sergeant felt a stirring of gale force proportions in his gut.

'Let's review what we know about this killer, Ncube. What can you say about him?'

'Er … not a lot, sir, but he is interesting.' 'Interesting' was another of Ncube's new responses to Sibanda's impenetrable questions and gave him room to manoeuvre.

'You're right, Ncube. The most interesting crime we've had on our patch for some time. We don't know how our victim was murdered or who she was but we do know she was thrown from a train, so our knife man had access to the railway.'

'A travelling man?'

'Possibly, but certainly a frequent train user or someone who works in or around the railway. This wasn't a random crime; our killer is organised. He planned the rape and murder. It makes sense that he knew how to dispose of the body at the most remote spot along the line. All passenger trains on this line are overnight, so it was dark when he threw her off. There are no villages either side of the track along that straight. The murderer was just unlucky an elephant chose to cross in front of an oncoming diesel.'

'It will be hard to find where he lives and works, there are four hundred kilometres of track between Bulawayo and Victoria Falls.'

'Yes, but only so many stations and stops. You had better list them all. The killer and the victim boarded the train somewhere.'

Sibanda walked towards the window and stared for a while at a flock of redbilled firefinches, scavenging for seeds on what remained of the station lawn. He took a few moments to search his brain for the parasitic bird that laid its egg in their nests. What was it? Ah yes, the steelblue widow finch. At least the chicks didn't murder their siblings like cuckoos, but settled in happily as a family member, matching red bills keeping the unwitting foster parents fooled. The nestlings even sang the same song as their adoptive parents during the rearing, completing the subterfuge. Did the killer sing the same song as his victim; somehow worm his way into her confidence? He dragged his thoughts away from the finches and their domestic arrangements. 'I've got a hunch they both boarded in Bulawayo.'

'Any evidence, sir?' he asked, although Ncube didn't need any confirmation. If Sibanda said they'd come from Bulawayo then he'd put money on it, spend a few dollars with old Tuesday Mpala who ran a book down at the Blue Gnu on all sorts of predictions. Sibanda was never wrong.

'The killer and his prey were travelling north and anyone north of Bulawayo would be travelling south to the city for shopping. No one would get on at a rural siding to go to Vic Falls; they'd rather go shopping than sightseeing. It's just economics.'

Ncube was confused and it showed.

'Our murderer reaches the Gwaai straight in the middle of the night. He awaits his moment and then heaves her off the train. He has packed up her clothes and belongings and taken some or all of them as souvenirs …'

'… Souvenirs? Why would he want to keep a reminder of such a filthy act, wouldn't he get rid of them?

'It'll become clear later Ncube, be patient.'

Be patient, and this from a man with not one grain of patience in his body.

'As he tosses her from the carriage, he isn't aware her panties are still underneath her body. They fly away. We know a train creates a backdraft pushing anything light – leaves, paper, rubbish – behind it. The victim lands and her panties sail behind her, lighter, more aerodynamic and floating on the turbulence. We found the underwear south of the body; therefore, the train was travelling north.'

'That makes sense, sir.' Ncube said. But whatever next? Flying knickers telling them which way the train was moving was a new one to him.

'You said he was a good knife man, Ncube, who are we dealing with here?'

'A butcher, sir? There's a young man at the Blue Gnu butchery who can take meat off a bone quicker than you can say *ukubengaimhwabha*.'

'Can't you think of anything but biltong and the making of it?' Sibanda snapped, 'and there are probably a hundred butchers between Bulawayo and the Falls.' This case was making him edgy. He didn't like the way it was stacking up. His sergeant didn't know the half and he wouldn't like it when he did.

It was time to escape. The detective was becoming crabby. Time for lunch. Ncube's stomach was complaining, his maize balls were a mere curd in a calabash of sour milk, and a container of amatshakada, a delicious mix of beans, peanuts and maize meal all cooked together with a little salt, was waiting for him. Suko, his third wife, used special smoky water. He had seen her burn empty maize cobs and sheaths last night and then add water to the ash. The residue settled over night and the strained water used this morning to cook the bean stew. His taste buds were panting. 'Profiling is very interesting, sir, but perhaps I'd better get to work on listing all the stations and sidings along the line.'

'What about skinners, Ncube, the guys who work in the hunting industry and remove animal skins for trophies? They have to be accurate and careful, particularly with head mounts.'

'That includes about fifty per cent of the population, sir. Most men around these parts can skin an animal. It's in their blood.' Now could he go and eat? Ncube stood as if to leave.

'There's something ritualistic about this crime.' Sibanda deliberately extended the syllables in *ritualistic* to get Ncube's waning attention.

'Not witchdoctors again, sir,' Ncube felt faint, and further rumbling, 'surely not …'

'… No, we're not dealing with muthi or magic here, Ncube. Skinning the victim is the murderer's signature. He's not a *nyanga* looking for human parts to cast a spell, but he is dangerous. I'm pretty certain we're dealing with …'

Ncube was spared the worst by PC Khumalo bursting into the office. 'Sorry to interrupt, sir, but this is important.'

'What is it, Zee?'

'You asked me to check out missing persons who may have been travelling north by train.'

'Go on.'

'I have a woman at the desk who was expecting her daughter five days ago. She hasn't heard from her, can't get in touch, and has come in to report her missing. This is her photo.'

Sibanda took the picture from PC Khumalo and could see straight away why she decided to interrupt him. It was a photograph of a young woman sitting at a desk, hands in front of her. The nails were red and long. He passed it across to Ncube. 'This could well be our victim, sergeant. Don't go too far away. We need to talk some more. Zee, bring the lady into my office.'

Mavis Khupe was slight, thin as a grass stalk and with bones that spoke of a spare life and self-sufficiency. 'This is a picture of my daughter, Lois, taken at her work, Universal Dream, in Bulawayo.'

Sibanda could see the pride of a mother whose daughter had done well. Universal Dream was a large international aid organisation dispensing food, water supplies and other necessities in hard times. They had been run off their feet in the last few years.

'She's a fine-looking woman, and coming home to Gubu, you say.'

'Thank you, detective, yes, she hadn't been home for some time …' she brushed aside the hesitation, 'we were expecting her days ago.'

'By train?'

'That's how she normally travels unless she can catch a lift with one of the UD vehicles coming up.'

'Have you checked with them?'

'They say none of their vehicles have come this way in the last week. Her colleagues are worried too. Lois hasn't been at work since last Friday and no one can contact her by phone.'

'Your daughter didn't visit home for a while; was there a reason, family problems?'

'She recently broke off with her boyfriend in the village. They had been together since school. Gideon was heartbroken and angry. He's a good boy from a nice family. Lois was uncomfortable and we don't know why she left him. Her sister thinks she has found someone else in Bulawayo, someone she works with. She had become secretive. Constable Khumalo knows Lois well,' she added. 'They were in the same class at Gubana Secondary.'

Sibanda broke the news to her as gently as he could, told her about the body on the railway line and the need to get a DNA sample. He explained that physical recognition would be impossible and it might not be Lois, but Mavis Khupe collapsed in a screaming heap on the floor of his office, she rent her clothes and tore at her hair in a display of grief that shook the whole station. Sergeant Ncube was beside the flailing woman, bent over, doing his best to console her and restrain her worst excesses. He feared she would injure herself, or him, her elbows were sharp and his stomach was soft. He was a sensitive soul and the right man for the job. PC Khumalo fetched a cup of sweet, milky tea; it went flying before the first sip.

'Thula, Mama, hush, we don't know …' Constable Khumalo was shaking, her eyes brim full of tears. Sibanda walked silently out of the office. He could do nothing. He didn't handle emotion well, kept it bottled at the best of times and didn't know how to deal with it with others. Anyway, he was surplus to requirements. As the messenger of bad news he was best out of it.

He walked outside into the freezing wind. The sun had the yellow intensity of late afternoon, the air was crisp, the wispy grass a natural winter blond, tipped with ashen seed heads, and the silvery colour turned his thoughts to Berry. What if she'd been found next to the track, raped and strangely exposed? He'd go mad, if not like the poor woman inside then like a raging, wounded buffalo on the tracks of the hunter. What had Lois Khupe suffered before her death? What kind of fear had she known? Anger was streaming down his arms to his clenched fists. He should keep a level head for the investigation, stay detached, rein in his temper. He was going to need every particle of restraint, every ounce of cool for the days and possibly weeks ahead. Gubu was in for a rough ride if his guess was right, and the trip had only just begun.

'PC Khumalo is on her way home with Mavis Khupe. She knows the family and can keep them updated. Are you all right, sir?' Ncube recognised the tension in the detective's jaw, even from behind, but there was something else, something about his posture and his hands twisted into fists.

'Yes, I'm all right, but this may be our last calm before the storm, Ncube,' he continued to stare into the distance.

Ncube looked in the same direction, up to the vast African sky radiating cloudless winter blue beyond the horizon. 'A storm in winter would be very unusual, a bit of drizzle from time to time or maybe a cold wind, but there is no sign of a storm.'

'Not that sort of storm, Ncube,' Sibanda's mouth managed a strained smile. There must be something terribly wrong. The detective rarely smiled. He normally snarled and snapped when Ncube misunderstood his meaning.

'What … what sort of a storm?' Ncube hardly dared to ask, although a strange peace had come over the detective.

'This murder is not just the normal, hot-headed attack motivated by greed or anger or jealousy, a one-off crime.'

'What is it then, sir?'

Sibanda turned to Ncube. 'This man has killed before. Everything we witnessed was too practised to be a one-off. See if you can find details of any similar crimes in the district or even further afield along the railway network going back as far as records will allow.'

'A lot of searching, sir, and record keeping has not been too good of late. The whole force from here to Bulawayo is out on roadblocks, standing around. It's near month end …' there was an apologetic tone to his voice. Everyone knew police topped up their wages from the roadblocks. As the driving population got wiser and wilier, and made sure they had the endless and growing list of essentials – fire extinguishers, red triangles, yellow jackets – the police got more creative with their fines. Ncube feared where it would all end.

'Do the best you can, Ncube. I'll rope in Chanza if he ever pitches up to work. We're all going to have to cooperate on this one.'

'How do you know so much about this man before we've even caught him? And why did he cut up that poor woman?'

'Profiling, Ncube. Plus I've seen this sort of behaviour before, and read about it. A killer who goes to the trouble of skinning a body, postmortem, has practice, has an agenda. Maybe the first time he murdered he sliced away a few pieces of skin, got away with it, enjoyed the extended buzz it gave him. With more experience and confidence his signature has got bigger and bolder and become set. The theme stays the same whether it's the first murder or one committed years later.'

'And the souvenirs, sir, why take the skin and clothes away?' he swallowed his distaste in a supressed belch, 'that's like a hyena walking around with a mouthful of duck feathers.'

'He keeps souvenirs to ward off depression after the murder. The skin is a trophy …'

'… Like those American hunters that stuff animal heads and stick them on a wall?'

'Exactly the same. Possessing the trophy gives the killer the same feelings of power he experienced at the time of the kill, lets him relive the moment. The killer's most treasured keepsake is her skin. I wonder if he salts and preserves them like leather?'

Ncube was frightened by Sibanda's words. 'We are dealing with the devil, a black chameleon on a moonless night, an evil creature who has wrapped two poor women in his long sticky tongue.' Ncube couldn't think of the horror any more. It was too distressing. He had to get some of his bean stew inside him and quickly.

'Did I say two murders, Ncube? There could be more.'

'More, sir?' Ncube's voice rose in disbelief. He didn't know which way to turn, didn't know which orifice would explode first.

'Yes, certainly more than two, and more to come; we are dealing with a serial killer.'

Chapter 3

Bert White checked his pocket watch, a battered but accurate substitute for the gold one he hoped to be awarded for long service, and blew his whistle. Doors slammed along the length of the carriage, a satisfying sound that underlined both the precision engineering of the Metropolitan Amalgamated Carriage Works of England and the punctuality of the Zambezi Express on its way to Victoria Falls from Bulawayo station. With all doors closed, the guard, Fred Sidebotham, a long-legged spider of a man, hopped aboard the guard's van and waved his flag.

The 7th class engine, no 43, that had been stationary for some time, steaming like a plum duff in a bubbling pot, now began a rhythmical chuff, chuff, chuff as the driver released the regulator handle and directed the build-up of steam to the cylinders. The cylinders in their turn released the used steam up through the chimney, giving the train its distinctive puffing breath and the station its addictive smell of wet soot. Coal was being used now to fire up the boilers. Wood worked well enough early on but most engines had been converted. Coal was readily available from the vast coalfields to the north and it certainly produced more steam for less energy. Engineers were starting to call all that pressure build-up a 'head' of steam; Bert supposed it was because the scalding vapour gathered along the top of the engine. This modern technology was spawning a whole new vocabulary and the station master was battling to keep up, but he knew the workings of a locomotive like the back of his hand.

Bert tasted another lungful of the polluted air. It still gave him a thrill after all these years because it spoke of travel and adventure. He saw the same gleam of excitement in the eyes of the passengers; they shone with the thought of exploring wildest Africa in what some Americans were calling an iron horse. He saw it too, reflected in the polished, bespoke and colourfully labelled leather luggage sitting arrogantly on the porter's trolleys, well-travelled, well-heeled and used to deferential handling. He heard the enthusiasm in the shouts of the tourists and their animated chatter as they milled on the platform, eager to display their moneyed travelling credentials, and he heard it most of all in the whistle signals of the drivers, each with their own signature. He recognised every one of them.

The chuff, chuff, chuff picked up momentum. The old station master could almost feel the heat of the fire box pumping white hot flames against the tubes transversing the boiler, keeping the water at evaporation point and creating the steam that powered the workings. The scalding air would be racing now through the veins and valves of the engine, heading under pressure to the pistons, pushing and pulling the great crankshafts that turned the wheels of engine no 43. And wasn't she a charmer, built by the North British Locomotive Works of Scotland and enamelled a highly polished green with cream trimmings, she stood out from the rest. The engine had been chosen to pull the luxury coaches of the Zambezi Express, only the best for the toffs. Oh, yes, she was a beauty all right, except the steam box, of course, the dirty nose of the engine siphoned off the waste smoke and steam and spat it out through the chimney in great black clouds, which was painted black.

The engineers loved no 43. She was an easy handler, they said, was styled to take the steep curves and flimsy 40 lb BSS rails of the recently laid track, handled like a dream, 'like a good woman,' said Arthur Jones, the scheduled driver, 'all smooth curves and sweet temperament.' He'd be tooting the whistle soon. His series of departure trumpets always sounded like the first bars of the recent music hall tune 'There's an Old Mill by a Stream Nellie Dean.'

Bert White was surprised at the accomplishments of the colony and its rail system and delighted with his decision to drag his family up to the newly opened country with all the promise of pushing the tracks up through the spine of Africa as far as the Mediterranean. It was Edwin

Arnold, a newspaper columnist, who first coined the saying 'Cape-to-Cairo', and Mr Rhodes jumped on that one right smart. The mining entrepreneur certainly knew a thing or two about marketing and raising capital for his vision. Now Cape-to-Cairo was a catch phrase peppering everyone's conversations. Transport meant riches and the opening up of the hinterland to mining and trade.

Most of all, Bert was chest-puffing proud that through his station passed some of the great and the good on their way to wonder at the magnificent Victoria Falls. Sometimes, the train was packed with Americans from the liners cruising into Cape Town. The railway side trip was included in their holiday – a package tour they were calling it, making the tourists sound as though they were going to be wrapped in brown paper and sent by post, whatever next? This lot were from the mother country. He could tell from their accents; they could shatter glass given a chance.

The carriages were beginning to roll, purring as they eased along the track, clicking as they negotiated the couplings with a rocking rhythm reminiscent of a childhood cradle. Once the excitement of departure died down, a few heads would be nodding off to this regular pulse, he could take bets on that. The first-class carriages were slipping by and Bert was about to doff his cap to Reverend Fogarty in the Chaplain's caboose, a habit he adopted in deference to the sterling work done by The Railway Mission ministering to the remote communities along the track, when he caught a movement out of the corner of his eye. It was the lad with the blond, curly hair racing down the platform, cap gone, curls bouncing, sprinting like a greyhound. Silly young bugger, he must have missed the train, now here was a to-do that he as station master would have to sort out, and then, just as the platform was about to run out of length, a carriage door swung open and a strong arm grabbed the lad's wrist and swung him into the compartment.

Bert grunted his relief. The next train wasn't due out for a few days and anyway the lad was too young to travel alone. He had noticed the father and son earlier, standing apart from the other nabobs and thought them a rum pair then, although Bert wasn't paid to think or make judgements about the first-class passengers. The father was tall with straight dark hair, spoke like a duke and carried a Malacca cane with a silver elephant's head handle, the trunk raised to take the palm of the hand. It reeked of the Indian colonial service. The boy was slim with the tipped nose and freckles of a street urchin, an accent that didn't quite match the polish of his father's and cheeky with it. That hair would pick him out anywhere; it was too good for a lad. His Maud could have done with a head of hair like that; hers was straight and lank despite sleeping in twisted rags. She'd never find anyone to court her. As the guard's van passed, Fred Sidebotham grinned and waved to the station master. His teeth fell about like moss-encrusted tombstones and his skin shone with boils, but Bert could make out curls under his cap. Must remember to ask Margie to invite him round for dinner, he might be a match for Maud. With that, all memory of the tardy boy and his father left him. The incident didn't even make it to the dinner table where he normally regaled Margie with the anecdotes of station life.

'Billy, what in tarnation do you think you were up to? Haven't I told you not to draw attention to yourself.'

'Sorry, Father,' Billy replied, the heavy irony underlined the fact that these two were not related at all.

'And cut that tone out or someone will rumble us and you will be shipped back to England and that miserable boarding house before you know it.'

The youngster sighed and kicked against the leather of the compartment seat. The truth was Billy almost made that very decision, almost missed the train on purpose and then relented at the last minute. Aunt Bessie said Billy could run like the wind, she wasn't wrong.

When Baron Montague of Bingley pitched up at Bessie Bawtry's Boarding House in Hammersmith, all swagger, crisp collars and sweet smelling courtesy, no one had been more surprised than Bessie herself. Used to commercial travellers and the odd London tourist, she hadn't hosted anyone titled before. She was pleased when the baron settled in almost anonymously. He kept himself to himself, was most undemanding, paid his board on time, ate the food she offered without complaint, and gave her not a moment's worry, altogether a good sort of a cove. None the less she sent for her sister's child, to help out with the extra chores a gentleman expected.

'Can't we cut the play acting now we're in the carriage, Monty,' Billy wheedled, 'it's bleeding 'ard work all this remembering to call you "father". We're well clear of the Cape; no one could possibly follow us up here to this wilderness.'

'No, we can't, we might make a slip, best to stay in character for the time being, at least until we're over the Zambezi,' the make-believe baron turned away in irritation and looked out through the window at a cluster of mud-daubed huts with ragged, tiered thatching, a far cry from the neatly combed roofs of the Hampshire villages of his childhood. Here and there a naked little boy took his interest or a bare-breasted maiden swayed to the gait of the water pot on her head, a bechu, the tiny traditional apron of the Ndebele, barely covering her sex and allowing luscious brown orbs to wiggle, unfettered by bloomers. The natives had been tamed since the rebellion, but thank the Lord the canting missionaries hadn't completely sanitised this landscape yet.

'Oh come on, Monty,' Billy complained, 'this is not some music hall knees-up, with you on tour in India in a turban, boot polish all over your face, playing an Oxford-educated Maharajah with a cardboard cut-out elephant. I'm getting bored. You promised me fun and adventure. I just want to be me again.'

'And we will have some fun, my little chicken, lots of it, as soon as we are away from prying eyes, as much fun as you want,' he rubbed his silver-tipped Malacca cane against the inside of Billy's thigh, 'in the meantime mind your manners and remember who we are supposed to be.'

Billy sat back in the seat sulking, while opposite Alf Watters or Monty, the baron, unfurled a copy of the *Bulawayo Chronicle* and began to read. The youngster read the outside pages for a while but it was just dreary stuff about the railway's native shanty compound and its unsanitary conditions. Ha! What did they know about freezing weather, an outhouse that stank, raw, split knuckles and endless dark days full of back-breaking work, falling asleep in the cold and damp and waking to the same? The natives should be so lucky, at least they had sunshine.

Boredom set in again.

When Monty first became friendly, it was flattering, but it didn't take Billy long to discover Baron Montague of Bingley was not all he was cracked up to be. Billy was rural but that didn't mean stupid. Aunt Bessie might be smitten by the milord demeanour, the waxed moustache and the hoity toi accent, but Billy picked the baron for a fake from the off, the vowels were a little too studied and the manners too precious. Up at the Big House, where Billy sometimes went to deliver the farm's produce, the strangled vowels of the servants, elongated and sharpened in an attempt to mimic their employers, sounded exactly the same. Bingley was definitely bogus. Blackmail appealed with the discovery of Alfred Watters's passport, among the baron's papers. It could mean a few spare bob on the side in return for discretion, but it didn't take Billy long to understand Monty had much more to offer than a few pence for keeping silent about a faked identity, and when the 'baron' suggested he and Billy run away together to Africa, it seemed like a dream.

Billy grew up on a small holding, a tenant farm, scrabbling hard in the dirt to raise a few hens, some potatoes, beets, and a crop of barley if there was money for seed and the weather was kind. Billy's dad was a hard man, free with his slaps, cuffs and curses, and mean with his love and praise. Mum pulled the plough, breaking the sods even when there was still frost on the ground; the cow was too old with her bones through her hind quarters and there was no money for a horse. Mum was a bent and crippled woman at thirty-five. When the letter came from Aunt Bessie in London asking for the eldest, it was decided the wage would help. Bessie was to send all the money to dad. Billy didn't care much, a square meal a day and escape from the relentless grind was enough for now. Little Tom would be the next carting the slop buckets, boiling up the mash on a freezing morning, and him with muscles like knots in cotton, poor sod.

Billy had never known luxury like this train journey before. The rich blue leather seats that squeaked with wealth and converted to beds made up with crisp white linen were both ingenious and comfortable. Billy had been used to an itchy, straw-filled pallet. The wood-panelled compartment shone rust-red with carved detailing, Greek urns and wreaths seemed the most popular. The etched glass light fittings overhead were held by a cluster of wrought acanthus leaves that endlessly fascinated the prone youngster who was previously used to staring at a wattle and daub ceiling and dusty beams. But it was the polished brass taps and basin that folded away neatly, an unheard of indulgence in a bedroom, that pleased Billy the most because it was a very convenient loo. Monty was horrified and said it was common to use it as such, but even he had to accept the value of its clandestine use.

The Braemar Castle out of Southampton had been an equal revelation in unexpected treats even though they travelled second class. 'We'll save as much as we can for the mining. We're going to need money for equipment,' Monty explained, 'and it's a long way to Northern Rhodesia.' Monty had won a gold-mining claim in a card game in Bombay from an old African hand, or at least that's the explanation he gave for the trip, but Billy suspected there was more to Monty's story than he was telling. Why did they need to pretend to be someone else? Monty was running from something, probably the man he cheated out of the mine with a marked pack. The baron's style. Billy learned over the last few weeks not to question Monty. Since Cape Town, he had become a man of moods and dark broody places, always with his nose in a newspaper. The latest outburst, the one Billy nearly abandoned him for, was because of the questions about the mining equipment. So far no equipment had been bought and surely none would be found up in the wild territories. Bulawayo was little more than a dusty village, what could they expect from the heart of the wilderness ahead, and why were they now travelling first class? Billy asked. Monty gave him a sharp cuff around the ears. Billy had swapped a bitter and broken father for an angry and twisted lover.

The youngster was brought back to the present by the folding of the newspaper and an unexpected grin from Monty. 'Cheer up my little dove, we'll head to the dining car for lunch shortly and then it won't be long until we enter the game park. By dusk we'll be in the heart of it and, who knows, we might see all manner of exotic creatures, lions, elephants, tigers ...'

'Don't be silly, Monty, everyone knows there are no tigers in Africa,' Billy smiled, the journey was finally beginning to get interesting.

Chapter 4

When Sibanda's phone rang, it was too early for any social chit-chat. Sunrise was stuck, frosted beneath the horizon, no hint of dawn and birds were still on their perches and roosts, fluffed up under their feather duvets, trapping warm air, beaks tucked under wings.

'What?' he answered abruptly.

'Sir, sorry to bother you at this hour, but the serial killer is prowling around your house. Be careful.'

'Who is this?'

'It's PC Tshuma, sir. I'm on night shift and there's a report of a dead body in your garden.'

'Garden? I don't have a garden.' The patch of bush in front of his house was wild, unkempt and boasted not a single plant of any flowering variety, let alone a lawn.

'In front of your house.'

'Is this a joke? Who put you up to this?'

'No joke, sir. Thulani Ngwenya was cycling past on his way home from his night shift at the Sweet Bun Bakery. He passes your house on the way. Sergeant Ncube has told me about a killer on the loose. I thought I had better warn you.'

Sibanda slammed his phone on the bedside table and cursed Ncube and his sharing imperative. He was like a social weaver with his large family of multiple wives and children and his flock of village friends and neighbours all living together in a vast, ragged nest of communal support. Did he know no guile? The most damning thing was this knowledge would now be with the Officer-in-Charge, Stalin Mfumu, who would perform a self-aggrandising song and dance about it resulting in another stand-off. There was no certainty in the case of Lois Khupe, a serial killer was speculation.

He pulled on his jeans, a thick fleece and a pair of pata patas. He eased his bed-warm body out into the freezing morning and lit up the front garden with a torch grabbed from beside the bed; handy insurance against the frequent power cuts plaguing the nation. He shook it, the batteries were weak; electricity supply during the last few days had been calamitous. Sibanda swept around 180 degrees for eyes, to make sure he wasn't about to walk into anything nocturnal, lingering and dangerous, but the bush was clear, the only movement coming from clouds of condensation billowing from his nose and mouth; the only noise from the frosted grass crunching under his rubber slip-ons. The flickering yellow light soon picked out a body lying among a stand of teak trees to one side of the patch.

Sure enough there was a body destined to complicate the days ahead, but this was no victim of the serial killer. He was a male, curled in the foetal position with all his clothes on and no skin missing. Sibanda bent over, torch in his teeth, both hands free to examine the scene, and then the body moved. The detective started, the torch fell on the body. He retrieved it and shook the crumpled heap.

'What happened? I thought you were dead.'

A groan came from the bundle of clothes, 'I'm fine, but as cold as a marriage bed. Do you have a drop of something to warm me up?'

Sibanda helped the man to his feet, a bit unsteady but otherwise unhurt. He reeked of stale Chibuku, the staple, cloudy beer of the township.

'Come on inside before you and I both freeze to death.' As he led the man towards his door, the first rays of dawn cracked like a sharding icicle across the eastern sky and a few early birds tested their songs on the stony air. Like any good choir they understood the distorting effects of the cold, they were out of tune and half-hearted.

Sibanda settled the shaking, shivering bundle into a chair and grabbed a briquette. He made his own when he had the time, old mealie cobs, shredded stalks, sawdust, soaked paper to make a mash, to this he added winter grass, weeds, dried elephant dung and anything else discarded and combustible which he compressed in an old brick-making mould. It was better than chopping trees. He got the fire going with a bit of kindling and blew on it until the briquette began to flare. It was remarkably smoke free. He set off for the kitchen, returning with a pot containing water and coffee grounds.

'How did you end up in front of my house?' Sibanda asked, as he balanced the pot on the fire over a grill.

'I live just down the road with my wife and her children. Lovemore Moyo, pleased to meet you.' He extended his hand.

'Likewise, Detective Jabula ...'

'I know. Everyone knows who you are.'

Sibanda shrugged. 'You could have frozen to death out there. If you are going to get as sodden as a wet floor cloth, then you need to go home first.'

'The river is full, it's better to shout over the water than cross it, or, as the English say, easier said than done.'

'Problems at home?' Sibanda was not normally interested in a person's private life, least of all his neighbours', but there was something about Lovemore Moyo. He seemed articulate, self-deprecating and completely at odds with his appearance.

'My wife is ... controlling.' He chose this word with thought. 'She objects to me having a few drinks. She has rules,' he drew out this last word in theatrical tones; he still had some drink inside him. 'If I'm not home by 9pm then all the doors are locked. If I miss my curfew then I might as well stay out and *go the whole hogshead* – forgive me, mixed metaphor. That's how I ended up in your garden. The teak trees looked inviting, one of the few groves left in the village.'

'You like trees?'

'Yes, I like all nature, but particularly trees,' he threw his arms out in an expansive gesture as if to embrace the wild world surrounding them. 'Don't know all the names, but enjoy the shapes and the colours, the way the light licks them warm in winter and suffocates them in summer, their caressing whispers on a windy day and their blessed silence in the still – my inspiration.'

'For?' Sibanda strained the bubbling hot coffee into two mugs, 'milk, sugar?'

'Black, fiery, dark and bitter, like my life – poetry, art.'

'Sorry?' Sibanda was confused.

'I write poetry, or at least I try to.'

Sibanda took a sip of coffee and threw another briquette on the fire. He wasn't a poetry reader himself, although Berry always used to quote bits and pieces to him and he enjoyed the cadence of the words when she did, more to do with the sound of her voice flowing over him like a warm hug than the poetry having an emotional effect.

'Are you published?'

'No, that's impossible, but I do readings from time to time. We have a small club, quite active. We meet in a corner of Mama Elephant's diner every Wednesday night. It's down the alley next to Barghees. You should come along next week.'

Sibanda sighed, he could imagine he and Berry with a cold beer and a barbecued short rib enjoying the ambience, she relishing the wordsmith, he just happy to be near her. Did Angel Better read poetry, he wondered.

'Unlikely, I'm afraid; it's a busy time for Gubu Police at the moment. Maybe in a few weeks.'

'Your loss.'

'If you're caught out in the cold again, just knock on the door. I'm usually up late. I can't offer much but it'll be warmer than the teak trees.'

'Thanks. Time to face the music, or rather atonal words uttered with the venom of a cobra – forked tongue, no rhythm, poisonous. Sorry to get you up so early, I'll pay you with a poem. It's about a rhino, they say you like wildlife, don't you?'

He began in a sonorous voice transporting Sibanda to the bush.

Silver dusk, grey darkling
Wrinkled by runnels of electroplated nickle water,
She puddles muddy pools
of lilly leaves floating,
Growing silently,
In imperceptible ripples
like a poacher's stealth.

She tosses horned treasure
To bejewel the envy

Of the erectile inadequates.
Silken, pearl sheets of an eastern moonlit tryst
Slither across susurrating thighs,
The dagger of desperation falls softly,
Drips.

She stands proud,
Curved in a hoary-beamed light,
For a brief second, a goddess illuminated,
An oxymoronic cornucopia of masculinity,
Before she disappears seamlessly
Among the reeds
Barely a puff of pollen
To mark her passing.

'I enjoyed the coffee, by the way, thanks.'

Sibanda watched as Lovemore Moyo rambled down the road, the chilblain flush of dawn lighting his way. He didn't seem too terrified of the vituperation ahead. Sibanda suspected he could hold his own verbally and that might be the cause of the marital conflict. A clever tongue tended to incite grievances. The poem brought back memories of the last case he was involved with. Poaching was a curse and Lovemore summed up the pointlessness of it all neatly.

Sibanda should get on his way as well. Early hours at the station were always the most productive before the clamour of crime opened its ugly mouth and shouted around the offices and corridors. When he arrived, the police station was an iceberg, cold and aimless – little going on above the surface at least.

'Morning, Tshuma.'

'Morning, sir, the body …?'

'… Was just a man who'd had too much to drink and fallen asleep, a killer on the loose is idle gossip. Lois Khupe may have died as the result of a domestic dispute. Keep your lips buttoned, you're worse than a flock of babblers.'

In his office, Sibanda scrabbled around in the piles of papers and files looking for his old notes to see what he had on serial killers. If he remembered the Nottingham college lectures, then serial killers rarely murdered people they knew. They might start out with a neighbour or acquaintance but they ended up with anonymous victims picked at random on the basis of some feature that attracted or angered them or a humiliating incident in the past. Prostitutes were fair game, easily lured away, and women in general, but serial killers weren't gender exclusive. Most multiple killings had something to do with sex but not all murderers were heterosexual. With only one body, he couldn't actually label Lois Khupe's murder as serial, but he knew damn well it was. The ritualistic nature of what happened to the corpse flagged it. The investigation would have to begin with known associates, the ex and the current boyfriends would be the obvious starting point, or some disgruntled lovelorn Universal Dream employee. He rifled through unfiled papers and uncompleted dockets without finding what he was looking for and sat back behind his desk to think of the next move.

'You're in early this morning, sir. I thought you might be.' Ncube's frost-nibbled nose made it around the door first.

'A bit earlier than I'd imagined, but it's given me some quiet time to plan where we go with this murder.'

'I have brought you breakfast, it's the Ncube special, mashed sugar bean pikelets with wild marula jelly, left over this morning, oh and this …' Ncube beamed as he handed the detective a piece of paper.

'What's this?' Sibanda asked, turning it sideways.

'It's a picture drawn by little Sobela, my daughter. She's at the Happy Giraffe Nursery. They are being taught about trees and … er … how important they are,' Ncube shuffled. He had been rude in the past about the detective's tree passion. 'I told her my boss liked trees too, so she drew this picture for you.'

'I'm glad to see she doesn't take after her father, maybe she'll be a conservationist,' Sibanda smoothed out the page and placed it on his desk. He could see now it was a baobab with a fat trunk and wavy arms like an octopus. It showed promise. 'I'll wager she can keep a secret better than you,' a note of anger crept into his voice.

'What do you mean, sir?'

'Even PC Tshuma believes we're looking for a serial killer. And Cold War won't like it. He'll try to interfere, probably insist the killer is some misguided soul straying from the Lord. We'll get no backup or resources.'

'I never told anyone,' he protested, 'I don't know where … wait a minute …'

'Go on.'

'Tshuma must have overheard me phoning other stations, trying to get records of a similar crime. I was here late last night and he came on night shift early. He's an *umgongomtshane*, a mopani fly, buzzing around anything juicy.'

'Make all your calls in here from now on and keep a lid on this until we're sure. There could be other consequences besides office tittle-tattle and village panic.' Serial killers, he remembered, often basked in their notoriety and enjoyed baiting the police. Sibanda didn't want to alarm his sensitive sergeant.

'There has been nothing yet on any similar crimes,' Ncube offered, 'I'm hoping someone will remember a related incident.'

'In the meantime, we'll check out Lois's contacts, starting with her recently dumped boyfriend from the village.'

'Do you have a name, sir?'

'Yes, Gideon Shumba. Do you know him?'

'He's the butcher at the Blue Gnu.'

'The good knife man?'

'Yes.'

Miss Daisy trundled through the village, Sergeant Ncube at the wheel. It was still early but the first of the school children from the out-lying areas were making their way to Gubana Primary or St Francis. The littlest of the learners were in school clothes so large their bodies were almost missing. The uniforms were on their third or fourth time around and washed clean of the pattern, but they would last for many more years of growth and patching to be handed on yet again, thinning as they went. Some of the lucky girls wore tracksuit trousers under the cotton dresses; some made do with socks alone. Nearly all the morning faces were shining, not with Shakespeare's eager glow but from the very practical application of Vaseline or Camphor cream to prevent winter chapping and cracking. Many carried miniature *izimbawula*, small braziers made of jam tins with a long wire handle and holes punched in the sides, keeping them warm on the long journey. From time to time the tins were swung vigorously in a circle to re-ignite the coals and then clasped in freezing fingers padded by overstretched pullover sleeves. Little communities of friends travelled together sharing the warmth, passing the tin from hand to hand. They would be exhausted and hungry by the time they reached school but the children were used to it or would be by the end of Grade 1. Miss Daisy took no notice; the trail of shivering scholars was part of the everyday landscape, besides which she had hardly warmed up herself.

'Is the Blue Gnu open at this hour, Ncube?'

'Not the cocktail bar, that gets busy around ten, but the butchery will be open early, particularly if a goat or a cow has been slaughtered.'

'Business may stutter for a while with all the elephant meat around. The butcher might be temporarily at leisure and it'll be trouble for us if Shumba's not at work. Do you know where he lives?'

'We'll find him, sir, no one gets lost in Gubu.'

Gideon Shumba was sitting around the corner from the Blue Gnu, sheltering from the wind, trying to soak up the sun's blustery start. He wore a blood-streaked, striped apron over a thick woollen pullover, and white Wellington boots that were about to part with their soles and through which peeped a robust pair of socks.

'Morning Ncube,' he waved as the Land Rover pulled up, 'Nomatter has already been here. She bought a slab of tripe still rich with stomach juices.'

Ncube glanced across at the detective. Some people washed off the stomach contents, worse still, he heard white people actually bleached the honeycombed stomach lining, but his family enjoyed the greeny-yellow liquor that came from the cow's guts. Blessing said it was only digested grass and was good for them since they could never digest it themselves. The rubbery stew had the powerful smell of cow pat as it boiled away in the pot. His stomach began to sing in anticipation. Sibanda took no notice of Ncube's potential supper or the sergeant's gastric juices that were doing their own bubbling; his eyes were fixed on a knife on a whet stone to the side of the butcher. Sergeant Ncube stayed close to Miss Daisy, just in case.

'We've come about Lois,' Sibanda said as he got out of the vehicle.

'I heard. What a terrible thing. Ayi, ayi, I can't believe she is dead.' Shumba's head was in his hands, Sibanda wanted to see his eyes.

'You weren't together as a couple anymore.' Sibanda got straight to the point.

'No, she left me over a month ago. We were almost engaged, been together since school.'

'When did you last see her?' Sibanda asked.

'She was going back to Bulawayo.'

'You didn't go after her?'

'No, why would I?'

'Because you still loved her, and you were angry.'

'No!' Shumba was becoming agitated.

'Sir,' Ncube interrupted with a polite cough, 'could I steal your ear?'

Sibanda walked back to the Land Rover. Ncube lowered his voice. 'There's been a radio message from PC Khumalo, an anonymous phone tip off.'

'What about?'

'Shumba travelled by train to Bulawayo last week. He went to win back Lois, according to the source, but the mouth on the other end of the phone could be a brush for driving away flies.'

'Diverting attention from the real murderer?'

'Maybe, but if Shumba did travel, why is he lying?'

'Let's find out.'

Together they walked back to the anxious butcher. He was standing now, watching the pair. 'Are you sure you've told us everything, Shumba?'

'What do you mean?'

'You were seen on the train to Bulawayo recently.'

Both Sibanda and Ncube were taken by surprise when Shumba took off. He dodged down the narrow service lane alongside the Blue Gnu and across the littered waste land behind, but he was never going to outrun Sibanda, least of all in a pair of gum boots with toes that talked. Sibanda was after him, sprinting with the ease of a star 1st XV winger. The detective was still a legend at Marula Tree School sixteen years after he scored his last try. His rugby tackle was a classic – low, hard and remorseless. Shumba planted his face in a tribe of weary plastic bags, holed and unwanted, tossed by the wind, but taking shelter against a clump of grass. The bolter was cuffed in less time than it took to say 'rubbish dump'.

Chapter 5

She sat beneath an old leadwood, the only surviving tree in the kraal, saved from the axe by the ferocious fight it put up against all comers. A few had tried over the years but the tree lived up to its name, the bole resisted with metallic vigour. No one swung the axe anymore and this generation came to appreciate the shade it offered in a yard swept clean and hardened against any future growth. There was no hope for any little and future leadwoods, the embryos perished in infancy before they had time to send down roots, no match for a proud Ndebele woman's broom.

Her back rested on the trunk, a blanket lay beneath her and across her tiny, bony knees a board acted as a desk. Her father had brought the flat wooden panel home. One side was painted with an advertising slogan for Mobil Oil. A red winged horse pranced across the sign, tail at full extension, legs frisking, powerful wings carrying it to distant lands. She never discovered where her father found the advert, but it must be old because no company called Mobil Oil existed in Zimbabwe. When she asked, her father told her the big petrol suppliers had been chased far away back to America and replaced with local alternatives, who sometimes had fuel and sometimes didn't. There had been change a few years ago and not always for the better, he said.

She loved that horse. He was often the only companion she had to talk to during the day and they had long conversations, told each other secret thoughts and sometimes cried when the pain was tough. Billibomvu cried too. He ached in his wings when he flew too hard and too long, and sometimes his long slender legs battled in the heavy clouds as he galloped or battled the strong winds to come home to her. Often, he cried for his home in America that had been chased far away. But mostly they sat quietly together, just being.

She wished she could fly, she wished she could rise from her dusty seat and soar over the earth on the back of Billi. He'd asked her to go with him and one day she would, but now wasn't the time. There were ambitions to fulfil and an important letter to write. Sometimes, like today, she turned the board over and wrote on the plain side. Dreams and horses were distracting and reality chastised.

Since she'd learned to read, been loaned books and learned of other horses, she realised Red or Billibomvu was a pretty simple, babyish name. Black Beauty sounded more elegant but the Ndebele didn't embellish colours with adjectives, except for white which was the holy of holy shades. Billi would always just be Billi. After several months of practising her writing, pencil pushing hard and sometimes through the paper, the red horse started to chip and scratch. His glorious coat and wings now had white flecks and graphite streaks. One of the marks made him look as though he had an evil eye in his cheek. She hated it. It made the red horse look threatening and less friendly. They argued more. He told her she was wasting her time with education and they should just fly away together, but she loved learning, all the more so because it had come so late and made her, for the first time in her life, a little bit normal, a little how the other children must feel. She had a younger brother and sister who complained about school, the long distance they had to walk and the beatings they got when they did something wrong. She couldn't help them yet with their homework, but she was catching them up quickly and soon they would talk to her, soon they would need her.

She begged her father for a pot of red paint and a brush to fix Billi, but he laughed and said he could find some white paint to cover the horse and make the board look smarter, but there would never be any red. When she cried, he walked away. Her mother came then, took away her pencil and paper and gave her a bowl of *indlubu* to shell. 'That girl comes here causing problems, just do your chores and stop reading and writing. It's a waste of time.' The words were a dagger in her heart.

That girl came again two days later and asked how she had been. She brought more paper and a new grade four maths book. 'You're amazing,' she said, 'and really clever with numbers. Look how fast you're progressing. You'll be a doctor one day.' Somehow she read her moods and cheered her up, but this time even the visiting girl noticed the deep, dark hole she had fallen into.

'It isn't the school work, is it? You're coping so well. I wish I had half your brains.'

'No, these books are my life. I would die now without them. It's Billi, look he's scratched and chipped and it makes him angry.'

The girl looked at her oddly for the first time since they met, but the glance was fleeting and quickly erased. 'I'll sort something,' she said. They spent their allotted hour together, the girl correcting her work, listening to her read aloud, showing her how to round her letters and make them equal. When the lessons were done, the girl talked to her in English, explaining it was important to be able to speak that language in the land beyond the village, and then she was gone on her bicycle and she took the sun with her. She came again the following week with more books and pencils and a story book about English children who had adventures. 'This was mine when I was younger,' she said, 'I want you to have it. I thought I would be forever young with a bunch of friends to explore with, share jugs of homemade lemonade with and a dog to follow me around ...'

'... What happened to your friends and your dog and your dreams?

'There was never a dog, I wasn't allowed one, and my friends, well let's just say they went in different directions. I made a few wrong choices and now I'm banished from their lives.' The girl seemed sad, there were tears.

'And what is a friend?' she asked picking at the corner of the blanket.

'I'm not sure I know anymore, but a very famous playwright whom I hope one day you'll study, said, "A friend is one that knows you as you are, understands where you have been, accepts what you have become, and still, gently allows you to grow".'

'It means you're my friend because you are helping me despite my problems.'

'It does,' the girl smiled, 'and you are mine.'

'Who said those words?'

'William Shakespeare.'

'I'll remember him. He is a special and clever man to put those thoughts on paper. I'd like to do that one day, make up words to help people to understand.'

'You might have another friend as well.' The girl was smiling.

'Who?'

'Billi, doesn't he know who you are and understand where you have been?'

'Yes.'

'And most importantly, accepts who you have become?'

'Of course.'

'Then, I have a present for you.' From her bag, an old satchel slung over her shoulder, the girl produced a small pot of red paint and an artist's paint brush. 'It's for your friend.'

She pushed herself up from the blanket, raised her arms and let the girl lean into her hug.

After the visitor had gone, she prepared Billi for his paint job. First she crawled across to the bucket of water sitting outside the hut and wetted her skirt. She dragged herself back to her blanket and began the task of washing Billi carefully with the hem, first his wings and then his body until not a speck of dust remained on his coat. She dried him off with the rest of her skirt and began to paint. She was hesitant at first but as her confidence flourished, so her brush strokes grew more assured. The red tone didn't quite match the original, which had faded to a pinkish red, but it was more vibrant and carried the hues of Africa – the brilliant red of a September sun, tinged with a hint of the yellow flowers blazing like butter on the sweet thorn Acacia trees in bloom and just a touch of the tingling blue of a clear winter sky. As she painted, she felt as though she were flying and Billi smiled again, and she truly understood what friendship was.

The girl returned the following week and was agog at Billi's transformation. 'Is there no end to your talent? You're an artist as well!'

She felt nothing for the praise that would normally lift her spirits because she had helped a friend and that was more important.

'Your steady hand has given me an idea for lots of fun,' said the girl, 'only it will have to be secret, for me at least.'

'What is it?'

'You'll have to wait for next week. It'll be a surprise.'

CHAPTER 6

'Er, well done, Sibanda,' the praise from Chief Inspector Mfumu, Officer-in-Charge Gubu Police, dictator in miniature and minister of religious cant, was as rare as the sighting of a crepuscular bat hawk, and undermined by a condescending tone. 'We have the murderer and can sleep soundly in our beds.'

Sibanda brushed aside the feeble attempt at praise. 'I don't like the way this incident is stacking up and I don't trust anonymous tip-offs. We haven't questioned Shumba, we don't know what he's got to say or if he has an alibi. Forensics have his knife and they'll let us know who or what he's been cutting up. I'm not sure we can close the case yet,' the detective was unhappy with the interview. He had been called into Mfumu's office after Shumba had been brought in. The killing was nowhere near solved. There might be a motive and circumstantial geography, but a stack of question marks hung in between.

'It all adds up,' said Mfumu, dusting off his hands as though they were cymbals and he was syncopating a triumphal march. 'Shumba, the butcher, was jilted by the victim, followed her onto the train, killed her and skinned her. Case over, make sure the paperwork is on my desk,' he gave a dismissive wave.

'I'm not closing the docket yet,' Sibanda was firm. 'Gideon Shumba doesn't fit the profile. I've got misgivings that he killed Lois Khupe.'

Mfumu began to splutter. He hated loose ends and this man, this detective, was the master of complication and mess. He revelled in it and then somehow, as if by sorcery, the crime was solved in the most unlikely fashion and the Sibanda myth would be added to and his superpowers whispered about in the corridors and offices. When in doubt Mfumu always referred to the Bible. It was his handbook for life's hurdles and men like Sibanda who were too clever by half and in league with dark forces. Quoting the Bible helped when he was on uncertain ground. The little man stood, his uniform creases and immaculate folds indicating sartorial OCD and a wife shackled to an ironing board, and leant across his desk.

'Revelations chapter 21, verse 8: But the fearful, and unbelieving, and the abominable, and murderers, and whoremongers, and sorcerers, and …'

'… Quite,' Sibanda cut him off before he could launch into a full blown sermon, 'I'll take care of the murderers, you take care of the others on the list.'

'Well,' a deflated Mfumu muttered, 'get that man charged as soon as possible.' His eyes darted around the office for a diversionary tidying job. He settled, as usual, for his pens, fiddling and rolling them. They stubbornly refused to balance with their clips upwards as directed. Sibanda used the distraction to leave. Mfumu looked up to find his office empty. He didn't care. There were other issues on his mind, exciting ones. Things were going to change at Gubu Police Station and the plans did not include Detective Inspector Sibanda.

Sibanda strode into the interview room. It didn't have a one-way observation window or even a clock to monitor the time of the interview. It was a plain unpainted cement cell with a table and chairs in the centre. A small window was high, mean and barred. Ncube would register any details on his notepad. Sibanda's phone would provide the time. He hoped his sergeant had a pen that worked. Last time it had run out and Ncube spent fifteen minutes trying to borrow one while a petty thief who made off with old Manyoni's bag in a snatch and grab sniggered.

Gideon Shumba was sitting with a doomed look on his face. Ncube was in front of him, pad and pencils at the ready. The tape recorder had long since vanished. Some said it had found a second life in a back-street recording studio. The truth was it had been ditched by the robber as unsaleable and obsolete.

'I didn't do it, I didn't hurt her, you've got to believe me,' Shumba's voice was high-pitched and stressed.

'But you did go to Bulawayo by train,' Sibanda began.

Shumba looked down at the desk and shook his head from side to side and then steadied it with his hands. He said nothing.

'We have a witness, Shumba, who saw you board the train,' Ncube added.

'Who told you? It's not true, I haven't left Gubu.'

'Can anyone give you an alibi?'

'For when?'

'The whole of last week.'

'I was at work every day. You can ask my boss, Tickie Mloya, at the Blue Gnu.'

'We'll check. And the weekend?'

Shumba took a long time to answer. 'I can't remember.' He put his head back in his hands.

'What, the whole weekend?' Ncube interrupted, how could anyone not remember what they were doing on their days off? Gideon Shumba was a strange one; even when there was no cockerel to crow, the day still dawned.

'I was … er drunk, out of it completely.'

'With no companion?' Ncube was almost speechless. He liked a drop himself but a man who drank alone would die a lonely death.

'I wasn't good company. I was drowning my sorrows.'

'Seems you have drunk the hot water to pluck the chicken with as well, my friend, and unless you can come up with an alibi, the *inkukhu* will still have its feathers on and we can't help you.' Ncube sat back in his chair.

Sibanda took out his phone and skipped to the photo of the corpse. 'Did you do this?' He pushed the screen under Shumba's nose. The skinned body loomed before his eyes, all muscle sinew and raw meat, like a medical chart for teaching human anatomy. The butcher turned his head and closed his eyes.

'No, no I didn't do this, that's witchcraft, get it away from me!'

'Look again, Shumba. Look at Lois's face, the face you say you loved.' Sibanda changed the picture to one of the skull. It was more hideous on the screen than in real life.

Shumba screamed, 'I didn't do this.'

'Then tell us where you were at the weekend.'

'I'm innocent,' he turned to look at Sibanda, 'you have to believe me, I can't tell you ...' he broke down.

'You'll find the holding cells might loosen your tongue, Shumba. Lock him up, Ncube.'

Ncube led the sobbing, handcuffed man to the cells; Sibanda headed for reception.

'Zee, any clues on who called in with the information about Gideon Shumba being on the train?'

'I don't know, he didn't leave a name.'

'So it was a man?'

'Yes.'

'From around here?'

'Hard to tell, but he had a Shona accent. His Ndebele didn't flow sweetly. The language was crushed like a butterfly on a chameleon's tongue.'

'Any idea of age?'

'Hmm, between twenty and forty is the best I can do. He wasn't an old man but not a child either.'

'Thanks, put him through to me if he phones again.'

Sibanda walked back to his office, checking on Chanza on the way. He still wasn't in. What was he up to? And why was Mfumu looking more than usually pleased with himself and more than usually ironed into his uniform?

Sibanda stared out of the window at a black-eyed bulbul, but he wasn't registering the bird and anyway it was already on his list. His mind was focused on Gideon Shumba and Lois Khupe. What had gone wrong for them? The reason for their split might be the key to Shumba's silence. Whatever had happened, it didn't add up to murder.

Ncube knocked on the office door. 'I've settled him in, sir, and he's not happy.'

The cells were little short of disgusting, flea-ridden, urine-soaked starvation boxes, with the temperature of a freezer. No one was going to be happy. Sibanda continued to examine the bulbul, which was now hopping around on the starved grass.

Sergeant Ncube waited for an answer. The detective was doing his window staring again. Whatever could he be watching in the courtyard to keep him so still and quiet?

'Are you going to charge him, sir?'

Sibanda remained frozen in concentration, although he heard every one of the sergeant's words. 'I met the Officer-in-Charge in the corridor,' Ncube decided on a change of topic, 'he was leaping around from one leg to the other like one of those whirling apostolics, minus the red robes and dancing attendants. He seemed to think we should have closed the docket, but maybe he is being previous.'

'Previous?' Sibanda queried. The word stirred a response.

'Er ... ahead of himself, sir, like a warthog racing away as though a pack of dogs is after him when in fact the dogs are still chained to the farmer's fence.' Ncube set himself the task of learning more English words, particularly ones of three syllables or more. He wanted to impress the detective. Nomatter, his second wife, had found a tattered Oxford English Dictionary at the SPCA charity shop on her last trip to Bulawayo. Ncube had been trying to learn a word a day ever since.

'Right, er, yes,' Sibanda decided on patience, 'he is being overly "previous". Gideon Shumba's not our culprit though.'

'Then why isn't he giving us an alibi for the weekend?'

'If we knew that then we could let him go.'

'You never asked Shumba about the wire ring, sir. That's a clue.'

'No, keep that to yourself, Ncube. Shumba is an unlikely killer of Lois Khupe and we may need that detail later. Any idea why Stalin Mfumu is so pleased with himself? What have you heard?'

'Nothing, seems no one's been throwing their ear down in the right places.'

'Keep alert, Ncube. Something's going on we don't know about.'

'What are we doing about Shumba?'

'Leave him where he is for now and keep checking with other stations for any similar unsolved murders.'

Ncube wobbled out of Sibanda's office. It was lunchtime. Fishing was poor in the cold weather, but *izimbambayila*, sweet potatoes, were being harvested. Not many he had to admit. Poor rains and a frightening drought had seen to that, but there were enough to put aside. He dug the storage pit for them himself, wider at the bottom and covered with a flat stone at the top. The potatoes would be raked out over the next four months as needed. The first of the starchy treats were in his lunch box, boiled and then fried in a little oil, brown sugar and cinnamon, accompanied by a few slices of sharp, barely ripe tomato; it made the perfect lunch. He hurried along the corridor but not to uncover a forgotten missing person's report. The absentee had waited for discovery for a long time and she could surely wait until he filled his stomach.

Sibanda picked up the phone and punched in the number of Universal Dream in Bulawayo. The speed of the connection surprised him – telephonic connections in Gubu were normally a hit-and-miss affair.

'The person in charge,' he barked. He waited, tapping his fingers on the desk.

'Hello,' a foreign voice came on the line, 'I'm Knut Von Bergen.'

'I'm phoning about Lois Khupe.'

'Ah yes, tragic affair,' the accented voice dropped in deference to death, 'she was a much appreciated employee of the Universal Dream team.' He made the victim sound like some kind of global Olympic basketball contender. Von Bergen's grief was contained and professional. Was there a poorly hidden hint of relief? In that moment Sibanda made the decision to get down to Bulawayo on the evening train.

'Is the entire "dream team" available tomorrow?'

'We are in important planning meetings all this week.'

'Good.'

'What do you mean?' Von Bergen spluttered.

'Good news because everyone who worked with Lois Khupe will be in the same place. It will make my life easier. I'll interview them all tomorrow.'

'But …'

'Tomorrow then, Mr Von Bergen, make sure no one is absent.' He put down the phone.

Sibanda would have to get on the train at some stage to visualise what might have happened to Lois Khupe and how. Train travel was not a favourite mode of transport. The carriages were overcrowded and less than wholesome, breakdowns and unreliability a fact of life. Still, anything was better than hours chugging along in that clapped-out Land Rover, Miss Daisy, with Ncube wittering about her long and glorious history or some arcane solenoid or pump or bolt connecting this to that or regulating something or other.

He started again to rummage for his college notes on serial killers and by the time Ncube returned happily filled with lunch, Sibanda was irritable with failure.

Ncube flicked through his own notes, licking his fingers, still sticky with sweet potatoes, to separate the pages. 'Some reports have come in. There have been a few unsolved murders or suspicious deaths on or around the railway in the last few years. One man was found dead in 2005 at Umgusa siding, but no one was sure whether he was hit on the head with a brick or suffered an unlucky blow from flying ballast as the train roared past. Then just outside Bulawayo, at Pasipas, a man was cut in half on the rails. He was drunk and went to sleep, but Bulawayo Central aren't completely convinced, seems he was a well-known drug dealer with a history of violence. Nothing else so far, but everyone's looking.'

'No men, just women in this case, Ncube, keep trying.'

'I've been in touch with every station along the western line.'

'We may have to check the whole railway network, there's no saying our killer hasn't been on the move further afield.'

Ncube's shoulders fell and his stomach sagged in sympathy over his belt. 'A lot of work, sir.'

'Get PC Khumalo to help when she can but tell her to make the phone calls from my office.'

'I thought …'

'You won't need the phone for the time being. We are going to Bulawayo on tonight's train to question Lois's colleagues at Universal Dream.'

'Sir, have you cleared that with Cold War?' Ncube detected the onset of a potbellied gurgle. This spelt trouble. 'He believes the case is closed and we'll need a travel warrant.'

'Leave that with me, sergeant. I'll meet you at the train station at midnight.' There was an edge to the detective's tone. He could handle the Officer-in-Charge without Ncube's preface of doom.

As it turned out, Mfumu didn't require much convincing. He signed the travel warrant and even upgraded the carriage to first class. When he suggested Sibanda take as much time as necessary to complete his enquiries, the detective became suspicious.

'We should only be gone for the day. We'll take tomorrow night's train back.'

'Don't stint on time. It pays to be thorough,' Mfumu ran his fingers along his crisp trouser creases, a sensuous pleasuring, all the while smiling like a lizard on a busy antheap.

'One day is enough.' Sibanda made to leave and then turned back. 'Where is Chanza? I haven't seen him all week. Should I be concerned?'

Stalin Mfumu looked up sharply, head cocked to one side, wary. 'He's, er, sick, terrible winter flu, it's a bug going around. He'll be back in a day or so, I'm sure.'

Sibanda left the office and headed home. Mfumu was lying, of course, or at least bending the truth and he wasn't any good at it. As he spoke, he twitched and wriggled like a half-squashed centipede, all frantic legs and arms. Lying was not Mfumu's forte, he was hiding something. Sibanda didn't waste time trying to work out the chief inspector's plan. Perhaps tonight's train journey would give him a clue as to how the killer had carried out his crime, subdued the victim, skinned the body unseen and thrown it from a carriage. His thoughts didn't go far or deep. The poet, Lovemore Moyo, was sitting on his veranda with what looked like a bottle of something decent by his side and a pair of pliers in his hand.

'Ah, Sibanda, welcome home,' he waved the bottle displaying a hairy-legged, kilted man mid jig. It promised at least a tenuous relationship with Scotland.

'A couple of glasses?' Sibanda walked through to his kitchen and returned with two chunky beakers. He sat next to Lovemore Moyo. 'Thrown out again?'

'No, in fact quite the opposite, I'm in the good books today.' He shook the bottle. 'See I have been rewarded. The viper had a fair week. She's a trader and with this bitter weather Gubu suddenly had a shortage of blankets. She got her hands on a bale, cheap, in Botswana. Her brother works at the Plumtree customs post ... voila, no duty and a handy profit, but I probably shouldn't be sharing that detail with you.'

'Smuggling is the least of my worries.'

'Bad day? I hear there's been a body found.'

Sibanda didn't share professional information with anyone, not even a likeable poet. 'Routine stuff, we have a suspect inside already.' He didn't believe a word, but it served the moment. 'What are you up to?' he asked, pointing to the pliers, some wire and a few empty cool drink cans on the ground.

'It's what I do when I'm not writing, wirework, I make animals from wire and old cans. Giraffe, elephant and geckos – they're particularly popular, tourists love a lizard.'

'Is it profitable?' Sibanda took another swig of the amber liquid. He couldn't define it as whisky, but it was a fair substitute and it was doing the job of easing his tense jaw.

'It keeps the venomous cobra off my back if I'm gainfully occupied. It means she concentrates on her kids.'

'*Her* kids?'

'I'm husband number three. None of the brood is mine. I've got some somewhere, just never managed to hang on to them or their mothers.'

'What made you settle down now?' Sibanda recognised a fellow traveller in failed relationships.

'Age, I'm getting on. I want a settled life. My restless poet's soul is beginning to wither. To be honest, I've hardly written a decent word since the terrible days of hyperinflation. Did you know we were second in the world to Hungary in the inflation ranks? Seems the Zloty beat us. I, for one, would have been prepared to suffer a few days more to get the record, be number one at something. Cynicism doesn't feed my muse.'

'Hit you hard, did it?'

'This little curio business used to thrive. I had a workshop with four employees, a stall up in the Falls, one on the road at the turn off, and shops in Bulawayo that couldn't get enough of the stuff. That's why Gloria took to me after her last husband died. The calabash was full, the pasture was sweet and the milk was fresh. It's all gone sour now, that's women for you, loveless, faithless witches.' Lovemore Moyo shrugged his shoulders and continued to bend and twist the wire, attacking the animal shape with aggression until a piece snapped badly and he threw the figure down in disgust. 'And you, any partner?'

Sibanda hesitated, could he share his complicated love life with this man? His relationships were as contorted and complex as the wire shapes the artist was working on. It was early days with Angel Better, the clinic sister, and talk of Berry was too painful and taboo. 'I almost had a fiancée once,' was as much as he wanted to divulge.

'What happened?'

He thought of Khanye, the beautiful, wilful girl who stole his heart and betrayed him. 'Work got in the way. It always does.' He rolled another mouthful of the tannic liquid around his tongue and gripped his glass in both hands, staring to the west. Distant trees were already warming their silhouettes against an inferno of blazing reds and flickering ochres. One thing Africa did best was sunsets, a rare A+ on a frequently blotted copybook. Sibanda turned up his collar against the evening nip and tuned in to the birds singing the day out. A scrub robin cut through the muted undertones of dove coos and murmurs, a lively, scolding song admonishing the neighbours to pipe down, it was bedtime. Black-eyed bulbuls warning with their bi-syllabic chit-chat told Sibanda they were alarmed, probably by an early rising genet on the prowl. In a thorn bush, a branchful of bronze mannikins, squashed wing to wing, like a sentimental mantelpiece ornament, twittered and wheezed in chorus, playing a game of fly away Peter, fly away Paul as one by one they peeled away and disappeared into their ragged grass roost on the branch below. Sibanda tipped his head back and washed down the last of his drink as a rufus-naped lark took ownership of a lonely stump and added a plaintive, melancholy whistle, a Last Post for the dying day. Lovemore Moyo piped up with his own chant in a hypnotic timbre:

The wind brushes, rushes, teases, tangles above the water.
Mahogany trees murmur sour nothings to the sweepings
Of crisped leaves.
"Tell father, tell father" insists the red-eyed turtle dove
But the boy is alone, staring into circulating ripples,
There is no father to tell.

The words echoed the mood and rhythm of the birds. Sibanda felt obliged to say something but he wasn't sure if he wanted to disturb the lingering sadness. It suited the moment. It suited his own melancholy.

'I'm having one for the road, my friend,' Moyo broke the spell, cheery again.

'I shouldn't, but I will, thanks.' Sibanda's glass was refilled generously before he could protest the long and difficult night ahead.

CHAPTER 7

Gubu railway station was a throng of chilled passengers and busy vendors, a bustle of blankets, thick jackets and tightly wound scarves. Red, white and blue taxi bags were stuffed with more of the same, zips bulging or long since broken, bound for security, with string or more pliable rekin. Vendors picked out their spots and set up their stalls. One enterprising trader had a brazier at the far end of the station, steaming with roasted mealie cobs, the grilled nuttiness travelling down the platform on the freezing wind, enticing a group of travellers to his stall. The lucky ones stood warming their hands against the fire, fingers splayed, every digit got their fair share of the heat, and brown skins glowed orange in the flare of the embers.

Most of the vendors were women with blankets wrapped around their waists like skirts, plastic buckets or basins balanced on heads. Each container full of boiled eggs, boiled sweets, oranges, bags of roasted peanuts and salted popcorn, sweet potatoes – an entire food court on the platform. The women were chatting, clustered in groups, rearranging their wares for better saleability, swapping stories, swapping samples, rocking hidden babies strapped to their backs, lost under thick wraps so the mothers looked like hunchbacks. How the little mites didn't suffocate was a mystery to Sibanda, who watched the midnight gathering from the shadows.

Lois Khupe left this station on a night just like this. Had she been upset at the breakup from Gideon Shumba or excited at meeting up with her new love? Had her killer skulked in shadows at a station somewhere along the line, even this one, or mingled with fellow travellers watching for an easy mark, a young woman to stalk and pick out for his warped theatre? Lois's murder was definitely a re-enactment and Sibanda was certain she wasn't part of Act I or the Epilogue. If he was right, there was drama still to come.

'Hello, sir, are you hiding? It has taken me quite some time to find you.' Ncube appeared in silhouette against the light, a ball of padding with two eyes peering from inside his balaclava. The detective was a strange one. Why was he back here in the dark, instead of with the giddy interest out on the platform?

'No, Ncube, just observing the comings and goings, the train is still a few minutes away.'

'I'll stay with my family until then if that's all right, sir. The little ones are very excited. They don't see the big engines often.'

Sibanda glanced towards the Ncube family gathering, a flock of brightly coloured nestlings, all chattering and clamouring, wide-eyed and wondering. He watched for a few minutes, reminiscing about the journeys of his own childhood. Travel was always a rare and celebrated event. Uncles and aunts, cousins and grandparents accompanied his family to the siding or the bus stop and waited with them, participating vicariously in the adventure, anticipating the stories told on the return. Somewhere along the line he lost that amazement, but there was no time to explore memories, or the world-weary jaundice dogging him these days, the train was approaching. He watched Ncube hugging his children as though he was leaving them for the far reaches of Canis Major and not just a day trip to Bulawayo. His wives kept a respectful distance, public displays of affection were deemed unseemly, untraditional and coarse; Thadeus Ncube and his wives kept to the old ways. A movement in the shadows beyond the Ncube clan flickered in Sibanda's peripheral vision, another anti-social observer hugging the station's dirty walls and alcoves. Was there a familiarity in the stance, in the jaunty tip of the head and the featureless outline of a baggy knee? He was sure it was Lovemore, the poet, whom he'd left a few hours earlier, but then the train pulled into the platform and, as one, the travellers and vendors surged towards the carriages, scrambling for good seats and the most likely customers who hung out of the windows shouting for this and that. When he looked again, the shadowy figure had disappeared.

'This is going to be a very comfortable journey, sir. We'll be like two lonely dumplings in a pot of stew.' Ncube looked around the four-berth compartment, at the banquette seats that converted to beds and the wealth of space. 'Will we be the only ones in here?' Ncube's previous encounters with rail travel had mostly been rescue missions to the regional capital for spares on behalf of Miss Daisy. Seats in the third-class compartment were crammed, upright and hard, with passengers squashed into every space and children sleeping on the floor.

'I expect so, Ncube.' Sibanda didn't much like the idea of sharing a stew with Ncube, particularly not one that was bubbling; the sergeant could produce enough gas on his own to fire up a whole village. 'Not many people can afford first-class travel these days, but our victim did, and possibly the murderer.'

'How do you know, sir?'

'Lois Khupe was raped and skinned – a long night's work – and you need privacy for killing. Murder is a secret, lonely and highly personal pursuit. The rest of the train is like a cattle truck.'

'What about the toilets, sir?'

'There isn't enough room in them to swing a cat, let alone skin one. My money is on a compartment like this.'

'But they wouldn't have put a man and a woman together in a sleeper. The rules are strict.'

'Obviously, and take a look at the lock, one of Barghees's keys isn't going to open that mechanism.' Sibanda flipped the robust lever lock and secured the four-berth compartment.

Ncube looked sheepish. His house keys had been vital in the last case, opening the victim's locked door. The same keys also opened half the doors in Gubu. Barghees, the village General Dealers, offered a stock of locks that could not be described as varied.

'If the murderer was in one compartment and Lois Khupe locked safely in another, how did he get in and murder her?'

'That's what we need to find out.'

The train pulled out of the station, gaining traction and banging couplings amidst a clamour of farewells. Ncube was already rummaging for a midnight snack, having seen Suko tuck a bag of home-roasted peanuts in his holdall. It was the season for the nutty *amazambane* and with a shake of salt they were addictive.

The sergeant was asleep on his bunk before the train passed the first siding at Impofu. He was snoring by the time they reached Water Loop and muttered in his sleep between Isilwana and Kennedy. By Ngamo siding his lips were vibrating in syncopation with the click of the rails. He drooled the rest of the way to Bulawayo. Sibanda didn't sleep immediately. He left the compartment, stood at the window in the corridor and stared out into the blackness. The rail line ran hard against the national park, defined the boundary. He didn't expect to see wildlife, the outside scenery was a blur, but looking into the winter-stark tangle cleared his mind. How had the killer talked his way into a secure compartment, or had he broken in? Maybe he had been in the compartment all along, the new lover from Bulawayo travelling with Loïs to meet her family.

His thoughts were interrupted by the ticket inspector. 'Your ticket, please.'

Sibanda showed him the travel warrant.

'Ah, police. That was a bad business, the woman found on the side of the track. A couple of hours south of here, was it?'

'Yes,'

'Murdered, was she?'

'It hasn't been confirmed,' Sibanda was spare with details. Railway employees were top of his list of suspects and the killer he was looking for could well be one who engaged with the police in a titillating game of catch me if you can.

'How often are you up and down the corridors?'

'Not often in the sleeper compartments, but there are passengers getting on at almost every siding. I have to check the tickets in second and third class after each stop.

'Could one of those passengers come into this section?'

The conductor shrugged his shoulders. 'All the carriages are connected.'

'Is there any way to open the compartment doors from the outside once they're locked?'

'Not unless you have one of these.' He pulled a chain out of his pocket with various metal pieces attached. He held up a multi-sided tube. It fitted snugly into an outside indentation on the carriage door and the inside lever lifted with ease. 'Very useful, you'd be surprised at the number of people who want to overstay their welcome.' The chain rattled in his hand. There was more than a key on it. 'My tool kit,' he continued, aware of the detective's interest. 'You need all sorts of bits and pieces on this job. Something's always jamming or sticking. These carriages are getting old.'

'I see you have a knife.'

'Yes, and you won't believe what I've used it for over the years.' The ticket collector turned to continue his trip along the corridor.

'You have blood on your collar,' Sibanda noticed a streak of red.

'Have I?' he clapped his hand to a series of parallel marks on his neck, 'must have scratched myself. I was clearing a field yesterday.'

'Your hand?' Sibanda caught sight of a fairly new bandage on the fleshy side of the palm, red and angry around the plaster.

'Same thing, caught it on the fence, trying to fix it.'

'Farming's a dangerous business.' Sibanda quipped.

'I must get moving, tickets to check, no time to chat.' The atmosphere changed. There was a flicker of tension. The ticket inspector was keen to move along.

'I didn't get your name.'

'Isaac Manhombo,' he said as he edged sideways down the corridor. His shoulders were too large to take it head on. Isaac Manhombo was a well-built man.

Sibanda stared into the dark and rubbed his jaw, his brain tumbled with thoughts. Why was the ticket inspector, holder of a key to all carriages, farming in the middle of winter? Now was not the time to be clearing fields and fixing fences. He had a full-time job. The flurry of part-time agriculture, in reality everyman's cultural patch of mealies, normally took place just before the rains. Why had he feigned ignorance of the scratches on his neck and yet put his hand straight on the bleeding marks when questioned? The wounds were too new to have been made by Lois, scabs would have formed by now, but she would have fought for her life, Sibanda was sure, not able to scream with fingers pressed around her throat, her windpipe closed, her brain fighting for oxygen. Maybe those long fingernails inflicted damage on someone, raked the killer's face or inflicted a few bruises from kicks. It was a detail to keep an eye out for.

Sibanda fell asleep around 2 am, disturbed hourly as the train pulled into each station or siding by the clamour of travellers and traders.

Ncube snored like a deaf tractor through every commotion. The detective woke at 7 am, irritable and cramped. His long frame only just fitted on the bunk and for most of the journey his knees had been bent.

'You slept well, sir,' Ncube was already upright and munching on a boiled egg and biltong, 'my wives sent this for you.' He proffered a plastic container with a variety of edibles. Sibanda, now propped on his elbows, didn't dispute Ncube's assessment of his night, but waved away the food, and then as if to disguise his lack of thanks, he stood, limbered his stiff legs, reached into his back pack for a bottle of water and asked, 'How far out are we?'

'Very close,' Ncube opened Sibanda's plastic container and was robbing the biltong.

'When we pull into Bulawayo, get hold of the station master and get a list of the train staff on duty on this western line. Forensics haven't confirmed a time of death, so check records from ten days before we found the body. I want every name and a trace on any police records, even a parking ticket, and get yourself straightened up, Ncube, you look as though you've been sleeping in a brothel,' Sibanda was back in investigative mode.

'I have never … sir. How can you suggest …?' Ncube wasn't in uniform and these were his smartest clothes. He tucked his shirt in, tried to smooth the concertina creases gathered around his crotch, took in a large breath and did up the button on a waist band some said was Saharan in its expanse, stretching from one side of Africa to the other. 'Start with Isaac Manhombo, he was on board the train tonight.'

'Isaac Manhombo from Gubu.'

'Do you know him?'

'Know of him. He has a reputation for being as vicious as a honey badger and not afraid to use his fists.'

'Trouble?'

'He's not long moved to Gubu on transfer, but there are rumours.'

'Check on him when you get back. He had a few cuts and scratches. He made up some story about them, but he was lying.'

'Will transport be coming to collect us, sir?'

'I'll get a taxi straight to the Universal Dream offices, you can stick around the station, talk to the staff, see if anyone recognises Lois Khupe from her photo. Maybe someone will remember her.'

'But how will I get into town to meet up with you?'

There was no answer. Sibanda was off the train before it had come to a halt and was at the taxi rank before Ncube bundled together his possessions and his precious supply of road food.

The Bulawayo morning beyond the station was raw; workers were scurrying, droves of them, walking since before first light from distant townships to reach the workshops and factories, the shops and street markets – an army on a pre-dawn route march. Traders were pushing homemade barrows welded together from old car axels, bits of scrap metal, anything to get a handcart on the move. They were off to the vegetable wholesalers to collect apples and bananas, or onions and cabbages, or whatever else arrived in plenty on the trucks. The vendors pushed and hawked around the streets and offices until last light saw final employees dashing home, grabbing one or two tomatoes from the carts to spice up the cabbage relish. The last cents squeezed out of a pinched populace.

Sibanda's breath condensed in smoky whorls as he strode to the rank. Had Lois Khupe walked to the station or had she taken a taxi? It was worth a shot. He flashed Lois's photo along the line of cabs. Some of the drivers were asleep, slumped over the wheel; it had been a long night. This was probably their last call. None of the cabbies recognised the photo, but then Lois Khupe didn't stand out from the crowd. She was of average height and weight and average looks. Her beautifully manicured hands would not have been in the driver's line of sight and, anyway, hands were not a man's lasting assessment. The last cab, belonging to a company called Tixi Taxis, was empty and parked a little back from the others. The driver arrived seconds after the detective. When shown the photo he smiled.

'Pretty girl,' he said, 'but I don't recognise her.'

Sibanda decided to use him.

'You can't get in,' he protested, 'you have to go to the front of the rank. I'll be lynched.'

'Rough lot you cab drivers?'

'No,' he laughed, 'we like to share the fares equally. They are a good bunch,' he was quick to defend his co-workers, 'it's just there's a system.'

'And I've just changed the system. Get going, Universal Dream offices.'

Richard Ngulube tucked his brightly patterned winter scarf tightly around his neck and started the cab. Putting the taxi into gear, he pulled away from the rank. He recognised a policeman when he saw one and he wasn't about to make him angry. Maybe it was time to knock off anyway after this trip. It had been another long restless night and he wanted to spend time with his thoughts. This cop interrupted some pleasant dreaming. He'd had a good week and he wanted to relive the thrills of the last few nights. His mind drifted. He was so familiar with the city he could drive with his eyes shut, could even draw an accurate pothole map, although the ruts and fissures proliferated and deepened daily with new craters springing from nowhere. Last night, again, had been special. He parked his taxi in darkness, waiting for a regular fare, shunning the feeble halo from the only street light working. He preferred the shadows. He remembered pulling a cigarette packet from behind his sun visor and fumbling for matches in the glove box. It had taken four matches to get one to light. The first three splintered and crumbled, not an unexpected statistic. Africa was doomed never to get it right the first time or the second or third. The fourth match flared, shaming the pathetic street light. Richard Ngulube killed the flame. He cherished these rare moments of anonymity after a day of sharing his space with a crush of bodies, endless chatter, sighing buttocks, screaming babies and demanding customers like this man in the back. He learned to live with the everyday discordant symphony of overcrowding and personal smells, but it wasn't easy. He liked a clean and ordered environment.

The regular fare he waited for was a second-rate politician with a wallet as fat as the neck rolls spilling over his collar. Over the last few weeks on this run he had found himself parking up earlier and earlier, finding the shadows and watching. Across the street, a neon sign was flashing 'open' over a faded blue door. A DJ and his muffled announcements seeped through the cracks and wafted across the street. He wound up his window, only the thumping base penetrated. He could live with that; it was a comforting heartbeat. The club sold sex, intolerable hot air and sleaze, making it and the politician a perfect fit.

'Have you been working the station long?' The detective's question disturbed his memories.

'A few years, sometimes I work the long-distance bus terminus, it depends.'

'On what?'

'Timings, passengers, wherever there are the most fares. I don't mind.'

'Heard anything unusual over the years? Anyone come looking for someone missing before?'

'Not since I've been on the rank, but these are hard times, people are on the move. Everyone has gone to South Africa, but there's unrest down there.'

'Any gossip among the other station cabbies?'

'Not that I've heard.'

Sibanda sat back in the seat and took in the gracious lines of the architecture that set Bulawayo apart from any other African city he had visited. A mixture of colonial grandeur and stylish art deco blended effortlessly. The charmless concrete monoliths of the sixties and seventies had mostly by-passed the city. Modernist steel and glass had been out of reach. Bulawayo retained its character through economic default, and with roads wide enough to turn a wagon and a span of oxen, he could have been on a slightly shabby Parisian boulevard until Richard Ngulube swerved into the oncoming traffic to avoid a deep pothole, swerving back as quickly into his correct lane.

'Nkomo's Crater, had to avoid it, sorry.'

'What?' It was Sibanda's turn to have his mood interrupted.

'We name the potholes,' the cab driver laughed.

Sibanda could only imagine what Joshua Nkomo, aka Father Zimbabwe, would think of his neglected city now.

Richard Ngulube returned to the right side of the road and his daydream, where was he? Ah yes, he had just lit a cigarette. He stared at the blue door. Would she come out? Several cars passed while he was watching. An ancient truck scuttled down the road, sideways like a crab, using the cover of darkness to move a load of forbidden cargo. And then there she was. She slipped silently from a side door in the filth-strewn service lane of vomiting bins and excrement. He exhaled a fug of smoke in a rush, unaware he held onto it so fiercely.

The child sits on the curb, spindly arms hugging knees. Her thin, white nylon dress is splashed with pink, painted by the overhead sign. The flimsy fabric is almost see-through. A wind picks up, outlining nascent breast buds poking against the nylon fabric. She is cold. She is staring into the gutter as if the answer to her life lies in the wind-blown detritus of a city's struggle. A crumple of yesterday's news nudges along the curb and grabs her ankle. She embraces it as a visitor and scans the columns of words. They hold no answers. The newsprint is tossed from her hands and tumbles further down the street, beyond the neon warmth towards the distant centre, an escape of sorts.

The blue door opens. The politician squeezes out still attached to a woman. Money changes hands. He hitches his trousers. The woman wriggles seductively and smiles through fat, rouged lips. Richard Ngulube chucks away his glowing butt and reaches for the ignition. The woman grabs the girl by the upper arm, long painted nails penetrating her young skin, and swings her violently towards the door. The lips shrink to a snarl as she beats the child with her free arm, screaming abuse. The girl looks back. Through the darkness her eyes lock on Ngulube's but then the looming bulk of the sated politician blocks the scene. The door slams, the taxi rocks and the girl is gone.

'How much?' Sibanda was leaning in through the window.

'What?'

'How much?'

'Er ... ten dollars,' Ngulube smiled. He didn't remember how he got to the Universal Dream offices, but that happened often with large swathes of his life. There were blanks. He drove on auto pilot and dreamed. Richard Ngulube's taxi metre hadn't worked for a long time, so he charged what he thought, but he could have asked for a higher fare. This cop had an aura, looked in charge, 'Here's my card,' he said, 'you might need me again.' Sibanda thrust a ten dollar note into the driver's hands and strode towards a restored old colonial. Richard Ngulube watched him go.

CHAPTER 8

'As you can see, Mr Sibanda, all our staff are in the meeting room,' Knut Von Bergen, a stocky man, wearing steel-framed glasses and balding badly pointed from his office to a room with an open door and a table with eight people around it. 'They are all waiting for you.'

'A word in private first,' Sibanda rose and shut the open door.

'We share everything here, detective, we are an open community. We keep no secrets from one another,' there was disapproval in the tone.

'A woman has been raped and murdered and her body dumped in the most demeaning of circumstances. I am here to investigate a crime, not participate in a bloody philanthropist's tea party.' Sibanda was irritable from lack of sleep.

'Yes, of course, apologies, what do you want to know?'

'Everything about Lois Khupe, her role in the organisation, her close associates, enemies, any detail at all that could be useful.'

'She was our liaison with the schools. Matabeleland North is the most educationally disadvantaged of all the provinces. The pass rate is woeful, lagging behind the rest of the country by some way, the teachers demotivated and depressed, and equipment non-existent. We help where we can, books, computers if there's an electricity supply, feeding schemes ...'

'... Did she travel to the schools often?'

'No, hardly at all anymore. She was a senior coordinator in the office, putting forward proposals, keeping track of the grants and the paperwork. Others did the leg work. We are going to miss her input greatly, a valued colleague. George Paradza is in charge here. I travel between the regional offices and Head Office in Copenhagen. He'll give you a much clearer picture.' He removed his glasses, placed them on the desk and rubbed his eyes. 'Who did this, detective? Will you catch him?' Sibanda couldn't decide if there was disinterest in the voice or just the inflexion of a heavily foreign accent. He stared at the glasses, they were missing the screw that attached the arm to the frame and were held together by a twist of wire. It was the same meticulously neat winding as the wire ring forced on Lois's hand, the same tarnished copper. He dismissed the coincidence. Anyone could do a tight spiral with a pair of pliers, possibly with the exception of himself.

Sibanda looked into the eyes of the man across the desk. Without spectacles they appeared hard, marbled with green, rimmed with black and strangely hypnotic. 'How long have you been visiting Zimbabwe, Mr Von Bergen?'

'Let me see, ten years or so, yes, at least that long.'

'You must enjoy it here.'

'I do, it's a troubled country at times, but there are many benefits.'

'Like?'

'Well, er ... the climate for one. Isn't it rated the best in the world? Look, detective, I didn't have anything to do with Lois's murder, nor did anyone else here for that matter. You are wasting time questioning me.' He was flustered and covering something.

'We'll catch the right man, Mr Von Bergen, you can be sure of that.'

The detective tapped the desk in the meeting room waiting for the last employee. He had interviewed the staff one at a time. They were like robots, each spouting a featureless assessment of Lois Khupe: no, they didn't socialise with her out of working hours, no, she had no enemies and no, there was no local boyfriend. They were familiar with nothing in her personal life. She was very good at her job, well liked.

A knock on the meeting room door broke the pattern.

'Come in.'

'I've brought your tea, boss.' A lady in domestic uniform of floral patterned dress with matching head scarf and apron entered. She placed a tray in front of the detective. Sibanda hadn't had anything all morning and he was grateful for the offering. 'Do you work here?'

'I do the cleaning.'

'Did you know Lois Khupe?'

'She was a lovely girl. We lived close to one another in Nketa Township, often caught the same transport home. She paid my fare when I couldn't afford it. They say she has been murdered. Who would kill such a kind person?'

'So you talked sometimes?'

'Often, you see we share the same name, Khupe, no relation but same totem. The others who work here are foreigners or from another tribe and ... different, she didn't trust them.'

'Why?'

Betty Khupe looked around nervously, 'I can't say, sir, my job ... I have children to educate.'

The door opened again and a man entered, 'Betty, you can leave now, the detective and I want to talk.' He waved her away.

Betty nodded and scuttled out of the room.

'Sorry to keep you waiting, detective, I'm the last man you want to interview. Oh, and there's a large police sergeant out there. He says he's with you.'

'I'd better check on him,' Sibanda found Sergeant Ncube chattering to a comely receptionist and pulled him to one side, 'Ncube, find the cleaning lady Betty Khupe ...'

'... A relative?'

'No, but she's scared of someone in this organisation and she was a close friend of the victim. She knows something. See if you can get it out of her. Let me get Mr I'm-in-charge out the way. I'll meet you in half an hour. There's a coffee shop around the corner.'

'George Paradza?' Sibanda was back in the meeting room, facing a smooth-faced individual, dressed a little too suavely for philanthropy.

'Yes, operations director, UD, Matabeleland.'

'You were Lois Khupe's immediate boss?'

'She answered to me. I oversee all projects in the region. Lois was in charge of our educational efforts. UD has many other areas of interest,' with the suavity came a hint of arrogance.

'Did you know her well?'

'As well as anyone here.'

'Did you notice any changes in her recently? Did she seem out of sorts in any way? Any problems at work?'

'Perhaps she was a little more subdued. I heard she had boyfriend problems.'

'A local man, someone she worked closely with?'

'What are you saying, detective?'

'A good looking man like you must have a way with the girls.'

'I resent this questioning. Our relationship was strictly professional.' Beads of sweat broke out on the top of George Paradza's lip, which lead Sibanda's eyes to a scab at the corner of his mouth.

'I see you've a nasty cut on your mouth.'

Paradza's assurance vaporised as he put his hand to his face. 'It's winter, my lips crack often. Look, have we finished here?'

'Not quite. What exactly did Lois handle at the schools?'

'I'm sure the others have already told you all this, detective.'

'Probably, but tell me again.'

'Lois was in charge of the distribution of books and equipment and, er … the bicycles.'

'Bicycles?' Sibanda noted the hesitation.

'We identified a need at some of the very remote areas. Often children have to walk kilometres every day to and from school. It leaves little energy for learning. We provide bicycles if the walk is more than two hours.'

'Is this a big project?'

'We have covered twelve secondary schools so far and we're hoping to cover another three by the end of the year.'

'Do you ship the bicycles in?'

'No, we use an importer in Bulawayo.'

'Who?'

'Is that important? Detective Sibanda, you are wasting my time. I have other matters to attend to.'

'I don't know if it's important, but tell me anyway.' Sibanda moved closer to the operations director until their faces were almost touching. Paradza was forced to step back and look down, the detective's eyes were strangely compelling. He didn't want to give him the name, but it spilled out all the same.

'Lion Cycles.'

'How many bicycles have been distributed so far?'

'Exactly?'

'A rough estimate.'

'Maybe five hundred or so.'

'And how much money is involved?'

'I can't say. I don't have those numbers to hand.' Paradza was visibly uncomfortable.

'I'll phone tomorrow, when they will be available,' Sibanda's underlining of *will* left George Paradza in no doubt.

Sibanda terminated the interview and made his way to the coffee shop around the corner. Sergeant Ncube had settled himself under a large umbrella outside. He looked out of place among the wealthy, white housewives and black businessmen who gathered in the upmarket establishment to dally away a few idle moments with a double macchiato. Ncube ordered a large glass of something foaming with cream, ice cream and sprinkles of chocolate. Beside the drink sat a Danish pastry; an apricot winked in the early afternoon sun from under a layer of glaze.

'You must have one of these, sir,' he suggested as he came up for air, sucking hard on the straw, dragging the liquid with some difficulty through the cloud of white, and pointing to the sticky tart.

'A long black please,' Sibanda answered the hovering waitress, ignoring Ncube's recommendation. 'What did Betty Khupe have to say, anything of interest?'

'She was very nervous and frightened of losing her job. She told me Lois had broken off her relationship with Gideon Shumba, but there was no new boyfriend. Lois was still too upset. She uncovered something about Shumba that worried her, but she didn't share the reason with Betty Khupe.'

'Maybe he was becoming violent.'

'Who knows? But I think we have the right man behind bars after all.'

'Perhaps ... so, no new boyfriend.' Sibanda rubbed his chin. Was he on the wrong track?

'There was something else, sir. Betty felt Lois was worried by more than the breakup with Shumba. She said something rotten is going on at Universal Dream, there are termites munching at the foundation.'

'Any details?'

'Just suspicions, but she was going to get the proof.'

'Knut Von Bergen is as blind as a mole, Ncube, there's something not right going on at UD and he needs more than glasses to see what's in front of his nose.'

'Blessing has an herbal remedy for bad eyes, sir, I could send him some.'

'It's insight he's short on, sergeant, and your wife can't cure that.' Sibanda's retort was laced with irony and irritation. Ncube, intent on his feast, missed the warning signs. He continued to suck on the dregs in his glass, not prepared to leave a single drop. The slurping noise was a cross between a dust-clogged vacuum cleaner and a sick crow, long in the dying. The lunch ladies looked up from their conversations in distaste, but they had never known hunger or the Ndebele joy of an achingly full stomach. The businessmen tucking into their plump burgers heard nothing out of place. Despite the trappings of economic success, they all started life in cramped township houses or mud villages where noisy eating and a clean-licked plate were a sign of appreciation and delight. Who knew when another meal would come?

Eyesight, insight, outsight ... the detective was getting in a tangle again, he often raced off like a headless chicken. Where was Sibanda going with this, Ncube asked himself, using his straw as a spatula to scrape the last of the tantalising foam from the sides of the tall glass.

'Ncube! For God's sake concentrate.' Sibanda grabbed the straw and crumpled it into an ashtray, his patience snapped. 'What did you learn at the railway station?'

Ncube's stomach mourned loudly, understanding the last of the froth would be wasted. He looked around to see if the detective's bad manners had been noticed by the other diners. It was terribly wrong to steal another man's food or at least prevent the eating of it, but the detective had not been observed. Ncube was glad, reputation and standing were everything.

'I spoke to the station master,' he fished a notebook from his pocket, 'Philemon Mathe, but he couldn't remember talk of missing girls at Bulawayo station. He has only been in the job a couple of years and said we should try and interview Tommy Bingley. He's the retired station master, worked on the railways for over forty years. Can you imagine, forty years of service? That man has put up with the tough meat and now he can relax and mop up the gravy.'

'He might be retired, but there'll be no gravy running down his chin in this economic climate, Ncube, where do we find him?'

'He runs the Railway Museum, over in Raylton.'

'Eat up and let's get going.'

The museum sat among a sea of rusting railway stock. Through the mesh fencing Sibanda could see row after row of windowless rectangles, transport from a bygone age, awaiting restoration that would never come; or should that be *wreck tangles*? The carriages and old engines were only good for scrap. He had to admit there was a sadness in the ghostly shapes, a lost glory in the faded paint, sagging bodies and corrosion, but he was unmoved. Anything with wheels of any shape or age was tedious. Ncube was distraught; here were the powerful and magical gods of his youth reduced to rubble, but rubble with potential. It wouldn't take much to put them right, would it?

'Can I help you gentlemen?' a stooped man with a pronounced limp shuffled up.

'Tommy Bingley?'

'Yes, and you are ...?'

'Police.'

'What have I done now?' The old man ran his fingers through grey hair, leaving them planted at the back of his head where they scratched in bafflement, creating a tangled thatch.

'Nothing we are aware of,' said Sibanda, 'we just need to delve into your memories.'

'Ah memories ... they're all I've got left. My wife is dead, my hips are shot and my kids are scattered to the winds. Diaspora they call it, *die-a-poorer* is my word for it. The kids can't stay, nothing for them here now, and I can't go if I want my independence. Never likely to see my grandchildren grow. I'm trapped here by the only house I'll ever be able to own, worthless in real world terms, an eroded pension that barely keeps me alive, and the social capital I've built up over forty years on the railways – mates. And if I'm lucky, a very occasional beer. Better than some, though, neighbours have been living on avocados alone. They have a tree, thank God, but there's not much in a pear to keep body and soul alive. Sold everything that moved to stay afloat, they did. Don't get me started or you will have to arrest me.' His hand dropped to his side. 'What memories do you want?'

'We are …'

'… We? There's only one of you.' Tommy Bingley snapped at the only government representative he'd been able to collar in weeks. He needed a new hip, all that walking up and down a draughty platform had worn it out. Surely they owed him that.

Sibanda looked around for Ncube but his sergeant had disappeared. He clenched his jaw. 'Have you ever heard of any girls or women going missing on the trains? Has anyone ever been to investigate before?'

Tommy Bingley's hand went back to his hair. Further scratching was converting the thatch into a haystack. 'Let me see … no, I don't think so … wait a minute, there was something, but … no, nothing to bother about.'

'What was the *something*?'

'A wild goose chase in the end.'

'Go on, Mr Bingley, let me decide.'

'Well, a few years back, my wife – Liz – was still alive then you see, and I remember talking to her about it. Liz had a sixth sense about these things, said the girl had run away, a lucky escape. Not healthy to live that sort of life, she said. She was a lively one, my Liz. Must have been five years back, now.'

Sibanda let the old man ramble. The memories were dissolving the clouds in his eyes, the frown on his brow and probably the ache in his heart.

'Who was she, the girl who had the lucky escape?'

'A nun, from a convent somewhere up the line.'

'A nun? She went missing?'

'Ran away, more like it. Seems she had enough of all that popery and no fun.'

'So why was there an investigation?'

'She left the convent, rumour was she was sent home on the train, but she never made it, did a runner, probably too scared to face her parents. They ate the walls of the church and she was a good time gal.'

'But the police investigated?'

'The nuns insisted they had put her on the train and her parents were waiting at Bulawayo station to meet her. The police never found a trace of her. In the end, they decided she got off in the night at one of the sidings and disappeared. Probably married with a tribe of kids by now.'

'Do you remember the name of the convent?'

The head scratching resumed, a whole flock of buffalo weavers could nest in the resultant chaos. 'St Patrick's? No, wait, it began with an M.' The weavers were now being roughly evicted, fingers snaking through the snarl. 'I have it, St Monica's at Gubu, that's where she came from. Sister Martha, her name was.' He beamed, delighted his dimming memory hadn't failed him for once.

'You've been very helpful, Mr Bingley.'

'Can I show you around? We've some interesting exhibits including Rhodes's carriage, very plush. Those Victorians knew how to travel. And you can't believe what two hundred tonnes of explosives will do to a train and a bridge. On its way to the mines, it was. We've got the twisted vestiges of one axle, nothing else remained, not even a tree for kilometres. Mind you, the locomotive was untouched. They built engines to last in those days.' His eyes roved over the more modern rusting hulks. 'During WWII. Sabotage, I'd say, but they never proved it. Couldn't, nothing left to examine.'

'No, I'll just wander. My sergeant has become lost.'

Sergeant Ncube had indeed become lost, in a world of mechanical dreams. The museum was even more exciting than a vehicle scrap yard. Everything was bigger and bolder – massive engines, heavy rods connected to outsize pistons, solid wheels on hefty axels, all stood testimony to engineering genius. If he closed his eyes he could see how each part talked to the other, sweetly, with respect twice repeated. He wondered if railways took on overage apprentices. Was it too late for him? He didn't have long to ponder.

'Ncube, where the hell are you?'

It occurred to Ncube he could duck inside one of the carriages and not be found until it came time to catch the train back to Gubu. He could spend the last couple of hours with his fantasy.

'I'm over here, sir,' he sighed, what was the point in hiding like a scorpion under a rock? The witchdoctor had thrown his bones long ago. He was a policeman.

Sibanda found his sergeant admiring one of the restored steam engines. 'We've got a lead from the old station master.'

'This is one of the oldest locomotives in the collection, number 43. Look at her, sir; she has to be admired, still around after all these years. Imagine the journeys she's made and the travellers she's pulled along behind her in one of those wooden coaches like Mr Rhodes's. She's a grand old lady like ... like one of those birds you admire, the big ones that fly fast, a black ...?' Ncube had no idea what name he was searching for. He hoped the detective would fill in the details. All birds seemed to be black, brown or white so he was on safe ground. The sergeant knew nothing about birds and didn't want to but Suko, his third wife, suggested he include them, the detective's passion, if conversation was getting tricky, and right now he could see by the set of Sibanda's jaw that he was in no mood for appreciating the finer details of engine number 43.

'It's just a heap of rusting scrap held together by a lick of paint. Now come on, let's get out of here.' Sibanda strode off without a second glance at the treasures surrounding him. Ncube hurried in his wake, hurt by the detective's dismissal of the historical collection while swivelling his head like a carriage bogie, trying to imprint in his mind the examples of fitting and turning dotting the museum sheds. It confused him that the last piece of memorabilia, situated just before the exit, was a chipped enamel sign reading: PASSENGERS ARE EARNESTLY REQUESTED TO REFRAIN FROM THE DANGEROUS AND OBJECTIONABLE HABIT OF EXPECTORATING. The warning caused him to hurry more than he wanted to. He recognised very few of the words but the one that stood out was *dangerous*.

Ncube never managed to catch up with the detective, the man was like a hare with a jackal on its tale. Besides which the sergeant had a few errands to run for his wives before he got back on the train. The row of little shops crammed into the colonially pillared and verandaed buildings along the street leading to the station provided a skein of crochet cotton, a large jar of camphor cream, and a treat for the children.

On the platform, Sibanda was pacing up and down at the far end talking into his phone. Ncube could tell from the agitated steps and the set of his arm hooked onto the waistband of his jeans against an unbuttoned jacket that it spelled trouble. The detective's body language was an open book. He took himself far off in the opposite direction to find a bench to set down his belongings. Maybe he'd made a mistake with the children's gift. It was bulky.

'Sergeant Ncube, I'm glad I caught you before the rush, it'll be as busy as an ant's nest in here just now.'

'Mathe,' Ncube greeted the station master.

'I've remembered something. After you left this morning, I chatted to a few of the old-timers here and they reminded me.'

'A missing girl?'

'Woman, more like. It happened soon after I was promoted. I was new to the job, didn't really understand the ropes …' he tapped his nose, '… if you get my meaning.'

'No, I don't think I do.'

'Well, you see, there are certain girls who work the trains.'

'Waitresses?'

'No, *amawuli*, prostitutes. They pay for their tickets up to the Falls and back, everything above board, but the staff here know what they are up to, they get a kickback.'

Ncube gulped. He tried to imagine what the customers got up to. It must happen in the toilets, an interesting task given the dimensions. 'One of the women went missing?'

'Yes, the guard complained she hadn't paid him his dues, said she must have got off up the line to avoid handing his cut over. Anyway, sometime later, a week maybe, the police came around asking if she'd been seen, but as far as I know they didn't pursue the case for long. She was a well-known tart, worked the clubs as well as the trains, but she wasn't worth any police effort; prostitutes never are.'

'What was her name?'

'We just knew her as Mama Stimela.'

'Sergeant Ncube,' Sibanda's voice echoed down the platform.

'Who's that? Whoever he is he's angry,' the station master was startled by the volume.

'My boss.'

'Sounds more like a big bully to me.'

'You don't know him, he can be as stubborn as a donkey and as angry as a black bull, but he is a good man.'

Philemon Mathe rolled his eyes as he walked away. 'If you say so my friend.'

Ncube watched Sibanda's progress towards him and steeled himself.

'Ncube, where did you get to? This case is breaking open and if we don't get a move on we are going to be left with egg all over our faces.'

Ncube could have done with a fried egg, one with not a trace of movement in either the white or the yolk, no liquid to get on his face. He liked his eggs rubber-solid, but he suspected the detective wasn't talking about food. He narrowed his eyes and tightened his lips. Blessing said wide eyes and an open mouth made him seem simple, as though he hadn't understood. Together they practised the look along with a shake of his head to add gravity. He said nothing.

'I've just had a call from PC Khumalo, another girl has been reported missing from the train.'

'When, sir?'

'A couple of nights ago, she was travelling back to Bulawayo after a job interview as a receptionist at Thunduluka Lodge.'

'Why do we only know now?'

'Seems everyone thought she'd stay longer for the interview. They weren't expecting her back and when she didn't arrive on last night's train her parents checked with the lodge.'

'No body yet?'

'No, but I bet I know where we'll find her.'

'There is talk on the station about a missing prostitute, about two years ago,' Ncube was felled by heartburn. He was paying the price for his *mukiwa* lunch of rich food and there were too many bodies to digest.

'And I've been hearing about a missing nun. Strange bedfellows, it doesn't add up, but it gives us four possible victims. I don't like this. Where are the links – an aid worker, a receptionist, a nun and a prostitute?'

'Figs, plums and nuts never grow on the same tree.'

'You're right Ncube, these murders are too random.'

'Sir, people are starting to board the train.'

'We can talk in our compartment.' Sibanda hopped on board and Ncube walked back to his luggage. He was battling with his super-sized bag of corn curls, almost as tall as himself and nearly as round. If he held the bag too tightly it might explode in a puff of salty orange snowflakes, too loosely and it slid from his grip. His children couldn't be disappointed. He had promised them a big treat.

'Sergeant Ncube, I thought it was you. How are you?'

Ncube peered around his bulky purchase to see Berry Barton standing in front of him. 'Miss Barton, what are you doing at the station?'

'Same as you, I should imagine, catching the train to Gubu,' she laughed. 'Here let me help you with the corn curls. It's a huge bag. You can't imagine how much I craved these things when I couldn't get them in the UK, but now I'm home I never seem to eat them.' Her smile lit up the station and her eyes flashed blue mischief.

'Do you always travel by train?' he asked.

'Not all that often, but I've been down in Bulawayo at a conference of history teachers. I don't like to drive on the roads at night, too many stray cattle, and this way I can be back in class tomorrow morning.' She helped him manipulate his corn curls up the step into the corridor.

'I'm, er, in compartment number one. I can manage from here.' Something had happened between his boss and this wondrous-looking creature with hair like the mane of a white lion and eyes the astonishing blue of the winter sky. The pair had been quite close during the last case but there had been a rift. The detective was hopeless when it came to relationships and he must once again have done something awful to damage this one. Sibanda had been as irritable as a dog infested with fleas these last few weeks; Ncube was sure Miss Barton was the cause.

'And I'm in number six. I'll see you at Gubu.' Berry waved and headed for her compartment.

He wasn't going to pick off any scabs by telling the detective of Berry's presence on the train. Neither of them would thank him.

'Ncube, what have you got there? Couldn't you have bought a bigger one?' Sibanda retreated to his seat to allow Ncube and his cargo to enter.

The irony went over Ncube's head. 'This was the largest I could find, sir. I'll put it on the top bunk.'

Chapter 9

Monty had gone quiet again. He was reading and re-reading the newspaper, picking it up, putting it down and muttering. The more he read the whiter and more drawn he became.

'You'd better put that paper down, Monty. It's not healthy to read in a train, it's making you sick and you won't want lunch.'

Monty glared at Billy. 'You don't know what you're talking about, silly child.' He glanced at his watch. 'In fact, I'm going along to the dining car for lunch now.'

'Without me?'

'Yes, without you. I need some time to think about our next move and to make connections with the other gentlemen on the train. There could be rich investors among the touring parties. You'll just be a nuisance.'

'I promise I'll behave, play me part, I am good at it, can speak like a toff when I have to. Look how well I've done so far.' Billy was getting restless. The compartment was becoming a prison and the dining car was like something out of a dream. White, crisp starched linen, glassware shining like diamonds as the sunlight flooded through the windows, silver cutlery with a polished mirror surface and food fit for kings.

'No, you keep using the wrong spoon for soup, the wrong knife for butter and you talk with your mouth full. You're getting us noticed and for all the wrong reasons. It won't be long until you're found out. I'll tell anyone who asks that you're sick.'

'But ...'

'No,' Monty was firm. He came over and put his finger on the protesting lips and then kissed them long and hard. 'I'll be back soon. I'll bring some lunch for you and then we can pull down the blinds, lock the doors and have … an afternoon nap together, you'd like that wouldn't you, my little chicken?' he pinched Billy's chin a bit too firmly.

Billy pulled away from his grip and sulked.

As Monty opened the compartment door a look flashed across his face that didn't speak of an afternoon of languid lovemaking. His brows furrowed. In the doorway, he turned back and smiled at Billy, reached down, picked up the newspaper and folded it firmly under his arm. Gathering his cane, he strode off down the corridor. 'Don't forget to lock the door behind me, and don't be chatting to any nosy parkers. There could be spies on board and you'll be locked up.'

Spies! Monty was becoming paranoid. Billy shuffled on the seat and stared out of the window. Enough of Africa, it was just miles and bloody miles of wilderness and blue-grey foliage. Trees of some height, but no distinction, seemed to go on and on. Billy wanted to see little farms and hamlets, meandering streams, lush grass and the twisted limbs of a great oak. The grass that sprang sparsely from this sandy ground was dry as straw and as tall as reeds. You couldn't grow anything edible and even cows would battle. There'd be no milk to churn into cream and butter. No wonder people were missing from the vista. What would they live on? It had been a while since even a few mud huts had been spotted. Monty said the population was only a couple of hundred thousand in the entire country. Imagine! There were as many people in Hammersmith alone. Billy was beginning to regret this trip, to miss the bustle of a big city and the larking around. Even Boggy Fen Farm and the daily drudgery began to look appealing. Why had Monty taken the newspaper with him? Billy could have read that and found out what was setting the baron on edge. Maybe there was an article on mining in the colony revoking licences or refuting claims. How would Monty be if he found out they'd come all this way for nothing? The youngster was beginning to understand Monty had a temper and if it was anything like dad's there could be suffering ahead.

The compartment was stuffy. With the window open, great swathes of stinking steam pervaded the carriage; slammed closed it was like a Turkish bath. Billy took off the tweed jacket that chafed and rubbed.

Not used to such clothing made the wearing of it a burden, particularly in this heat. Monty had bought the suit, claiming it would complete the disguise. 'We need to fool the toffs we'll be travelling with,' he had said. At first, Billy had been excited and intrigued. There had been no money for new clothing at home. It was all rags and cast-offs, but now, in this heat, the old cast-offs seemed preferable, looser and what Billy was used to.

Most of Monty's luggage was in the guard's van. Billy just had one battered suitcase on the rack above him, holding old clothes, a facecloth, a nearly toothless comb, a toothbrush which was a real novelty, having only used twigs before, and one special outfit to be worn when they arrived at their destination. But overhead, in the netting luggage rack opposite, lay Monty's carpet bag, a large colourful portmanteau he had purchased in India. He said the whole thing could double as a rug for draughty railway carriages, never let it out of his sight and, normally, never left it unlocked. Billy had been warned off with the threat of a good caning. But alone in the compartment, the lock tantalisingly open, Billy couldn't resist; maybe there would be a cooler shirt in there, surely in India Monty hadn't worn a suit. The youngster was quick and nimble, on the seat reaching up to the rack and rifling through Monty's pomades, past his stud box and spare smalls to the bottom of the bag. Ever curious, exploring fingers pulled out a heavy drawstring sack wedged in the corner. When the strings were untied, a sight lay on the banquette that would startle those young eyes until they forgot to blink and grew large with amazement. Jewels of every shape and colour blazed in the African sun, returning an intensity of light and splendour that spoke of unfathomable opulence and the mysteries of the East. Great claws of gold punched out in elaborate shapes, or wrought with filigree work, clasped the stones in awe. The workmanship was sublime. Another smaller drawstring bag held further gems, every one the brilliant red of brothel velvet. They spilled and rolled as drops of blood among their multi-coloured cousins.

How had Monty got his hands on this stuff? He couldn't have earned this sort of treasure prancing around on a stage, or even in a late-night card game with a miner. Monty had to be a thief as well as a liar. This must be the healthy bank account he was talking about. No wonder he was nervous and edgy carrying all this wealth around in something that doubled as a blanket. Billy could be light fingered at times, Aunt Bessie's boarding house gave plenty of opportunity for pilfering, but never too much, a shilling here and there from the careless guests, but this loot was theft on a grand scale. Somebody would be missing these pendants and rings, and probably somebody powerful and well connected. The jewels spelled trouble. What had the baron got them in to? Billy didn't want to be labelled an accomplice and locked up in some foreign jail. How to get out of this muddle? The baron deceived with all this lofty talk of love and a new life in the colonies when he was nothing but a liar and a rotten lover to boot.

With the jewels safely returned to their hiding place, Billy sat down, put the jacket back on and began to worry. By the time Monty returned with a lunch of poached sheep's brains in onion sauce, Billy was back to normal and with a look that wouldn't have gone amiss on the choirboys from St Peter's in Black Lion Lane, a hop, skip and a jump from Aunt Bessie's boarding house. It wasn't only Monty who could act.

'I've brought you the menu to look at, Billy, cheer up. Look, it's got pictures of all the animals we're going to see.'

'I'm fine now, Monty, honestly I am,' Billy noticed Monty bought the cheapest food on the menu when he could have bought a mutton roast with all the trimmings for an extra sixpence, and the queen of puddings and custard sounded tasty.

'It's just as well you didn't come to lunch, one of the gentlemen asked where my pretty son was. Best to lay low from now on.' The fact was no one had mentioned his missing son at all. Monty sat alone, watching, observing the comings and goings in the dining car, pretending to read his newspaper while listening in on the conversations around him. No one else had the newspaper, which was an immediate relief, and anyway the picture of him was blurry. He'd changed his appearance since then and travelling with a son was an inspired disguise. He honed in on a couple of young gents dining not far away, picking up key words like *north, mining, emeralds.* They were young and wet behind the ears, easy pickings. Behind him sat a missionary couple, equally as naïve, and he thought briefly about introducing himself, offering to join them in their saving of black souls, and disappear for a couple of years to reinvent himself in the wilds. It could be interesting and offered endless possibilities to indulge his fantasies. The colonies were more relaxed about the age of consent; elders often arranged marriages pre-puberty and people always trusted their children with a preacher. He certainly had enough knowledge of the bible, bashed into him on Sundays of fire and brimstone, but he also understood part of his nature could never be tamed, nor did he want it under lock and key, the thrill was addictive. The missionary couple would never do. He needed to hook up with a sophisticated gent, one who understood the lure of young flesh and the occasional 'accident'.

'Are we slowing down, Monty?'

'Yes we are,' he said, knowing the little urchin would be too stupid to latch onto the irony of the double entendre. He was tiring of Billy who had grown up during their adventure, gained a little too much worldly knowledge and lost seductive innocence. He didn't need the subterfuge of a son anymore; he'd got away with it all. Billy had been the perfect camouflage for getting out of England and onto the boat, where they were anonymous among a sea of travellers and Billy an amusing distraction to ward off the boredom of the voyage. No one had been looking for a father and son. But this train journey was a little too intimate, soon he would need to travel fast and light. Billy's hours were numbered and Monty was looking forward to the endgame. He licked his lips.

'Is something wrong? We aren't there yet, are we?' Billy was alarmed.

'Nothing wrong,' he soothed, 'just a water stop for a refill, all this steaming is a thirsty business. I'll get down and stretch my legs; shouldn't be more than fifteen minutes or so. An army of natives will already have pumped into the overhead reservoir. It's just a case of opening the valves and letting the water flow by gravity into the tank. You stay here. It's safest, and don't put your head out of the window. Lay low.'

With Monty out of the carriage, Billy began to think clearly again. He hadn't taken the newspaper with him. Where was it? A corner of paper was peeking out from the back of the seat. Monty must have lost track of it during his daydreaming. How long until he came back? How long to scan the fine print? Billy could read, had done a couple of years in the local school room, but the skill was a slow painful progression accompanied by a tracing of letters with fingers, and a determined tongue poking out. It didn't take long to find the article because it was highlighted by a photograph of Monty under the name of Edward Brixton, travelling entertainer. It didn't look all that much like Monty because Edward Brixton had a beard, and longer hair, but Billy would recognise those eyes anywhere. Underneath the picture was a long article and the youngster battled with some of the words, while others stood out like bonfires in the night: *treachery, cheating, trickery, fraud* and then *torture, torment, cruelty, mutilation*. Edward Brixton had committed all manner of evil in India and it had taken some months for the news to reach England and longer still to get to the Cape and beyond. The report stated five girls and three boys were his victims and the authorities linked them through the distinctive nature of the heinous crimes and the coincidence of his travelling shows. The last of his victims managed to escape and alert the authorities. Billy couldn't read *heinous* but got the gist. And then there was a second photograph. It was of a young girl, stripped of her clothes, brutally slashed, her eyes gouged, her face almost unrecognisable with most of her features removed and her belly slit from the breast bone down. The paper didn't go into details, said they were 'too vile to report and had been edited to protect sensitive readers', but Billy knew where the cut had gone. Baron Montague of Bingley, Alf Watters and Edward Brixton were one and the same. The name the paper gave him in extra-large letters was The Rupee Ripper.

Billy opened the window and vomited on the rails. Sheep brains, with the onion still attached, cascaded in three great heaves. Billy slammed the window shut and rinsed his mouth out in the basin, grateful, more than ever, for its presence; the splashed water cooled the terror.

Billy spoke aloud to the empty carriage. 'How are you going to get out of this one? Think calmly.' But with a pounding heart and shortness of breath the instruction was almost impossible. 'If only this were Victoria Falls, I could get away, but where to?' There was no escape from this train, there was nothing but wilderness for thousands of miles and Victoria Falls was just a big waterfall in the middle of it all, not a city to hide in.

'Dear God, protect me from this evil monster and give me the wits to escape.' God was the only person to turn to. There was no one else, not another soul on this blighted continent to offer help. The adventure was dissolving into nightmare.

Billy was resourceful, used to hardship, but this was a challenge where everything was at stake not just a few hours skiving off from drudgery and a good thrashing. 'Think hard, you idiot, your life depends on it.' And then an idea struck. 'Yes, of course, money, nothing like a fat wallet to get you out of a pickle.' The youngster leapt on to the seat and felt back inside Monty's carpetbag, fishing out the smaller of the drawstring sacks containing the rubies. Monty wouldn't miss those straight away, wouldn't miss the weight.

'Now the newspaper, he can't know I have read it.' Billy folded *The Bulawayo Chronicle* carefully and replaced it down the back of the seat, pushing it out of sight for good measure. With the rubies tucked away in a jacket pocket, Billy sat back, willing heart and breath to slow down, trying to act unconcerned. One more night and they would be in Victoria Falls. One more night and Billy would skip the train and be rid of Montague Bingley, Alf Watters, Edward Brixton, The Rupee Ripper – free, with a bag of rubies to fund a future.

'What the hell did you think you were doing with your head out of the window?' Monty was furious. By luck, and Billy's late arrival, none of the other passengers knew the little pest was on the train and he wanted it to stay that way.

Billy had nearly been caught red-handed, but still had time to come up with an excuse. 'Being sick, that's what. Those sheep's brains were rotten. It's all your fault buying the cheapest meal on the menu. I might die of food poisoning.' Struggling to subdue the horror taking hold, the youngster felt attack was the best form of defence.

Engine no 43 chose that moment to start her journey again, jerking a little as she took up the slack from the carriages, causing Monty to fall backwards onto the seat. He steadied himself with his cane, caressing the silver elephant's head as he did so. The heavy rounded handle and Malacca stick had been one of the few things not stolen. He found it in a Bombay bazaar being made by a silversmith of exquisite talent, who tapped away at the ridges on the trunk and wrinkles on the ears that seemed alive and flapping when the sunlight caught the mirror metal. It served him well, initially as protection from the dacoity rife on the Indian highways and byways he travelled as an entertainer, and then as his subduer and inflictor of pleasure and pain. When the head was removed from the handle, attached was a sharp sword-like blade.

'Don't fret, Billy, I have a bottle of Mrs Winslow's Soothing Syrup in my bag. It'll cure anything. Do you want some?'

'No, no,' Billy didn't want Monty rifling in his bag. 'I'm better now I've spewed me guts.'

Monty winced at the guttersnipe language. He checked his pocket watch. It was already late afternoon. Night fell early in these parts and as soon as it did his theatre could begin. Such a pity Billy would never set those beguiling eyes on the Victoria Falls, he heard they were one of the Seven Wonders of the World.

Chapter 10

'Sparrowhawk.'

'What, sir?' All Ncube's coping strategies went out of the train window. He had absolutely no idea what the detective was talking about. They settled into their compartment, the banquettes had this time been made up with surprisingly white sheets and Ncube was looking forward to settling down for the first half of the night at least.

'You asked about a big black bird that flies fast. The black sparrowhawk fits the bill. It's fast and powerful, like your steam engine, although it doesn't snort fire. In fact, in some ways it's similar to our killer.'

'To our killer?'

'Yes, the black sparrowhawk takes its victims, normally doves, by surprise, hiding in the tree canopy, using stealth and then chasing its prey at speed rather than swooping on it. But even more interesting, it plucks the dove's feathers, stripping it bare and carrying it naked above the trees to a suitable perch to devour it. There are parallels here, Ncube. We're looking for our own black sparrowhawk.'

'But only one of the missing women has been found without her skin. We don't have any other bodies.'

'No, but we will. I know we will. Tomorrow morning, I want you working on the missing receptionist, Kerry Williams.'

'A white girl?'

'Our sparrowhawk doesn't only hunt doves.'

'What about the prostitute, Mama Stimela? She's important too. People are not like water, they follow different paths.'

'You're right, Ncube, liaise with Bulawayo Police. She may have turned up or changed her lifestyle. See what you can find out. I'll look into the missing nun.' Sibanda turned on the tap in the corner basin but no water came out. He closed it and sat back. The carriage was a little shabby but elegant, lined with wood panelling and not the Formica-clad compartment of the trip down. This must be one of the earlier cars still in use. He hadn't taken much notice when they boarded.

'There'll be problems with Cold War, sir. Once he thinks a crime's solved he'll never open it up again, he's as obstinate as a *tshongololo*. Gideon Shumba is behind bars for Lois Khupe's murder. Mfumu will have wrapped up the case and I'll be assigned elsewhere.'

'Let me take care of the Officer-in-Charge, remember a *tshongololo* is easily squashed.'

Ncube winced, he didn't like the underfoot crunch and disgusting goo that resulted when he stood on one of the large carapaced centipedes that flocked indoors in the summer months. 'What about suspects, sir?'

'There are a few, but once we make the links between the girls we'll have a better idea of who's in the mix. The ticket inspector, Isaac Manhombo for one. He's been up to something. See what you can dig up on him. There are a couple of guys at Universal Dream I don't like the look of either, but Gideon Shumba is certainly not our man. For now, get some sleep. It'll be a broken night, we need to be on our game tomorrow, and ...'

'And what, sir?'

'Never mind, Ncube, I'll tell you later. For now, get your head down.'

Ncube did sleep, dead to the world like a hibernating tortoise, head tucked in, limbs retracted and then the moon's high beams shone in through the window and fooled his eyes into thinking it was morning and his stomach into thinking it was time for breakfast. He lay for a few minutes trying to decide if he could make a very small hole in the top of the bag of corn curls and sneak a few out as a midnight snack when he heard the noises, at first sleepy protestations, then shouts and finally screams.

'Sir, sir, wake up,' he shook Sibanda's shoulder. 'There's screaming from further down the train, and Miss Barton is in compartment number six.'

Sibanda's eyes focused like a leopard on an impala as if he wanted to rip its intestines out. He was on his feet in seconds and through the door. He reached Berry's compartment in a heartbeat. She was standing at her door, shaking, but still with enough presence of mind to point out the direction the intruder had taken.

'Sergeant, stay here with Miss Barton,' he barked, as he sprinted shoeless and shirtless down the corridor. The passageway was dark, the moon was in the east and the western side of the train was in moon shadow. Sibanda's shoulders and hips bounced on the corridor's sides as the train swayed along the tracks and he fought to keep his balance. At the end of the carriage, the door that normally led to the platform was wide open and banging. Sibanda stuck his head out into the ice-cold air. Had the assailant leapt off the train? Impossible, the bush was racing past. Moon-tipped trees and shrubs flashed like ghostly eminences. No one could survive a fall at this speed. He pulled his head back, his eyes were blurred from watering and his naked torso was freezing but he felt nothing. He ran through the next carriage, a shared compartment, bench seats with sleeping bodies strewn at every angle; some grumbled as he kicked a stretched leg or stood on a toe, others never stirred. Sibanda didn't know who he was looking for. He scanned faces, but these people all looked well bedded down. Could one of them be the killer? He ran on through two more carriages crammed with sleepers and their shopping. Ncube's giant corn curl packets were obviously popular – several lay propped up or lying down. In the half-light, they looked like extra passengers. In the third carriage, a baby was crying. Her mother was searching for a breast under layers of clothing.

'Did you see anyone come this way in the last minute or two?' Sibanda asked.

The young mother was startled. A man was streaking through the carriage, half dressed with eyes as mad as a rabid cow. She hugged her child closer, guiding her nipple into the nudging mouth and looked around for help.

'Police,' he added, 'has anyone come into this carriage?'

'No, it is quiet. Everyone is asleep, no one has moved.'

At the end of the carriage was a door carrying the notice: *Private, staff only. Unauthorised entry will be prosecuted.* Sibanda hammered on the door. People began to stir and grumble in the carriage, releasing a fug of sour sleep smells into the atmosphere. Not even the cold air could mitigate the concentrated odour of relaxed bodies. Sibanda thumped harder and was rewarded by a shout from the other side of the door

'Go away, do not bother me, go back to sleep. I am busy.'

'Police, get this door open now or you will find yourself busy behind bars for obstructing an investigation.'

The door opened slowly and a head peered through the opening. 'It is the middle of the night, what's this about?'

Sibanda pushed the door open to reveal a half-clad man at the door and a naked woman lying on a makeshift bed. She pulled her clothes around her but the van reeked of recent sex and stale sweat. 'Get your clothes on, and you,' he said, pointing to the guard, 'get about your duty. There's an intruder on this train and he's broken into one of the carriages. Check everyone's tickets again, check everyone is where they are supposed to be, particularly in the first-class compartments. Get onto it now.' There was no brooking the command in Sibanda's voice.

The guard zipped up his fly, pulled on his jacket and was through the door like a rat out of a burning hut. Sibanda stepped aside to let him through and to give the woman time to dress. When he turned back she was clothed but her lipstick was smeared and her mascara had run, she had the face of a clown but the jester's baggy uniform was replaced by an ample body in tight lycra.

'I take it you are working the train?'

She nodded, she had no alternative. 'Stay here and don't move unless you want a solicitation charge. My sergeant will be here to question you in a few minutes.'

Sibanda made his way back though the carriages, checking every face for signs of a killer, questioning passengers, now awake, about movements in the carriage but no one had seen or heard anything. They all looked like ordinary travellers living ordinary lives and that was the problem. Serial killers could blend like chameleons. They survived because of ordinariness, the ability to harness bland and to change colour as they moved across the landscape, adapting to change just as the black sparrowhawk had. Faced with a diminishing environment and disappearing forests, the fearsome raptor had taken a liking to the tall pine trees and exotic gum plantations that ballooned around habitation, nesting happily in their canopy. The species was thriving while many of its less malleable cousins were on the brink of extinction. But how had this murdering scumbag got away? Had he flown?

He found Berry and Sergeant Ncube in her compartment. Ncube was chatting away while Berry listened. To anyone else she would have appeared recovered and relaxed but Sibanda studied every contour of that face and every syllable of Berry's body language since they first met, the face shapes were misspelled and the body syntax was jumbled. Berry was stressed.

'Unfortunately, Miss Barton didn't get a good look at her attacker, sir, seems he came in through the window and was well wrapped up. Miss Barton said she left the window slightly open for fresh air. He must have forced it and come in from the next compartment. I've checked either side, both are empty.'

'It all happened so quickly, Jabu, one minute I was fast asleep and the next someone was standing over me. When he put his hands around my throat …' Berry began to shake.

'Sergeant, I'll stay with Miss Barton. Go to the guard's van; there is a woman who may be able to help us with our Mama Stimela enquiry,' he gave Ncube a knowing look and raised his eyebrows. 'I've sent the guard to check on all the compartments, see if he comes up with anything.'

'Right, sir, I'm on to it.'

'And Sergeant, I'll travel the rest of the journey with Miss Barton. I'll see you in Gubu.'

The sergeant's face remained professional as he left the carriage.

Sibanda sat next to Berry and put his arm around her shoulders. She had started sobbing soundlessly; each ragged intake of breath was a dagger to Sibanda's heart. He would kill whoever had done this.

'I'm all right, Jabu, honestly,' she cleared her throat, 'just a bit of delayed shock, I guess.' Her smile was a little crooked and her normally bright eyes were clouded.

'Was he black or white, Berry?'

'I … I couldn't tell. He was completely wrapped up, face covered with a balacalva, gloves on. I didn't have time to … I'm sorry. It would have helped, wouldn't it?'

'Don't worry. You screamed, how did you do that if he had you by the throat?'

'I managed to knee him where it hurts and he let go. I learned the strategy at one of those self-protection courses. The university recommended it because there had been a spate of attacks on Nottingham students. Glad I did. I'll be fine now.'

'I'm not leaving you, Berry.'

'It was probably just a robber. He won't come back now he knows there are police on the train. I'll be okay.'

'I'm not leaving you.' There was no point in telling her the intruder could be a serial killer, he just held her tightly.

'But Jabu, really …'

'Shhh, don't talk, try and sleep. There're still another two hours or so until we reach Gubu.'

When he felt the shaking lessen and her body slacken into his, he lowered her gently until she was lying on the banquette with her head on his thigh; aftershock set in and the lethargy associated with it. Berry would sleep deeply now. Sibanda pulled the blankets over her and some over his naked torso. The night was cold, probably nudging zero, and the adrenalin of the chase was leaving him. Imperceptibly, so as not to disturb the sleeping girl, he edged his body into a lounging position, put his shoeless feet on the opposite bunk of the coupe and began to run his fingers gently through Berry's tangle of curls, an instinctive calming reaction, and something he had longed to do since that first meeting when drops of English rain sparkled on the white blonde locks. This was the first time he had touched her in other than a hugged greeting. It was dangerous, but he couldn't resist. Was she completely asleep? He detected a slight movement of her head to guide his hand to a favourite spot, or was it just a natural adjustment in her sleep?

When the alarm on his phone woke him a few hours later, his hand strayed close to her right breast and she placed her palm on his thigh. She slept through the alarm and Sibanda indulged the sensuous moment for another minute before moving her hand and his own rough-skinned fingers and gently shaking Berry awake. 'Berry, we're nearly there, time to wake up.'

'Is it really that time already?' her eyes regained some of their life and Sibanda detected the beginnings of a smile. Berry had, in fact, been awake for some time but she lay still despite an annoying kink in her neck, not wanting to disturb the perfect moment. Jabu's thigh was like a rock and a very unsuitable pillow, but she was in love with this complex man and this nearness to him was as close as she was ever likely to get. She tried to get over her obsession, tried to forget the disappointment of finding him with another girl when she thought there might be a chance of finally breaking through the hard shell he wrapped himself in, but it was hopeless. Could she risk being hurt so badly again? Last night she had thought for a moment as he stroked her hair that the caress was more than just a soothing action. His fingertips on her scalp and the slow and restful rearrangement of her curls set her head tingling. She thought she would never sleep, but she did.

'I need to put on a shirt and shoes, but I'm only a few metres down the corridor.'

'I really am okay, Jabu, but thank you, I did sleep better with you here.' Her eyes were fixed on his until he turned away. Sibanda slid open the carriage door and then slammed it closed again and turned back to face the bewitching girl, it was time. 'Why didn't you come for the drink at my house, Berry? I thought we were friends. Didn't I at least deserve a phone call?' There was steel in his voice.

'I did come, but you were … otherwise engaged.' Berry could fight her own corner. Love didn't mean capitulation.

'What?' She had him on the back foot.

'You had someone else with you, another girl.' Berry tried to keep jealousy and hostility from her voice but there was an unavoidable edge.

Sibanda searched his memory for who could have been with him that night. 'Oh, just the clinic sister. She came to dress my wound, remember, the one in my thigh, and you believed …?' Why had he dismissed Angel Better as a distraction? She deserved more than that.

'It looked very cosy, I didn't want to intrude.'

'I suppose it did, but I invited you over. You could at least have come in.'

'My name might be Berry, but I'm not a goose.' Were they having their first argument? You didn't have this sort of interchange if there was no emotion involved.

'A goose?'

'Gooseberry, I'm not a gooseberry.'

Sibanda laughed; Berry laughed with him. The train driver chose that moment to apply the brakes as he headed into Gubu station; couplings collided, buffeting backwards and forwards, jolting the pair into each other's arms. They clung to each other like baby vervets to their mothers as the slowing wheels squealed on the rails, neither willing to let go, both still chuckling.

Sibanda was the first to break from the embrace. 'Berry will we ever get our timings right?'

'What do you mean?'

He shook his head. 'Never mind, I have to get dressed or be forced to stay on this train all the way to Vic Falls. I'll phone; we can meet up somewhere. There's a club in Gubu, Mama Elephant's Diner, how about a drink there? We can talk, like we used to in England.'

'I'd like that, promise you'll phone.'

Sibanda held Berry's gaze, his hands on her shoulders. 'I promise.' He'd broken many arrangements before, a murder enquiry always took precedence over his personal life. 'Is anyone meeting you?' he changed topic; the moment passed.

'Dad, he doesn't seem to mind coming to the station at 2am. He's not a good sleeper and he says it's a great time to see nocturnal species on the way in, but I know he's just being kind.'

'Give him my regards and tell him I'd like to spotlight with him one night.'

'He'd enjoy that.' Berry skipped onto the platform. She felt happier than she had in weeks.

By the time Sibanda had dressed and gathered his backpack, Berry had left the station. Sergeant Ncube was waiting for him on the platform.

'I'll debrief you in my office tomorrow morning, Ncube. Be early, we've got a lot to sort out.'

Ncube looked at his watch. It was already 2am. He sighed, by the time he got home there would be barely enough time to put his head down before he would have to be up again. Did that man never get tired? He needed a family to go home to. Ncube might work on that. He didn't approve of mixed-race marriages, but maybe Miss Barton would be the one to settle the detective. It might be in his own interests to play the role of *sidombo*. Matchmaking was a calling, one that shouldn't be taken on lightly, and required ancient skills. He was a novice in these matters. He would talk to his wives. Together they would come up with a strategy.

Sibanda jogged away from the train, a warm glow fending off the freezing lash of the small hours. On a whim, he turned and ran backwards for a few metres, staring towards the carriages. The engine was pulling out on its way to Victoria Falls. The carriages were silhouetted by the moon and suddenly Sibanda knew exactly how the killer got away and he cursed his own stupidity. How close had he come to capturing the evil monster? This was an older model rail car to the one they travelled on from Gubu, one with a completely different profile. He hadn't noticed the carriage's external features in Bulawayo; PC Khumalo's call kept him distracted until boarding. He saw now how the killer's escape was possible and he could have kicked himself. He would be ready for The Black Sparrowhawk next time. The killer wouldn't fly away again.

Chapter 11

Gubu Police Station was as busy as a beehive in spring and as focused as a dog chasing two tails. Officers were scurrying to dismantle benches and stands, others were waving used paper plates and discarded cups, calling for rubbish bags. PC Khumalo was on her hands and knees rolling up a hand-woven sisal mat that passed as Gubu's version of a red carpet.

'What's going on, Zee?' Sibanda reached the station early, but not as early as the rest of the station staff.

PC Khumalo tilted her head in the direction of a brand-new police vehicle. 'Sorry I couldn't tell you, but I didn't know, seems Chanza and Mfumu have been cooking up this event for some time. You being away was a godsend. The pair of them were like squirrels in a box of peanuts.'

'What event?' Sibanda's eyes were fixed on the Zimbabwe Republic Police badge plastered to the outside wall of the station. Normally chipped, faded and barely worth a second glance, it had been picked out smartly in blue and gold paint, and the motto, *pro lege, pro patria, pro populo*, was for once readable, although Sibanda wondered how many of the Gubu population could decipher the Latin, or would believe it if they could.

'Yesterday, there was a ceremony, that vehicle over there has been donated by the US embassy in appreciation of our unravelling that last case involving their national, Tiffany Price. Chanza has been in Harare organising the whole thing and taking all the credit for solving the murder. Anyone would think he knew one side of an investigation from another when we all know he's just a dumb ox and was chasing the wrong man. It's not fair, sir. It was your case and it wouldn't ever have been cracked if you hadn't been here.'

'It's not an issue.' And it wasn't. Sibanda preferred to operate under the radar. He'd had his share of laurels that plunged him into serious political hot water and while he didn't mind a good scrap, he was wise enough to avoid them if they were unimportant. Rural Gubu and anonymity suited him. 'Where's Sergeant Ncube? He's the one that should get the slap on the back.'

'He's with the new vehicle, sir, and not happy.'

'Why?'

'We had a feast for all the dignitaries. He missed out.'

Sibanda smiled and walked over to where Sergeant Ncube was checking out the latest addition to the Gubu fleet.

'Take a look, sir. Can you imagine driving this? Ah, the smell of the new upholstery is greeting my nose like a rose garden and look at the paint job.' The white pick-up had the same blue and gold stripe along its sides and across the bonnet as the police badge. It gleamed with pride.

'Shut your jaw, Ncube and don't slaver. You or I will never drive this and, anyway, it's designed for tar roads. It would be absolutely useless in the bush. Mfumu won't let the keys out of his sight, and I don't care as long as the vehicle we have starts at the turn of the key and gets us to the crime scene. The good news is we now have the more reliable Santana and Miss Daisy can go out to pasture.'

'Like an old cow? Miss Daisy is of good breeding, sir,' Ncube bristled. 'If she really was a cow she would be a Nguni and her beautifully marked hide would be used for the shields of Mzilikazi's crack regiment.' Sergeant Ncube felt guilty about his moment of jealousy. The new vehicle was as seductive as a comely virgin, but a man could have more than one love, couldn't he, and more than one wife? Miss Daisy might be older, more complex, fragile and cantankerous but she was loyal and she was not going to rot in any paddock if he had his way.

'Get over it, Ncube. My office, now!' Sibanda could only pander so much to Ncube's ridiculous obsession. He strode away, rubbing his own jaw which was a taut as Ncube's was slack.

'We missed it all, sir.' The pair were back in Sibanda's office. 'The American ambassador was here and the governor, Micah Ngwenya, they say he was asking for you. Even Minister Muchacha came for the handover. There was a party …'

'The Minister for Cultural and Rural Affairs, Cuthbert Muchacha?'

'Yes.'

'Then it's as well I wasn't here. He and I have history and it doesn't read like a romance. Now, Ncube, what did you find out from the hooker on the train?'

The sergeant let the comment pass. He didn't read much and the only book he understood was his notebook. He licked his fingers and turned the pages. 'There's some kind of a roster, and a queue of women eager to get on the waiting list.' He raised his brows. 'It's a very, er … profitable run. Cherish Mabena was given her place on the trains, Thursday up, Friday down, when Mama Stimela disappeared. She was the next on the list.'

'What does she know about Mama Stimela?'

'Everyone was shocked when she left the business. She had been one of the organisers of the group and successful with a way of enticing the travellers. Cherish said she was a strong woman. From her description, she sounded big and round like a watermelon. Soft, sweet and juicy on the inside, firm and perfectly formed on the outside. I'm not surprised she was popular.'

'And you wouldn't have minded cutting off a few slices yourself, I suppose?' Sibanda snapped. Sergeant Ncube's dual fixations of food and women dovetailed perfectly in this missing woman.

'What are you saying, sir? I have never ever hurt any woman, never cut one …'

'… Forget it, Ncube. How did the girls operate?'

Ncube was muttering. The detective's words were set like a branch of hook thorns placed to snag the unwary. 'If the client had a compartment or coupe, they used that, if not, then they rented the guard's van.'

'Did you find out her real name?'

'She was known to everyone as Mama Stimela.'

'So, Mrs Steam Train lived and died by her name.'

'Interesting.'

'What?

'Er, nothing, sir.'

'Talk to PC Khumalo and see what information she has on Kerry

Williams and check which train she left on and if Isaac Manhombo was on duty that night. He has fresh scratches on his neck and what looked like a bite mark on his hand. Kerry Williams fought for her life. She has marked someone.'

'But he wasn't on duty last night when Miss Barton was attacked.'

'No, but all railway employees can hop on and off trains with impunity. Could be he stalks the station, watching for a potential victim.'

'I'll go and find out what PC Khumalo knows.' Ncube thought it best to get out of the room. He nearly asked who 'Impunity' was and if she was also a suspect, but he was learning to keep his mouth shut. Impunity had a pleasant ring to it, maybe the next baby could have that name.

'And Ncube, get Miss Daisy started, I'm off to the convent. I want you ready and waiting when I get back.' Sibanda would first have to check in with the Officer-in-Charge and debrief him on the Bulawayo visit. It was time to let Gideon Shumba out of the cells.

'Such a pity you weren't here yesterday. Did you see the new vehicle?' Stalin Mfumu, otherwise known as Cold War to those in Gubu Police Station, was preening himself like a red-billed teal just flown onto a waterhole, flicking his tail and running his beak along gleaming feathers, chasing drops of water. His tone was condescending.

'Very smart, I hope it lasts longer than the previous one.' The detective reminded Stalin Mfumu that his nephew, Chanza, had driven that new vehicle smack into a cow, writing it off and nearly himself with it. The detective could do *condescending* just as bitingly. The loss of the station's new and much prided vehicle was the reason the rattle trap Miss Daisy, ex the junk heap, had made a hurried appearance.

Mfumu was flustered briefly. 'Er, yes, very unfortunate incident, but only I shall be driving this new vehicle. Now how did the trip to Bulawayo go? Complete waste of time, I take it?'

'No, and we should let Gideon Shumba out of the cells. He didn't murder Lois Khupe.'

'Of course he did. There are no other suspects.'

'No firm suspects, but we do have more women missing from the train and Shumba couldn't have killed Kerry Williams. He was already in the cells.'

'Kerry Williams, the missing girl? She is just missing. Lots of people go missing.' Mfumu threw up his hands for effect. 'Without bodies, this is all speculation. Don't waste your time or police resources pursuing this case further. Shumba should have read his bible before he committed murder. Exodus 23:7. Keep thee far from a false matter; and the innocent and righteous slay thou not: for I will not justify the wicked.'

Mfumu had him and Sibanda knew it, with no further bodies there was no proof. Gideon Shumba would have to wait a little longer to get out of Gubu's flea-ridden lock-up. He changed the subject. 'The nuns have reported a break-in, just a small matter but I am off to investigate,' a lie, but a white one. The nuns would forgive him, he hoped. He was investigating one of their own.

'Yes, yes,' Mfumu waved him away; he didn't like the nuns. They were his rivals for Gubu's souls and it was a tight-run contest. They offered all sorts of perks he couldn't compete with, including an old-age home and a primary school. Women had no place in religion. 'You will have to take the old Land Rover. Chanza has the Santana out in the village gathering more evidence against Gideon Shumba. Believe me, that man will face the noose.' Mfumu turned away and then, as an afterthought, 'Oh, the minister asked after you,' he added with deliberate spite.

The detective didn't bother to respond. He left the office knowing his reputation would have been blackened further. These were difficult times. He had heard Muchacha was again rising up the political ladder. It was only a matter of time until he set about revenge.

The convent of St Monica sat on the corner of the road leading to Gubu's commercial centre of Barghees General Dealers, the Sweet Bun bakery, the Last Drop garage and a host of little one-room, one-pavement businesses clustering like piglets around a sow. The convent didn't boast any arches, stained glass or a single gothic gargoyle. Instead, a large, squat '60s house, converted for the use of the nuns, sat squarely in a garden of bougainvillea, dull as a cardboard box in a Frida Kahlo wardrobe.

'Welcome to St Monica's, Mother of Virtues, mother of the blessed St Augustine of Hippolyte, and Africa's first female saint.' Sibanda sat in front of a tiny Irish nun, of indeterminate age. Sister Emmarentia was clad in a modern, dove-grey habit, her round blue eyes and plump cheeks creased as she smiled. The white band on the wimple above her brow emphasised the weather-worn tan of her skin. She had been in Africa a long time.

'Thank you, Sister,' Sibanda smiled pleasantly, although he was gritting his perfect teeth and hoping he wasn't about to be subjected to Mfumuesque cant.

'So, detective, you are here to enquire about a missing nun?' Sister Emmarentia spoke the words with the calming pace and lilt of a litany, an appealing sound, but this twinkling personage in front of him had a spine of steel. Looks could fool and Africa had never been a destination for the faint-hearted.

'I heard one of your young nuns left by train some years ago and was never heard from again.'

'Ah, yes, she was a postulant, detective, hadn't taken her vows. Sister Martha, and … well, let's say she wasn't suited for the cloister, or a life of dedication to others. She made the right decision to leave.' The old nun stared through her window, as though searching for answers in the purple petals of the most vigorous bougainvillea. The flowers were more than a match for Africa's blistering light.

'But Sister Martha never made it to Bulawayo.'

'So I believe, and I'm hardly surprised. She was … a lively girl, with a mind of her own.'

'Did she ever contact her parents again?'

'They're both dead now, so I don't know. The father went quickly, poor soul,' Sister Emmarentia made the sign of the cross, 'and the mother a year later, may her departed soul rest in peace. Very sad, they deserved more from their daughter.' She sighed, 'Arghyro was her baptismal name, it's Greek for silver, beautiful don't you think? And she was as mercurial as quicksilver, a happy scatterbrain of a girl. She lacked the gravitas to be a nun.' The smile in Sister Emmarentia's eyes was genuine. 'She was a late and only child, you see, born into a good Catholic family. I met the parents when she first came to the convent, nineteen she was, and as fresh as a daisy. Lovely couple, Mr and Mrs Spyrios, dedicated to Arghyro and delighted at her choice of a religious life.'

Her fingers fiddled restlessly with a string of rosary beads worn around her neck. The skin on her hands, splodged with sun damage sank into the spaces between her metatarsals leaving bones radiating like spines towards fingers that bent at the ends from arthritic good deeds.

'Is there anyone else in the family I can contact to see if she returned home?'

'No, no, you see Mr Spyrios was recruited from Greece to work on the railways, his wife followed a couple of years later.'

'To work on the railways?' Alarm bells rang for Sibanda.

'Yes, as an engine driver, no one else from their family came out and they were somewhat isolated. The Church was their family until Arghyro arrived.'

'And you definitely put her on the train?'

'Didn't I go with her myself and wait at the station until the train pulled out? I gave her a little rosary, fitted in a tiny, hollow ivory egg, a present from my first Communion, and told her to pray for her vocation. Of course, some say she got off at the next siding and made her way back to Gubu.'

'Why?'

'It's just talk, detective, idle prattle.'

'Tell me, anyway.'

'They say there was a boy, an apprentice safari guide. He used to attend mass. But I never saw anything. We have rules … I don't think …'

'…Do you have a name?'

'No, I never really knew him. Nice-looking chap, though, with eyes that could fetch the ducks off a pond. You're easy on the eye yourself, detective, don't you go turning the heads of any of my sisters will you?' she chuckled.

Sibanda ignored the comment. 'When did all this happen?'

'About five years ago, let me see, it was August. I remember because we were preparing for the Feast of the Assumption.'

Sibanda sensed the interview was over. 'Thank you, Sister, for your help.'

'Anytime, detective, we discharged our duty by the girl, you know. We can't be held accountable for her disappearance. God doesn't call everyone.'

Sibanda nodded agreement and exited through a little hallway, painted in seminary blue and well furnished with lace doilies, exposed hearts, halos, cruciform suffering and a plaster statue in long, black nun's garb that he assumed was St Monica. In the corner, a round table had been covered in a very familiar tablecloth. Sibanda smiled, he remembered Miss Daisy's ice cream-striped upholstery fabric had been left over from a job done for the nuns. Sergeant Ncube would have been delighted to see it there. The Order might be less pleased if they knew the brightly coloured fabric had been involved in a murder.

He stepped out into the winter sun. The cold atmosphere in the convent was not only due to temperature; godliness sent shivers down the detective's spine. By the fence, a young nun was tending to a bed of lettuce. She looked up, caught Sibanda's eye and looked back down again, trowelling the weeds with dedicated concentration. There had been something in that look, enough to make Sibanda stroll towards the kneeling nun.

'Good morning, Sister ...?'

'... Mary Bernadette,' she offered.

Such a long European name for a short African nun, 'I see you enjoy gardening.'

'We all have to eat, detective. You're here about Sister Martha.' She had been waiting for this moment for a long time.

'Yes, did you know her? Were you here when she was here?'

'We joined the Order at the same time, me from a local village, her from Bulawayo. An odd mix but we became good friends. She was fun and joyful and made those early days easier. You see, I missed home and all my brothers and sisters. She genuinely became my sister in Christ, but ... I ... I don't know where she is now.'

'Do you still remember her well?'

'We shared a room.'

'Do you know the name of a young man, a safari guide, she was reported to be interested in?'

'It was nothing, just a friendship, there was never talk of ... well she didn't run off with him. She was only going back to Bulawayo to consider her vocation. She meant to return, at least that's what she told me. Look, detective, I don't know what you've heard but she was a dedicated nun, a bit modern in her outlook for some ...' she looked around as if Torquemada might be in earshot.

'Do you know the name of the guide?'

She looked around again as if spouting heresy, 'Barney Jones.'

The name jolted Sibanda. If there was any name that could ruffle his feathers it was this one. Barney Jones had been Berry's high school sweetheart. The relationship was over, but the thought of them together still rankled. He almost tried to pin a previous murder on the man. 'Barney Jones is not in the country and Sister Martha isn't with him.'

'No, of course not, Sister Martha was a bride of Christ. It was the only marriage in her heart. Can I ask, detective, is this a cold case investigation? She's dead isn't she?'

'I don't know, but there have been a couple of other disappearances from the train. We are checking for a link.'

The nun stood and murmured a prayer through silent lips, clasping the crucifix at her breast. Sibanda gave her space.

After a moment, she said, 'I have something of Sister Martha's, a box, she left it with me for safekeeping, for when she returned. I would like someone else to take care of it now. Will you wait here?' The nun rose silently and floated, as if on a moving walkway, towards a second entrance door. Sibanda watched her ghostly hover in fascination.

He drove back to the police station with Sister Martha's box. The wooden container was firmly shut with a stout but rusty lock. It sat on the seat beside him. Even a key from Barghees universal lock supply would be no use on this one. It was a job for Ncube and a screwdriver.

CHAPTER 12

Before dawn on Saturday morning, the Ncube household was in chaos. Children were running to keep warm, their noses were running with cold and the household was on alert. Sergeant Thadeus Ncube was going camping for the first time in his life.

'Camping? Can I come too?' young Sampson asked.

'You mean you want to sleep on the ground under a bit of flimsy material in this weather that would surely turn the marrow in your bones to ice and freeze your toes off like jigger bites, and with wild creatures on the prowl waiting to eat you?'

'Yes, baba, it would be so exciting. Are you sure I can't come? I want to sleep in the bush in a tent.'

Ncube looked down at his young son, whose face still bore the creases of sleep, and wondered if they were actually related.

He shook his head, not only in denial; there was a hint of bewilderment in the movement. 'Not this time, Sampson, I will be working, but maybe when the weather is warmer.' He hated lying to his children.

Why had he ever agreed to the detective's suggestion? The trip would be as useless as a pot with a hole and as dangerous as walking on the crumbling edge of a crocodile-infested pond.

'What are you doing tomorrow?' Sibanda had asked.

'It's the weekend, sir, and I'm off duty.'

'I know, and you can't be fishing, it's too cold, but are you busy?'

Ncube suspected this line of questioning would lead to disaster but he didn't know whether it was better to say 'yes' or 'no'. He punted for the latter.

'Good, then how do you fancy a spot of camping? We could pop by Thunduluka to check on the details of the missing receptionist and then camp along the railway line. There's old kit at the station we can use. This way we should be able to cover quite a distance. It's a long shot, but I'm convinced there's more than one body on that remote stretch of track. We'll be back by Sunday evening.'

'Actually, I am … my wives have asked me to … two days, you say, I'm not sure …' the sergeant tried to wriggle out of it, but he had been unable to think of a single excuse. Two whole days in the bush … he had stabbed himself with his own spear. Why hadn't he said 'yes' when the detective asked him if he was busy? Surely the choice of one silly little word would now haunt him forever. His life might come to an end as a frozen corpse or lion breakfast or he might be driven to insanity by the deathly howling and screaming of wild things after dark. He had barely closed his eyes last night.

'Ncube, I have packed your medicines in the blue bag.' Blessing was carrying a small bag full of bottles and jars. 'This is for your stomach. Don't forget to take some after you have eaten. The ointment in the jar is for stings and bites. And this bottle will help you sleep. Do not drink from it until very last thing when you are already in your blankets. It is powerful.'

Ncube was finding it hard to concentrate.

'Here are your blankets, my dear,' Nomatter was next with her offering, 'and I have borrowed a foam mattress from Manyoni, next door. Her husband used to work for a safari camp. This is what the foreign *mukiwas* use when they go fly camping.'

'What is fly camping? Sleeping on a rubbish tip with *izimpukane*?' Ncube was stressed and unusually snappy.

Nomatter laughed. 'In this cold weather surely there will be a few insects and no flies around. Calm yourself, my dear, all will be well, you are with Detective Sibanda. He is untouchable.'

Oh yes, Detective Sibanda might be untouchable, surrounded by some kind of otherworldly electric fence, but that meant every famished creature would be staring at him. He, Sergeant Thadeus Ncube, was the sacrificial lamb.

'This will cheer you up,' Suko interrupted his fears. 'We have baked and cooked many of your favourite dishes and here is your breakfast to eat on the road.

Another Ncube baby woke and added its high-pitched decibels to the mix. Suko smiled, handed her husband a box of containers and packages, and set off to tend to the latest complainant. 'Just think, it will be so peaceful in the bush with no babies to bother you,' she added as she left.

Ncube snorted, baby's squeals meant you were alive, bush squeals meant either you or something else was dying or being ripped to pieces. He pulled his green balaclava over his head and struggled into a thickly padded jacket. Blessing handed him gloves, knitted from the same green, she was accomplished with three needles. In dawn's freezing silence, he heard Miss Daisy coughing and spluttering in the distance. Ncube knew her well. She might be all heat and steam under the bonnet but in the cab she would offer no comfort. Icy winds would leak through her crevices, through the bullet holes in the door and through the new knot hole caused by a rampaging rhino, sucking away whatever warmth he managed to hang onto. It would be ten o'clock before he could unwrap. Miss Daisy bellowed as she reached the house, announcing her own displeasure at the early start. Detective Sibanda was on time.

'I've had a devil of a job getting this rust bucket started, Ncube. We are stuck with the thing for the time being but I'll have my hands on the Santana soon.'

'It's the heater plugs, sir. They don't like the cold.'

Sibanda cranked the key, Ncube crossed his fingers, Miss Daisy remained schtum.

'What now, Ncube?

'Gently, sir, give the plugs a moment to warm up. Should I …?'

'… No, look at the mess the last time you drove to Thunduluka. You nearly got us killed by a rhino,' Sibanda pointed to the hole in the bodywork behind the driver's seat.'

Miss Daisy started after a few choking splutters, expelling air pockets like popping corn, her exhaust gases scenting the fresh morning air, and none too soon. Both men were becoming irritated, Ncube with the unfair accusations and the stress of Miss Daisy's possible acting up, and Sibanda with the pre-dawn start.

The drive to Thunduluka was uneventful. Mist rose in swirls of condensation from the valley as the pallid sun puffed her warm rose-tinted breath into the air. A small group of zebra snorted and stamped against the cold and a pair of scouting jackal, noses to the ground, searched among the tussocks for overlooked titbits before heading home to their underground burrows, where noses tucked under tails and communal breathing would soon have them dozing.

They found John Berger, the manager, standing with his back to a camp fire, warming his hands on a mug of coffee.

'I've been expecting you, detective. This is an awful business, again. I'm beginning to think the lodge is cursed. Can I get you both a coffee?'

'Black, no sugar, thank you. You have had a run of bad luck of late,' Sibanda agreed.

'White and, er … four sugars please. We're hoping Kerry will turn up. Perhaps she changed her mind and didn't get on the train.' Sergeant Ncube was making himself at home in front of the fire poking at the coals with a log to encourage flames. He only made more smoke.

'Tell us what you know, John, from the beginning.' Sibanda took a sip from his coffee.

'The lodge is hiring a new receptionist. Kerry applied. She looked good on paper. We normally ask employees to come for two days. It's a long way to travel into the bush and we need to assess a person's suitability before we, or they, commit to the position.'

'What happened with Kerry Williams?'

'She arrived by train last Tuesday and planned to leave on Thursday. I collected her from the station, but from the outset it was obvious she was not suitable.'

'Did you terminate her trial period?'

'No, she did that. She was a bright girl and recognised she would be a square peg. She chose to go home a day early on the Wednesday.'

'She wouldn't have fitted in?'

'Too sophisticated, too high maintenance – a bit of a townie. There are no beauty parlours for hundreds of kilometres. She thought we were a spa-type establishment, glamorous like those high-gloss South African safari lodges, but we're just a bunch of bushies. She laughed, we laughed. She was lovely.'

'Did you put her on the train?'

'No, one of our guides, Trywell Dube, was going on off days. He gave her a lift in to Gubu.'

'Can I speak to him?'

'We haven't been able to get in touch since he left. We've tried his phone, of course, but it's out of range. Everyone's hoping ...'

'... That she's with him? What can you tell me about Trywell Dube?'

'Enthusiastic, hasn't been guiding long. Great diesel mechanic, always useful to have someone like that on board. Did his apprenticeship with the Railways.' Sibanda and Ncube glanced at one another.

'How old is he?'

'Forties maybe, but still in great shape. Good at his job too.'

'Was he working last week, the week before?'

'He had a couple of days off, about eight or so days ago, I'd have to check, said he needed to go home to collect some of his stuff, but otherwise he was here.'

'Did he come back with any cuts or bruises?'

'No, why ...?'

'... Yes, he did, John, remember,' Mrs Berger arrived and joined the conversation, 'the poor wee man. I put some cream on it myself. Quite red and open it was, and with this braw weather, painful as well,' her thick Scottish accent was incomprehensible to Ncube, bringing memories of the last time he questioned her and the tangle of answers that made no sense. He returned to poking the fire.

'You're right, there was something. Coming back from his days off, he went into the bush following a drag mark, a leopard kill, he said, and got a whipping thorn branch right across the cheek for his pains, took a few days to heal. I remember now.'

Sibanda looked at his watch. He wanted to be along the railway line before the sun got too high. 'Let the station have any contact details for Trywell, maybe we can chase him up in his home village, and let me know if either of them get in touch.'

The sun burnt off the mist and added a few grudging degrees as Miss Daisy trundled back down the valley towards the rail line.

'You are deep in thought, sir.'

'This is a tough one, Ncube, my head is all over the place. Do we have more than one murder? Are we chasing a serial killer? What suspects do we have?'

'We've got Gideon Shumba.'

'He's still locked up, so who attacked Miss Barton on the train?'

'Could be anyone, there are plenty of tsotsis out there, sir. Maybe it was just a robber.'

'Shumba might not be coming clean about his actions, but he didn't kill Lois Khupe, and Miss Barton's intruder had her by the throat. He was intent on more than robbery.' Sibanda clenched his jaw. The thought of what might have happened to Berry if she hadn't been quick-witted and they hadn't been on the train stressed him even now.

'So what suspects do we have?'

'Isaac Manhombo has definitely been up to something and there were a couple of guys at Universal Dream who could fit the bill.'

'Are there any clues?'

'Circumstantial stuff, a bit of wire, a guilty conscience, opportunity, and Lois Khupe was on to corruption at Universal Dream. Maybe she was disposed of because she knew too much, was threatening to derail someone's personal gravy train, but you're right Ncube, I'm clutching at straws.'

Ncube looked across at the detective, he clutched at his straw in the coffee shop, rather rudely. Was this going to become some kind of habit? The detective looked worried and what was all this about gravy on the train?

'What about Kerry Williams's disappearance?' Sibanda asked.

'Perhaps she's with Trywell Dube.'

'Or murdered by Lois's killer. I don't like it, Ncube, we have no clear suspect. Trywell Dube worked for the railways, would know the insides of a train like the back of his hand, and he came back from leave with a scratched face. If we can synchronise the time of Lois's death and Trywell's off days, then we might have a match.' Sibanda lapsed back into silence.

Sergeant Ncube saw them first, he just happened to be looking at the tree line when the herd of elephants broke cover and lumbered towards a waterhole in the middle of the valley. Sibanda hadn't noticed the group. He was still far away in thought. Ncube wanted to glue his lips together, wanted the lumbering grey menace to disappear, but Miss Daisy was behaving rather noisily over her little pocket of air this morning. He could sympathise, suffering from a similar infliction himself, but he wasn't sure the detective could. This might be the way to reinstate her in Sibanda's eyes and make the detective feel better about this confusing murder.

'Elephants, sir, over there, do you want to visit them?' The words were out, they could not be sucked back in and Ncube regretted them immediately.

The detective never replied. He simply swung Miss Daisy off the dirt track and headed towards the wallow.

Ncube didn't know elephants had eyelashes, or that they were so long – if they had been human, the lashes would have tickled their nostrils, nor did he realise elephants are hairy all over and their skin deeply crisscrossed with a pattern of wrinkles resembling a tangle of wires. He never had cause to examine them before from point blank range. The monsters were so close to Miss Daisy, he was sure the wheezing noise he heard from her engine was hyperventilation, and he couldn't blame her. The sergeant sat like a statue barely allowing a breath to escape. His buttocks were pinched together as firmly as he could manage; he didn't want any breath escaping there either. The elephants were not so polite, they plopped gassy bubbles at will. Gurgles and rumbles from their bellies spoke of both enviable and liberated digestion, and chatty waterhole conversation.

'It's okay, the herd is relaxed, don't worry,' Sibanda whispered to his sergeant, but the whispering alarmed Ncube more, the detective never normally spoke quietly. It confirmed they were in a desperately dangerous situation. His tightly squeezed eyes opened to a slit. The situation couldn't have been worse. They were surrounded, sandwiched by mountains of grey flesh pressing in on the Land Rover. Every direction was swamped with grey. Trunks waved, water dripped, mud was slapped against leviathan bodies, dappling the dusty hides with battleship grey. The only sounds were of splashing and blowing until a large pair of tusks appeared to the right of the windscreen, the owner emitting an ear-splitting scream. A slightly smaller but no less threatening ivory curvature appeared from the left, with a trunk the size and weight of a fair-sized tree outstretched between the tusks. Ncube couldn't contain himself, 'Sir, they are angry, they are going to fight, club one another to death and spear one another with those … those weapons. We must get away while we can.' He tried to keep his voice down, but it cracked into a falsetto of blathering terror.

'Shh, Ncube, for Heaven's sake, get a grip. They aren't fighting, this is a handshake,' he murmured. 'Look, the younger bull is putting his trunk into the mouth of the older one. It's a greeting, showing subservience.'

'Won't that big one bite the trunk off?' he mouthed as if to a deaf man.

'They don't have those sort of teeth, Ncube. They can't cut anything.'

'So how do they eat?' Ncube couldn't imagine a life without canines and molars. Biting and chewing was a joy.

'They have one tooth on either side of their jaw. It's an elongated plate with ridges. An elephant grabs food with his trunk and sticks it in his mouth, which is a bit like a mill. As one set of teeth wears out with the daily grind of processing several tonnes of vegetation so another set erupts from the back of the gum. They only get six sets. If they outlive their teeth, they die of starvation.'

Ncube could think of no worse fate. He must remember to buy a new toothbrush. Suko had been nagging him that his was worn and useless. He said nothing more until the elephants moved away and Miss Daisy was again maundering along the dirt track; the thought of death by malnutrition kept him occupied for a time, until he rummaged in his bag and produced two doorstop ends of Suko's special sour dough bread, hollowed out and filled with sweet and spicy sugar beans followed by a layer of cooked tomatoes all topped with a fried egg and a slather of chilli for good measure. This was far better than a sandwich because there was no danger of any mess dribbling out of the sides. It was the perfect travelling food. He handed one to the detective.

They munched away in silence for a while until Sibanda returned his unfinished breakfast back to the sergeant who wolfed down the remains. Ncube also took a precautionary swig of Blessing's stomach drops – beans were an irritant.

'Not long now to where we found Lois's body, Ncube.'

'I know we are looking for Kerry Williams, but is there anything else we should keep an eye out for?'

'Bones. If I'm right then our serial killer has been using this stretch of track as his own personal hyena sink hole. Who knows how many girls he's murdered and tipped off the train over the years?'

'Is he speeding up his activity? There has been barely a week between the last two murders, assuming Kerry Williams is a victim as well.'

'Maybe, and don't forget Miss Barton, she was lucky to escape. Serial killers get more and more familiar with their crime and more careless.

They almost want to get caught, want the publicity for their deeds.'

Ncube shuddered along with Miss Daisy as she came to a halt. Who would want to be famous for murder? 'Shall we set up camp first?' he asked, as he clambered out of the vehicle.

'No, let's get started with the search. You walk close to the railway line. I'll keep to the bush side. Call me if you find anything unusual, anything at all, and keep me in sight. I don't want to have to go searching for you as well.'

Ncube had no intention of doing otherwise.

Some people enjoyed words – Berry was an avid bookworm – but Sibanda read the bush. The shape and depth of spoor and any disturbed ground were his story, the light's uneven reflection from the turn of a leaf, the angle of grass or a broken twig were the punctuation marks that made sense of it all, a rare tree, an unusual nest, uncommon birdsong, the anecdotes that added interest. The bush was Sibanda's library.

The pair walked, zigzagging, stopping every now and again to upturn something of interest.

Sergeant Ncube got very excited over a scattered rib cage. 'Here, sir, I have found bones.'

Sibanda walked over. 'Just an old impala kill,' he said, pointing to a pair of lyre-shaped horns near by, but it gave them a moment to take a drink.

The sun was high in the winter sky and there was no better time to be walking in the bush, warm sun, a cool breeze and not a cloud as far as the eye could see. Ncube dumped his jacket, scarf and a thick, hand-knitted pullover in a heap. He would pick them up on the way back. He looked across to the detective who had left the vehicle in shirt sleeves. How did he do it? He had an inbuilt cooling and heating system that switched modes at will. A kilometre further on, Ncube was sweating and wiping his brow with a handkerchief. He hadn't signed up for a route march. This exercise was ridiculous and probably as pointless as a blunt pencil. He muttered under his breath as his armpits streamed, his thighs burned with step after chafing step, and a few blisters began to form. It was then that he spotted something. Sibanda had roved further on and it took quite a loud shout to get him to turn back. Ncube saw what looked like a hand, or at least finger bones, still more or less together, no skin, but a few sinews intact. Was it a baboon's?

He didn't want to appear stupid again. He should have known the difference between human and impala ribs. Sibanda's withering look said as much. He picked up the hand by the wrist to have a closer look. A small cream-coloured egg fell out of the palm. Ncube let it drop, was surprised the shell didn't break, and wondered which bird would find comfort nesting among old bones. There was bound to be one, the bush turned up the oddest of habits.

'What have you got, Ncube?'

'Not sure, sir, but it could be a human hand.'

'Well spotted. It's a human hand all right judging by the size, not a baboon's, where did you pick it up?'

'Right here, sir.'

'It has wire twisted around the ring finger, our Sparrowhawk has a signature all right. Let's fan out. Mark every bone you find in the area. Put a stick in the ground and tie some of this on to it.' Sibanda produced a roll of yellow duct tape.

The detective found the skull twenty metres from the hand, not far away was a femur. He could see his sergeant placing sticks to mark bits of skeleton. They had found one of the missing girls.

'Ncube, can you walk back to Miss Daisy on your own? Walk along the railway line. You'll be safe. Radio the station. Tell them we have found another body. PC Khumalo should be on duty. She must get hold of Forensics to come and secure the scene. They are going to have their work cut out on this one. These bones have been picked clean but jackals, hyena, porcupines or even rats could disturb them further.'

'What are you going to do, sir?'

'I'm going to keep searching, but I'll be back at the camp site before dark. You get the tents up and a fire going.'

Ncube was grateful to be turning back. He had reached the limits of his endurance and tucked away in his bag was a delicious and well overdue lunch of samp, consisting of bits of dried maize broken into crystals, cooked until soft and creamy with powdered milk, herbs and spices, and topped with a delicious tomato and onion relish. What he didn't like was the idea of walking alone or waiting as the waning sun enticed all sorts of mischief to come out of the bush.

Sibanda figured he could search for another hour, maybe longer, before he would have to return to the camp site. He understood Ncube's sensitivities but the man would have to hold it together. There were more bodies up ahead, he was certain of it and he would be vindicated. Mfumu would be forced to reopen the investigation, and when he found Kerry Williams, and he would find her, Gideon Shumba would be released.

The detective walked briskly but carefully, covering Ncube's ground and his own, prodding possible finds with a stick. He was rewarded for his stealth by the appearance of a trio of giraffe strolling out of the tree line as though wading through water, their limbs below the knees seeming to take more time than was natural to catch up with their thigh movements. He stood motionless. The lanky creatures stopped and peered with supercilious disdain at the intruding, inefficient biped before returning from whence they came. Sibanda moved on too, weaving between the rail line and the tree line, glancing up from time to time to check he wasn't walking into a carnivorous ambush; there were no fresh tracks, but it paid to be vigilant.

He would have to turn back if he was to get to Ncube before sunset, but there was something interesting in the ground just ahead of him. He fossicked with his stick, unearthing a few putty-grey bone fragments, disappointingly indeterminate. He scraped together a pile of the aged and weathered splinters from under their covering of grass and leaves, some so old they had crumbled. Next to them he found a few links of rusted chain and a shard of blue and white china. Sibanda almost ignored them, the bones were outside the time range of his search, decades old at best and probably an animal kill, but a jaw bone lay in among the pile with a few teeth still embedded, the canines looked too small for a baboon's, the dentition remarkably human. Was he dealing with some kind of time-travelling serial killer? He dug further and uncovered a hard shape. What on earth was a black rock doing in the middle of the Kalahari sands? He scraped around it with his foraging stick. The top of the stone was smooth and smaller than he imagined, but as he dug down further the shape revealed some intriguing man-made bits. Once Sibanda cut away grass roots and brushed off the dirt and leaves, in his hand he held what appeared to be an elephant's head with a dagger on the end.

CHAPTER 13

Ncube made it back to Miss Daisy in one piece. He had never been so glad to see anyone in his life. He walked along the tracks trying to get an even gait, two steps to every sleeper, but it didn't work and he ended up skipping and hopping to find a rhythm, all the while looking over his shoulder and scanning the bush for unwanted companions. When that became tiresome, he tried balancing on a single rail but fell off after three steps. He had read in *The Bulawayo Chronicle* that some foreigner claimed to have walked on a tight rope over one of the gorges at Victoria Falls, but it had to be trick photography. All that churning water and a swaying rope? Not possible.

The sergeant was exhausted by his walk and shut himself into the old Land Rover with his lunch. He radioed PC Khumalo, who held out very little hope of raising Forensics on a Saturday, and then dozed off into a deep sleep. When he woke the sun had already turned pinkish-golden in preparation for its spectacular bout of winter bloodletting on the horizon. Ncube panicked. He hadn't even begun to put up the tents and having never put one up before, he didn't know where to start. He dragged a hefty bag from the back of Miss Daisy and unrolled the contents. Several beetles scurried from the canvas, unhappy at being exposed. The tents had not seen daylight for years. The sergeant scratched his head. What shape was he supposed to achieve? Where did all the poles and pegs go? He tried his best, tying himself in knots with guy ropes, disappearing through an opening in the tent and ending up trapped and smothered in musty-smelling canvas. Was this what it was like zipped up in a body bag? He called out for help but no one was in earshot, just a curious kudu cow, all pink ears and almond eyes, fascinated by the wriggling shape. When the peculiar creature shouted, she took off for safer territory.

Sibanda arrived back at the campsite, having jogged the last few kilometres to find Ncube sitting around a fire, jittery, jumping at every noise and eyeing up a handy burning log that could be used as a weapon. A few moments before the detective appeared he had heard rustling and then a call that sounded very much like lions.

He could have hugged Jabulani Sibanda as he emerged from the gloom. 'Sorry, sir, I failed with the tents,' he blurted with relief.

'They won't take a minute, here, give me a hand. Did you hear the ostrich booming just now?'

'Ostrich? Oh, er … yes, interesting call.'

'They fool a lot of people, sound a bit like a lion at times. Hold that pole steady while I hammer in the pegs.'

Within twenty minutes, Ncube felt more relaxed. The campsite was now cosy. Two tents, called pups – he supposed any bigger version would rightly be called a bitch – sat with their backs safely to Miss Daisy and their doors to a roaring camp fire whose flames licked the sunset and flared amber against Sibanda's glass. Ncube was nursing a can of orange, glowing nuclear in the fire's light. Almost homely.

'What's that you have in your hand, sir?'

'I found it near some bones that could be human. I've marked them for Forensics. It's possibly silver, but it must have been there for years looking at the tarnishing.'

'A moulding of an elephant's head?'

'But not from Africa, look at the small ears and the slope of the forehead. This is an Indian elephant.'

'Is it some kind of a weapon?'

'The whole thing is too clumsy for a dagger. This blade was designed to be hidden. My guess is it was concealed as a walking stick with the head as a handle. I've heard of sword sticks.'

'But how did an Indian elephant walking stick get here to the Gwaai straight?'

'From a passing train, carried by some Indian gent or ex-colonial and lost through the window, thrown through a door, who knows, but it's been here for years. Not part of our current investigation.'

'I wonder what it was used for and how the tip got broken off.' Ncube had taken the blackened head and was staring at the blade.

'We'll probably never know, and just as well, that edge could have sliced through brick in its time. We have enough on our hands.'

They ate under an African tablecloth of touchable stars, the crisp night air distilling their brilliance, some salted and scattered like silver-white dust, some clustered like crystals in a geode others lost in the swirling clouds of the Milky Way. Sibanda produced a slab of steak he set to grill slowly over the glowing coals and Ncube rustled up a pot of mealie meal along with Blessing's relish of choux mollier and home-stamped peanut butter.

They ate in companionable silence, Sibanda catching the deep grunting hoots of a giant eagle owl and the faint, tinny whistle of a pennant winged night jar; Ncube catching the last morsels of Nomatter's sour milk scones with marula jelly. He brushed the crumbs off his platform gut, feeding a platoon of stalking ants, and then slapped his lips and patted his stomach. Rarely had he eaten such a large portion of tender meat, maybe this camping wasn't so awful after all. 'The bones we found, sir, have we any idea who they belong to?'

'Not a clue, there should be enough material left to extract DNA, but neither the nun nor the prostitute seems to have any relatives to compare with. We may never know. We'll have to leave that up to the boys in the lab.'

'Will the Officer-in-Charge understand he should keep the case open now we have found more evidence?'

'Probably not, Mfumu will never make the link. He'll say the connection is too messy. Kerry Williams is the key. We'll set off first thing in Miss Daisy and get as far as the last search spot and keep looking for her from there.'

'What was in the nun's box I prised open? Any clues to lead us to a suspect?'

'Just papers, a couple of photos, letters from her parents. I've read them, nothing out of the ordinary, some female stuff and that is it.'

'I'll turn in then, sir,' Ncube was beginning to hear noises: squeaks and roars, shufflings and crackings. He didn't want to leave the warmth and comfort of the fire but he did want Blessing's drops and a deep sleep if he was to be walking some distance again tomorrow. He had aches in places he never knew he had muscles.

Sibanda sat for a while soaking up the atmosphere. It had been months since he spent a night in the bush. He added a couple of logs to the coals and drew in closer. One log caught and flared, the sudden light casting shifting shadows around the bush and sending bright sparks into the night sky like tracer bullets destined for the stars. The log was not silent as it sacrificed its hundred years of growth, it crackled and snapped in protest. Louder splintering and cracking sounds came from deep in the bush. Sibanda recognised elephants breaking branches, stripping bark and extracting what nutrients they could from the winter landscape. Tonight would be blisteringly cold and sleep would be hard come by, but he didn't mind as long as Africa kept up the nocturnal noises quiz.

When he finally crawled into his bed, he lay for a while staring through a rotted hole in the canvas roof perfectly aligned with Crux. The five-starred kite formation of the Southern Cross had been his friend since childhood and along with the Alpha and Beta Centuri pointers had guided him home when he wandered at night. With a pair of binoculars, the Jewel Box at the heart of the Cross would be visible, a cluster of red and blue giants twinkling like rubies and sapphires, but he fell asleep staring into the Southern Cross's Coalsack Nebula, forming questions and looking for answers that never came as the dark, dark hole in the dark sky swallowed him.

He woke in the early hours as the southbound train raced past, the canvas flapped and the displaced air nipped his already frozen ears and nose. He pulled his blankets further over his head and tried to get back to sleep. He may have dozed but the northbound train repeated the exercise forty minutes later. He was wide awake when the lions called, not a full-throated roar but a series of muted moans floating through the air, saying, 'The ambush is set, you take the flank, we'll drive them into the trap, stay focused.' The cats were close and hunting. He stuck his head through the tent flaps because he heard something else, a few soft, contented grunts and chewing of grass. The moon had come up to backlight a buffalo herd grazing quietly on the cleared firebreak.

'Ncube, are you okay?' he called out with just enough volume to carry. His sergeant would be nervous, but there was no reply. In between the lion's calls Ncube was snoring rhythmically. He was dead to the world.

The tents were downwind of the herd and the lions were upwind of the buffalo which meant he and Ncube were in the path of a stampede. That was a lion pride's standard tactic, get the herd running and then pick out the laggards in the confusion. Miss Daisy had their backs covered, but headlong panic was unpredictable and their own flanks were unprotected, particularly Ncube's; his tent was directly in the line of flight. Sibanda barely had time to consider the options before all Hell broke loose. The lions made their move in a snarling pincer movement. The herd was spooked, bellowing loudly, and pounding the earth in their desperation to escape. The ground shook as most of the buffalo headed at speed straight for the tents, guided as though in a dip tank race. To the right lay thick bush with few escape routes, to the left the steep embankment of the railway line. The herd would want to wheel and get the wind as soon as they could, but it wouldn't be easy. Some animals did peel off. Sibanda could hear the crashing of branches and trampling of bushes as they found an escape route in among the trees, but the main herd ploughed forward like a thousand horsemen of a thousand apocalypses.

'Ncube, get out of the tent now!' he roared above the thunder, as the phalanx of horns and hooves bore down on them. 'Get into Miss Daisy.' There was no movement from Ncube's tent. 'For God's sake get out of there, you idiot,' he tried again. With seconds to spare, Sibanda raced to the exposed side of Ncube's tent, throwing his arms wide open, jumping up and down, yelling and shouting at the galloping herd. For a moment, he thought they would both be trampled to pulp, but at the last second the leaders veered away, eyes wide, white and rolling with terror, narrowing their escape route, crushing bodies one against another like sandpaper on rough wood. Sibanda could smell adrenalin on the hides and acrid fresh dung splattering from fearful bowels. The bellowing was deafening and thumping hooves pounding the frosted grass reverberated through his body.

The lions picked their mark carefully, a thin, old cow with no tail, worn horns and a battle-scarred hide. She had seen off lion claws before but now was her time. She staggered past Sibanda, a lioness clinging to her rump, and one pacing alongside, heading for her throat. The herd came to a stop a couple of hundred metres beyond the camp. They turned and stared at the old *salukazi*. The danger was over for them, but her extended family, generations of her calves, and calves of her calves, watched with guilt and relief as she stood in defiance, shaking her head to dislodge the throat grip, desperately trying to keep her withers upright. Once she was down she was done for. An extra lioness leapt on her back tipping the scales. She bellowed plaintively as her back legs collapsed and she sank to the ground. The throat lioness changed her grip to cover the nose and mouth, giving the cow one last breath, one last yell at life. The victim would suffocate in a few minutes such was the power of the cat's jaws. Death was not easy or painless. A pack of half-grown cubs caught up with the chase and began live disembowelment and the rump and back lionesses swallowed chunks of her anus before she finally gave in. Sibanda watched the whole drama. The kill happened a mere thirty metres from him. He hoped adrenalin and shock had numbed the old girl's pain, but this was the way of the wild, unforgiving, unforgettable and, he had to admit, thrilling. He had rarely been so close to the raw drama of a lion kill before.

The noise of the hunt soon abated, reduced to the ripping, snarling and panting sounds of satiation spiced with the violence of a family dining dispute as the pride settled in to a night of feasting, scrapping and the teaching of table hierarchy. The cubs, with the faint ginger rosettes of birth still visible, were well below the salt. They would have to wait for the scraps. Sibanda's own pounding heart slowed. The moment had been a near run thing. He watched as a handsome black-maned lion strolled onto the scene. Where had he been lurking? Now was his time to assert supremacy over the females and cubs. There was nothing like a kill to get his natural power and authority to the fore. Pa always ate first and got the choicest titbits.

Ncube continued to snore in his tent. Sibanda contemplated waking him, but the lions were close, too close for Ncube's comfort. Let him sleep. It was barely 4 am. Sibanda wouldn't go back to bed, the pride was focused on the kill but he would keep an eye on them anyway. A few leadwood coals were still smouldering; he added some gagu kindling to get a flame, wedged an old coffee pot on to boil and warmed himself as the fire caught and flared.

The detective used the still of the early morning to try and draw the threads of the investigation together. What was he missing? What was it about this disparate group of women that got the Sparrowhawk's murderous juices flowing? What did Berry have in common with a nun, a prostitute, an aid worker and a receptionist? Did there even have to be a common denominator, could the attacks just be opportunistic, wrong place, wrong time? Three coffees later followed by a sunrise that would have outshone the fiercest of tequilas, he was no closer to an answer.

'Good morning, sir, you are up early.' Ncube emerged from his tent, only his eyes visible through layers of clothing, a blanket wrapped around him doubling as a cloak. 'Ayi, it is colder than the grave of a snake.' He shivered, rubbed his hands and made his way to the fire.

'You slept well. Didn't you hear anything? Want a coffee?'

'Thank you, sir. I heard the ostriches again, not long ago, as I woke up. They have a strong voice for an early morning.'

'Not ostriches, look over there.'

'What … what is that? It's not … It can't be ...'

'Lions, Ncube, you missed quite a party last night …' Sibanda didn't finish the sentence. Without another word, Ncube took off at pace, his cloak flapping, for the safety of Miss Daisy.

Sibanda produced a long link of sausages and set a frying pan of eggs on the fire. The smell of blistering fat fanned towards the Land Rover, penetrating her various body piercings. He heard Miss Daisy's squeaky window being rolled down, it sounded like the screech of a barn owl, enough to set anyone's teeth on edge. 'Sir, sir,' the voice was whispered and urgent.

'What, Ncube?' Sibanda was abrupt. His dawn calm was dissolving on the waters of Ncube's irrational fears.

'Do you think it's safe to be out there?' Sausages charring on the fire were a cruel tease.

'Or stay in Miss Daisy and starve, you mean? I'm not going to wait on you, make up your mind.'

Ncube was tormented by the waft of grilling meat and bubbling eggs and terrified by the teeth tearing flesh, crunching bones and wolfing down their own bloody breakfast on the far-too-close edge of camping insanity.

'Put it this way, Ncube. If you don't get out of the vehicle and help with breaking camp, I'll personally turf you out of Miss Daisy and leave you here to find your own way back to Gubu.'

Miss Daisy's door creaked on her arthritic hinges and Ncube slid out, he had no option, when two elephants fight, the grass gets trampled, and he was the unfortunate turf underfoot. From that moment until they moved on, he watched the cats. He didn't care that the big male lion was a particularly magnificent specimen or that he might be a darling of the world's wildlife lovers, posted on websites from Tunbridge Wells to Indian Wells, wherever they were. To Ncube he was just another meat-eating killer to be avoided at all costs. Hadn't an old lion just like this recently eaten a young boy in Mabale? The sergeant wolfed down his breakfast, knowing that indigestion would be his penance. Matters only improved when the sun prised free from the eastern horizon and floated upwards in a pale pink watercolour wash. The lions took that cue to move, the big male lion in the vanguard, his wives and children in his wake, all bloated like blow flies, staggering to the nearest water for a drink before sleeping off their raw banquet.

Miss Daisy's diesel had thickened in the night to sluggish fudge and her heater plugs were as effective as using a match to melt an iceberg.

'Don't tell me we are stuck here, Ncube, I don't have the patience for this.'

'No, don't worry, just a little delay and remember, sir, patience can cook a stone.'

'Get on with it, we don't have time to melt rocks. Kerry Williams is waiting,' Sibanda snapped, and strode off towards the site of the kill. Ncube rekindled the fire and put a pot of water on to boil. He would scald some of the reluctance out of the old girl.

Miss Daisy responded well to her morning bath. Twenty minutes later Ncube and Sibanda were bumping along the deeply sanded firebreak road that hadn't seen a drop of water for some months. Miss Daisy struggled at times to grip and she whined with the effort, but the detective was keeping her clear of the worst of the sand traps. Sibanda had enjoyed his time examining the lion kill, checking the spoor, finding where they buried the entrails, noting what body parts had been left. The head, of course, was not touched – as he had expected – and the lungs were still intact. Neither were favoured felid morsels. As he heard Miss Daisy splutter into life so a bateleur eagle arrived for the choice pickings, vultures would not be far behind and the minutiae of recycling could begin. Soon Miss Daisy was steaming past the first set of human bones and the yellow banded marker sticks. Fifteen minutes later they came to the second site, the pile of ancient remains marked with only one stick.

'We'll walk from here. It's not far to where Lois Khupe was found. This seems to have been Sparrowhawk's favoured dumping stretch. Same procedure as yesterday.'

'Right, sir, I'll take the railway line.' Ncube was stiff, sore and could hardly move. Blessing had included some balm in her first aid kit, but although it smelled foul – always a good sign when it came to her remedies – the relief was minimal. He wasn't sure how much walking he could manage. The sleeping drops had worked a little too well, particularly since he had doubled the dose. Sibanda had told him the full story of last night's drama. He couldn't make his mind up if it was better not to have known anything about the terrible danger or to have been awake and saved himself. He pondered the conundrum of abject fear versus blissful oblivion as he walked, prodding here and there with his stick and using it to assist his aching muscles when he could.

Sibanda was in his element, the bush was both alive with activity and dying from winter's grip. Against the rich green backdrop of teak trees still hanging on to their ageing summer foliage were layered the already yellowing leaves of an ordeal tree highlighted by the winter orange and brown of a cluster of duiker berries. A lone mukwa stood stripped bare, an early winter casualty, hairy, fried-egg-looking pods clinging to the distant crown. Beneath him across a bare patch of sand he could see the marks left by the trailing quills of a porcupine and a few scrapings where it had searched for a midnight snack. Ahead and from several metres inside the tree line he caught sight of a tawny eagle flying up from the ground. Large flapping wings, a heavy body and limited runway made a clumsy and noisy event out of the take-off. Once in the air the raptor soared with ease. Sibanda paused, what had it been up to? Tawnys didn't hang around on the ground for no reason, he thought, and triangulated the spot. Walking warily, he came across the drag mark first and recognised the accompanying spoor as a pair of hyenas. Whatever they had killed and pulled into the thicker vegetation was substantial. He followed the drag deeper into the bush until he came across the kill.

Kerry Williams lay partially eaten and, bar the hands and feet, totally skinned. The tawny eagle had been taking advantage of the hyenas' daylight absence to steal a few mouthfuls. The hyenas had fed for several nights on their find. Kerry's thighs and buttocks had mostly disappeared, but the choice internal organs would have been wolfed down first. In a few days, the victim would have been reduced to a heap of chewed bones and some of those bones would have been taken and buried for later. In a few weeks, she would have been scattered and untraceable. He slipped the wire ring off what remained of her fingers, nibbled and ripped by some predator, maybe a jackal. The wire evidence was for his and Ncube's eyes only.

After covering the remains with his jacket, he followed the drag marks back to the open area. The story of the tracks was written in the large print of a Grade 1 reader, it led Sibanda to the middle of the cleared firebreak where Kerry Williams's body landed when it was thrown from the train. Any predator would have taken advantage of a free meal, couldn't blame them, and Sibanda had the tawny to thank for advertising the hidden spot in the thick bush.

'Ncube,' he shouted. Where had his sergeant disappeared to?

'Over here, sir.' Ncube had clambered up the embankment and was standing in the middle of the rails. When he lost sight of the detective, he panicked.

'There are no bones in the middle of the tracks, what are you doing up there?'

'To get lost is to learn the way,' he blurted in excuse.

'You can't get lost along the railway line; it's impossible, even for you.'

'I was making sure of my bearings, sir,' he huffed.

Ncube scrambled down faster than his legs wanted to move. They had stiffened up and felt like wood.

'I've found Kerry Williams, Ncube.'

'Where?'

'In the tree line. I've marked the spot with a stick. She was dragged into the bush by hyena. Don't go in, you won't like it, she has been eaten.'

Ncube blanched, 'And skinned?'

'Yes, exactly the same MO as before, down to the wire ring on her finger, or what was left of her finger.'

'So, Gideon Shumba is innocent after all.'

'Definitely, time to get back to Gubu and let him out.'

Chapter 14

'What?!' Stalin Mfumu's voice echoed with the practise of pulpit oration down the grubby corridors of Gubu Police Station, causing PC Khumalo to look up mid form-filling and the queue of complainants to shuffle nervously along the cement bench regretting the warm spot they had worked hard to cultivate and inheriting their neighbour's less enticing patch. 'The paper work is completed and the police are on their way from Detaba to transfer the prisoner to the provincial cells for trial. Do you know what chaos you have caused? Detective Inspector Sibanda, you are an abomination, a pestilence, a plague on my house.'

Sibanda watched the spittle fly from Mfumu's mouth and settle in foam droplets on his cleared and empty desk. Mondays, he reflected, were never good days for Mfumu if the congregation of the Brethren of the Lord's Blood had been sparser and less enthralled than usual. Rumour spread that the pews had been particularly empty on Sunday. The freezing weather was not encouraging to the faithful. Even the promise of fire, brimstone and a social chit-chat did little to cheer their winter melancholy. The church hall was an icy tomb. It hadn't helped that the Covent of St Monica instituted Mary-blue uniforms for the female faithful with a fetching white hat and a spectacular collar to crochet. Word had it Mfumu's congregation was defecting in droves.

'We can't convict an innocent man, no matter how far along the process, how complete the paperwork. Gideon Shumba is innocent. He never murdered Kerry Williams, he was locked up here and the MO is identical, a skinned body thrown from the train, which means he had nothing to do with Lois Khupe's death either.'

Mfumu huffed and removed a speck of hair from his shirt and then continued to dust away with the back of his hand at imaginary detritus. 'Have Forensics confirmed the time of death?'

'Not yet, they were slow to arrive at the scene, but the girl was alive before Shumba was arrested. The longer we keep him locked up, the longer the serial killer has to continue his carnage.'

'A serial killer?' Mfumu's voice rose to the treble range.

'We found another body along the track, just scattered bones and possibly the remains of another victim, a much older crime. We don't know how long this man has been operating or how many girls he has raped and cut up.'

'A serial killer?' Mfumu muttered in disbelief.

'I'm afraid so and I'm going to need all the resources we can muster at this station; the killer is ratcheting up his activity. There was another attack on the train on Friday night but the victim managed to fight him off.'

'This can't be happening; a serial killer in Gubu?'

'We don't know he's from Gubu. He operates between here and Bulawayo.'

'Then we must hand the investigation over to Bulawayo, they have the resources to investigate multiple murders. Consider our statistics, if they get any worse, I'll be doomed to moulder in this Godforsaken village.' Mfumu rarely shared his fears, particularly not with the smugly, irritating detective, but his guard was down, Sunday had been a disaster and Mrs Mfumu was away tending to her ailing mother, leaving him to look after himself. He took pride in an immaculate house, but not on the effort it took to keep it looking that way. Already the polished floors were cloudy and scuffed. How did his wife keep the sand, grit and filth of this rural eyesore from every surface?

'We can't hand over, the murders are all on our patch and when we can catch the killer it'll be a feather in Gubu's cap. It could mean promotion,' Sibanda baited the hook.

Mfumu drew his thoughts from the fluff balls lurking under his bed and looked up at the tall, elegant man in front of him, a detective with dark powers who solved impossible crimes. He narrowed his eyes and tried to assess if there was hope of a reprieve from the dusty

Matabeleland bush and lack of clean, paved spaces, or if he was being tempted by the devil dangling a sinful escape route in front of him. On reflection, the detective's efforts had, after all, brought them a new vehicle he could drive with some pride, as befitted his status. Maybe the capture of a serial killer would finally bring the accolades he deserved as Officer-in-Charge, and a move to a bigger station with cement, tar and at least a two-storey building. He cleared his throat.

'Let me see. What do you need? I can't spare much manpower and certainly no vehicles.'

'If Assistant Detective Chanza can take some officers and cover the area further along the railway line, he'll find more bodies – one set of bones at least. I'll brief him. And can you put someone on the front desk to cover for PC Khumalo?'

'Why do you need her, a female PC?'

'I've heard the Universal Dream team are visiting Mabale, a Food for Work meeting to resuscitate the dip tank and the dam. I want it checked out. A couple of Lois Khupe's colleagues are up to no good. One of them could be her killer. Lois discovered corruption at her work, maybe someone wanted her silenced. It's one lead we're folllowing. They'll recognise Sergeant Ncube and me, but they won't have seen Zanele Khumalo. She can mingle with the crowd, pick up any undercurrents.'

'Highly irregular, a woman? Are you sure? They aren't really designed for such work.'

'Yes, I'm sure.'

'I suppose PC Tshuma could cover for her, wouldn't you prefer him.'

'No, PC Khumalo has more experience, and a woman will blend in better.'

Sibanda left Mfumu in his office, puzzling over the detective's choice of assistant. Women were only good for cleaning, cooking and washing. He was obliged to tolerate the rise of females to elevated ranks in the police force and their inclusion in politics. This he did, like most of his colleagues, with a smile on his lips and a scowl in his heart. It wasn't in the natural order of things. The bible didn't have women leaders, God didn't intend it. Women only got a mention as mothers, daughters and sinners. The bible was the rule on all things, the blazing truth set in stone. And these people called themselves Christians. Ha! They would burn for their heresy.

'You're with me for the foreseeable future, Zee.'

PC Khumalo produced a smile stretching the length of the charge office desk. 'Why, what's going on?'

'I need a fresh face to mingle in the crowd at the UD Food for Work meeting this afternoon.'

'Me? Work as a detective?'

'For the time being, but don't get carried away, it's only temporary.'

'Wow!' the thought of getting out from behind the desk and investigating crime was the best thing that had happened to her.

'Just take yourself off to the Mabale meeting. No uniform of course; and you'll need a cover story in case you see anyone you know.'

'Easy, I have an aunt who lives in the district. She's away looking for work in Johannesburg. If anyone asks I'll say I'm coming to find out details for her.'

Sibanda briefed PC Khumalo, told her to keep an eye on George Paradza. 'That man has got some sort of money-making scheme going and Lois Khupe may well have died to keep the embezzlement from exposure.'

'But aren't we looking for a serial killer, a random murderer?'

'We are, so be careful. This isn't going to be a jaunt, Zee; stay well undercover. Could just be Lois threatened to reveal what she had discovered and set the man off again on a killing spree. Serial killers go dormant, sometimes for years, and then an incident triggers their activities. Kerry and Lois are his most recent victims, but five or six years ago a couple of other girls went missing and there may be others we don't know about. Our murderer was lying low for a while. George Paradza could well be our man.'

'I'm a good actress, sir, don't worry.'

Sibanda raised an eyebrow.

'I was the lead in the Christmas pageant last year as Mary, don't you remember? Everyone says I should be on the stage, could be famous.'

Sibanda raised the other eyebrow, 'And keep an eye out for Knut Von Bergen. There's something not right about that man.'

'Lois's funeral is tomorrow morning. Her colleagues are staying over for it. I want to be there.'

'Keep away. I'll cover that with Sergeant Ncube.'

'But Lois was my friend.'

'She'll understand.' Sibanda spoke with such conviction PC Khumalo felt Lois heard.

'And, Zee …'

'Yes, sir.'

'Just keep your eyes open, don't do anything stupid.'

Zanele Khumalo boarded a Kombi plying between Gubu and the Mabale turn off. She was wearing her winter best: a padded silver jacket over a cerise blouse and flowered skirt. Her black knee-high boots were genuine leather and soft, bearing the name Clarks, which didn't seem to be a Chinese make. They were new … well … new to her at least and a revelation in comfort. She had bought them, along with the rest of her wardrobe, on a recent trip to Bulawayo, at the Bendovers. This was a market of unimaginable excitement where every weekend an eager crowd descended on a street near the City Hall. Here, the hawkers arrived with their massive, compressed bales of donated clothing to set up stall by placing large tarpaulins on the ground, ripping open the hessian covering and disgorging the bale contents into a volcanic heap, a continuously expanding lava flow of discarded fashion. There were over fifty mountains to choose from. Cries of 'fifty cents, fifty cents, fifty cents' or 'dollar, dollar, dollar' reverberated around the markets, 'tops, trousers, T shirts, skirts, skirts, skirts', echoed from every corner as the traders warmed up for the melee, enticing the buyers to their particular heap of merchandise. PC Khumalo burrowed like a mole through the crumpled, gnarled piles looking for suitable items. So intent was she on a bargain that the crowd density went unnoticed. The excavation work was back-breaking and the market well named. The constable came away a couple of hours later armed with a new wardrobe for under $10 despite having her dignity severely dented by a shove on her not inconsiderable rear end, resulting in a swan dive into the middle of a pile of second-hand pyjamas. She burst out laughing at the memory.

'What have you got to laugh about?' asked the lady squashed in next to her on the back seat of the Kombi. 'These are desperate times.'

'You're right, mama. It was just a good memory.' And that's all it would probably ever be. The government were threatening to ban the import of second-hand clothing, claiming it was a health hazard, even though no one ever got sick. Politicians certainly knew how to suck the last marrow of joy from the bones of adversity.

PC Khumalo let her guard down with her musings. She must concentrate on the task in hand if she was to do the job properly. A detective wouldn't daydream on the job. She would chat to this lady and use her as cover at the meeting. 'We don't have many of those anymore, do we?' she added.

'No, I'm going to register for the Food for Work programme just to put something on the table for my kids.'

'Me too.'

'Where are you from? I don't recognise you as local.'

'Gubu, I'm getting information at the Universal Dream meeting for my aunt Patricia Khumalo.'

'I know Patricia, but hasn't she gone down to Johannesburg?'

'No work and Xenophobia, she will be home soon.' PC Khumalo thought the white lie was probably the black truth anyway, no need to cross her fingers.

The pair chatted until the kombi dropped them at the Mabale turn off and then they walked along the old tar strip road gathering more desperate souls as they went. When they reached the dip tank clearing, which served as the local village green, over two hundred locals were gathered to hear news of the programme. Goats that normally flocked in the clearing and neatly trimmed the foliage on the base of the trees to back-leg-standing height were sulking, bleating and ringing their bells of displeasure in the distance. They had been displaced.

The community meeting was not only an opportunity to stave off hunger but also an outing, an excuse for a social get-together. Each participant was dressed in their Sunday best: jackets and ties for the men and multicoloured, crumple-free fabric for the ladies, nobody had time or energy to waste on ironing, and anyway, cotton faded quickly and lost its brilliance in the African sun. By the time the meeting was underway, PC Zanele Khumalo was just another local supplicant, as embedded as a blood-sucking bug in a mattress seam.

She made her way steadily towards the Universal Dream vehicle, dragging Mamoyo, her new friend, along as cover. She recognised the white man first. It had to be Knut Von Bergen with steel-framed glasses and the proportions of the Gubu station outhouse, solid and square with a faint whiff of the unsanitary. The detective had told her to keep an eye out for him. When she questioned why, Detective Sibanda replied 'gut instinct' and that was enough for PC Khumalo to keep him in view.

'Do we need to get so close? It makes us look greedy and desperate, and there's good shade under this tree.' Mamoyo wanted to hang back.

'I, er, don't hear so well,' PC Khumalo improvised.

'But look, that man over there has a megaphone.'

'Well, you stay here. I want to be first in the queue.' It was time to ditch Mamoyo. The man with the megaphone looked slick and too smartly dressed for a rural gathering. His long, chisel-nosed shoes were already clouded with Kalahari dust and his shiny suit made him glisten like a snake that had just sloughed its skin. That must be George Paradza, another one of Sibanda's hunches.

She wormed through the gathering throng until she reached the third row to the side of the main event, out of the line of sight of the two men she had been sent to spy on. Shiny suit man picked up the megaphone. Waves of charitable speak washed over Zanele Khumalo; she caught a few words: 'together', 'community', 'hard work', 'achievement'. It irked her. She looked around at the gathered villagers, who toiled every day to put a meal in a pot, who walked great distances to find wood to heat the pot and who lugged gallons of water on their heads to wash the pot. How had the snake man lost touch with his roots? His words were an insult to the aching muscles, calloused hands and sun-starched skin of the rural poor who stood in front of him. George Paradza sat in a smart office in Bulawayo, drove an expensive vehicle that never featured in the wildest dreams of the villagers and had the gall to talk to these people about hard work. What a joke. PC Khumalo seethed under her silver padded jacket and turned her attention to Knut Von Bergen. He was standing apart surveying the crowd. Was he judging them? Was he looking for his next victim? His eyes found a tall, young woman. Her clear-skinned beauty and model proportions were out of kilter with her surroundings. PC Khumalo watched him watch her. She could see the lust in those weirdly coloured eyes; even through thick glass they signalled desire.

'They talk a load of rubbish, don't they?' Mamoyo sidled up silently, come to claim her place near the front of the queue with her new friend.

PC Khumalo was startled by the intrusion, 'And we have to stand here and listen to it,' she improvised. 'I suppose it's the price we have to pay for food. Anyone would think we're kids in a classroom and he's the teacher with a big stick. And the local councillors are here, I see, claiming all the glory for their political persuasion. Doesn't it make you sick? They cause the problem and claim the solution. Who is that girl over there?' she added.

'Which one?'

'The tall, skinny one, looks like that super model, Naomi.'

'Miranda Siziba, poor girl.'

'Why do you say that?'

'Both parents dead – you know from what – and she is left with her three younger siblings to bring up. No wonder she is here looking for work.'

'Can't anyone help her?'

'There are lots of men who'd like to but she's a good girl, loves her brothers and sisters, the youngest is still a baby. The suitors, and there are many, get nowhere with her. She chases them all. Why are you asking?'

'No reason, just, she's a striking girl,' but she watched as Knut Von Bergen's eyes roved over the young body with unmasked desire. Not that lust lead to murder; if it did, most of the female population of Gubu would be dead in their beds, but if Detective Sibanda thought Von Bergen might be a suspect then she better keep an eye on him and on the girl.

'Come on, time to register,' Mamoyo nudged her. During her distraction with the girl, Miranda, George Paradza put down the megaphone and moved off. Another man and woman were beginning to write down names on a clipboard.

'No, er, I've heard enough. I'll pass on the information to my aunt.' PC Khumalo was kicking herself. Where had the man with the megaphone gone? She edged away from Mamoyo, who surged forward with the queue, and scanned the area. The winter sun was gaining midday strength; one of its targets was Paradza's suit that reflected like a thousand mirrors of mica against the grey dust. He was standing thirty metres behind the UD Land Cruiser, chatting intently to a man she hadn't noticed before. Their stance alone told PC Khumalo they were up to no good. How could she get closer to listen to their conversation? She cursed the goats that had stripped the area of any cover and the hundreds of cow hooves that had trodden the ground clean and scoured of the possibility of regrowth. To her left and ahead was a tree of sorts, in truth, more of a sapling, but if she made for it and pretended to need the shade, little as it was, then she could amble further on towards the drinking trough commandeered as a bench by a couple of the older, plumper ladies, for whom the day had already been too long. From there she could wander towards a large ant hill that might keep her from sight if she crouched, and that would allow her to reach the ruins of an old pump house and within ear shot of what the two men were discussing. Why had she worn pink and silver? Her serviceable brown fleece would have been better camouflage. Learning to curb her vanity would be essential if she was to be any good at this surveillance stuff.

The constable made it to the tree unnoticed where she fussed with the zip on her boot and stole a sideways glance at the two men who continued to chat animatedly. The ladies at the trough never flickered from their gossip as she strolled past. The ant heap had served as a comfort stop for a couple of women before her, so hunkering behind it alerted no stares. The transit to the pump house was the most difficult. Her heart was in her mouth as she watched the two men chatting, voices tantalisingly out of range. This next move was essential and would be a matter of timing. PC Khumalo hesitated and was about to make a dash for the half-collapsed pump house wall, when the megaphone piped up requesting everyone have their IDs ready to speed up the registration process. The two men turned towards the announcement, PC Khumalo took her opportunity and sprinted. She was breathing hard when she reached the wall, not from exertion but from a surge of adrenalin. Her ears were thumping with blood but she still heard the conversation.

'Look, as I said, it's not as easy as it used to be, someone got wind of that last deal.' George Paradza scuffled the dirt with his unsuitable shoes.

'Are we safe?'

'This time, yes, the problem has … um … disappeared,' he hesitated, 'just be more cautious in future. I can't afford another cock-up.'

'What about this next lot?'

'Same deal, but for God's sake be more careful with the paperwork. We both lose out if I get fired.'

'How many this time?'

PC Khumalo never heard the answer. She was struck from behind by a blow that felled her.

Chapter 15

With Billi's face to her knees and a sharpened pencil in hand, Thula began to write. It would take most of the day because she wanted to choose every word with care, they must not only reflect her feelings but they needed to impress the girl with the progress of her learning. The handwriting must be neat and well formed. She practised and practised from a very old copperplate writing primer the girl had given her, found, she said, among a stack of old books where she lived. Her natural abilities had, over the months, given the strokes a style of their own. Thula was proud of her control and talent for keeping each letter the same slant, size and all on a level. Her writing had become a work of art. With materials in place, she began to martial the thoughts that had been forming for weeks:

I miss you more than the moon can her beams, more than the wind can miss the clouds, more than the sun can miss the warm shine on an old man's brow, but I knew when you came to say good bye that I wouldn't see you again. You said you would come back soon, but there was a troubled distance in your green flecked eyes. Did I tell you yours were the first eyes other than African I had ever seen? I will never forget them; they are badges of bright light pinned to my heart forever. You said Shakespeare had called eyes the 'windows of the soul' and when I came to read some of his work I would see he had a special magic that could pierce a person's being and reveal their worth so that hundreds of years after his birth he would still touch generations with his poetry and insight. I am no English playwright, nor even a Ndebele soothsayer, but I saw your soul that day as I glanced under your curling lashes and through the tears gathering on irises the colour of a summer river in flood. Your very essence was stripped bare like a tree in winter. I could see your spirit was troubled and you needed to go away and heal your anguish. You who breathed in special air reserved for the Godly, you who were untouched by sin and mortal pain, you who had held my hand through my aching hurt, and squeezed it when my bones bit like dogs and my muscles screamed, you, of all people, endured a hidden torture of your own shared with no one. But I knew your pain that day and I never thought to say this, but it was worse than mine could ever be. Yours was an agony, not of Jesus' thorns or scourging or hammered nails, but more the pain of Our Blessed Lady, of unimaginable loss and grief.

It has been two years since you left and I still think of you every day. You'll be proud to know I have read my first Shakespeare play, The Tempest. *It was difficult to understand without you but it talks of magic and exile, warring brothers and wronged kings, colonialism and subjugation, so not too far from our own Ndebele history. I sympathised with the crippled Caliban although I don't think I was meant to, crippled = evil in Shakespeare's imagination and he's certainly with Africa on that, but I understood Caliban. "I cried to dream again," he says, and those words have stayed with me. I do that sometimes when my dreams transport me and take me running across the hills or dancing with a boy. And then I wake to who I am, to the reality of my life and I too want to fall back to sleep to find that joy again. Does that sound ungrateful? I am so much more since you have come into my life, not just a bag of bent and twisted bones but a living breathing entity with potential or po ten shul as you pronounced it, giving weight to every syllable.*

I don't look at the gift you gave me very often. I keep it hidden. It is in the hollow arms of my wheelchair. No one else knows this and I'm telling you in case I die (who knew I'd live this long? 'You're only lent,' my mother says often) then you can have it back again. Soon, I will sell the gold chain and start my business. I will keep the gold cross for a rainy day, or for when you come back. Your parents gave it to you, so it must be precious, more so because of the love it carries and the symbol of sacrifice it embodies. I promise to repay everything when I am a lawyer defending the rights of the disabled and downtrodden. That is my new ambition, I hope you are proud. I still have a long way to go but I will get there.

I think often of our last meeting, how we giggled, how I took out the little bottle of colour and we chatted about the first time you came to the village with nail polish, the surprise of it and how much fun we had experimenting over the months with different shades and glitter. I painted your nails for one final time that day. You had let them grow and they were long and beautiful. 'I'm leaving it on,' you said, defiantly, 'They can rant all they like but I'm going home and I'm going to start again, find what I've lost and fight for it.' I saw combat in those eyes and I cheered.

I don't know what you lost, you never told me or if you ever found it again, but my hope is that you did and have come to a place of joy in your life.

Your friend for ever,

Thula

PS Billi sends his love

Chapter 16

Sibanda was at his desk, watching a female sunbird preening in the foliage of a Zimbabwe creeper continuing to creep despite the adverse season. The bird was a dirty olive and drab compared to the brilliance of her mate. Sibanda hadn't spotted him yet but he would boast a scarlet chest with iridescent emerald sprinkled on his throat and crown. Even the rest of his plumage was sleek and black while she had absolutely no finery to display. Given her obscure appearance, marking her in birder parlance as a 'little brown job' or LBJ, it was her beak that helped identify her: long, thin, curved like a scimitar and adapted to probing corollas for their nectar. When the floral tubes were too long, Sibanda watched the species pierce the base of a flower with their pin sharp beaks and capture the sweet liquid. Odd, really, they also ate spiders in their webs and foraged for ants on the ground. What sort of a system did they need to process all that variety?

Sergeant Ncube rapped on the office door. 'You called, sir?'

Sibanda drew his eyes from the window and his mind from the sunbird's digestive tract. 'Yes, I've been trying to phone PC Khumalo but she's not answering her phone, have you had any contact?'

'No, she's not coming in, is she?'

'I told her to take the day off and to stay away from the funeral, but I would have expected her to report any findings from the dip tank meeting. See if you can get hold of her.'

'Sir,' PC Tshuma put his head around the door. He couldn't manage to get past the large presence of Sergeant Ncube who took up the entire width of the doorway.

'What?' Sibanda snapped. He was edgy, where was Zee?

'I've had a phone call …'

'… From PC Khumalo?'

'No, from Forensics.'

'Ncube, get on your way and stop blocking up my door, you're hanging around like a ball of ticks in a dog's ear.'

'Well, I …' Ncube couldn't find the right words to express his indignity, he hadn't found one in his new dictionary yet, but he muttered all the way along the station corridor.

'What did Forensics have to report?'

Tshuma looked down at the notes. He read carefully, running his finger along the lines, 'The two victims, Lois Khupe and Kerry Williams were both strangled by a … a lig ... liga ...'

'… Ligature. Get on with it.'

Tshuma cleared his throat and continued. 'The lack of skin has made it hard to determine the type of lig-a-ture used but there is bleeding in the strap muscles and around the larynx and the … the … hyoid bone is fractured,' he looked up hoping he had delivered the anatomical assessment correctly. 'There's more detail, should I go on?'

'Just the basics.'

'They were both sexually assaulted before death.'

'I know, what else? Any news on the bones we found?'

'Yes, both sets are human.' Tshuma referred to his notes again. 'The most recent of the remains are female, probably between 20 and 35 years of age. They can't narrow it down without more sophisticated testing. The woman had given birth at some time in the past, Forensics found, er … parturition pits on the pubic bones,' he stumbled over the last few words, ending with a raised voice question mark of confusion. What in God's name were parturition pits?

'Must be our sex worker, Mama Stimela. And the older bones?'

'Definitely human but they can't determine age or sex, the bones are too degraded. Local Forensics is sending both sets down to Bulawayo to the National University of Science and Technology; they have a forensic anthropologist on staff.'

'He should come up with more detail. Heard anything from your cousin?'

'Who, sir?'

'Your cousin, Assistant Detective Chanza, remember him? He works here, or at least sometimes he does.' Sibanda's sarcasm often made an outing under pressure, a release from the tension building up over PC Khumalo. Had he been wrong to send her to that meeting alone?

'He's not … I mean … how did you know?' Tshuma's face turned purple.

The Mfumu/Chanza/Tshuma nepotism was the worst-kept secret at the station. No one had been fooled by the appointment. 'It doesn't matter, just do your job, and let me know if Chanza finds anything more along the railway line. I take it he's still out there?'

'As far as I know.'

'Good, and send Sergeant Ncube back here.'

Sibanda glanced through the window, the sunbird had gone, no one had taken her place. The Gubu police yard was deserted. He turned his attention to his phone, scrolled down and hit Zee's number. There was no reply. He scrolled back up to Berry's number, hesitated and then thumbed out a quick message about the poetry club tonight. He hoped PC Khumalo pitched up by then otherwise he would have to cancel. Where had she got to?

Ncube popped his head around the door. 'We should get going to the funeral, sir, just in case Miss Daisy is a bit slow. The wind is cold enough to freeze the fire out of a bird's eye chilli,' he thought it best to prepare the detective for any misbehaviour.

'Right, and we'll swing by Zanele Khumalo's house on the way.'

Miss Daisy snorted and puffed, hopped and coughed, stuttered and screeched as Sibanda turned her ignition and pumped her pedals, but she found her steady note and soon relaxed if not to a purr then a gruffling snore as the pair drove towards the township.

'What have you got on Isaac Manhombo?'

'A violent man, by all accounts, and he was on the train to Bulawayo last Wednesday night. I got the information from the Gubu station master; he was only too pleased to let me know. They're all scared of Manhombo. They'd like him moved on.'

'We'd better pull him in for questioning.'

'He's on duty. He'll only be back on tonight's train.'

'That puts him here in the early hours. Let's hope the women on board are safe. At least National Railways now have extra security on the train.'

'I'll do that, sir. Have they been told we suspect a serial killer?'

'We have enough evidence to back that up, two girls skinned and two sets of bones in the same area. What about Trywell Dube, any news there?'

'No one knows where he is. He didn't go to his home village and he isn't answering his phone. I've got Tshuma doing a background check.'

'Good man.'

Ncube looked up sharply; what was this, rare praise from the detective? What had put him in a good mood? He didn't ask and he never found out because Miss Daisy pulled up outside Zanele Khumalo's house.

'Hop out, Ncube and check if the family knows where she is.' Sibanda checked the message from Berry, it was responsible for his good mood. He wanted a repeat of the warm glow. "Will be there, can't wait xx." It was the two crosses he liked the look of.

'Sir, PC Khumalo is not at home,' Ncube had been quick.

The warm glow was replaced by a nagging ache. 'Do they know where she is?'

'They're saying she planned to stay over with cousins in Mabale after the meeting. They haven't heard from her. Her phone battery must have died and there's no electricity that side.'

'Let's get going to the funeral.'

Miss Daisy made her way towards the funeral as though it was her own. She puttered along the road liked a reluctant hearse and barely made it up some of the steep hills that twisted and snaked through the granite ridge. Sibanda crashed down the gears with little concern. Ncube pumped continually on an imaginary passenger clutch and made a note to check the poor lady's fluid levels on their return; she was beginning to wheeze.

Lois Khupe's home village lay north of Gubu, not far off the main road. The family home showed signs of wealth – a brick-built house of some stature sat among fallow fields. Several vehicles were parked in front of the house and a large gathering of people congregated in the shade of a well-established syringa. A pastor had the microphone.

'Ncube, let's split up. You take the left side of the crowd. I'll take the right.'

'What am I looking for?'

'A man on his own, someone out of place, anyone suspicious and keep an eye on Knut Von Bergen and George Paradza from Universal Dream, their vehicle is here already.'

He looked across to the smart Land Cruiser bearing the interlocked UD letters in a stylish, turquoise triangle. He looked back to Miss Daisy ticking, steaming and dribbling some or other liquid from her undersides in a bout of incontinence and shook his head. He set off towards the crowd.

Several young men separated from the congregation and were hanging back, consulting smart phones rather than the pastor's words. Sibanda passed them unnoticed and unnoticing, the serial killer would want to participate closely if he was here; this was, after all, one of his finest moments. Closer to the crowd of mourners were a few of the UD employees from Bulawayo. Each acknowledged his presence with a nod of the head or a nervy smile. No one made eye contact, tension was visible in the body language, were they the suspect? Would the bones be cast in their direction? Sibanda moved on, into the crowd, and as he did the toes in the shoes of the UD employees uncurled.

'Detective Sibanda?' He felt a tap on his shoulder and swung around to find himself face to face with Betty Khupe, the tea lady from the UD offices in Bulawayo. 'I thought it was you, detective, have you found Lois's killer?'

'The investigation is ongoing, we're making progress.' He was intentionally vague. But are we making progress? He looked into the face of the concerned woman, wrapped up against a biting wind whistling with the monotony of an orange breasted bush shrike, a rhythmic keening giving no let up. It gave him a brief, happy glimpse of summer and the rains that came when the bird's call was prolific. Betty Khupe was leaning into the wind, frail and battered. Sibanda felt she might take off with the leaves in the next swirling flurry and instinctively put his hand on her shoulder. What suspects did they have? Isaac Manhombo was a violent, twisted personality by all accounts, but a serial killer …? Trywell Dube was still untraceable and the last person to see Kerry Williams alive. Knut Von Bergen and George Paradza bothered him, both had issues, that was obvious, and continual contact with Lois Khupe, but could they have raped and skinned her and the other women? Von Bergen was in the time frame and hiding something, but was he a warped murderer? And Paradza was up to no good. Had Lois got in his way? Betty Khupe was talking to him. He focused. 'Sorry, mama, I missed that.'

'You should know George Paradza has just bought a new car and a plot of land in Zvishavane.'

'How do you know this?'

'He is a boaster, like a strutting pigeon with a puffed-out chest. He thinks I am invisible, just the tea lady, but he is careless with his secrets, talks loudly on the phone and throws papers in his waste basket. I know his life inside and out.'

'Do you spy on all the employees at UD?'

'No, just him.'

'Why?'

'He was unkind to Lois. He was trying to have her fired, accused her of stealing equipment meant for the schools.'

'But she hadn't stolen anything?'

'No, she was honest and dedicated. She felt for those children. And she was clever too.'

'How?'

'George Paradza was trying to get at her because she had something on him, I just don't know what, so she kept every single paper, got everything signed, did extra stocktakes. I helped her sometimes. If it gets out I've told you these problems, I'll be fired.'

'Your secret is safe with me, mama.'

'Thank you, detective.' She looked into his eyes, and knew reassurance, safety and strange warmth.

Sibanda's phone chirped in his pocket, 'I have to answer this.' He took his hand from her shoulder.

Betty Khupe felt oddly undone when he removed his hand, as though a heater had been switched off. She threw her thick scarf around her neck. The wind would be much colder away from the touch and aura of the detective.

'Jabu, it's Angel. I have someone in the clinic who wants to talk to you. It seems important.'

'Who?'

'Your colleague, Zanele Khumalo. She's not too well. I just put stitches in her head. She has something to tell you and she won't sit still until she has.'

'Keep her there, I'm on my way.'

Sergeant Ncube could see Detective Sibanda slicing through the matted, sorrowing crowd, like a panga through maize stalks, head and shoulders above the mourners. Ncube guessed he was looking for him. He could read the stress in the man's body as taut as Blessing's washing line, which she never allowed to sag and which he had to retension often in the interests of marital harmony. The sergeant had been keeping an eye on Knut Von Bergen and what he saw gave him cause for concern. He wanted to linger and check further but he recognised Sibanda's urgency. His passage was not as easy as Sibanda's, no one gave way for him, no one noticed he was trying to move. He was bumped and jostled, pushed and tripped and altogether flustered by the time he met up with the detective.

'Ncube, we're leaving now. PC Khumalo is at the clinic.'

Ncube never mouthed his regrets about the funeral feast under preparation where flame-seared chicken skin and roasting beef juices were sending warm and tantalising wafts on the stiff breeze. It wasn't the time.

Miss Daisy raced back through the twisting granite landscape, taking the snaking bends and steep curves with the grip and torque of a pro; well, that was Ncube's take on the journey. He worried as the tyres squealed on the curves; didn't the detective know the spare was useless? He closed his eyes as Miss Daisy strayed over the double white lines to avoid a straining donkey cart, full of wood for sale in the village. His heart almost stopped as a ribby Brahman half-breed considered strolling across the road to search for greener grass. She had spied a dry, spikey, half-eaten tussock covered in road dust and then judged it not worth the risk as Miss Daisy roared towards her with no intention of slowing down.

'Is PC Khumalo okay, sir?'

'All I know is she has a head injury. I'm sorry I ever sent her to that meeting.'

'Don't be, she was excited and if she has found something out then the deed is greater than the one who risked it.'

'Not in this case, Ncube. Did you pick anything up at the funeral?'

'I watched Knut Von Bergen. He was looking for something or someone, scanning the crowd. He had no eye for the proceedings, no heart for the deceased.'

'Looking for his next victim?'

'Maybe. He was searching the faces of the women rather than the men, looking for something, some common feature making him want to murder and slice off their skins,' the sensitive sergeant shuddered.

'A sexual predator? I wonder ...?'

'What, sir?'

'You've just given me an idea, Ncube.'

The sergeant, glowing with importance, didn't have time to ask what genius he sparked because Miss Daisy pulled up outside the clinic and Sibanda was out of the vehicle before the sergeant could find the right words. He recently acquired 'magnitude' from his charity shop dictionary and it was on the tip of his tongue but he couldn't manoeuvre it into his sentence. He was concentrating on three-syllabled learning.

'I'm all right, sir, honestly, just a small bump. I was so stupid.' PC Khumalo was lying on the clinic bed.

'Is she well enough to talk, Angel?'

'It's not serious but she should get some rest.'

'What happened, Zee?'

'Knut Von Bergen had his eyes on the young women, a real creep. George Paradza took himself off to talk to somebody, away from the meeting. It was all a bit secretive, back of the hand stuff, so I tried to get closer. I was out of sight, behind an old pump house, until someone hit me on the head with a brick. When I came to the crowd had dispersed and my bag with my phone had been stolen.'

'I told you not to do anything rash, there's a serial killer on the loose.' Sibanda was sharper than he intended but he had been more stressed than he realised by PC Khumalo's disappearance.

'I know you told me not to, but it was too good an opportunity. I could see the pair of them were up to no good and heard enough before some tsotsi hit me.' Her fingers reached to explore the stitches. She winced as she discovered the bald spot Angel Better had shaved around the cut. She would have to spend money on a weave to cover it. 'Have I failed badly? Will you let me do this again? I promise I'll be more careful next time.' She wiped away a few threatening tears.

'What did you hear, Zee?' There was no chance he would send her off alone on risky surveillance again.

PC Khumalo related the conversation. 'It sounds to me as though George Paradza got rid of Lois Khupe because she knew too much about some deal or other.'

'Would you recognise the other man talking with Paraza if you saw him again?'

'I have a good memory for faces.'

'Sister, make sure PC Khumalo gets all the rest she needs.'

'I'll be fine in a day or so, Sister Angel says I can go home in a couple of hours.'

'Take it easy. I need you back at the station and in one piece. You did a great job.'

PC Khumalo basked in the praise. Detective Sibanda had taken her headache away single handedly. She felt ready for anything.

Angel Better followed him out to the vehicle. 'Will I see you tonight, Jabu?'

'No, Angel, can't make it tonight, this case is breaking. I'll be busy for a few days. I'll phone.' He watched her eyes cloud with disappointment and wondered what sort of a tangled personal mess he was getting himself into. Tonight he would be with Berry. He didn't have time for this intrigue.

'Do we have our man in George Paradza, sir, and do you think it was another accomplice that attacked PC Khumalo?'

'Hard to say, Ncube, but Paradza's come into money. Direct from some donor to his pockets. He's got a scheme creaming off UD somehow. I don't like the sexually charged behaviour of Knut Von Bergen either and he has a pair of pliers if the repair of his glasses are anything to go by. Both those guys are in the mix at the moment.'

Ncube could not imagine anyone who didn't have a pair of pliers. How did anyone get by without such a basic tool? He didn't comment.

'So, we have a magnitude of suspects. Did you pick up anything at the funeral, sir?' What a relief. Having that word inside him awaiting its moment was like a stomachful of retained post-bean-eating discomfort.

'Only Paradza's recent wealth; nothing else.' Where had *magnitude* come from? He didn't comment either. Ncube was a babble of incomprehension at times. But had there been something at the funeral, some face he recognised? Something in the periphery of his vision? What was it? It would come to him.

CHAPTER 17

'I'm waiting at the front of the alley way.'

'I'm coming now.' Sibanda left his table at Mama Elephant's Diner and went to collect Berry. They had probably never seen a white woman in such a place, one reserved for the cultural heart of the Ndebele. Her looks alone would be enough to cause a stir. He hadn't wanted her to walk alone into a room full of stares. So far the poetry had been in Ndebele, traditional praise songs and some modern attempts, but Lovemore told him it would liven up later and would be mostly in English. A dancing group was about to perform – poetry in motion, he supposed.

'Thanks for coming.'

'I wouldn't have missed it.' She kissed him on the cheek, he went for the double in European style and their noses banged in the confusion, it was clumsy.

'Sorry.'

'More timing issues?' she grinned with no trace of discomfort.

He laughed and led her down the narrow alley to the sound of drums accompanying the dancers. From the moment she entered Mama Elephant's Diner, Berry's eyes never left the performers. She was hypnotised. Sibanda ordered two beers. Mama Elephant's didn't have much call for wine. Berry swigged from the bottle like a shabeen regular.

'Look, Jabu,' she pointed to two men swaying around the room together locked in an embrace, transforming them into a giraffe on the plains, the gait perfect, and the neck and head stretching towards an imaginary branch capturing the essence of the species in an uniquely African ballet. She gasped as the 'giraffe' splayed its legs and lowered its head down to water. 'Amazing, I'm actually watching a giraffe drink.'

Her enthusiasm was catching. 'Wait, the best is yet to come.' Sibanda had seen this group before. When they transformed themselves into a troop of baboons with all the sound effects and mannerisms, the room erupted in laughter. Berry had tears running down her cheeks and was clutching her sides. Sibanda loved her more than ever in that moment. To witness her joy gave him a happiness he hadn't experienced for a long time. Was he beginning to live again after an age of numbness? Was he opening himself to emotional vulnerability?

'These guys should be on a London stage, they're brilliant.'

'They wouldn't be able to raise the bus fare to Bulawayo, let alone London. We live in hard times, Berry.'

'I know, but one day, surely …'

'… Shh, Lovemore is up next. You'll enjoy his stuff too.'

The poet made his way to centre stage and picked up the mike, it squeaked like a squirrel so he blew into it in time-honoured fashion, at which point the squirrel protested further at its fate with a scream that had everyone covering their ears.

'Sorry,' Lovemore continued, as the squirrel died a whimpering death, 'the mike is a bit like me today, old, out of sorts and short of nuts.' He settled himself onto a stool. The laughter in the room died down, the poet waited for his moment, for a still and focused audience.

Whisper to me my darlin'
Caress my stopped up ear
I won't betray your secrets
If you don't betray my fear.

Summer's gold has melted
In the forge of winter's grip
The gown I wore is ripped and torn
Bodice, lace and slip.

Shredded like a promise
From lips that spoke of joy

But gave us only emptiness
And a plastic Chinese toy.

So I'll not be planting maize again
I'll not be hoeing corn
Drought will fill the furrows
The child will stay unborn.

Whisper to me my darlin'
Curl me in your hand,
For us no carpe diem
Just an hourglass trickling sand.

The room erupted in applause and some approving whistles. Sibanda glanced across at Berry, she was clapping too. 'Very brave,' she said.

'Why on earth is it brave?'

'It's a bit critical of government. I hope there are no politicos here, none of your friends from CIO.'

'Political?' Sibanda glanced around, but saw no one from the dreaded organisation that monitored political dissatisfaction and protected the image of government against all actions and comers. He couldn't imagine how a poem about a torn dress and what was it? Chinese toys? could be subversive. He obviously had a lot to learn about this poetry stuff.

'Yes, and all misery, your poet friend doesn't see much of a future for any of us in Zimbabwe.'

'Come, Berry, forget the gloom for now, it's the interval. Let's grab a bite to eat. I can smell something sizzling.'

Mama Elephant, a woman who more than most lived up to her name, was toiling over a barbecue, waddling between grilling meat, roasting mealies and a pot of plopping maize meal. She took the money and gestured to a pile of plates. This was a self-service meal.

Lovemore intercepted them. 'Hi, detective, grab your food and come and join me. I'm at a table over there. Glad you came; you must need a break from your serial killer investigation.'

How had the word got out about the killer? Sibanda cursed the gossiping staff from the station. It would be around Gubu district and probably further afield by now. Thankfully, Berry hadn't heard the comment. He wished he could have dined with her alone.

'So, you are writing political stuff now, are you?' Sibanda said to the poet, as he sat down, nodding to Berry in acknowledgement of her interpretation.

'It's just a poem – words, a rhyme scheme. Read into it what you will.' Lovemore was defensive and changed the topic. 'Aren't you going to introduce me to your friend?'

'Berry, this is Lovemore Moyo, poet, artist and avid whisky connoisseur. Lovemore, this is Berry Barton, history teacher, daughter of a fellow birder and …' there was an awkward silence, Sibanda didn't know how to categorise their relationship. He had talked himself into a corner.

'… Extraordinary beautiful woman,' Lovemore filled in for him.

'Thank you, Lovemore,' Berry demurred.

'I'll toast that,' Sibanda felt rescued.

'Can't join you in a toast, I'm afraid.'

'I can understand you not eating, but turning down a drop of the good stuff?' Sibanda waved a hip flask in front of the poet.

'Can you believe it? I never thought I'd say that, but I'm not too good. I've had this awful pain since the weekend.' He rubbed his stomach. 'Must have overdone it. I've sworn off the stuff. Haven't been able to eat or drink since.'

'Well enough to give us some more poetry, I hope?' Berry chipped in.

'Oh yes.' Lovemore picked up the microphone again.

A solitary tear of September rain
Falls, dribbles, pleads to be let in
To a land damp with only tamped expectations.

But the earth is cracked hard, tattooed
By winter's ink, marked and branded,
Like a red-nailed whore on the road to addiction.

She knows this land cringes and cows to the belting summer rain
That drums like the needles of a dictator's spit,
On soft hide, skinned, pulled tight, seasoned

And stretched across a hollow tree
Resonating to the beat of hands
Calloused by tradition, segged with greed.

But let spring trickle
With the drops of an incontinent puppy
squirming for acceptance,

And this spineless land lusts the opium
Of summer's pimp, heated on a spoon.
An addict lost, the syringe her final straw.

September's drizzle dries unwanted, unaccepted, unused
Like the drool of this homeless vagrant
Reviled, shunned and despised.

'Gosh, your friend does have some issues,' Berry said when they were alone at the table. In the background a solo mbira player was playing, expertly plucking the African piano's keys of cut and flattened nails set inside a well-seasoned gourd. The plinking was strangely soothing, the atonal melancholy suited the moment.

'Lovemore? He may have a few domestic problems.'

'I'm not surprised; his poetry is a bit self-pitying and quite violent.'

Sibanda tried to remember some of the other poems he heard in his back garden. Was there a dripping dagger mentioned? Mostly he remembered murmurings, birdsong and puddles. He was useless at this sort of creative stuff, deciphering imagery and the like.

'Just a few problems with his wife at the moment.'

'It's more than that, Jabu, and there's a deep-seated hatred of women in those words, quite disturbing, in fact.'

Sibanda looked around for Lovemore, but he had gone, probably home if he wasn't well. Berry's assessment stirred suspicions. Had he seen him lurking on the Gubu platform the other night? Could he be a suspect? He worked with wire. He put the thought aside; poets might be tortured souls but they purged themselves with words not deeds. Still he might keep an open mind, keep an eye on the man.

Berry was glancing down at her watch. 'I have to go, Jabu, it's late.

I have classes tomorrow. It's been a fabulous evening.' She picked up a much thumbed and tattered book lying on the table. 'This is Lovemore's poetry book, he's left it behind.'

'I'll get it back to him tomorrow. I've work to do tonight.'

'What, at this hour?'

'Crime doesn't sleep; criminals might, but detectives can't.'

'Who are you chasing this time? My attacker?'

'No, another baddie, but I'll get your mugger.' A lie, but he didn't want to burden her with the serial killer theory or the fact she might have been one of his victims. 'And a couple of niggling problems to work out plus a suspect to pull in for questioning before my day is over. I'll walk you to your car.'

It felt good next to Berry, his hand lightly resting on the small of her back. They reached her car in silence, each aware a boundary had been crossed. She turned to say goodnight, he took her hands, 'Berry, I …' he desperately wanted to kiss her, the moment was perfect, but then he stopped abruptly. 'Oh my God, it's been staring me in the face.'

'What, Jabu, what is it?' She leaned in ready for the embrace.

He pulled back from her, 'I have to go, Berry, I'm sorry, it's this case I'm working on,' he bundled her into the car, 'and don't go travelling by train on your own, not for the time being at least.' He leant in through the car window and planted a kiss on her lips, not the slow romantic caress he planned, more of a hurried peck, but it still warmed his lips like the summer sun on fields of maize, and then he turned and sprinted towards Buffalo Avenue.

He barrelled through his front door and headed straight for his bedroom and Sister Martha's box next to his bed. He threw aside the photos and letters and rummaged among the rest and there it was, a small insignificant bottle of dried-up colour. Ncube had been right to remind him he needed to look at features, only it wasn't in the colour of the skin or the eyes or the shape of the nose or the curve of the lips that marked the girls for murder, it was their hands. Looking down at Berry's fingers had set the train of thought in motion. He had never seen her with varnish on her nails before, usually she wore them natural, but she must have had a manicure in Bulawayo. He vaguely noticed them on the train, they were now long, red and glamorous. Lois had long red nails, probably Mama Stimela too, and although Kerry Williams's fingers and nails were gone, John Berger had mentioned she was the beauty parlour type, which meant she probably looked forward to a regular manicure. And now here was the proof that Sister Martha coloured her nails with … he looked at the bottle again … *Scarlet Passion*. She must have painted them for one last time, indulged in one act of vanity after months of plain living, before she caught the midnight train to her death.

He lay, fully clothed, on his bed for while, trying to sleep, but his head was full of girls with nails. Was the killer a nail fetishist? Did such a fixation even exist? He didn't like long painted nails himself, saw them as claws steeped in blood, hated the smell of the chemicals involved, but someone got high on them, someone needed those lacquered spikes to achieve sexual arousal. And what was the significance of the twisted wire ring, and why the train for his macabre theatre? These thoughts rumbled through his brain until he dozed off. He woke to a poacher's moon shining through his window. It was time to head to the railway station. Isaac Manhombo would be finishing his shift.

The cold in the early hours was brutal, the air cracked like a slave master's whip, sharp, imperious and tipped with lead. Sibanda turned up his collar and stepped up his pace. A Scops owl trilled from a nearby branch and Sibanda found himself counting the predictable seven-second interval between chirrups. He measured the interstice with a 'white elephant' muttered under his breath, but the diminutive owl was obviously hyperactive – the call came every six seconds. In the distance a hyena was whooping to a silent pack, the volume of her call to arms intensified in the thin night air to an eerie, extra-terrestrial echo rolling unanswered around the moon-swept bush.

Sibanda checked over his shoulder, he sensed he was being followed, but he shrugged it off, the bush was fidgety tonight and he was picking up on the restlessness. Walking hard into the wind, he turned for a second time, the gusts drumming in his ears as he strained to pick up the faint sounds behind him.

'Lovemore is that you?'

He was sure he could hear a regular crunching on the winter-crisp leaves tumbling in the road. He stood for a while, waited for the follower to catch up and flashed his watery torch down the road, but all he saw was a pair of jackals that stared at him briefly before skittering into the long grass. He turned back towards his house, struggling to see in the dark. Shadows loomed as the trees waved wands across the road and dark shades danced in fear. The bush was deathly quiet; insects clam up when they detect movement and the unnatural silence magnified the threat. Sibanda rarely used a weapon or drew one from the armoury, but he felt naked without one. He stopped to listen, heard again the crunching footsteps and headed into the bush, crouching, stealthy, edging through the tangle of undergrowth. Despite the dangers, he would have cover and the upper hand. The wild African night was preferable to a deranged killer.

He circled until he came opposite his front door and watched, but Buffalo Avenue was as quiet as the grave, just a whispering wind coaxing the leaves to fall and bidding the grasses to wave them farewell. He waited, every breath ragged and far too loud. There was nothing, nobody, no movement. He crept closer to the road and tracked back, keeping to the bush for camouflage, peering through the remaining foliage, but the road was as empty as the country's coffers. He didn't know who got more of a fright, himself or the duiker munching on a low bush. They stared at each other for a microsecond, enough time for Sibanda to register the large brown eyes and the black tear drop glands before both leapt sideways and the duiker ran in a low profile, allowing him to negotiate the jumble of shrubs and bushes in his path.

Sibanda took stock. What was he doing? There was no one following him, he was just twitchy. The case was getting to him. Ten minutes later he was on the bustling platform at the station, awaiting the arrival of the passenger train from Bulawayo.

In the early hours of the morning, Gubu Police Station was deserted. A single, naked, fly-specked bulb burned feebly in the polar reaches of the charge office. PC Tshuma was asleep at the reception desk, his arms cradling his head, his shivering body wrapped in a blanket, his breath rising in misty updraughts; winter midnight crime was negligible.

'What is this all about? I am just a hard-working man. It's been a long night. I have to work tomorrow night again and I need my sleep. Why am I at the police station?'

'Just a few questions, Manhombo.'

'Couldn't this wait 'til morning?'

'You were working on the train last Wednesday?'

'Yes, I work Sunday to Thursday.'

'Kerry Williams was murdered last Wednesday on your train.'

'I didn't know,' Manhombo looked around wide-eyed, 'on my train?'

'And you heard nothing, saw nothing unusual on that trip?'

'No, nothing.'

'Maybe you didn't need to hear or see anything because you killed her yourself.'

'Wait a minute, I had nothing … don't you go pinning a murder on me.' Manhombo's anger rose and his fists curled.

'You've got a quick temper. What is it about women that makes you angry?' Sibanda goaded.

'What do you mean?' the guard's eyes narrowed.

'You've got scratches on your neck and a wound on your hand. They aren't agricultural scars, are they? Why did you lie about them? What are you hiding? Kerry Williams fought for her life. Did she defend herself, did she bite you? And what about Lois? She didn't fight did she, because she knew you, recognised you from the village?'

'No, no, that's not how …'

'You weren't on the train back from Bulawayo on Thursday night. Why?'

'How do you know? Are you sure of your facts?' The guard was becoming confused with the speed and direction of the questioning.

'I'm sure because I travelled back on the train that night and it wasn't you in the guard's van. Your replacement was having a very cosy night of it.'

'Manhombo's hefty shoulders slumped. 'I … I swapped shifts, I had business in town.'

'Or, having murdered Kerry on Wednesday night you thought it might be too obvious to attack another woman on the train the following night, so you gave yourself an alibi and then jumped on the train as a passenger. Very convenient.'

'I said I had business in town. I wasn't on that train. Don't you listen, detective?'

'I'll listen all right, as long as you tell the truth. What business?'

'I ... I can't say. It's private.'

'Because no one can back up what you were doing, can they,

Manhombo? You got back on the train that night and attacked again, only this time your victim defended herself with more than scratches and bites, didn't she?'

'I wasn't on the train on Thursday night, I came back on Friday. I worked that shift, you can ask anyone.'

'Don't worry, I will. But you could have been a passenger on Thursday night up to Gubu and then passenger down again on Friday in time to work your duty. No alibi, Manhombo. You'll need to tell me where you stayed on Thursday night. So, how did you get the wounds?'

Manhombo remained silent.

'I've got all night. In half an hour or so dawn will be breaking and then I'll have all day.' Sibanda stared through his window. If Manhombo was going to be stubborn then he'd get Tshuma to put on the spray. He could while away his time watching for early morning drinkers.

'It was my wife.' Manhombo's narrow eyes shifted.

'She attacked you?'

'Yes, and she'll vouch for that.'

'Because if she doesn't you'll beat her up again, won't you, Manhombo? Hasn't she been into the station a few times? Haven't I seen her sitting at the front with a black eye?' Sibanda had no idea who Manhombo's wife was or if he had seen her before, but daily women came to the station with domestic disputes, bearing cut lips, smashed teeth and bruised eyes. Manhombo had a reputation. His hunch was right.

'A mistake, she ... she fell.'

'We'll check that, too. Now where were you last Thursday night?' He looked through the window as dawn crowned the horizon and birthed a pink glow into the eastern sky. The silence lengthened. 'They tell me our cells are not a pleasant place to be on a cold night.'

'You can't lock me up.' He seemed shaken.

'Then start talking.'

'I was staying with a friend.'

'Name, address? Our Bulawayo colleagues will investigate.'

Now Manhombo stared out of the window at the burgeoning dawn as if the details of his overnight stay might be written on the blush, or perhaps he could float away with the fading stars.

'Evidence Rusere from Selous Mine in Esigodini. He'll vouch for me.'

'A miner?'

'Yes.'

'Known him for long?'

'No, he's ... a new friend.' Manhombo looked down; the detective's gaze was becoming intolerable.

Isaac Manhombo was a wife-beating bully and up to his eyes in something, but was he responsible for the deaths of the women on the railway line?

'Can I go home now?'

'We will be watching you, Manhombo.'

'There are two guards on each train until this serial killer business is sorted out. We watch each other,' he spat the words. He wanted to hit this smug detective, smash that handsome face to a bloody pulp, but he'd keep for another time.

As they made their way to the front office, Sibanda could hear there was a change of shift. Tshuma was moaning and mumbling about cold and fatigue, another voice was telling him to harden up if he wanted to make it in the police force. It was PC Khumalo.

'Zee, what are you doing back at work?'

'I wanted to be here, sir, there's a lot going on, plus I want to find out who attacked me, and you heard Sister Angel, she said it was only mild concussion.'

'Manhombo, don't go anywhere aside from work, and get in touch with me if you see anything out of place on the train.'

Now that he was walking out of the police station, Manhombo threw his shoulders back and attempted to reassert his standing. 'You won't hear the end of this, pulling me in for questioning in the middle of the night. I have friends ... Minister Cuthbert Muchacha is a cousin.'

'Why does that not surprise me?' Sibanda's irony went unnoticed as the railway man walked out into the dawn morning.

'That's him, I'm certain of it.' PC Khumalo had an excited look on her face.

'Who?'

'The anonymous phone call about Shumba.'

'Are you sure?'

'It's that raspy catch at the back of the throat. Isaac Manhombo is the one who reported Gideon Shumba.'

'If you're certain, get hold of Shumba, ask him how he's connected to Isaac Manhombo and why he might bear a grudge. And check on Manhombo's wife …'

'Kindness?'

'You know her?'

'She's been in a few times reporting domestic violence, but then she always withdraws the charges.'

'See if she bit and scratched her husband sometime in the last ten days or so, and take it easy, don't work too hard, Zanele, Gubu can't afford to lose you.'

He walked out of the station, detoured to switch on the spray for the birds and then headed back toward Buffalo Avenue. A shower and a strong coffee would set him up for the rest of the day. It was time to track down Trywell Dube. A few phone calls established he'd been fired from the railways with a record of drunken violence and public disorder.

The wind was settling but the sun had yet to rise and the morning was still smothered in gloom as he walked back along the dusty path, checking to see what had been out and about in the night. He made out jackal spoor and the joined up chevron dashes of a nocturnal rodent scurrying across the road. He found his own shoe prints clearly outlined. Over the top of them was another set of footmarks, laid down after his in the small hours. Was this his stalker from earlier? He followed the tracks as they stopped, turned back and then led straight to his gate. Sibanda was alert, every sense heightened.

He looked around to check where an attacker might hide. He checked the grove of teak trees, their shadows swirled in the wind, invading his peripheral vision like bats darting on a waterhole. Satisfied there was no one lurking, he moved to recce the outside of the house first. Catlike, he skirted around the walls, each foot fall was as gentle and precisely placed as a genet's stalking a guinea fowl. The windows were secure. Was the intruder still inside? Every one of his nerves was stretched. He cursed his lack of weapon, a log or even a brick would help, but his fists would have to do. He clenched them and listened. He wanted to pin point the intruder, get the advantage. Leaves rustled behind him, the pulse in his neck throbbed, he could feel it in his throat. He sidled, back to the wall, checking behind and scanning the way ahead. A barn owl screeched with the edge of nails dragged across a blackboard as it flew away, disturbed by what or who? He paused and held his breath to listen. Silence. The tracks lead to his front door and the signs of entry were obvious, it had been shouldered, the lock had given in easily, splinters lay at his feet. Another of Barghees's Chinese security specials, he concluded wryly.

In the hallway, he yelled, 'Come on you bastard scum, I know you're in here and I'm armed. I'll kill you if you don't show yourself!' But the house was still, only the dripping of the bath tap he should have fixed weeks ago greeted him.

He switched on a light. He was alone in the house with the howling wind and saw the marks straight away. It would have been hard to miss them, blood-red droplets shining against the scuffed and worn wooden floor. They dripped through to the kitchen where a large red blob, arterially bright, hardened in the beginnings of the dawn light. Sibanda bent to examine the substance. He knew before he touched it that it was nail polish, the acrid smell of solvents gave it away. A quick check through the rest of the house affirmed nothing had been taken, everything was in place. The killer came to leave a message, a chilling one. 'This isn't over,' he was saying and, 'Catch me if you can, and watch your back.'

Sibanda put a pot of coffee on to boil and sat down to consider his next move. The Black Sparrowhawk had unwittingly given Isaac Manhombo an alibi. He had been with the train guard when this taunting was done. Manhombo left his thoughts completely as he focused on the rest of the suspects, but returned with a vengeance two nights later when the railway worker called Sibanda at 3 am to report a body being thrown from the train.

Chapter 18

'Tell me about Victoria Falls, Monty,' Billy wanted to keep the murderous man opposite from any amorous advances. The thought of it would make a body sick in the light of what the youngster now knew. Night time had fallen. Through the window, looking upwards, Billy could see stars stretching to infinity, a gown of midnight blue velvet strewn with millions of sparkling dots. Where did they end? What did it all mean? Billy had never contemplated higher matters before, the drizzly sky at home on Boggy Fen Farm had rarely been so clear and so full of questions. All this travelling was beginning to play scary tricks with the youngster's mind.

'A very big waterfall, maybe the biggest in the world and discovered not so very long ago by David Livingstone,' Monty explained.

'Everything is very big in Africa, isn't it? Too big to put an 'andle on and I don't like it.' Suddenly, cosy familiarity with a few cuffs and back-breaking icy mornings featured in Billy's imagination like a picture postcard of Victorian rural sentimentality. The farm hand wasn't cut out to be an adventurer. 'Who is this Livingstone geezer?'

'A missionary and explorer, Scottish and very brave to have hacked his way for months, on foot, through this brutal land. They say he once walked seven hundred miles with malaria and there were no roads or railways then.'

'So where's he now?'

'Dead.' The word fell like a stone in the bottomless pit of Billy's fear.

''Ard luck 'im, killed by the natives, 'acked? You didn't say they were dangerous.' Billy's efforts to hang on to aitches as well as courage were deserting. Dad always said Billy couldn't manage two things at once. Billy could do with him now. Dad would know what to do.

'No, probably from malaria or black water fever or some other tropical disease, his body weakened from years of living among the natives and far from civilisation. Some say he died from bleeding piles, but that's ridiculous.'

'Shouldn't we be worried about malaria and stuff, then?' But the legendary high-fevered disease caught from breathing in tainted air would be the least of their problems.

'You have nothing to worry about, Billy. I will take care of everything,' Monty was licking his lips with the glazed look in his eye that had preceded their intimacy in the past. The Rupee Ripper was about to lunge.

'He can't have been the first to discover it, though?' Billy stalled.

'What do you mean?'

'With all that water in the middle of nowhere, someone must have been living nearby.'

'The first European then,' Monty snapped.

'The natives don't count, I suppose.'

'Of course not, don't let them worry your lovely little head, they're just savages.' At that moment sharing a carriage with a 'savage' would be far safer and probably more comforting than the civilised European on the opposite banquette.

'Come, my little dove, move over here,' Monty patted the bed, 'I have some new adventures for us to try out tonight.'

'What sort of a waterfall is it, this Victoria Falls?' Billy was time-wasting and not wanting to imagine what these new adventures might be.

'A waterfall is a waterfall, just a big hole in the ground with water crashing into it. What's this all about Billy?'

'I mean, how did the hole in the ground happen? I'm interested, Monty, you said I should learn stuff.'

'I don't know,' Monty was short and exasperated, 'someone said the water found a crack and wore away a soft patch in the rock over millions and millions of years until a huge ravine was created. The water's done it several times before, left steep zig-zag gorges and then moved on to a more promising fissure.' He took a moment to fantasise about Billy's promising fissure and what he was going to do to it. 'Just imagine all those years, all those lifetimes,' he continued, 'now, my chicken, give me a taste of those hot, fleshy lips and your tongue, that eager, darting little snake. I've never known such pleasure.' He was panting. Billy struggled to keep a face that didn't show fear and disgust.

'In a minute, Monty,' the breathy response from an adrenalin pumped heart, coupled with abject terror, passed for passion. Billy's tongue flicked provocatively to keep Monty interested.

'Oh you little tease, so you'd rather play the long game tonight. Well, so would I.' Torture was far more rewarding when strung out and gently managed. There were hours of amusement ahead, he could wait. 'What else do you want to know?'

'Tell me about the hotel, tell me … tell me … about all the fun we're going to have there.' Billy was getting desperate. The story about the hotel better be a long one, long enough to buy some time and a plan. Sitting in a carriage with The Rupee Ripper was unnerving; making love to a murdering body slasher would be beyond even Billy's acting skills.

'It isn't The Savoy, of course, there will be little luxury and no electric lights or running water. It's probably more like your Aunt Bessie's guest house, although even her establishment is built of bricks. The Victoria Falls Hotel is just a wood and iron building, 16 rooms at most, I'm told, with an old railway dining car tacked on as a dining room. Now come over here and let's get comfy.'

'In a minute. Will we have to share a bathroom with others?'

'Of course, who ever heard of a lavatory inside a bedroom?'

'Aunt Bessie said they had them at some of the posh London hostelries.'

'Very unhygienic, give me an outhouse any day. Toffs are a rum lot.'

Billy's mind was drifting as Monty rambled on about the decadent upper classes. Where was The Rupee Ripper's knife? There was nothing in the carpet bag and Monty's body and clothing had been explored several times; there was no weapon hidden on his person. Billy had to find it and quickly.

'Hope there's a decent bloke running the place,' Billy hedged. 'Aunt Bessie put a lot of store in cleanliness and good service. I should know, I gave you very good, clean service, didn't I?' There was deliberate cheek and flirtation in the comment. How much longer could Monty be strung along for?

'Oh yes, we've had some enjoyment, haven't we, my little chicken. Now time for some more.' He pounced across the seat, Billy shifted sideways, Monty missed his mark.

'What now?' he rasped.

'The manager?' Billy pouted, lips bitten to appear red, swollen and seductive.

'Dear God, you are tantalising me.' His patience was wearing thin, but the wait would be worth it. 'Someone called Pierre Gavuzzi, must be Italian or French, or both – a very good mixture for hospitality aren't they? Suit you well enough?'

'Dunno, Aunt Bessie was always wary of foreign types, said they had dirty ways, "unclean 'abits" she called it.'

'Bessie Bawtry was no more than a whore herself, a brothel hostess. You must have seen stuff going on at that boarding house.' Monty was getting snappy, the heat was rising.

'Steady on, Monty, that's me dad's sister you're talking about,' Billy jumped up, fists ready. Defending the family honour, or anyone else's, was not something Billy was used to, but it seemed right to shield his blood folk at this moment of bursting tension.

'Settle down, I didn't mean it, silly,' Monty's voice was soothing, almost comforting and the youngster was desperate to believe Monty was not a mutilator of children, that it was all a case of mistaken identity, but Billy had seen the killer's hand stray to the stick with the silver elephant's head, gripping it with intent when he thought he was under threat, somehow there was a blade hidden inside.

'It's me, er … guts again, Monty, I need the khazi.'

'Can't you relieve yourself in the basin?'

'No, I need the crapper this time. Those sheep's brains are gurgling round me innards fit to explode.' Billy had come up with a plan to get out of the compartment, sit somewhere public, maybe in the lounge, mingle with people. Monty couldn't do much then.

'Ugh, you have the vocabulary of a street urchin, don't be so common, Billy. If you have to go then I'll check the corridor, make sure it's all clear and follow you. I'll guard the door and let you know when it's safe to come out. We wouldn't want the passengers knowing our secret. You'd be thrown off the train; the world doesn't like pretty little boys seducing older men.'

Not a bad plan, although screaming and carrying on would rather get Monty thrown off the train, and when they all knew the truth, the real truth, hidden for months since long before discovering the newspaper article, then surely it would be the older man to blame. But the train was very noisy – all the chuffing, puffing, grinding and shrieking on the rails would cover any screams and by then Monty would have made a plan to stifle the noise, and anyway, what certainty was there? This murder stuff might still be a figment of the imagination, maybe that wasn't a picture of Monty in the paper or maybe Monty had reformed and was truly in love as he whispered every night.

'Hurry up then before I burst a bum string.'

Monty winced, rose, opened the carriage door, checked the corridor and looked back with distaste. There was something else in the look confirming Billy's worst fears, pure and unguarded evil.

Chapter 19

'Manjelengwa is a long way, sir.'

'Trywell Dube is staying in that village.'

'Hiding out?'

'Could be, he hasn't pitched back for work at Thunduluka.'

'Are we travelling through the park?'

'The roads are better, Miss Daisy might be happier.' Sibanda turned right at the T-junction, leaving no doubt as to their route.

Ncube shuddered, the detective wasn't the least concerned for the Land Rover; he just wanted to go game viewing. His own recent experiences with the detective were nothing short of terrifying. He hoped they would all survive the journey and swallowed a belch. It was the end of the month and there was no spare cash for fizzy drinks so he was reduced to one of Blessing's bitter, eye-shivering flatulence remedies. With luck and no dangerous animal sightings, he wouldn't need it. 'How do we know Trywell Dube is at Manjelengwa?'

'No certainty, but PC Tshuma has had word from a cousin that Dube has been hanging around the area.'

'I hear he has a record.'

'Petty stuff, according to PC Khumalo's digging, but significant if it kick-started this killing spree. He's used a knife before.'

'Stabbed someone?'

'No, but threatened. It got him fired.'

'Thunduluka can't have done a police check.'

'Maybe they did, maybe he paid someone to make his record disappear.'

The corruption plagueing the police force kept them occupied for some time as Miss Daisy lumbered along the gravelled road. Occasionally, Sibanda would stop, reverse, and check a tint of orange in the long winter-brittle grass or a deep shadow next to an ant heap, but they turned out to be dappled logs disguised as leopards or antbear-raided termite mounds with broken clods of earth doubling as lion cubs. They spent a few moments at a waterhole close to a grove of leadwoods where Miss Daisy ticked with impatience. She wanted to get a move on, find Trywell Dube and get home. All this stopping and starting was causing havoc with her fuel delivery. But Sibanda waited and watched and scoured the landscape for early visitors or lingering predators. As they sat, a stiff breeze in partnership with a sparkling morning sun brushed a diamond mesh over the water casting a net for fish, but any barbel present had long since wormed themselves deep into the bottom mud in preparation for the worst of the winter dry to come. A pair of blacksmith plovers, aware of Miss Daisy's tetchiness, gave up on their stilt-walking between mounds of insect-rich elephant droppings and fluttered their wings entincingly like a pair of Japanese geishas. They tink-tinked as they fanned, tapping on the forge giving them their name while a grey hornbill mourned with a lyrical dirge from the top of a nearby tree.

Ncube cleared his throat several times. He heard and saw nothing of the life of the pan but feared that if they hung around much longer a herd of elephants would appear. Even he could see this was a favoured waterhole. Sibanda took the hint and moved Miss Daisy along as the hornbill launched herself, dipping on the wave of the wind as she flew.

Ncube felt guilty. Somehow this man derived pleasure from watching nothing, from just sitting and staring in anticipation. The detective wasn't happy to be moving on. Ncube shuffled on the seat, wanting to talk, but the detective seemed stony faced; he should have let him wait for his elephants.

The road grew sandier. Miss Daisy bounced and bobbled from side to side, but their two-hour journey was pleasant. The sun, through the windscreen, warmed the sergeant's cold bones and relaxed his acres of flesh. Sibanda was lost in his wildlife world of wonder and discovery, only Miss Daisy was out of sorts as the ruts yawned and the corrugations shortened to resemble Nomatter's washboard.

'Can we stop for a moment, sir?' They were over the park boundary and the first of the villages were popping up here and there in a picturesque parkland setting.

'Manjelengwa's close, can't it wait?'

'I'd better top Miss Daisy up. I don't trust her gauges.'

Sibanda, who didn't trust anything about the ageing wreck, pulled over and parked under a grove of acacias. He walked for a few paces to stretch his legs. The truth was Miss Daisy was holding up well as far as liquid was concerned, although her rattled innards were nauseus, but Ncube wanted to reach his lunch, which had skittered out of reach due to the hazardous roads. He didn't expect much joy. It had been a tough week financially, the twins needed new shoes, Samson had an ear infection, antibiotics were expensive and they had been obliged to buy new blankets for the bigger children. Blessing told him his lunch would be healthy, never a good omen, but Nomatter winked, which augured well. He strolled across to the detective, leaning with his back to a tree, surveying the landscape. 'A bite to eat, sir?'

'Bit early isn't it?'

'Yes, but I expect we'll be busy from now on.' He offered the plastic container to his boss. Inside was a mound of white mealie meal smothered in a slippery green sauce, made from wild foxglove leaves, a drought staple. Ncube was not fond of the texture, but it was food, foraged and free.

Sibanda scooped a pinch of the cooked meal and mopped up some of the gooey sauce stretching and wobbling through his fingers like a slimy green jelly.

'Why do foxes need gloves?'

Sibanda shook his head and moderated his response. 'A story for another time, Ncube.'

The sergeant continued to dig his chubby fingers into the sticky lunch. 'What are we expecting from Trywell Dube if we find him?'

'An alibi and an explanation as to why he's disappeared, or an observation, maybe he noticed someone at the station, someone he recognised or someone Kerry recognised.'

'Is he our main suspect, sir?'

'I don't know, Ncube, but Isaac Manhombo's off our list.'

'I thought he was top of it.'

'He didn't murder those girls.'

'How do you know for sure, sir? Didn't he make the anonymous phone call to point the finger at Gideon Shumba, point the witchdoctor's stick away from himself?'

'He had nothing to do with the murders. Leave it, Ncube.' Sibanda didn't want to alarm his sergeant with the nail polish visitor the previous night, he was edgy enough himself.

'Right, sir.' The detective had obviously had another vision. The old spirits were aware of everything. 'So that leaves us with Dube, Paradza and Von Bergen.'

Sibanda didn't answer; he was staring into the distance searching for something, some clue, someone tantalising just beyond his grasp.

They reached Manjelengwa village half an hour later.

'Where do we start to look, sir, where was Dube seen?'

'We'll call in with the headman first. He'll know who's in his district.'

'This must be the kraal right here.' A gathering of villagers was milling around a centre building like spectators at a cockfighting ring. 'The headman's holding court, sir, and it doesn't look peaceful. Is that a scuffle going on in the middle of the kraal?'

Sibanda was out of Miss Daisy in seconds and in the middle of the fray in a couple of strides. The headman had taken flight, pursued by several women. Some old enough to be grandmothers, one particularly hefty specimen of womanhood was wielding a frying pan. The headman was bleeding from a cut over his eye and screaming retribution in the form of heavy fines. Sibanda's presence brought instant calm to the situation, as though a violent wind suddenly dropped and the eye of the cyclone arrived. The villagers sensed a powerful aura, it was displayed in the confidence of his stance, all confirmed by the waddling run up of Sergeant Ncube in full uniform. The warring genders fell apart, mumbling, cradling bruises and wiping cuts. One woman lay dazed and wailing on the ground. 'Sort this out, sergeant; I'm going to talk to the headman.'

'Just a little disagreement over a judgement,' the headman winced as his wife bathed the cut. They moved into the village court house, a circular mud construction with half walls and a thatched roof. The walls were lined with earthen benches. The headman's seat was an elevated high-backed throne of sculptured mud, plastered with ochred designs. Sibanda stood while the injured man received treatment.

'Anything I need to be involved in?'

'No, just petty local issues, it will blow over. I will blow it over. There will be punishments. Times are trying to change, but we stick to tradition and our Ndebele culture here. The women in this community are lively, they need a steady hand. How can I help you, detective?' The wizened man with facial creases making erosion gullies look like a conservation project had regained his dignity lost while fleeing the angry women. The mud chair did that for him, its much-stroked arms restored his power.

'I'm looking for a man called Trywell Dube. We have information he's in this area.'

'You are in luck, he's right here. I've just ruled against him in a damages case. He's probably in the middle of the uproar outside. Wearing a red check shirt, tall man, you can't miss him.'

'Damages? What for?'

'Impregnating a young girl from the village, and not the first time, but he will think twice about doing it again.'

'You fined him?'

'Six cows to the parents and one cow every year for maintenance of the child, plus school fees.'

Sibanda left the mud courthouse and walked over to Sergeant Ncube, who was chatting to the large woman with the frying pan. He called him aside. 'Trywell Dube can't be far away, he's just been fined in this court. Let's go.'

The pair hurried back to Miss Daisy, followed close on their heels by the headman's wife, carrying a bucket. 'Thank you, you arrived in time to stop a nasty situation getting out of control. My husband … doesn't always understand the mood of the village or the independence of women. Please take these goat intestines. They were confiscated from a previous case, Mpofu's dogs killed Mabhena's goat, both parties were found to be in the wrong.'

Sibanda wanted to reject the gift in his hurry to pursue Trywell Dube, but Ncube grabbed the bucket, knowing a gift provides the sweetest meat. The pair set off in Miss Daisy and followed the confusing criss-crossing sandy tracks. Manjelengwa was a rural line of villages.

Each house was set far apart with plenty of space for cattle and goat kraals and a field of mealies. They came across groups here and there discussing the recent fray and asked which direction Trywell Dube had taken. He was on foot, they said, and headed that way. They pointed to a distant cluster of huts.

'What's his problem, sir?'

'The usual, Ncube, hit and run.'

'With a vehicle?'

'No, with a girl. She's carrying his child. He's abandoned her.'

'Ayi, a terrible thing. He sounds like a cold-blooded killer.'

'Because he gets women pregnant? If that were the case then most of Gubu would be suspects, you included, sergeant. If I remember rightly, wife number three came with your child on her back.'

Ncube spluttered, 'But I married her, sir.' He was furious, the detective could not pass judgement, wasn't Sibanda himself involved with two women? There was talk of him dating Sister Angel Better, and Miss Barton was definitely in the mix. Miss Daisy's cab fell still as she negotiated the bumpy tracks in silence.

'So what was all the fuss about at the *inkundla*, Ncube?' Sibanda was unaware of his excommunication.

'Chicken pieces,' Ncube was short and still nursing his injustice.

'The headman was holding court on bits of chicken?'

'A husband dragged his wife there because she had eaten some chicken breast and thigh when, as you know, sir, those pieces are reserved for the head of the household; a wife may only eat the entrails, the head, wings and the feet.'

'Is that still the way even now?'

'Well, the headman agreed, fined her a chicken and fined the mother too for failing to teach her daughter how to treat her husband properly. That's when it all started. The women in the community weren't happy.'

'I bet they weren't. I see our man ahead, in the red shirt.' Sibanda put his foot down, Miss Daisy ramped over a particularly bad hump, became airborne and slithered to a stop just ahead of Trywell Dube.

The tall man stopped, alarmed at the sudden appearance of the Land Rover. 'You're going to kill that vehicle driving like that,' he shouted over Miss Daisy's idling clatter, 'the springs are shot, I can hear them, the injectors are sick and what is that coming out of the exhaust? I'd take it easy if I were you.'

Sibanda got out of Miss Daisy, 'Trywell Dube?'

'Yes, who's asking?' The suspect was a tall man, with an unusually round face and the bulging cheeks of a nut-smuggling squirrel. Sibanda noted the healing scratch, barely there, but it could easily date to Lois Khupe's death. His forearms were those of a wrestler.

'Detective Inspector Sibanda, Gubu Police.' Sibanda watched the hands, strong and capable of heavy locomotive engineering, fingers that could snap the neck of a woman or slowly asphyxiate her with ease.

'I've just been hounded in the *inkundla*, the local court, what do you lot want me for?'

'Just a few questions, Dube. You took Kerry Williams to the train last Wednesday night?'

'Yes, I dropped her off,' Dube looked confused.

'And you haven't returned to work since, why not?'

'Not illegal is it? I was due some days off and then this court nonsense happened.'

'You never informed your employers.'

'No phone signal.'

'But you could have got a message to them.'

'They're *mukiwas*. Would Berger have understood the *inkundla*? And the minute I'd have mentioned "court" they'd think I'd committed some capital crime. I'd lose this job, so I'll just tell them I've been sick when I get back, seriaaarrrrse sick.' He laughed as he elongated the syllables.

'And have you committed a capital crime?'

'What?' Dube was confused.

'Kerry Williams was murdered on that night train …'

'… Murdered? No … Ayi … Murdered …? How was she killed?'

'I'm asking the questions, Dube. Did you follow her on to the train? You've got a record of violence plus you like the girls, the headman says this is not your first run-in with angry parents.'

'… Steady on, detective, what are you suggesting?'

'We're not suggesting anything, Dube,' Sergeant Ncube intervened to calm the rising anger. He levered himself from the Land Rover with difficulty after rescuing the goat's guts that jumped from their bucket with the jolt and distributed themselves in black and green dripping ropes over the pastel upholstery of the back seat. Ncube could play good cop, not with intent or knowledge of the psychological subtlety involved but from the simple fact that he avoided confrontation wherever he could. 'We just need to know your movements the night you dropped Miss Williams off. Can anyone give you an alibi?'

Dube began to talk. 'In the middle of the night? It was one o'clock, remember? I went to my house in Gubu, slept for a few hours and then drove down here the next day.'

'No one saw you?'

'I live alone.'

'Surely not alone, Dube, you have a reputation to uphold with the ladies,' Sibanda took over. 'What time did you get down here?'

'Quite late, I … er … had a breakdown in the park. By the time I got going again it was too late to call on anyone. I slept in my car and then came to visit Sibongile. I wanted to talk to her parents.'

'So no one can give you an alibi until the Friday morning?'

'I suppose not,' he shuffled his feet.

'Didn't you come through the park gate? They would have a record of time of entry,' Ncube suggested gently.

Dube shook his head, his cheeriness deserted. 'I went the back way, avoided the gate, entered via the road past the staff quarters. I suppose that's another fine I'm up for.'

Sibanda was into his stride now. 'You could have followed Kerry Williams onto that train, murdered her, got off at a siding down the line, caught the later northbound train back to Gubu and still made it down here sooner than you did …'

'… But I didn't do it.'

'Having worked for the railways and with your specialist knowledge of trains and carriages, this is not looking good, Dube; a fine is the least of your worries.'

'You've got nothing on me, detective, not a shred of proof.' Dube was growing agitated. 'I didn't kill Kerry Williams and you know it. Go and find someone else to harass. You police are all the same. What are you looking for, a bribe? I've got no money to spare. With this *inkundla* judgement, I'll be broke for years.'

'Help us with our enquiries, Dube, and do not insult the crocodile while your feet are still in the water. Who did you see at the station that night?' Ncube asked. 'Anyone you knew, or anyone Kerry Williams recognised, anyone she spoke to?'

'I can't remember. It was busy on the platform and freezing cold. I was keen to get home. I didn't see anyone I recognised except for Lovemore, the poet guy, but he's always hanging around the station looking for a drinking partner. There was a white man travelling, though. I remember because I thought it might be nice for Kerry to have some company, someone from her own tribe.'

'What did he look like?' Sibanda asked.

'Shortish, quite stocky, going bald, oh yes, and he wore glasses.'

Sibanda and Ncube shared a brief, knowing glance. 'Age?' Sibanda snapped.

'Heading for fifty, maybe.'

'What are your plans? When are you going back to work?'

'I'm going to discuss the fine with Sibongile's parents first, they live over there,' he waved his strangler's hands in the direction of a distant cluster of huts. 'I'll have to marry her, that's what the parents are angling for. I've no other option, they think they've caught a big fish but they've foul-hooked a Zambezi shark. They'll regret this day and so will she.'

'Trywell, that is no way to start a marriage, you can't do that; consider the coming child,' Ncube looked to Sibanda for reassurance.

'Not our problem, sergeant, but you, Dube, had better report to Gubu Police as soon as you are back at work. I want a full and detailed report of your movements for the last couple of weeks backed up with an alibi for every single hour of every day.' Sibanda turned and strode off toward Miss Daisy. A bewildered Ncube followed.

'Sir, this man is our serial killer; he doesn't have an alibi for the time of Kerry Williams's death and he is aggressive towards women. Why aren't we arresting him?'

'We'll keep an eye on him; he's certainly in the mix, but is he our Black Sparrowhawk? We only have circumstantial evidence and would a serial killer be so open with his emotions? Dube is an angry man and multiple murderers are masters at concealing turmoil, that's how they get away with their violence for so long.'

'What now, sir?'

'Back to Gubu, Ncube and as quickly as we can, it's getting late and

Dube has just flagged Knut Von Bergen. I want to know why he was at the railway station last Wednesday night.' He kept his thoughts on Lovemore, his poet friend, to himself.

Ncube rolled his eyes. Miss Daisy had taken a heavy beating on the journey out; would she survive 'quickly' on roads that rattled like loose teeth in an old man's gums? She didn't, of course, she lasted for a while, just far enough to put them beyond help from Manjelengwa, out of reach of Gubu and in a spot without phone signal, but then she'd had enough of being treated like a ping pong ball.

It began with a strong smell of diesel wafting around the candy-striped cab. 'What's going on, Ncube?' Sibanda barked. 'Am I smelling leaking fuel?'

Despite the fast-sinking sun and the early creeping cold, Ncube had beads of sweat in every crevice. When Miss Daisy began to hiccup and stutter, he knew they were in trouble.

'We should pull over, sir. I'll take a look.'

Ncube lumbered out of Miss Daisy and lifted the bonnet. He didn't suppose the detective would notice he had finally replaced the support arm, having his head trapped in the engine well with a deadly monster python had finally made him prioritise the job. His brother at the Central Mechanical Engineering Department had been unable to find a replacement, so he asked Hilarious Dlamini at the Last Drop garage to weld him something from parts of an old metal bed. Hilarious was happy to do the favour, since Blessing, with her traditional muthi, had successfully dosed his family for the worms that had been causing his children's itchy bottoms. That was the last pleasing thought the sergeant had for some time. Miss Daisy was awash in diesel and it didn't take him long to discover the source of the leak. One of the injector pipes had snapped in rebellion and been pumping fuel all over the engine block. Miss Daisy was running on three cylinders. He and the detective weren't going anywhere until he could fix the problem. The night had fallen moonless and black, so unless detective Sibanda had a torch to shed light on the repair, they would be stuck in this freezing, dangerous and godforsaken wilderness until morning.

'Oh, Miss Daisy,' he whispered, despair creeping into his voice, 'what sort of a mess have you got us into this time?'

Chapter 20

Sibanda stared at his phone for the twentieth time. The battery was too low for the flashlight function. He would need battery life in the morning when he walked to find coverage. Trekking in the dark was not a good idea, a midnight rendezvous with an elephant herd was ill-advised, the tracks of numerous groups criss-crossed the road making towards a string of water points. The bush was bone dry, hadn't seen a drop of rain for months and water was king; no one should get in the way of a burning thirst. They were stuck for the night.

Ncube had given up under the bonnet, the begrudging and late rising moon, as thin and curved as a mostly eaten potato chip, shared a few crumbs of light, but barely enough to see his own hand. He was stamping his feet and rubbing his frozen fingers. Night had not only fallen dark and heavy but it promised further misery in the form of plummeting temperatures. 'We need a fire, do you have a match, sir?'

'A match? Yes, Ncube, your fat backside for Miss Daisy's rubbish ability to move!' he snarled. As much as anything he was angry with himself for not foreseeing the situation. The ancient crock had been rattling along reasonably over the last few weeks. He should have known the second honeymoon couldn't last. 'And I'll tell you something else, Ncube, this vehicle is off to the scrap heap as soon as we get back to Gubu. The station has two perfectly good runners, so we don't need Miss Devil Thorn Daisy Weed any more. Her days are done.'

Ncube's face fell and his jowls crumpled. He had been expecting trouble, Sibanda was as cranky as a burnt snake when it came to Miss Daisy and her occasional lapses, but this was a disaster. He hadn't understood the reply about 'matches' but he understood from the tone the 'yes' actually meant 'no' and it came with an offensive quip typical of the man and his short fuse. As to calling Miss Daisy a weed, that was unforgivable. The night would be unpleasant with the detective in a mood, and probably life-threatening as well. Miss Daisy would have to keep them safe.

'So no fire then, sir?' It could have cheered them, kept evil creatures at bay and thawed the creeping hostility.

'No,' he barked. Sibanda could have lit a fire if they really needed one, having done it often as a herd boy by rubbing sticks together, but he would have to find a soft-centred wood to produce the ember dust to ignite the kindling, and none of the likely species grew nearby. His favourite was *umtshwankela*, the chocolate berry, but he might bumble around for hours in the dark before he found one. Besides which, he looked down at his palms that had lost the hard-earned callouses of his youth, these hands would bleed before they produced a spark.

They sat for a while together in the cab, discussing the case, or rather Sibanda bounced his thoughts off his silent, deeply hurt and increasingly nervous sergeant. Miss Daisy's deckchair-striped upholstery did nothing to calm the continued fury of the detective or the near panic of the sergeant – uncertain noises were beginning to chirrup and slither their way through the African night.

'Move into the back, Ncube, and try and get some sleep.' Both were aware there was little chance of Ncube's bulk squeezing between the seat and the steering wheel. 'And get rid of those goat's guts, they're stinking the cab out.'

Sibanda would have to do battle with the gear box. The only advantage was the proximity of the engine still shedding heat through Miss Daisy's ill-fitting floor boards. Ncube, his balaclava in place, leaving only wide and alarmed eyes visible, his padded jacket zipped up and his scarf wrapped several times around his neck, settled himself as best he could on the back seat. For a while, since his stomach believed his throat had been cut and grieved at the thought of impending starvation, he tossed and turned, causing Miss Daisy to rock and fidget.

Sibanda said nothing despite his resting head bouncing against the metal cab, he had already let his temper get the better of him. There would be no hope of sleep anyway. He buttoned up his jacket, turned up his collar and stretched his legs into the well of the passenger seat, edging around the gear stick.

Ncube settled flat on his back with his knees in the air.

Sibanda must have dozed. He woke around 2 am cramped and frozen, a stiff breeze had blown up and was needling its way through the patched up holes and leaky seals. Sibanda shifted as gently as he could so as not to disturb the fitfully snoring Ncube. The detective was far too cold to consider sleeping again, so he lay shivering, eyes closed, churning over clues. He discounted Isaac Manhombo who had an alibi for the nail polish incident, and Trywell Dube's story was plausible. That left him with George Paradza and Knut Von Bergen, or some completely unknown suspect who had yet to emerge. Could any of them be a murderer who throttled and skinned his victims? It would take either an extremely cool head or a complete psycho to slice away carefully at a corpse, running a sharp knife under the skin to separate it from the fat and then taking the hide away to dry and worship as a trophy of manhood, or keep as some kind of warped revenge against a perceived wrong.

What long-nailed siren had humiliated the Black Sparrowhawk and set him on his frenzy of peeling and paring? One thing he did suspect was that the killer had a link to Gubu, could find his way around and knew Sibanda's front door, plus all the victims either boarded the train at Gubu station or were on the way back to the village. Paradza and Bergen had business in the area, but it was Lovemore who lived in Gubu and his name was cropping up more than it ought to. Was it a coincidence the poet had curled up in the detective's back garden or was it subtle, serial killer stalking? Sibanda didn't trust coincidences.

He remembered he had brought Lovemore's notebook along, meaning to return it when he got back and possibly share a shot of scotch. With nothing better to pass the time he rummaged around in the glovebox and pulled it out. If he angled the jottings against the window, there was just enough moonlight to make out the words. As he rifled through the pages even he, a poetic philistine, recognised the work was patchy at best. Somehow Lovemore's baritone timbre had given life to dross. After an hour or so of laboured interpretation he had a few ideas and they were setting off alarm bells. If he accepted an element of the autobiographical in the work, then Lovemore was a fatherless impotent with a hatred of women. Berry had picked that up. The profile could easily fit a serial killer; sexual impotence and inadequate parenting often featured.

His college notes – finally unearthed a few days ago in a box in his bedroom – refreshed his memory as he reread the carefully highlighted words of the psychologist Joel Norris:

"*The image of a fiancée who rejected the killer, the echo of the voice of the hated mother, or the taunting of the distant father; all remain vividly in the killer's mind after the crime. Murder has not erased or changed the past because the killer hates himself even more than he did before the climax of emotion … it is only his own past that is acted out. He has failed again. … Instead of reversing the roles of his childhood, the killer has just reinforced them, and by torturing and killing a defenceless victim, the killer has restated his most intimate tragedies.*"

Did Lovemore hate himself? Was the witty self-deprecation a disguise for self-loathing? '*There is no father to tell*' was a line of Lovemore's poetry. Had he lost his father early or been abused by him? Some of the imagery was violent, as Berry suggested. Sibanda particularly didn't like the reference to the skinning of hides and stretching them over trees. That was close to the bone even if it did refer to a drum. But it was the discovery, on the last page of Lovemore's most recent doggerel, dated about a month ago, that sent the gently humming alarm bells into fire truck clanging mode:

Born, breath in, inspire.
Grow in leaps,
Chirp and tweet,
Seethe like fire.

Grow in bounds,
Claw the air,
Seize the day,
Accept the dare.

Grasp the day,
Twist the wire,
Plead for air,
Suck, scream, expire.

Sibanda sat up sharply. He needed to get back to Gubu and in a hurry. He took his phone out and glanced at it again but there was still no signal. He cursed, rubbing his jaw and clawing at the overnight stubble in frustration. In that moment he made the decision to start walking. It was still a couple of hours until dawn, but with his wits about him he would be fine and the exercise would pump some heat into his freezing veins. He might even jog for a while, or would he? Something was going on close to the vehicle. Snuffling and background giggling noises began to penetrate his concentration. He had been so focused on Lovemore's poems and trying to overlay them on the psychology of serial killing he had failed to notice what was going on outside. Hyena, a pack of them, were chortling with the glee of a free meal. He had heard a few whooping hollers earlier and ignored them. The predators were excited by something, and they were close, too close. He twisted and looked over the rise and fall of Ncube's stomach mound and his well-padded knees. Through the left rear window, the large round coal-black eyes of a brazen hyena met his and then ducked. Behind the alpha female were the rest of her clan, more hesitant, advancing gingerly. He could have admired their cohesion, their wholesome family values, their handsome, wide-eyed faces, but their proximity spelled trouble.

'Ncube,' he yelled, 'wake up!'

'What? What's happening, are we there yet?' Ncube hadn't a clue where he was or what was going on, so deep was his sleep.

'Hyena.'

'What? Where?'

'At your feet, just outside the door.'

Ncube sat up quickly, his gut, that had moaned and gurgled all night with the deprived resentment of the previously pampered, exploded, with such force the hyenas stopped mid cackle and took up with a snigger, or at least that is what Ncube recounted later. 'My goat,' was all he could manage in the aftermath.

'The *amatumbu*?'

'Yes, I put the bucket of innards outside.'

'Well, it's brought the hyenas to the tyres. Once they've finished the intestines, and they'll wolf those down in seconds, they'll start on the rubber, they love it. We've got to chase them.' The giggling got higher, accompanied by a few muted whoops and whines. Hyena, a sharing, caring bunch, make sure everyone partakes of anything available, particularly the sick and the young. They are the socialists of the veld.

'Those creatures are going to eat Miss Daisy?' Ncube was becoming hysterical, 'if we lose the tyres we'll be stuck here forever.'

'Open that back door and bang it, make as much noise as you can and hurry up.'

'Open the door? Have you seen their fangs? Witches ride those things, they are evil. If our bones aren't crunched to splinters, then we'll be cursed and doomed.'

'Don't be ridiculous, do it now, sergeant,' he yelled, his patience dissolved. He manoeuvred his long, lithe body across to the passenger side and was hanging out of the window and hammering on the door, but the hyenas were bold, the smell of ripe blood and guts was too much for them to ignore.

One snout-scarred and battle-hardened individual, her spots well faded from age, stood her ground. She had taken part in many a scrap, including plenty of lion wars in her time. She was a wily adversary and backed by strength in numbers, only Ncube joining the cacophony convinced her to retreat. She made off with the bucket, loping away, chuckling and snickering, hoovering up what was left of the ropes of entrails, biting chunks out of the plastic bucket with her powerful jaws until all that remained was the handle, abandoned as unpalatable.

When Ncube could speak he gasped. 'Thank you, sir, if you hadn't been awake and with brave thoughts, we could both be dead or bewitched and Miss Daisy in bits.' Ncube marvelled at his boss, the man was superhuman with the eyes of a leopard and the ears of an elephant.

'We were perfectly safe Ncube, but Miss Daisy might have taken a beating.' He opened the Land Rover door. 'I'm going to walk down the road until I can make a call. We have to get back to Gubu, I've got a hunch about who our Black Sparrowhawk is and the sooner we stop him in his tracks the better.'

'You can't get out in the dark it isn't safe, you'll be eaten. Won't the hyenas return?'

'No, I'll be fine, but stay in the vehicle, Ncube, at least until day break. I'll be back with help.'

Sibanda was out of the vehicle and jogging in a flash. Ncube watched him go until the tall loping shape was swallowed by the gloom of the

African night. The sergeant felt very alone. Where did the man's courage come from? He didn't ponder the question for long as the burning ache of hunger prompted him to remember Nomatter's wink and set him scrabbling around in his lunch box. Tucked away down the side was a stick of biltong. He began to munch.

Sibanda had underestimated the distance he would have to travel to get signal. The sun was over the horizon before he made contact. There was blood back in his limbs and he had even worked up a sweat. His jog had been uneventful, only having to skirt one herd of elephants, and he made good time.

'Zee, thank God it's you. The Land Rover has broken down in the park. Ncube is still with it. Can you send Chanza in the Santana to pick us up and organise a tow.'

'Chanza's not here yet and …'

'… and?'

'He won't be doing any rescuing. He's going to be busy today.'

'With what?'

'They found more bones along the line late yesterday evening and he and Cold War have organised interviews with the press, taking centre stage as usual. This Sparrowhawk story is going to be headline news.'

'Damn it, Zee. Can't you stop him? It will only goad the killer to reward himself for his notoriety with another death.'

PC Khumalo remained silent. There was no need to answer; the detective understood the situation as well as she did. Chanza was the favoured nephew of the Officer-in-Charge and she was just a lowly PC. Sibanda's battery died. He looked at the screen in disbelief and took a moment to register that the newly found bones must be those of the nun, Sister Martha.

He was in for a long hike to Gubu. What was needed was a vehicle to tow the Land Rover back to the station where she could finally be retired and used for scrap. Miss Daisy, he thought with some satisfaction, you're a goner.

An hour later, with the sun well up and several more kilometres under his belt, Sibanda heard the welcoming sounds of a vehicle. Hitching a lift would save him a couple of hours and they could be critical. The truck grew closer, and it had to be a truck making that racket, it was on its last legs, but a third-class ride was always faster than a first-class walk. He looked back to see a ball of dust and fumes heading in his direction. When Miss Daisy pulled up alongside him he was astounded. 'What the ...? How did ...?'

Sergeant Ncube's cheery face greeted him. 'Hop in sir, I daren't stop.'

'How did you fix her, Ncube?' he felt obliged to ask and for once he had a passing interest.

'I crimped the broken pipe using a rock and a piece of wood to hammer on. Of course you can hear her battling on three cylinders and she's lost a lot of fuel,' he spoke as though she had haemorrhaged her life blood and he'd applied a tournequet, 'but even if we don't make it back to Gubu on what's left in the tank, we'll get close enough to find help. Did you manage to phone anyone?'

'Yes, and there would have been no rescue for us, Ncube. Chanza is occupied going viral with the news of the serial killer.'

'Oh, right,' Ncube narrowed his eyes and closed his mouth in his practised look of comprehension, but he couldn't understand if Chanza was sick or if serial killing was catching, he had never heard of a virus in connection with murder.

The rest of the journey was mostly in silence. Miss Daisy, never a purring runner at the best of times, took noisily to her three-cylinder gait. The din in the cab would have broken every health and safety rule a first-world country could dream up; in Zimbabwe, as she steamed triumphantly and tractor-like through Gubu, she didn't even raise an eyebrow. One conversation did take place along the road with Ncube trying to curry favour on behalf of Miss Daisy, anything to rescue her from oblivion. It had to include trees or birds or both.

'They must have had big winds here last night, sir,' he offered.

'Why?'

'Look at those clumps of dry grass blown up into that thorn tree.'

Sibanda looked at his sergeant witheringly. 'They're nests, Ncube, whitebrowed sparrow weavers and if they were blown there, why are they on the opposite side to the prevailing wind, there's a question for you?'

Ncube sat up in his seat, he had accidentally asked a perfect question, now to somehow make it more detailed. 'Nests? That can't be, they're just a bunch of wind-blown weeds, like rubbish against a fence, the birds must have abandoned them years ago.'

'They're current.'

'Then why so ragged and untidy?' He was doing well so far.

'The weavers like them. Not all houses are as neat as yours, Ncube. The birds use them as roosts and work on them all year to keep their homes at the ready. They can mate as soon as conditions are right and don't waste time building again. The leeward side of the tree offers more protection.'

Ncube accepted the good housekeeping compliment. 'Looks to me as though the eggs would drop out, it's just a ball of loose grass.' A good comment.

'The nests have two entrances at the bottom, but once the breeding pair decides on which nest to use, and usually only one pair get to breed, then they seal up an entrance. Any other questions?'

Ncube sighed with relief; the detective was back to what passed in his world for cheerfulness, maybe he would give Miss Daisy a reprieve. And now that he thought about it, he did have a sensible question about birds to ask him but he would keep that for the next tricky moment.

CHAPTER 21

Sibanda headed straight for Lovemore Moyo's house on Buffalo Avenue, not far from his own. It was still early morning and a breeze was stirring the crisped leaves, the dried elephant dung and the polystyrene detritus of a mixed demographic. Overhead a few birds on bare branches chirped and fluffed to trap the first of the day's warmth. Low down, in a roadside bush, he heard the zirrupps and churrs of a trio of marico flycatchers, perched, waiting to hawk a flypast of insects. Like all flycatchers, they rarely hunted.

Lovemore's front door was chipped and scuffed but the yard was well swept and showed signs of life, washing was draped over the sagging fence and milk hedge, and a couple of hens scavenged and scratched at crumbs left over from breakfast. He knocked. The door was answered by a plump teenager, bundled up and ready for school.

'Who is it?' a cheery voice called from the kitchen.

'I don't know,' the boy grunted.

'Detective Inspector Sibanda to see Lovemore Moyo.'

'He's sick, you'd better go in,' the teenager spoke, as he edged past Sibanda.

A comely woman came down the hallway to greet him. 'You're looking for Lovemore? He's still in bed.'

'Can I talk to him?'

'If he'll talk. He hasn't said much for a while.'

'Is he seriously ill?'

'No,' she laughed, 'he's just making the most of the bed, he often mistakes laziness for poetry.' She led him into a room at the rear of the house.

Lovemore lay on his back, bedding discarded, despite the cold; pale and sweating. 'I'll leave you with him, detective.'

Sibanda planned a sharp interrogation, but this man seemed genuinely ill.

'What's wrong, Lovemore?'

'My stomach, it's worse,' he could barely speak, his hands moved down to the affected spot.

'Have you been to the clinic?' Sibanda's eyes followed Lovemore's hands.

'Do I look as though I can walk? Anyway, that's my drinking days over. I've sworn off the stuff. Gloria,' he nodded towards the closing door, 'says it must be my liver, she says I've pickled it, and if I rest and drink water it'll come right, but nothing's happening, I don't feel better.'

When he took his hands away from his naked torso, Sibanda noticed severe bruising on the poet's stomach.

'Did you fall or bang yourself somehow? Were you in a fight?'

'I don't know, but I was pretty out of it a couple of days ago. Gloria was in the money. I bought two bottles. I suppose I could have fallen, but I would have remembered a scrap.' Lovemore groaned in pain. 'Pass me that water will you?'

'I've got to ask a few questions.'

'What about?' The invalid sipped sparingly from the cup and winced as though each drop were acid.'

'The recent murders.'

'If it didn't hurt to laugh I'd be splitting my sides. You don't suspect me do you?'

Sibanda handed him the poetry notes. 'I've been reading these, you left them at the diner.'

'Ha! So I've converted the barbarian.'

'I wouldn't go that far, but I've scanned them. Some of your poetry is pretty violent and misogynistic.'

'What if I don't trust or particularly like women? Gloria has made sure of that; it doesn't make me a murderer. Okay, maybe I have lived out a few fantasies in those words, but it's not a crime to dream, is it?'

'You've been seen hanging around the railway station a few times late at night.'

'It's a social place to be in the early hours. I do my thinking there.'

'And do you ever travel on the trains?'

'No, never set foot on one.'

'Can Gloria give you an alibi for the nights in question?'

'She could, although some evenings I've been missing, like the night I spent in your garden, but *would* she, is the question you should ask.'

'Why wouldn't she?'

'She'd love to see me behind bars or, better still, dangling on the end of a rope.'

'Surely not.'

'So, she's fooled you as well, with her I'm-a-lovely-person act. No matter how long you leave a dead branch in the water, it'll never grow leaves. Gloria's a witch.'

'Tell me about your father.'

'My father? What about my father?' Lovemore sounded confused.

'Was he kind?'

'Sometimes, but he could wield a sjambok with some skill when the mood took him. Worked hard, provided for his family, ruled the roost, same as every other dad.'

'And your mother, was she …?'

'… Was she what?'

'Sophisticated?'

'Are you trying to kill me, detective, by making me laugh? She was a rural housewife, chopped the wood, carried the water, hoed the fields, stamped the maize, cared for her children, did without so we could have. She was as unworldly as a cow that never left the kraal. What sort of questions are these?'

Sibanda could see the effort of talking was taking its toll. 'It may all be circumstantial, but you're a suspect Lovemore, so don't go anywhere without informing the station.'

'Now I know you're trying to kill me. Does it look as though I'm likely to sprint off?'

Sibanda left the house and headed home. Lovemore was either completely innocent or as cunning and scheming as he claimed his wife, Gloria, to be. Was he faking that illness? Did he injure himself murdering Kerry Williams? Did she kick and punch? The poet had been confined to his bed for a couple of days, and off colour before that, which coincided with a lull in the killings. Could he be the Black Sparrowhawk? The jury was out.

Sibanda was wary as he approached his house and unsurprised to see his replaced latch smashed and bright red nail polish drizzled down his door like blood seeping from a raw wound. Lovemore could certainly have dragged himself a hundred metres down the road during the night; this didn't let him off the hook at all. Trywell Dube could have made it back to Gubu using the main road. Were George Paradza and Knut Von Bergen still in the area? Whoever this was could have murdered him in his bed if he hadn't been stuck in the wilderness. Maybe he should thank Miss Daisy.

Had the killer come back to do him an injury or just to taunt? The Black Sparrowhawk was ratcheting up the ante. Chanza's publicity campaign would only add fuel to the fire. Sibanda's hand might have gone to his chin, but it was his back he would have to watch.

A quick shower, change of shirt and a couple of mouthfuls of coffee saw Sibanda set up for the day, and it was going to be a long one. Before he left home, he put a few arrangements in place. He wasn't going to be caught out by the Sparrowhawk's visits again.

Sergeant Ncube arrived at the police station shortly after the detective. He had spent the little time available at home bewailing the loss of his goat *amatumbu*. By now his wives should have cleaned the guts and set the tougher large intestines to boil and bubble along with onions and tomatoes for a delicious evening stew. The smaller tubes would have been sliced and fried, and breakfast would have been filling and tasty. As it was, all they had for him was two-day-old bread and black, sugarless tea. Heaven knows what they found to put in his lunch box. He shouldn't complain. There were many on the point of starvation. Pitiful rain earlier in the year meant the drought was beginning to bite with the teeth of a python. Even paid employees like himself were feeling the pinch. The unemployed were anxious and dependent on relatives, or money sent home by the diaspora. Everyone shared where they could. Desperate women had started to appear on the verges, spending back-breaking hours collecting the tiny red seeds from under the *umtchibi* trees. The boiled husk produced a nourishing drink and the seeds, when roasted and pounded, made an acceptable starch. They needed several buckets full to feed a family. It was a worrying time.

When Ncube reached Sibanda's office, he found him deep in conversation with Zanele Khumalo.

'Come in, Ncube, we've got a lead on Constable Khumalo's attacker,' Sibanda was already behind his desk.

'Yes, sergeant, and we've the internet to thank,' PC Khumalo was beaming. She considered herself the technology expert in the station, being the only one who could work the dodgy, old, virus-ridden desktop.

Ncube pinched his lips and squinted, his rehearsed expression of understanding was becoming second nature. 'The internet?' Repeating the question put him on safe ground.

'Yes, social media to be exact. I've got some young cousins who live over at Mabale, my very own junior detective agency. Reason, he's the oldest, put an alert out on Facebook to find my phone. I told him to offer a reward. The phone's an old one and pretty worthless, but it has all my contacts on it, and I can't afford one of those smart ones.'

Ncube jaw dropped and his eyes popped, why would a phone be 'smart' and whatever was a 'face book'? 'Facebook, you say, amazing,' he tensed his mouth muscles.

'Yes, and it worked, within the hour, a guy pitched up with my phone. Reason, Jeremiah, Thea – she's the clever one – and little Praisegod went with him back to where he found it, thrown in a ditch. And, here's the good bit,' she looked at Sibanda for approval, 'Jeremiah, he's a brilliant bushman, well, he picked up the spoor and back tracked to the antheap where I was attacked, just to make sure he had the right set, and then followed the tracks all the way to a nearby kraal.'

Sibanda took over. 'We've got our link to George Paradza and his little fraud scheme. The man that hit PC Khumalo over the head was Biggie Nkomo. The boys ...'

'... And the girl.' PC Khumalo was very fond of Thea.

'They *all* asked around and found out Biggie Nkomo works for Silence Chihuri who imports bicycles for Universal Dream. He owns Lion Cycles in Bulawayo.'

'It was mostly little Praisegod who got that information. He played the dumb, wide-eyed child and the old gogo at the house told him all about the business. When Biggie found out, he was furious with her. The kids all witnessed the argument and little Praisegod's part in it. No one is too small to make a difference – try sleeping in a room with a mosquito!' Zanele was immensely proud of her cousins, even the littlest one.

Ncube, keeping his eyes narrowed, was beginning to pick up the thread. 'So Biggie Nkomo was keeping watch for Paradza and Chihuri while they cooked up their plan.'

'Yes, and Detective Chanza has gone to Mabale to bring him in.'

'Now we'll get to the bottom of it. I overheard Paradza talking about getting rid of someone. He killed Lois and we'll get him,' PC Khumalo straightened her shoulders, tipped her chin and looked as though she would rip his head off on her own.

Once the constable left for her desk duties, Ncube asked, 'So George Paradza's our Black Sparrowhawk, sir?'

'Too clean and too easy, Ncube. He could be, but so could Knut Von Bergen and I haven't discounted Trywell Dube. He has form against woman, and there's someone else.'

'Who, sir? I thought you'd excluded Isaac Manhombo and we know it couldn't have been Gideon Shumba.'

'No, neither of them. In fact, according to PC Khumalo, who's been snooping around, Shumba is having an affair with Manhombo's wife, Kindness. That's why he made the phone call to point the finger, and that's why Shumba was too frightened to tell us the truth of where he'd been; he's terrified of Isaac Manhombo and with good reason. It doesn't pay to get on the wrong side of that family of mongrels.'

'Aren't you going to charge Manhombo with wasting police time and giving false witness?'

'No, he has powerful friends and relatives in government. It could derail our investigation.'

'Ah, you are so right, sir, leave well alone.' Ncube couldn't believe the detective was finally learning caution. 'You should never pull a lion by the tail unless you're a lion cub.'

'I'll pull that tail, Ncube, rest assured, but when I take him down it won't be for a malicious phone call, and the whole of his rotten clan is going with him. For now, we have a murdering scumbag to concentrate on.'

Ncube shuddered and hoped he wasn't around when that investigation started; the detective was too reckless for his own good. 'I suppose Lois must have found out about the affair between Gideon and Kindness, which is why she left him. There was never another man involved. So who's the other suspect, sir?'

'Lovemore Moyo.'

'The local poet?'

'Yes, but let's not spread that about. As soon as Chanza's back with the culprit we'll take the Santana and go after Knut Von Bergen first; Lovemore is on his back and too sick to move far.'

'Where's the new vehicle, sir?'

'The Officer-in-Charge has taken that to Bulawayo to publicise the serial killer and blow his own trumpet. The Black Sparrowhawk will be headlines in *The Chronicle* tomorrow. I just hope Cold War has the sense not to put a picture of himself in the paper.'

'Why not? It will be good for his image, help him move to a bigger posting. Wouldn't that be positive? The elephant moves on and the mongooses drink in peace?'

Sibanda groaned at Ncube's lack of understanding. 'If it was only that, Ncube, I'd pay them to give him the entire front page, but the killer is in Gubu and dangerous, the less he knows about who's investigating the better.'

'Here in Gubu? How do you know?' Ncube was glad breakfast had been humble. His stomach was oddly at peace with the alarming news. 'Will my family be safe? My wives ... I should go home.'

'I just know,' Sibanda said with finality, 'and unless your wives have taken to painting their nails and travelling by train, they're safe. And, Ncube, if I catch you wasting your time trying to resuscitate that old wreck outside, I'll string your guts around the village goalposts.'

'But ...'

'... No buts, Miss Daisy is history.'

'Really, sir, I can fix ...'

'... Get out of here, Ncube, while you still can, and send PC Khumalo back in. She has proper work to do. And you could be useful too if you can find out where Knut Von Bergen is.'

Ncube huffed out of the office with his long-suffering tolerance teetering.

The constable appeared a few minutes later. 'You need me, sir?'

'Tell me where would you buy nail polish in Gubu?'

She looked down at her sadly unloved nails and shrugged, 'I never do.'

'But if you did, where would you get it from?'

'Not Barghees, any cosmetics on those counters have been there so long they would be dried to dust.'

'So where?'

'There's a nail bar, of sorts.'

'Whereabouts?'

'In the little shop next to the Last Drop garage.'

'I'll find it. Call me when Chanza gets back.'

Sibanda left the station, crossed the railway line and was at the nail bar in less than five minutes. He arrived at a tiny establishment tucked in between the garage's mechanical workshop and the local hairdresser. The air for fifty metres was redolent with a heady mix of fuel fumes, solvents and chemicals.

At first there appeared to be no one in what was little more than a dark cupboard, and then a head appeared above a desk in the corner, haloed by an anglepoise lamp.

'Come for a manicure?' a small voice chirped.

'No, just to ask a few questions. I'm Detective Inspector Sib ...'

'... Sibanda, even I know who you are.'

He approached the desk to find a badly disabled body wedged into an ancient wheelchair. If she stood she would hardly reach Sibanda's waist. Her legs were atrophied sticks, but her upper body while misshapen and bent was in proportion. Her face was untouched by whatever disaster had befallen the rest of her, it radiated a rare beauty. She was reading, she closed the page and looked up.

'You have the advantage; I don't know your name,' Sibanda said.

'Nokhuthula Nxumalo, but everyone calls me Thula. Sit down, detective.' She waved to a chair in front of her, 'I might as well give you a manicure while you ask me whatever it is you need to know. Good practice and on the house,' her eyes sparkled.

As Sibanda sat, Thula grabbed his hand and placed it on a towel on the desk in front of her. She began to massage cream into his cuticles. 'Very dry and neglected,' she frowned.

For the first time in days, Sibanda began to relax, his scalp tingled, his shoulders dropped and he battled to keep his eyes open. He was dog tired, but there was no hope of a good night's sleep until this case was solved. 'What do you know about nails?'

'Not a lot, I just paint them. There's not much to know.'

'So, you weren't reading up on your trade when I came in?'

She laughed. 'No, I'm studying, *Macbeth* by William Shakespeare. It's a good murder mystery, mixed with magic realism and a sprinkling of horror, perfect reading for a detective.'

'Could never come to grips with Shakespeare, myself. Do you like the plays?'

'They're full of truths and man's faults. You should give them another go.'

'Are you still at school?'

'I never really went to school, detective. In fact, for the first fifteen years of my life I barely saw the light of day,' she shrugged. 'You know what it's like … I was hidden, locked away from sight, a shaming example of some misshapen misdeed. Oh, I was put out to air in the yard every day, placed on a blanket, but no one talked to me except for family. When you look like I do, everyone assumes you're intellectually impaired.' She continued to massage his hands, moving onto the left one. 'Do you see the tree outside?'

'The teak?' he glanced at the tall specimen casting its shadow as far as the doorway.

'People meet under its shade, chat to one another, reveal secrets, bare their souls and even now they still assume I can't hear or understand. If I were a gossip …'

'So how ...?'

'… Did I get this far? My father got religion. About six years ago, he converted to Catholicism and the whole family were baptised. Every Sunday he'd hoist me on his back and take me to church.' The light of a good memory came into her eyes. 'It was my first-ever outing.' She began to poke his cuticles with a stick.

'And then you went to school?' he winced; the stick found a tender spot.

'I did try, the nuns from St Monica's got me this wheelchair, but starting Grade 1 at fifteen looking like this and having to travel many kilometres over rough roads was not easy. I gave up after a few months, or rather my chair gave up. It broke so many times it's more weld than chair,' she laughed.

'So how did you get to reading Shakespeare?'

'There was a young nun, she got me books, came twice a week and checked my work. She saved my life, if it weren't for her I would still be a bundle of rags at the back of my parents' hut.' Thula started filing, admiring the long fingers and pale pink, shapely nails as she did so.

'What was her name?'

'Sister Martha. By the end of that first year she had me up to Grade 5. I couldn't get enough of learning.' As she filed, motes of the detective's keratin floated on a shaft of daylight, settling invisibly on every surface.

'You knew Sister Martha well?' he never changed the level of his voice.

'She wasn't much older than me and we had a lot in common. We talked, giggled, shared secrets. In fact, she got me painting nails. We used to paint each other's. Of course, her colour was removed at the end of the session, wouldn't do for a nun, vanity is forbidden. Sister Martha was very beautiful, could have been a movie star. Anyway, she suggested I start this bar, said I was gifted with a steady hand and it could bring in some money while I studied and saved to get to university. She was convinced I would make it. I wish she could see me now, I'm half way there.'

'Do you know what happened to Sister Martha?'

'She had a wobble with her calling and went home to Bulawayo.'

'And you haven't heard since?'

'No, but ...'

'But?'

'There had been an incident in her past, something she was atoning for, or at least atoning for at her parents' insistence. "Expiation of sin", they call it in the church. I hope she's found peace wherever she is. She used to cry sometimes. It broke my heart. She wanted to look at options other than a life of religious devotion.'

'Such as?'

'Working for a NGO. She spoke very passable Ndebele, and I'm living proof of what she could achieve.'

'Did she mention any particular NGOs?'

'Why so much interest in Sister Martha?' Thula started buffing the nails on his left hand.

'She sounds like an interesting person, maybe I could track her down for you.' Sibanda didn't want to tell Thula what he suspected, not until there was absolute certainty.

'Universal Dream. She mentioned her family knew the director.' She let go of his hand. 'There, all done and they look much better. You should take care of those fingers and nails; they're beautiful, for a man.' She looked him in the eyes, with a hint of regret and a thousand what ifs.

'Thank you,' he stood and glanced at his nails, now shiny, smooth and even.

'What did you want to ask me?'

Sibanda almost forgot what he originally came to the nail bar for now that he had heard details of Sister Martha's plans and the link to Knut Von Bergen and UD.

'Has any man been buying bottles of nail polish from you, particularly red, maybe for a wife or girlfriend?'

'You're the first man to set foot in the place, but there was an odd incident a week or so ago. A young girl came in with a twenty-dollar note and asked for five bottles of my reddest red. I only had three and then I battled for change but it was unusual for a child in this village to be trusted with so much money for an indulgence. I watched her leave, came from behind the desk and looked through the door. She met up with a man far down the street and passed it over to him. He gave her a tip for her trouble.'

'Did you recognise the man? Is he from Gubu? Black or white?'

'No, can't say I recognised him or his colour. He was bundled up and too far away, but then I'm still a bit of a recluse, don't get out much.'

'And the child?'

'She was one of Mandlovu's brood from Mama Elephant's Diner.'

'Thanks, Thula, you've been a great help.'

'Come back whenever you want, detective, it's been a pleasure; and if you find Sister Martha, tell her I miss her, and ... a favour, detective.' It was time to let go of her memories. 'Could you give her this.' She passed over a thick wad of paper. 'It's a letter. I wrote it long ago. If you find her, please pass it on.'

Sibanda nodded as he walked away. He did think about paying Thula as a contribution to her fees, but as someone constantly on the receiving end of pity and charity, it was empowering to own the luxury of a kind gesture. He wouldn't demean the gift with an offer of money.

He left the nail bar with the thought he might expect a third visit from the Black Sparrowhawk if the number of bottles of nail polish were relevant. His phone rang half way back to the station. He wanted it to be PC Khumalo with news the Santana was back with Biggie Nkomo in custody. It was becoming even more imperative he found Knut Von Bergen, and quickly. Instead, it was Berry and his heart missed a beat.

Thula watched him leave. She lifted the towel off the board on her desk. 'So, Billi, will he ever come back?'

Chapter 22

'Hurry up, Billy. I can't stand around in this corridor all night.'

'Oh, ahhh, ugh,' the moaning was loud, 'I'm trying to hurry Monty, but I've got the gripes.'

Billy searched the small bathroom compartment for anything that could help. There was no way out, the window was too small, squeezing through was not an option. And anyway with the speed and the rails, escape that way was dangerous even for a lithe young body. Standing on the lavatory seat meant the cistern could be reached. Billy was currently working hard to disengage the pull chain. Towards the top there was a gap in the join of one of the links. The youngster's farm-strong hands and fingers were wiggling the metal back and forth to weaken it while continuing with the groaning sound effects to buy time.

The link snapped, leaving a good length of chain and a dainty porcelain handle, hand-painted with delicate blue flowers. It fitted under Billy's baggy shirt as a sort of chainmail waste band. Billy could have it unravelled in seconds and get it swinging to good effect, but anyone coming to the khazi now would have to jump to flush. Billy almost laughed.

'I'm a bit better, Monty, I'll be out in a minute,' the youngster shouted through the door while looking in the mirror. Monty was right; it was a pretty face, clear skinned, curly blond hair and long lashes. There had never been time for vanity on Boggy Fen Farm, for keeping clean and groomed, and mum and dad had been no role models. If Billy could get out of this fix, there might be a career in those looks.

The water from the basin tasted slightly stale not like the sweet water that burbled in a merry, rock-strewn stream along the northern boundary of the farm, but it quenched the thirst.

The chain clinked as the links butted up against each other, but the noise of the train would drown out a brass band. Billy continued to groan anyway.

'Oh shut up,' Monty said, as he ushered the sufferer down the swaying corridor, and then, after a moment of reflection, 'I've got something to take the pain away and make you better.'

With the carriage door firmly latched behind them and the blinds blocking prying eyes, Monty pulled down his carpet bag and rummaged among the pomades and lotions. Billy figured there was no point in worrying about the discovery of the missing rubies. The Rupee Ripper had more on his mind than jewels.

Through the window, night had fallen fast. For all the light and heat that swanked and preened during the day, the African sun disappeared as fast as she could with no dallying or lingering regrets. She high-tailed it like a mare smacked on the rump, off to the northern hemisphere where she might sulk occasionally and fight with rain clouds, but where you knew her heart was because she stayed awake, propping her eyelids half open, to watch evening picnics and cricket matches on the green, to spy on lovers in the hay and oversee children playing as late as they could, even when she and they should be tucked up in bed.

'Here, drink this,' Monty proffered a glass of viscous brown stuff that looked like treacle.

His lover's thoughts moved from home and out into the thick black night. Miles and miles of dense bush swirled past, drinking up the sooty smoke billowing from the engine, absorbing the scream of steel racing on iron, sucking up the flickering lights from the carriages and dousing them within a few metres of the track. Billy felt a hopelessness far greater than the purgatory of Boggy Fen Farm.

'Drink, this, I said.' Monty was becoming insistent. Billy glanced at the full beaker and knew it was poison or at least some kind of tincture to make you drowsy. Mum had only ever doled out medicine by the teaspoon, and rarely. If you got sick you got better on your own. Medicine and doctors were for the rich. So this must be how Monty lured those poor kids to … to … Billy shut the grisly thought off, it wouldn't help.

'No, I'll be fine now, Monty, honestly.'

'Oh, you stupid child, drink it or I'll whip you with my cane. You don't want a beating, do you?'

'Stop acting, Monty. It's over, I know who you are.' It was almost a relief to say those words.

'What do you mean?'

'You're not Baron Montague of Bingley or Alf Watters, your name is Edward Brixton, The Rupee Ripper. I've read the newspaper, and if you lay a hand on me I'll scream so loudly everyone on the train will know,' false bravado, but there was no alternative.

'What a silly Billy,' he soothed. 'You're delirious, you must have a temperature. Come, drink this up, my precious, it will bring you back to your senses.'

Monty stood and approached with the liquid. At the last second, he leapt forward, grabbed Billy's head and tried to force the fluid down. Billy spat out the thick brown medicine over Monty's suit and started a scream. In seconds Monty had a hand over his companion's nose and an arm around the tender throat he once praised as swan-like, trying to pour more liquid into the youngster. Billy gagged and lashed out, smashing the glass and spilling the sticky liquid everywhere.

Monty cursed and moved his hand over his lover's mouth. 'You fool, the opium would have made it easier, now you will feel pain and terror like you've never felt before and I'll revel in your suffering. I am going to be very creative with you, my little blossom. We have all night to play. You will be my clay, my Carrara marble, and I will sculpt and mould your body until I find perfection. Now where shall I start, those glorious eyes? No,' he shook his head, 'you're right,' Billy's head was waving frantically from side to side, 'maybe they should be last. I need someone to witness my supreme artistry and I want to look into them as we make love for one last time. Your pain will be my aphrodisiac, your panic, my Kama Sutra, your terror, my virgin child's wonder.' Monty's voice was changing, he adopted some kind of foreign accent. Billy recognised he was mad.

The young victim struggled, trying to prise Monty's hand away, kicking with every fibre of strength, but Monty was a grown man. The choke hold was firm; each breath was becoming more difficult.

'Don't struggle, little one, don't flee from perfection. You will be transformed from Billy, the filthy farmhand, into Billy the glorious creation. Embrace your destiny. Aren't you the lucky one?'

With his free arm, Monty reached for his walking stick, but he hadn't banked on farmyard strength. Billy abandoned the attack on Monty's hand and arm and changed grip to the walking stick. They wrestled for its ownership, the youngster with two hands, Monty with his left. Billy thought he had won and Monty had let go, but the cane fell away and the elephant's head came free. Attached to it was a long silver blade, gleaming with the light of razor-sharp mutilation. The captive would have gasped, but all Billy managed was a sucking in of breath that slid past the side of Monty's hand and across his palm before reaching the partially closed throat and screaming lungs.

The youngster was tiring, wanted to give in, give up to the monster, let him have his way, but Billy hadn't toiled long hours with hay bales, heavy buckets and back-breaking hoeing to be considered a weakling or a quitter and the thought of being gutted and pulled like a chicken triggered reserves of strength.

The Malacca cane was to hand. It may not have a blade or much weight to it any longer, but it was a weapon of sorts. Billy, locked in front of Monty, began to beat him about the head, swinging the cane backwards and then, as the murderer ducked and took cover, the blows changed to Monty's legs, targeting his knees. More struggling and wrestling ensued but Billy had little oxygen to draw on, little strength left, just a tiring body and desperate lungs. Monty put the blade down on the seat and wrenched the Malacca cane away. He wasn't talking anymore, the little brat had more strength than he had imagined. But the end was in sight as he felt Billy's body weakening, a few judicious, non-fatal wounds with the knife would subdue his subject and then he could begin, carving a tracery of designs and gouging out a few holes while his victim looked on in wonder at the power and the glory of the workmanship. The Indians taught him all about design and filigree work. They were masters of the art, all curls and dots. He felt himself hardening.

Monty, in changing his grip, moved forward slightly. It gave the diminutive victim one last chance. Billy kicked hard against the facing banquette now in range and the impetus caused them both to fall backwards onto the seat behind them. Billy fell into Monty's lap, but it was a futile move; Monty's grip remained firm and Billy had expended every ounce of energy with only enough oxygen left to dream up visions of mum shooing the hens, flapping her apron to chase them from the vegetables, the old whitewashed cottage leaning into the wind, soft blue light over the distant hills, gentle rain on the hedgerows and little Tom lulling himself to sleep sucking on a bit of rag he kept to soothe himself. Monty had fallen right next to his elephant head blade. It couldn't have been better placed. He caressed the curves with his free hand and picked it up. Billy's peripheral hallucinating vision caught a last flash of silver as the point descended.

CHAPTER 23

'I have your man, Detective Sibanda, but he doesn't look like a guilty party to me. I'm not sure my uncle would approve of a suspect brought in on the evidence of a bunch of rural *mafikizolo*.' Chanza said this as though there was a bad smell under his nose. 'Uncle Stalin likes cases investigated by the book and I would remind you he is in charge of Gubu, for the time being, at least.' The diminutive detective adjusted his presidential glasses, nudged them back up his nose with the help of a squint and could not keep a smug grin from cracking his cheeks. He and his uncle had big plans.

'Biggie hit PC Khumalo over the head with a brick. He's guilty and he's up to his armpits in corruption along with his boss, Silence Chihuri from Lion Cycles in partnership with George Paradza from Universal Dream. I want a confession and a conviction. Biggie Nkomo knows what's going on and he may even hold the key to the murders.' Sibanda's temper was on hold for the time being. He refused to be baited. The phone call from Berry had left him floating. She suggested a weekend away, somewhere private, where neither of them were known. Somewhere they could talk.

'The murders, what do you know?' Chanza intruded rudely, 'I may need any information you've got. The Officer-in-Charge is in Bulawayo right now briefing the press. He will want every detail for his interview.'

'Well, he's getting nothing from me. This investigation is sensitive, so far we have two bodies and two or three sets of remains. The more publicity this case gets the more likely there will be another woman murdered. Stalin Mfumu will have blood on his hands. He may even put himself at risk if he makes out he's the lead investigator, and don't you go sticking your head above the goat kraal or you could be next.' A little fear went a long way in taming Chanza's arrogance. Sibanda had his number.

'How … how do you know?' The heavy glasses slipped again as growing perspiration caused them to slide like rats down a drainpipe.

'Chanza, believe me, I just know, now hand over the keys to the Santana and send Sergeant Ncube in. He'll help with the interrogation.'

'The keys, but my uncle said they must remain with me.'

'I am ranking officer while Chief Inspector Mfumu is in Bulawayo, so hand them over or I'll have you up on an insubordination charge,' Sibanda snarled, his patience had done well, probably broken all records, but enough was enough. Chanza scuttled off. Sibanda would pay later for the outburst.

'Sir,' Sergeant Ncube popped his head around the door, 'what did you say to Detective Chanza? He's seems nervy, like a grasshopper hiding from a treefull of crows.'

'A murder, actually,' Sibanda couldn't resist.

'What, sir?'

Sibanda hadn't seen Ncube's eyes pop and his jaw fall for a while and he missed the sergeant's misunderstandings, it was oddly endearing. 'It's a murder of crows, Ncube.'

'Oh, er, right, sir, a murder, of course,' he squirmed.

'Chanza's got the jitters over the Black Sparrowhawk. Hold his hand through this interview with Biggie Nkomo, and don't let him make a mess or use his heavy tactics. I'm going after Knut Von Bergen. I've just found out he knew Sister Martha, a family friend. She phoned him before she left for Bulawayo, told him she was travelling down because she wanted to work for Universal Dream. Von Bergen could easily have come up to Gubu and boarded the same train. Sister Martha was a good-looking woman by all accounts and an obvious target. With Lois, that's two links to UD.'

'He's booked into the Gubu Safari Hotel. My friend is a waiter. He says Von Bergen stays at the hotel often, has his own room with his own stuff in it. I was coming to tell you.'

'Good work, Ncube.' He was out of his chair and along the corridor before he called over his shoulder, 'And keep PC Khumalo well away from Biggie. She's too emotionally involved and she'll be needed as a witness.'

Ncube winced as he heard the Santana race out of the car park, dust churning, stones flying and rubber burning. If anything was being murdered it was the vehicle and not the crows. Of course, everyone wanted to murder crows, they were ugly, irritating cacklers that sounded like sick goats, the detective really was a bit simple at times. Ncube was grateful the vehicle screaming out of the car park wasn't Miss Daisy. Her new pipe was already on the way. His younger brother at CMED had worked miracles. Ncube hadn't questioned the source; the part was certainly pirated. He blocked out the name of the unfortunate police station and their suffering vehicle. The walk to the interview room brought on a sigh. How on earth was he going to keep a rein on Chanza who could eat him for breakfast? Maybe his newly learned word, 'codswallop', would help. He loved the sound of the fish in it, if only he could remember what it meant.

Sibanda reached Gubu Safari Hotel in a record twenty minutes. Built in the early '70s at the very birth of safaris in Zimbabwe, it now stood testament to a changing industry. One hundred and twenty identical, air-conditioned rooms faced a large lawn dotted with thatched umbrellas and an elephant watering hole. Sibanda rapped hard on room 79.

'Detective Sibanda, this is a surprise.'

'It's not a social visit.'

'Then you'd better come in,' he ushered Sibanda towards a seat with a view of the waterhole. 'I take it this is about Lois?'

'And Sister Martha.'

'Arghyro Spyrios? What has she got to do with this?'

'She also went missing from the train.'

'But that was years ago.'

'Yes, and we have found her remains by the side of the track.'

'Arghyro? Are you sure?'

'Not yet, but there's a good chance it's her. You knew her?'

'I knew her parents, we went to the same church in Bulawayo.'

'She phoned you before she got on the train?'

'It's all so long ago, I can't remember.'

'Well, start thinking. Two women killed on the Gubu–Bulawayo train had links to you, more than coincidence?'

'Of course, it's a coincidence, I would never … Detective, this is ridiculous. I am a Christian, murder is a mortal sin. I work for a charitable organisation.'

'Lots of killers cloak their intentions with good works. They find justification in religious texts.' He stared into Von Bergen's bespectacled face. 'Did you talk to Sister Martha before she got on the train?'

'I might have. She phoned me a few times. She had become an unhappy girl. As a teenager she was bright and cheery and then something changed her. I didn't see her for a long time until she appeared at church as a nun.'

'Are you married?'

'What?' Von Bergen was startled by the change of interrogation.

'It's a simple question.'

'No … no, I'm single.'

'So you're a bit of a loner.'

'I was married, but my wife died.'

'How?'

'I didn't throw her from a train.' There was an edge of sarcasm in his voice. 'She died in a car accident, and I wasn't driving.'

'Did she rake her nails down your back, Knut, scratch you like a she-cat? You like finger nails, don't you? Did you arrange the accident?'

'My wife is dead, leave her memory alone and she always kept her nails short. Whatever, you believe, detective, I am not a killer.'

Von Bergen was a cool customer and not easily rattled.

'So, did Sister Martha phone you?' Sibanda was getting frustrated.

'Yes,' Von Bergen took a moment and rubbed his hand over his face, 'she phoned to ask for a job. Look, I couldn't help her, I had nothing available. The Board wouldn't have approved anyway, so I brushed her off.' He walked towards the window, a herd of wildebeest were drinking; their appearance against the cold, misted water was bearded, narrow-eyed, roman nosed and darkly sinister, hardly living up to their reputation as clowns of the veld. In contrast, a few impala were waiting their turn at the water, pronking like wooden horses, rocking through the foggy morning for the joy of it all. He turned back into the room. 'She took her own life, didn't she? That's why she never arrived in Bulawayo. Her phone call has caused me sleepless nights.'

'What did her parents think?'

'I never mentioned the phone call to them. They believed she had run away. Arghyro and her father fought about something. I didn't know what, not my place to ask. I'm glad they believed she was alive and well until they died. Her father blamed himself. He'd already retired from the railways and for months after her disappearance travelled up and down on the trains, stopping at every siding, questioning anyone who would listen. It killed him in the end.'

'Do you travel by train often?'

'No, never.'

'Why are you lying, Knut?' Sibanda joined him at the window. 'What have you got to hide?'

'What do you mean?' Von Bergen was alarmed by the stealth of the detective's arrival at his shoulder and the threatening hissing in his ear.

'You were seen boarding the train the Wednesday night before I came to Bulawayo to interview you, the same night another girl was murdered and you never mentioned it.' Sibanda's voice was hard and uncompromising. 'That connects you to three of the victims and gives me more than enough evidence for an arrest.'

'Arrest? You can't arrest me, I'm a Danish national.' Von Bergen stepped away as if distance could prevent the arraignment. 'My embassy will have something to say about this. Do you want to cause an international incident?' The director's European entitlement reared its head, something he struggled to subdue on a daily basis.

'I care nothing for international incidents. That's a problem for the politicians. I'm here about a spate of killings and you, Knut Von Bergen, are at the very heart of them. Tell me, did you enjoy torturing those women? Let me show you a picture of Lois, your employee. Do you remember what she looked like once you finished with her?' Sibanda took out his phone and flicked through to the picture he took on the railway line.

The photograph of the skinned head and bulging eyes shook the UD director. He sat down, put his head back in his hands and groaned.

'Doesn't look so sexy after a few days in the elements, does she?'

'What do you want to know, detective? I thought I had seen it all. I worked for the Bosnian War Crimes Tribunal, thought I had witnessed every despicable deed that man could inflict on man, but that …' He fell silent.

'Great act, Von Bergen, but you don't fool me. Come clean, I might be able to get you transferred to a Copenhagen jail, although scum like you belong in the cesspool of Hwa Hwa,' Sibanda said, referring to the notoriously brutal prison.

'I didn't murder Lois or Arghyro. Is that what happened to her as well? Was she skinned? God help the poor girl.'

'And the rest of them. How many are there? How many did you slice up?'

'I didn't kill anyone.' There was resignation in the tone.

'I need more than that, Von Bergen. Why were you on the night train to Bulawayo last Wednesday and why did you lie about it? UD has a big enough fleet. You don't need to travel by train.'

'I try not to misuse the transport. This was a personal trip.'

'We've been watching you. Enjoy the ladies, don't you, Knut? Do you use their services on the train? A single man like you has his needs.'

'I wanted some privacy.' He was agitated. 'I didn't want the office to know I was coming up here so often. Mostly I travel at the weekends but …'

'… You were desperate to murder again, to cut up those women, couldn't wait for Saturday. Where's the knife Knut?'

'There's no knife, detective, but I apologise, I did lie to you.'

'Ah, so now we get to the truth.'

'I am married. I married in secret a couple of weeks ago.'

'You were on the train, because you are married?'

'Yes, my wife lives in Mabale. I visit and she comes to stay here with me. Sometimes I use the train.'

'Why the secrecy?'

'She's an orphan and I met her through our AIDS support programme. So, you see how it looks, not good, as though I'm taking advantage. She's not a child, she's over 21, but she has young siblings she cares for. We decided to keep everything secret until her papers came through. We are going to live together in Denmark. I am adopting the children.'

'Who is this wife? Can we contact her? Your story had better check out.'

'Her name is Miranda Siziba. Here,' he gestured to a manila folder of papers on the table, 'this is all the paperwork. I came to Gubu to get their signatures and speed up the residency applications.' As an afterthought he added, 'We do love one another, detective. You must know what that feels like. This is not a marriage of convenience and, contrary to all evidence, I'm not a dirty old man.'

Sibanda drove away from the Safari hotel at a more leisurely pace. Knut Von Bergen's story seemed reasonable and, if it held up, he was probably off the list. That only left Lovemore, George Paradza and Trywell Dube in the frame. His mind drifted to Berry. It was hard not to read too much into what she suggested and much too hard not to fantasise. Knut Von Bergen was right; he did know love and it was threatening to overpower his judgement. It was going to be even more difficult to keep his attention on the case.

CHAPTER 24

'Ayi ayi ayi, this whole Lion Cycles thing is a codswallop.'

'A what?' Sibanda was debriefing Ncube on the Biggie Nkomo interrogation.

'Yes, sir, a codswallop, you know, a fishy and violent affair,' Ncube was on firm ground and preening, it was the detective's turn to be confused and see how it felt to not understand words. 'Biggie is locked up and has admitted to hitting PC Khumalo, said he just wanted to steal her bag. He insisted he didn't know anything about Silence Chihuri, George Paradza and Lion Cycles.'

'Didn't Detective Chanza get anything out of him?' The depths of Ncube's eccentricities were unfathomable. He ignored codswallop.

'No, sir, we were wasting our lungs on dead embers,' Chanza said. He knew all along the children were lying, children always lie. 'He told me to do the paperwork and charge Biggie with assault since he didn't actually steal anything, issue him with a fine and let him go.'

'But you didn't, if he's still in the lock up.'

'No … er, after Detective Chanza left to go and greet his uncle, PC Khumalo came in. I did try to keep her away, sir, but there's no stopping an angry woman. When she heard the flimsy charge, I thought she would kill Biggie. She can be very dangerous. I am now seeing her through the eyes of a mouse in an owl's nest.'

'Fearsome was she?'

'Biggie came clean. He couldn't stand the screaming. It was enough to pierce the ears of old man Dhlamini and he's deaf and lives on the far side of Mambanje. Biggie admitted to being asked to keep watch for

Chihuri and Paradza. He didn't realise PC Khumalo was a police officer, thought she was just snooping. He could tell us nothing more and I believe him. No sane man could have withstood the spitting venom coming out of PC Khumalo. Biggie told us all he knew.'

'Is he involved in the fraud?'

'No, but he's witnessed false invoicing and irregular paperwork. Silence, together with George Paradza, inflated the prices of bicycles to Universal Dream, skimmed the money like fat off the top of the stew.' Ncube was sorry he said that. He could have done with a swipe of mealie porridge smothered in a rich, meaty sauce. Wasn't it lunchtime?

'How long has it been going on?'

'For so long, it's become a tradition. I decided I'd better keep him here so he can't tell Paradza we're on to him.'

'What does he know of Lois Khupe and her murder?'

'Nothing.' Ncube shook his head, his wobbling jowls magnifying the negative. 'He's just an employee paid to turn his head and watch Chihuri's back.'

PC Khumalo's head popped around the door. 'Sir, do you have a minute?'

'Tell me it's good news, Zee. We need a break in this case.'

'Mixed. Cold War is hopping around like a springhare that's stood on a scorpion and wants you in his office now, and Trywell Dube has been in. He's given me a list of his whereabouts over the last couple of weeks. I'm cross-checking with his contacts.'

'Good, and one more thing, see if you can get hold of Miranda Siziba.'

'From Mabale?'

'Yes, do you know her?'

'Know of her. She was the young beauty Knut Von Bergen had his eyes on at the Food for Work meeting. She hasn't been …'

'… Killed? No, but it's unusual, she's Von Bergen's wife, or so he says. Make sure that's correct. Get the details.'

'Ncube, it's lunchtime,' he pointed to the sergeant, 'and I owe you for getting us back to Gubu in that rust bucket. How would you like to visit Mama Elephant's Diner?'

'But what about the Officer-in-Charge, shouldn't you …'

'… Later, Ncube, he'll keep.'

Ncube was torn between official disaster and the burger he would choose. Mama Elephant was famous for her peri peri chicken liver burgers, but he had heard of her newest menu addition – the mealie burger, layers of refried mealie meal alternating with chilli braised slices of meat and a spinach relish – all his favourites in a bun.

The diner wasn't roaring with trade, in fact it was barely whimpering, the wind whistled around an empty courtyard of tables, and the small inside space had two diners and a woman queueing for a takeaway. A young man stood behind the counter. 'We'll take two peri peri chicken liver burgers and I'd like to speak to Mandlovu if she's around.' Sibanda didn't give Ncube the choice, his sergeant was a ditherer, choice confused him. He hadn't even been able to settle on one woman.

They sat at one of the tables and in no time the burgers bulging with content and dripping with juices were placed in front of them. Mandlovu delivered the plates. 'Did you and your girlfriend enjoy the other night?'

'It's a bit quieter today,' Sibanda had no intention of chatting about his personal life.

'Business is bad. No one has any money. What do you want to see me about?'

'Your children.'

'What have they been up to now?'

'Nothing wrong. One of your daughters might be able to help with our current investigation.'

'I only have one daughter, detective, Shalott. Brian,' she shouted to the lad behind the counter, 'run and fetch your sister.'

'Charlotte?' the detective quizzed.

'Yes, Shalott. Her father didn't stick around so Lovemore named her, he said Shalott came from a poem about a beautiful and magical lady and no one else in the village has it. Sounded good to me. And now the new English princess has the same name. Terrible news about Lovemore,' she added, 'I take it you've heard.'

'That he's sick?'

'No, he's dead.'

'I saw him only early this morning. What happened?' Sibanda was taken aback, he hadn't seen that coming.

'He died an hour ago. Gloria says it was his liver but she's a cunning one, that woman. You know he's her third husband. The other two died as well, and who knows how many she's cursed before she came to the village. Lovemore always said she was a witch.'

Ncube, relishing the spongy, spicy livers and the tangy juices seeping into the soft white roll, failed to make the connection between Lovemore's diseased liver and the delicious burger he was finishing off, only the mention of witches brought his chewing to a halt.

'A witch, where?'

'There are no witches, Ncube, they don't exist, just eat and keep quiet,' he snapped, and turned to Mandlovu. 'Did the others die in their beds?'

'Yes, and suddenly, too, like Lovemore. Last week he was fine and full of fun. I know he wasn't so well at the poetry club meeting, but that was only a couple of days ago. Ah, here's Shalott.' Mandlovu's face lit up as her youngest and most precious child came into the diner.

'You called for me, Mama?'

'The detective has some questions for you. Don't worry, you're not in trouble.'

Shalott was a slight child with a closed face. Sibanda had never been any good with little ones, and suspected he might need Ncube's help; after all he had eight of his own. He glanced across to his sergeant for support but Ncube was licking his fingers and refusing to look at the detective. The man had insulted him a second time when he was eating. The sergeant made a pact with himself not to dine with the detective ever again. Eating obviously made him crabby, he hadn't even touched his burger yet.

'Hello, Shalott, don't be afraid,' Sibanda towered over the tiny scrap. She stuck a finger in her mouth and retreated to her mother, hiding her face in her skirts and clinging to her legs.

Ncube raised his brows and relented, he couldn't bear the terrified look on the little one's face, the detective needed lessons in children. 'Come Shalott,' the sergeant said, in a gentle voice, while going down on one knee until their faces were on a level. 'I've got something to whisper in your ear.' The child moved forward, listened and set about giggling. 'Now sir,' he looked up at Sibanda, 'what is the question?'

In the Santana, on the way back, Ncube was perplexed. 'A man buying nail polish. Why was it important to find out about him, is he linked to our Black Sparrowhawk?'

'He is, and I believe that young girl came face to face with the serial killer.'

'But she couldn't identify him, except to confirm he's a black man wearing a bright scarf. She didn't recognise him.'

'His face was disguised by that scarf, probably deliberately.'

'Everyone is wrapped up these days. This weather is cruel. I pity those with too few blankets. But why is the nail polish so important?'

The detective was far away in thought. There was something he was missing, something just beyond his line of sight.

Ncube asked, 'We can tick Knut Von Bergen off our list. The Black Sparrowhawk is definitely black, and what about Lovemore, can he go too?'

'What?'

'The poet, he's dead and surely no longer a suspect.'

'If the murders stop now then maybe he has done us all a favour.'

'And the nail polish, sir?'

'It's complicated, Ncube, but the killer is fixated with the stuff, just go with me on this.'

Ncube glanced across at Sibanda. He had been strangely silent the whole journey. As ever, Ncube was in awe of the man who sat beside him. Irritable at times, but a man of such intuition it was hard to believe he was human. Perhaps he wasn't, maybe he was a spirit come to guide them. Wasn't the fact he never ate proof of this? Ncube cradled a bag containing the detective's peri peri chicken burger, entrusted to him for his wives. They already worshipped the detective and Ncube could understand why.

At the reception desk, PC Khumalo stood to greet them. 'I've got some information back from Forensics, sir, and the Officer-in-Charge is rabid, pacing up and down like a caged lion.'

'Give me the forensics first.'

'The old bones you found are very ancient. They can't give us an exact date, maybe eighty to a hundred years, but they were able to extract enough material from the remains of the teeth. The genetic markers suggest the bones come from a Caucasian male.'

'So, nothing to do with our serial killer and too old to pursue. The case is stone cold, could even be some old hunter or explorer up in these parts before the railway line existed, probably died a lonely malarial death, or got himself gored by a buffalo. And the other remains?'

'Same profile as the last set of bones, a woman between 20 and 25.'

'Must be the nun.' He turned to his sergeant. 'Ncube, go home early, we are off to Bulawayo tomorrow to check on George Paradza.'

'On the train?'

'No, we're driving in the Santana. I've had enough of train travel for a while.' Sibanda strode off to Mfumu's office.

'Ah, Detective Sibanda, at last, I've been waiting.' Mfumu was almost bursting with the news of his interview with *The Chronicle* and other papers. He even managed a very satisfactory meeting with the Commissioner of Police for Matabeleland, July Chimombe, who seemed delighted the focus of news had swung from police corruption at road blocks to a bone fide serial killer. Before he left he had seen the billboards advertising 'Cannibal killer on the loose', 'Human skins tanned for bags' and, in the scurrilously creative tabloid, *B-Mirror*: 'Flesh eating rapist fries liver in front of live victim.' He didn't think he'd said that.

'I've been pursuing leads on the killings.'

'But you have someone locked up, Biggie Nzimande. He's your man isn't he?'

'No, just part of a fraud case we're investigating.'

'But you are about to make an arrest?' Mfumu could feel tension in every bone. He'd promised the commissioner the case was wrapped up. His tension didn't show because his starched and regimentally ironed uniform never followed a single bodily contour or barely touched a patch of flesh, it lived a separate rustling life.

'Right now, our suspects are falling away one by one. We're heading to Bulawayo tomorrow morning to interview the last man on our list. If he doesn't fit the profile and one of the others doesn't break cover, then it's back to the drawing board. I'm taking the Santana.'

'I've told the journalists an arrest is imminent,' Mfumu spluttered, but never queried the use of the vehicle. He wanted the killer stopped as soon as possible if he was to get promotion out of this stinking hole of a stagnant pond.

'What else did you tell them? Is your name mentioned?'

'Well, of course, I am in charge of the investigation.'

'Not a good move.'

'Why?'

'Because the killer is stalking us. I've had a couple of incidents and if I'm not around he might focus on you.'

'On me?'

'Yes, are your wife and children at home?'

'No, they're at my mother-in-law's.'

'Good, tell them not to come home for the time being and make sure you lock your doors with a stout lock.'

'I'm under threat?'

'You could be now the murderer has your name. He's a police stalker and he may resort to violence. There's also a fair chance the killer is dead. One of our main suspects died of natural causes mid-morning. I'm going to his house now. I suggest you focus your prayers on yourself.'

The body lay in the bedroom. It had been boxed and laid out, just the face was visible. Lovemore's brow was smooth, the lines of suffering Sibanda had witnessed in the morning were gone. The detective was alone with the corpse. He could hear the wailing of the widow and the hymn singing of the women who had come to comfort her in the next room. The vigil would continue through the night. Gloria had done well to organise the coffin and he understood the burial would be tomorrow. Funerals were a persistent feature of life in the village and Gloria had already buried two other husbands, so she'd had plenty of practice.

He looked down at the face again. 'Are you our Black Sparrowhawk, Lovemore? Did you have it in you to rape and skin those girls and how many have disappeared at your hands? Where do you keep the skins and the girls' clothes?' Sibanda spoke as if he expected the corpse to respond. He did a quick and silent inspection of an old wardrobe, but there was nothing, no skins, no curing salt, no spare bottle of nail polish, no knife and now was not the time to ransack the rest of the house for clues.

'Come on, Lovemore, give me something,' he whispered through clenched teeth. 'We're making no progress here.'

He listened at the door to make sure he wasn't going to be disturbed and then apologised to the body. 'Sorry, my friend, but I have to look at those bruises one more time.' Sibanda carefully folded back the shroud and unbuttoned Lovemore's shirt. The bruises had developed further while he still lived. They were purple, livid and perfectly round, with no signs of imprinted knuckles or heels or nail scratches. The poet hadn't been punched or kicked. With signs of movement in the next room, he rearranged the covering and then, as an afterthought, took Lovemore's battered poetry notebook from his jacket pocket and tucked it between the corpse's clasped hands. He took one last look at the face. 'I really hope you aren't the killer, Lovemore, and at least you've got some familiar words with you for comfort wherever you are going.' He left the room, muttered further condolences to Gloria and set off for home.

Dusk fell early in winter. It was 5:30 and already dark. Sibanda had no intention of sleeping in his bed. The Sparrowhawk might take things further. He made his way as normal to the house, entered through the front door and then snuck out through the back door and over the fence. He circled for a few hundred metres and came back via the bush until he was opposite his front door again but hidden from view by the undergrowth. Early that morning, under a large and still leafy teak, he had stowed a sleeping bag, a bottle of water and the one-eyed binoculars he'd held onto from the last case of the murdered American researcher. It would be his observation post.

He sat down and put his back against the tree. A couple of hours later, as the viciously cold weather closed in, he zipped himself into the bag and pulled it up around his shoulders. He didn't want to be too comfortable, having barely slept in the last 24 hours; if he dozed off the whole exercise would be pointless.

The falling cold began to eat at his bones like a hyena gnawing on a knuckle end. Once settled he could not risk any movement by drawing his sleeping bag closer around his shoulders or blowing on his freezing fingers. Any stamping of feet or slapping his body for warmth were luxuries that might give his position away. The Black Sparrowhawk was a wary bird.

He drew in deep breaths and exhaled with measure. The stony cold of previous night surveillance jobs before he was posted to Gubu had taught him to conceal the condensation of warm breath in cold air by releasing it agonisingly slowly. His body wanted to shiver involuntarily, to raise hairs that might trap a scintilla of warmth, but his trained skin stayed smooth, at ease. He kept his eye glued to the binoculars. The freezing circle of metal burned his cheek; the rubber eye pieces had long perished or been worn away by constant use. Rising condensation began to form ice on his eyebrows. He couldn't have picked a colder night. Only his body warmth kept the water bottle from freezing, but he never moved; his discipline was matchless.

Around three in the morning his stealth was rewarded by the appearance of a leopard walking past him almost within touching distance. He certainly made the grade as a spotter, measured by a harsh environment and judged by a wary critic.

The cat rasped as she walked, her breath ballooning white mist in front of her. When she reached Buffalo Avenue she lay down, making the most of any heat retained in the tarmac. She began to clean herself, licking and purring in the middle of the road. She had hunted, eaten and drunk and was now resting in the warmest place she knew. Sibanda relaxed a little and enjoyed the spectacle. There was no one else around and moving because the leopard was unperturbed and her olfactory skills left his in the dust. The still burning lights from his house picked her out like a spotlight. If she moved then he would begin his surveillance again.

He let his mind slip through the tortured tangle of the case, but oddly it was Lovemore's bruises that kept circling, something about them was familiar. The leopard was finishing her toilet when her ears pricked, she sat and then stood and then ghosted away into the bush as though she'd never been there. Sibanda's eyes strained through the binoculars, scanning Buffalo Avenue for signs of life. He saw someone about fifty metres from his front door walking normally, lips pursed, in a soundless whistle. Could this man just be a night worker returning home? Wasn't it the night shift baker who spotted Lovemore asleep in his garden at about this hour? Sibanda heaved himself up from the tree, his limbs had almost locked, he wasn't getting any younger. At his gate the man stopped, glanced furtively from side to side and lifted the latch.

'Got you,' Sibanda murmured.

The Sparrowhawk was about to take the pathway to Sibanda's door when an elephant bull screamed close by. The piercing, high-pitched trumpet would have impressed hard-blowing Satchmo. Sibanda jumped, where had he come from? The stealth of the giant creatures never failed to amaze him. He watched in frustration as the Sparrowhawk turned and took off down the road in terror. The elephant took off in pursuit. The killer had some speed but the elephant was faster, not yet at full tilt but fast enough to be gaining, and he was angry. Sibanda was after them, running hard, damning the situation as he ran. Would he have to try and turn the elephant away, divert its attention to himself? Sparrowhawk was obviously a novice when it came to wildlife. He was going to get himself trampled. The killer had no choice but to divert into the bush, the elephant hot on his heels.

And then the bull stopped, rocked his front leg from side to side, lowered his head, flattened his ears and rolled his trunk under, the signature prelude to a full-fledged charge, but something changed his mind. Instead, he kicked at the dirt, sending a shower of stones into the air and head butted a fair-sized sapling, ripping it to shreds in a rage of displaced aggression. Sibanda was close enough with the aid of the waning moon to see the cause of his irritation. The bull had been raked down his side by automatic fire and the wounds were suppurating great gobs of blood-streaked pus. Automatic fire didn't produce enough knock-down power to kill an elephant outright, just enough penetration through the thick leathery hide to lead to a slow and agonising death. Sibanda couldn't follow the killer until the elephant moved off. The bull was in pain, incensed and primed to kill anything in his way. The detective cursed the bad timing. Should he make a detour around the elephant and try to bisect the killer's tracks? The chances would be slim at best.

There was no hope at this hour of rounding up a team to search the bush and it would be dangerous with a wounded bull on the rampage and a bunch of amateurs with a stick for protection. He had no choice but to head home until daylight and the elephant headed off to water. The old boy would probably make for the sewage ponds. They were a magnet and a steady supply of water at this the driest time of the year. There, he could wallow and throw cooling mud on his wounds to try and ease the pain. Sibanda was angry, Sparrowhawk had now eluded him twice.

Back at his gate, Sibanda checked the spoor and took note of the footprint. In the house, he put some eggs on to fry and threw a piece of steak in the pan. It had been a while since he ate and tomorrow was another long day. His stomach rumbled and gave a few sharp stabs. It acted as a sort of aide memoire to Lovemore's illness. He left his meal on the table, found a book from a pile on the floor and began to flick through it as he ate. The book, *Forensic Scientist,* by Paul Johnson was tattered and without a spine. His brother Xholisani gave it to him when he was posted back to normal duties. Heaven knows where he had found it, but he thought it might cheer Sibanda up with the weird and interesting crimes covered from the very early days of forensic investigation in Africa. 'See, it won't necessarily be boring,' he said, 'and you might actually enjoy yourself back on the beat.' Sibanda couldn't dispute that, so far there had not been a dull moment. He continued to browse looking for a particular section dealing with traditional and customary crime. As the first light of dawn hovered in a layering of pinks and oranges bleeding to salmon, and clawed its way up from the horizon, he found what he was looking for.

Chapter 25

'Zee, I want Lovemore Moyo's funeral stopped.' Sibanda burst in through the front door of Gubu Police Station.

'But it's today, isn't it?'

'Yes, so we don't have much time. Make sure the body isn't buried before I get back here tomorrow.'

'What's the problem?'

'I want a postmortem done on Lovemore's body. He didn't die from alcohol poisoning or liver failure.'

'A lot of paperwork, sir.'

'I know, but do it and get hold of National Parks, tell them there's a badly wounded elephant bull on the loose, probably hanging around the sewage ponds. They need to kill it before it kills someone.'

'Anything else, sir?'

'Yes, is Ncube here?'

'No one but me, I'm an early bird.'

Sibanda strode off towards his office. 'Nice hair style, by the way.'

PC Khumalo glowed. She didn't think the detective had noticed. He had been so preoccupied and dictatorial, but she didn't mind, she was used to his moods. For three hours last night she had been at the salon getting the weave done and the real Brazilian hair had cost her the best part of a week's salary, but at least it covered her shaved bald spot. She loved the style, it was very glamorous but loose enough to let Sister Angel take the stitches out when the time came. She sighed and wondered who could be sent to the Moyo household to delay the funeral and take charge of the body. She would have to persuade

Assistant Detective Chanza, oh lordy, lord, lord, how could anyone spoil her day so early?

Sibanda glanced briefly through his window at a chinspot batis. It was the female of the family with her rufus chest band and chin spot. The police yard territory belonged to a pair that had probably been here as long as he had and he spotted them often. He'd watched the monogamous duo raise a brood last year. Their nest was a pleasingly built cup, camouflaged with stitched on lichen and built in the fork of a tachoma, more of a bush than a tree, but the largest structure in the police yard. They'd nested late in the year. He'd monitored the two fledglings and watched as the female bossed the male with her constant buzzing call, at which summons he would feed her or the chicks or both on demand. Now there was a bird who understood equality, what would the headman and the *inkundhla* think of that?

In his pocket, as he observed the birds, his fingers played absently with three bright strands of wool found freshly snagged. He had set out early and easily located the spot where the killer dived into the bush to get away from the elephant. The spoor matched the footprint by the gate and the frightened man's feet dug in hard as he sprinted away. Sibanda tracked the Sparrowhawk a couple of kilometres to the burnt out bole of an old *umtchibi* tree. In his panic, the killer probably hadn't noticed he left a marker behind on a thorny Chinese lantern bush, a strand of each colour, red, yellow and purple. He followed him on to the tar road where it was impossible to track him further. The tree he'd cowered in was still alive with some small lifeline of bark remaining to wick up nutrients, but the fire had eaten out the centre of the trunk, leaving a hollow big enough to hide in. The killer had waited out the rest of the night in terror, urinating on the same patch, too scared to leave the protection of his wooden cave. 'So, you can dish it out but you can't take it, Sparrowhawk, interesting to know.'

'Who are you talking to, sir?'

Sibanda hadn't noticed Ncube come into the room, he didn't answer.

'The Santana is all fuelled up and ready to go,' Ncube offered.

'Then let's get on our way. I hope you're all fuelled up too, Ncube, because you're driving.'

The sergeant beamed, this was a good day. He could feel it in his water and in the weight of his lunch box. Sibanda slept all the way to Bulawayo.

'We're almost there, sir, what's our plan?' Ncube noticed Sibanda had stirred. He wouldn't have disturbed him otherwise; the poor man was obviously exhausted.

Sibanda hadn't had time to make a plan. He had barely had time to think straight in the last 24 hours. The development with Lovemore was a complication, and Berry hadn't even been allowed to negotiate a mental synapse. 'Let's take it as we find it Ncube.' They pulled up outside the Universal Dream Offices. 'But I'll take a bet George Paradza isn't in the office yet.'

'How do you know, sir?' Ncube hadn't any intention of betting against the detective. He was always right. He definitely heard him talking to his ancestors when he went into the office.

'Because the Black Sparrowhawk was in Gubu last night and we are going to catch him on the hop.'

As predicted, George Paradza was not in the office, but Betty Khupe was. 'He's often late, particularly if Mr Von Bergen isn't here, sometimes he's not in until lunchtime.'

Sibanda checked his watch. 'It's lunchtime now, we'll wait, thanks Betty.'

A rare smile spread across Sibanda's impossibly handsome face and Betty Khupe felt urges that hadn't bothered her for some years.

Sibanda and Ncube moved into the meeting room, which overlooked the street. Betty provided a tray of tea and Ncube reached down for his lunchbox. His wives had done him proud, given the family's current straightened circumstances. In the middle of the box lay a brown loaf-shaped blob of *amabele* surrounded by a relish of *indlubu* mixed with tomato and onions. The sorghum was traditional Ndebele fare eaten long before the Portuguese introduced white maize. As a hardy annual plant it withstood drought. Ncube wished they had planted more of the tight-seeded, red-headed grass this year. Some called it Zambezi mud, but the brown porridge had a delicious nutty flavour and an interesting speckley texture. The *indlubu* beans too, didn't mind poor soils and minimal water, they flourished on difficult ground. These had been stored in ash to discourage pesky weevils. The mites could eat their way through a village's entire food wealth before you knew it if not kept in check. The beans had been boiled in salted water to a creamy softness, shucked from their hard nut-like shell and mixed with tomato and onion. Ncube reached across and offered the first portion to the detective.

He shook his head. 'I had a big breakfast and I want to focus on the window and George Paradza's arrival.'

Ncube had barely taken his first mouthful when the Universal Dream Land Cruiser pitched up with George Paradza at the wheel. He pulled in behind the Santana and then pulled out again just as swiftly in a scream of burning rubber.

'Ncube, the keys, Paradza's making a run for it.'

Ncube tossed his boss the keys and ran after him. He only just wedged his body into the passenger seat before the Santana was away and speeding down the road in pursuit. Ncube managed to close the door half way through the first intersection. A car that had had its right of way usurped hooted loudly; Ncube felt horribly exposed to the bare-toothed, one-fingered venom of the driver. The Santana was honking loudly, advising pedestrians at zebra crossings not to risk it and vehicles at intersections to stay where they were.

'Sir,' was all Ncube managed to squeak after a particularly close encounter with an overloaded pick-up full of cabbages. The sudden breaking caused several of the wilting vegetables to bounce off down the street, shedding leaves as they went.

'Keep your eyes open, Ncube, and warn me of anything coming.'

The best Ncube could do was keep his eyes at a squint to cut down his vision of impending doom. He wished they had a flashing light and a blaring siren to advertise their chase but Gubu Police didn't run to the sophistication of audio visual alarms. The Land Cruiser was making ground in the distance weaving in and around slower vehicles, causing mayhem with the traffic. Suddenly, Paradza pulled a hard left turn almost on two wheels and disappeared from sight.

'We're losing him, Ncube,' Sibanda slammed his foot down and managed a few extra clicks of speed. The Santana's engine was screaming and Ncube's stomach was moaning in sympathy as Sibanda sped through the next intersection missing a large L-plated truck from the Forever Safe Driving School by the width of a coat of paint. The terrified learner driver's wide eyes never closed for a week and he abandoned all ambitions of becoming a long-distance truckie there and then.

The Santana took the left hand turn with less grace than the Land

Cruiser. It didn't have the same stability and nearly toppled. Ncube was flung against the passenger door, adding his considerable weight to the momentum. The Santana teetered like a lemming on a cliff edge, but righted itself in the nick of time, its two groundless wheels spinning wildly.

'Hang on, Ncube,' Sibanda yelled above the hooter. An unnecessary warning, Ncube had himself wedged and hooked against anything he felt might hold him upright and minimise the wobbling of his flesh slapping around the cab like sheets on a windy washing line.

They raced down the road with no view of the Land Cruiser.

'Where has the bastard gone? We can't lose him Ncube. I won't lose him again.'

'Again, sir, what do you mean?' But there was no answer.

'Be careful this part of town is busy, not everyone can drive like you.' Ncube was oblivious to the irony of his comment, but cars were flashing headlights and the cacophony of irritated hooters was becoming orchestral. It wouldn't do to upset the detective with advice now.

'Never mind, Ncube, keep your eyes on the road.'

'What's happening ahead?' In the distance they could see a commotion. A black saloon car had been clipped by another vehicle and was facing the wrong direction. Men were sprinting down the road followed by a posse of varied taxis and civilian cars.

Sibanda stopped next to a bystander, who pointed to the road ahead. 'Hit and run, some idiot speeding down here in a Land Cruiser nearly caused a serious accident. The guys are after him. He won't get away.' By the time they reached the Land Cruiser about a kilometre down the road it was boxed in by vehicles and surrounded by people. George Paradza had been dragged from the cab and was on the receiving end of a severe kicking and beating.

Sibanda pushed his way through the gathering crowd. 'Police, we'll take over now.' He was in time to hear a bone crunching kick for good measure. Ncube stumbled along in his wake, gas escaping from every orifice in a series of squeaks and gulps; this must be what they call seasickness, his stomach had rolled and twisted like a tub on water, and he'd left Blessing's muthi back at the UD offices.

As the crowd calmed down and backed off, Sibanda picked George Paradza up from the pavement. He was a sorry sight, his suit was shredded and his face was pulp. Blood was streaming from both nostrils, a front tooth was missing and one eye was a swollen purple bulge. He was cradling his ribs. Sibanda didn't condone vigilante behaviour but sometimes it was satisfying and this might just be one of those times.

'Right, George, let's sort this out, shall we, or do you want me to set the crowd on you again? They're pretty angry by the looks of it and they aren't going anywhere.'

Paradza scowled and tried to wipe the blood from his mouth. Sibanda dragged him back to the Santana and cuffed him, 'It's me or the posse George, come clean.'

'I haven't done anything,' he lisped through the new gap in his teeth. 'Okay, I hit that car, but I was in a hurry. Since when has a car accident been a criminal offence?' the last word came out as offenth.

'You'd be surprised, but a dangerous driving charge is the least of your worries. What about the bicycles, George?'

'What do you mean?'

Sibanda leant across him and opened the passenger door. 'You're on your own,' he gestured to the sergeant. 'Ncube, call in the crowd, George hasn't learned his lesson.'

Ncube, examining the Land Cruiser, looked alarmed. He abhorred violence and mob violence was the worst. He took the cue, however, knowing the detective pushed these situations to the limit, but rarely carried out the threats. 'Right sir.'

'No, no,' Paradza's face was a deathly pale, which made his bruises more dramatic. 'I may have taken a couple of bithicles.'

'Your friend Silence Chihuri's creative paperwork shows more, but then you knew we were on to him and we had Biggie Nzimande behind bars, that's why you took off when you saw our vehicle at the UD offices.'

'No ... er ... I just remembered I had an important meeting elsewhere.'

'Really? The crowd don't believe you and neither do I.' The mob was closing in again. Word had it the woman driving the black saloon was injured.

'But it's the truth,' he screamed.

'And Lois Khupe?'

'What about her?'

'You murdered and raped her and skinned her body because she knew what you were up to.'

'No, you can't pin Loith's murder on me!'

'Oh yes we can, George, and she wasn't the first, was she? How many had you murdered before her and what is it with the skin thing? Give you a buzz does it, to strip women naked of their flesh and pitch them off the train like a lump of meat?'

'What … are you mad?'

'No, but you are a sick, warped psychopath, George, with a nail fetish. What were you doing up in Gubu last night?'

'I wasn't in Gubu, I haven't been there since the funeral.'

'Then where were you?'

'At home. What are you accusing me of? I want a lawyer.'

'And you'll get one, eventually, once we've gone over your life with a fine-toothed nit comb.'

With the arrival of a local police contingent, the crowd was encouraged to disperse. Ncube was in conversation with a counterpart, pointing to the Santana and relating the incident.

'Okay, George, let's find you somewhere cosy for the night shall we?' Sibanda said.

With Paradza safely ensconced in the cells at Central awaiting charges, and all inter provincial protocols taken care of, Sibanda and Ncube set off with a local detachment to search his house. The aid worker lived at Nketa, a high density suburb not far from the city, a warren of cheek by jowl houses which gave new meaning to the word proximity. Most were neat and well-kept, although the verges along the roadside were littered with plastic bags, bottles and broken buckets disgorging more bags and bottles, tins and indistinguishable organic matter, a festering heap of fly-blown, rat-attractive, germ-ridden trash. City living had its drawbacks.

George Paradza's house lay at the end of a narrow laneway surrounded by a grey pebbledash pre-fab wall. Sibanda had the keys. He wanted to enter the house alone, get a feel for the way Paradza lived.

'Ncube, deploy these guys to the neighbours, canvas them for any information on George Paradza and his movements. I'll take a look at the house.'

Ncube didn't like the sound of the word canvas. It brought back horrible memories of his night camping in the bush and his war with the tents. Thankfully, one young local officer prompted, 'So, should we get going sergeant, this is a crowded neighbourhood?'

'Right, yes, get to it, and quickly,' Ncube regathered his authority.

Sibanda entered the house. It was the usual three-roomed house, kitchen/diner, bathroom and bedroom. Next to the sink in among a stack of pots and pans lay a lethal-enough-looking knife. He ran his finger down the blade, it was blunt and would barely cut through an onion let alone skin a body. Were the pots from last night's meal? That would put Paradza at home when the Sparrowhawk was hiding in the tree in Gubu.

Sibanda moved through to the bedroom. It was reasonably neat and tidy for a single man. He opened the drawers in a chest squashed between the bed and the wall. The wood had warped but in the bottom drawer after some yanking to open it he discovered three pairs of ladies' panties. The wardrobe yielded nothing of interest; two cheap suits, three polyester shirts, a pair of jeans and a couple of T-shirts, hardly the uniform of a serial killer, no obvious blood stains.

The yard gave up nothing, not even a piece of rusty wire. Sibanda stood in the late afternoon sun, a bag with the panties in his hand, and began to doubt his suspect. To begin with, the panties were a hefty size and none of the victim's descriptions came in as steatopygic. There was nothing woollen in the wardrobe, not a scrap of evidence to tie Paradza to the Sparrowhawk. There had to be another hang out where he stashed the skins and souvenirs, his working clothes and the paraphernalia of his murders. Did Universal Dream have a warehouse or storage facility? He waited for the police team, all the while fingering the strands of wool, all the while realising nothing about this case felt right.

'What have you got, Ncube?'

'No words to set the rooster crowing on the dung heap, just the usual, kept himself to himself, has a girlfriend, new clothes, plenty of money. But he didn't seem to be here overnight. No one saw the UD vehicle in his yard.'

'Gather up the team, I want to go back to the UD offices, Paradza keeps his souvenirs elsewhere.' Ncube couldn't wait to get back to the offices, he had left his uneaten lunch there and his stomach was howling like a jackal in the desert.

They arrived to find most of the employees had left. Betty Khupe was there, picking up papers, emptying baskets and collecting used mugs and plates. 'Did you get him?'

'We did and he's behind bars for now.'

'Good, I hope he rots for what he did to Lois, hanging is too kind for men like him.' She handed Ncube his lunch box. 'You left this.'

'Thanks, mama,' Ncube looked longingly through the clear plastic lid at his lunch and wondered if he could steal a few mouthfuls. 'We're looking for evidence to tie Paradza to the murders. Is there a store room somewhere, or maybe a room only Paradza had access to?'

'There's a lock-up garage at the back, but I don't have the keys.'

'Don't worry Betty,' Sibanda interrupted, 'Ncube is good at breaking locks.'

'Sir,' Ncube protested, as he tried to keep pace with Sibanda's strides across the UD yard, 'you make me sound like an illegitimate.' This was one of several crime-related words in the sergeant's charity shop dictionary. It meant criminal and seemed impressively long as a counter to the insult.

'What? Ncube, I don't give a toss what your mother got up to, now what have you got to jimmy this lock?'

Despite his wives coaching, Ncube's eyes popped, 'Jimmy who? Is he a locksmith?'

'For God's sake, Ncube, just find something to smash this lock.'

Ncube left to fetch the tyre lever from the Santana, muttering with outrage at the insult to the blessed memory of his mother, while Sibanda tried to peer through an old key hole in the door.

Nothing. They stared at the empty garage which held a few non-working printers, out of date computers and quires of old paperwork. The lock had been child's play.

'I don't like this, Ncube. If Paradza is our man, then where has he stashed his cache of skins and the victim's clothes?'

'There must be another location, maybe we should let Paradza out and follow him, hunger lures any fish out of its hiding hole in the river.'

'And you'd know all about that wouldn't you?' Sibanda snapped. He was edgy, this case wasn't coming together. They needed a break, some evidence; they couldn't keep Paradza inside forever without charging him. He'd get bail on the fraud case.

'Maybe Betty Khupe knows of another place if she thinks hard enough?' Ncube offered. Sibanda just nodded.

They made their way back to the office. Betty was locking up. 'I've phoned Mr Von Bergen, he's coming back on tonight's train. He told me to keep the keys. He is shocked Paradza is the murderer.'

'We don't know …' Sibanda stopped mid-sentence. 'Have you been in Gubu recently, Betty?'

'No, not since Lois's funeral and that was my first time there.'

'Then how do you explain this?' Sibanda pulled the three strands of wool from his pocket. They matched exactly the colours and texture of the scarf Betty had around her neck. Sibanda knew he had seen those colours somewhere before, they were hard to ignore.

'I don't know, but I haven't been to Gubu, and see,' she unwound her scarf, 'there are no snags or holes so those bits of wool aren't from me.'

'Sir …' Ncube interrupted, his mind a jumble, where did the wool come from and what had it got to do with the case? This poor woman was too frail and innocent to be a murderer. What was the detective up to?

'Back off, Ncube, this wool came from the bush outside my house. I trailed the Sparrowhawk last night and these strands came from the killer's clothing. So, Betty, have you knitted anything else from this wool, something for a male relative perhaps?'

'No,' Betty was pale and weepy, 'I don't knit, sir, this was a gift from Lois.'

'Lois?'

'Yes, she had knitted herself an identical scarf and I admired it, so she made one for me.'

'Lois had the same scarf as yours? Was she wearing it when she set off back to Gubu on the train?'

'I don't know for certain but she had worn it every day since she made it.'

Sibanda had his hand on his chin and was deep in thought. He'd seen that scarf on someone else; who was it?

Ncube had his arms around the cleaner's shoulders comforting her. 'It's all right, Betty. The detective knows you didn't kill Lois, but he also knows, thanks to you, whoever murdered her took her scarf.' And that was as much as he knew, too. How had the detective linked someone's knitting to a murder? The man was as mysterious as a hedgehog, one minute all spikey and prickly shuffling in the undergrowth, the next, rolled up in a secretive ball. Yes, the name *inhloni* suited him. He had heard him called Chameleon in the station because he could look over his shoulder, eyes swiveling in every direction, solving crimes no one else could even see. Whichever name, the man was a weird creature.

They dropped Betty off at her township home and headed towards Ncube's brother. 'Be up early, Ncube, I want to get back to Gubu tomorrow morning.'

'But shouldn't we wait here in Bulawayo and question Paradza further. He's our man isn't he?'

'He's not our man, Ncube. Paradza would never wear a home-knitted scarf. I checked his wardrobe, not his style. As soon as Central find out where he was last night then I bet his alibi checks out. We are back to square one. No, the answer lies in Gubu. The Sparrowhawk must be a local man.' Ncube's brother lived not far from Betty. Sibanda dropped him off for the night.

'And Ncube, don't waste your time looking for spares for Miss Daisy. She's finished.' The sergeant walked towards his brother's door and never replied. He had already planned a midnight excursion to the CMED yard.

Sibanda headed towards his own brother's house in the leafy eastern suburbs.

'Too long, Jabu, the children don't recognise you.' Xholisani Sibanda grabbed his brother at the door and hugged him.

'Rubbish! Come Lisana, I see you Umkhonto.' Two small children raced from behind their mother's skirts to greet their uncle, squealing as he launched them in the air and chased them down the corridor roaring like a lion.

Later, when they had eaten and he had been chastised by their mother, Thandie, for spoiling them with chocolate bars, she took them off to bed and the brothers chatted over a glass of red wine. 'Time to settle down, Jabu, you are so good with the children, you need some of your own.'

'You wouldn't say that, Xholi, if you had seen me yesterday. I nearly frightened some poor child out of her wits. My sergeant had to rescue me.'

'Yes, but your own …'

'You are as bad as our mother, leave it Xholi.'

'There is someone, isn't there? I can see a change in you.'

'It's complicated, and anyway I'm in the middle of an investigation going nowhere.'

'You mean Mr Police Star is stumped by a mere rural criminal?'

'A serial killer, actually, and four murders at least.'

Xholisani winced. 'Ouch, and no suspects?'

'Plenty of suspects, but no hard evidence. And I'm haunted by the idea I've had him in my grasp and not realised it. Twice, I know I've been close but I couldn't get him. You've read about that Russian, Andrei Chikatilo? They arrested him in 1984 but let him go. He went on to murder another 20 victims. He killed 56 in all, in the most brutal and savage tortures imaginable.'

'Depressing, don't tell me about them. I've got children.'

'Our guy goes for women. He throttles them, rapes them and then skins them. The murders occur on the train. The bodies are thrown in the bush. Chikatilo used the railways as well. People travelling alone are easy meat.'

'I've been reading headlines about some cannibal freak, the Black Sparrowhawk, must be your case. Only you would give a serial killer a bird's name. It's not like you to advertise.'

'My case, but not my journalism – Mfumu grandstanding.'

'Oh right, still giving you grief?'

'He tries. How's the law business these days?' Sibanda moved the topic from office politics.

'A minefield as usual, nothing's changed. A few of us are taking on human rights cases pro bono.'

'Could be dangerous. We're not big on personal freedoms in this country.'

'It's okay, so far it's pretty low profile stuff,' he laughed, 'and you're becoming paranoid.'

'Take care, Xholi, it's no joke, you've got the children to think of.'

Xholisani took a sip of wine and looked away, as if what he was about to say next was trivial. 'You know if anything happens to Thandie or me you are the kids' guardian. It's in our wills.'

Chapter 26

Sibanda took a long time to drop off to sleep despite the glorious quality and generous quantity of the red wine on offer. He couldn't get his brother's words out of his head. He'd always known Xholi would go in for the law, he was a sucker for justice even as a young boy, doling out any treats equally, sharing chores when he could have beaten his younger brother into submission if he had chosen to. What was he getting himself mixed up in?

When his phone rang, Sibanda believed he hadn't even closed his eyes. He was short as he answered it.

'Detective, this is Isaac Manhombo. I'm phoning you from the train. Screaming has been reported and now we appear to have lost a passenger.'

'Someone's missing?'

'Yes, a young woman travelling first class. We've searched the train and there's no sign of her.'

'Where are you?'

'About three hours out of Gubu.'

'Heading south?'

'Yes.'

'Have you stopped at any sidings since the screaming?'

'At Sawmills, and we are just about to stop at Igusi.'

Sibanda cursed again. If the Sparrowhawk had been spooked by all the noise and activity he had already had plenty of opportunity to get off and get away. 'I'll meet the train in Bulawayo. Try and get me the name of the missing passenger.'

'I'll radio Gubu. She got on there. We arrive in Bulawayo around 8 am.'

'I'll be there.'

Sibanda barely slept the rest of the night. He was up at first light, pacing silently, not wanting to wake his niece and nephew. By 6 am he had refused breakfast, had a quick cup of coffee and was on the way to pick up Ncube.

Ncube was awake but bleary eyed. He had been scrounging in the CMED yards for some hours in the middle of the night and he was delighted with his finds – replacement windscreen wipers, it might rain this year; a serviceable door handle, a must if the detective was going to hare around corners, he hated to think how Miss Daisy would have performed on the car chase; a winder for a back window stuck closed since Miss Daisy arrived in Gubu; and the best prize of all, a radiator with cap. After the python had invaded the engine and destroyed the previous cap when they were on the trail of the murdering poachers he'd been obliged to reuse the original, which was so battered it barely maintained any pressure at all. His biggest worry was how to repatriate the finds without Sibanda knowing.

His brother had made a plan with a friend who drove one of the big trucks along the Vic Falls road and on up to the Congo. He would drop the precious parts at Cross Gubu and Ncube would organise with one of the *tshova* taxis to bring the treasures the last 15 kilometres to his house in Gubu. It was good to have a network.

'Why so early, sir?'

'There's been another incident on the train. Isaac Manhombo phoned me in the small hours, someone reported screaming. We're going to round up our detachment from Central and meet the train at the station, check everyone and the carriages. This has got to stop. She has to be the last one.'

'Poor, poor girl. Have they found the body?'

'No, but I've phoned Mfumu. He's agreed to send Chanza along the line this morning to search.'

'In that new vehicle? A delicate butterfly on a rotten cabbage leaf. The rough going will destroy a beautiful thing; it's not a Land Rover. How did you get him to agree?'

'He got the fright of his life when he woke up to nail polish splashed all over his front door. When I explained it's the Sparrowhawk's signature and he knows where Mfumu lives, he caved in. For once the Officer-in-charge wants the right killer behind bars as much as we do.'

They both spent the next few minutes imagining the two-wheel drive pick-up bouncing down the railway easement. At the very least it would return with flattened springs. Ncube had the extra conundrum of the nail polish on Mfumu's door to explore. What did that mean?

Central Police Station was already a hum of activity when they arrived. Bulawayo was no stranger to crime.

'It was you, wasn't it?' A comely woman ran up to Sibanda and began to hit him with a bag; the blows were feeble. 'You took my George into custody. He was with me last night. I swear it on the bible, he was with me.'

Two charge officers emerged from behind a very busy counter and led the shrieking woman away.

Sibanda turned to Ncube. 'Paradza wasn't the murderer because he was in lock-up last night, but, Knut Von Bergen is on that train.'

'But, he's white.'

'All indications are the Sparrowhawk is a black man, but maybe we're wrong. Maybe the man who sent Shalott to buy the nail polish was another decoy. For now, gather the men. I want to intercept the train.'

'The scarf?'

'I'm working on it.'

The police contingent arrived as the train rolled up to the platform. Sibanda knew the diesel engine would be pulling the older carriages, the ones with wood interiors, gutters and a windowed ventilation panel protruding along the top. This was how the Sparrowhawk negotiated his way unseen until he reached the carriage window of his victims and broke in. Sibanda had worked that out when the murderer had escaped him last time he'd been on the train. For a man to risk his life on the top of a speeding train, he must be fit and agile. The Sparrowhawk was turning into a formidable opponent. But it did give Sibanda one advantage; he could manipulate the killer's journeys by dictating which carriages ran on the Gubu route. A plan was forming in his mind. He would lure the Black Sparrowhawk with his favourite prey and set a snare to trap him.

The men from Central questioned each passenger who alighted and searched through every bag, checking for a weapon and the grizzly possibility of human skin. They found nothing of interest, only a small stash of marijuana in the bag of an old Tonga tribesman who had smoked it since it was legal in the fifties, and a set of lethal-looking carpenter's tools in another. Neither gave cause for arrest.

Sibanda personally sidelined Knut Von Bergen for questioning, but he had travelled with his wife, the beautiful Miranda, and his future family. They had been together in their coupe all night. A faint hope anyway. Isaac Manhombo wasn't able to add any extra details. Sibanda had the name of the girl, though, Michelle Woodford. Manhombo carried her back pack, left behind in the compartment. Sibanda checked out her sleeper but there was nothing to suggest violence – just an open window and no blood. If the man skinned the body in here he was a master of the art.

'Where to now, sir, Gubu?'

'Yes, but first I want to visit the line controller's office.'

As they drove back to Gubu, Sibanda would have liked to concentrate on the teak forest lining the road, there were still some magnificent aged specimens despite the ravages of the illegal axes, the stalls of carvings and the neatly stacked cords of wood to tempt the traveller, but his mind was awash with plans. The Sparrowhawk's days were numbered.

Ncube munched away on a pie the detective had bought for him before they left Bulawayo. Despite the extreme flakiness of the pasty, not a single crumb escaped his attention. He wet the tip of his finger and chased each morsel until they all succumbed. When the silence became boring, he searched for conversation and came up with birds again. 'What bird lays its eggs among bones, sir?'

Initially startled, Sibanda was heartened by his sergeant's interest. 'Well, I'm not sure it's a habit, but I've seen a spotted dikkop's eggs in among some old elephant bones.'

'A dikkop?'

'Now known as a thick knee.' He pictured the slender-legged stilt-like birds with large, round nocturnal eyes and couldn't imagine how any classifier came up with such an ugly name. 'They make a basic scrape in the ground as a nest, but they like a marker, a rock or a small sapling, to guide them back to it, so I suppose this pair made use of the elephant bones as their beacon.'

'Interesting,' Ncube warded off a yawn.

'Have you found a nest?'

'I don't know, but an egg fell out of the hand bones we found along the railway line.'

'I doubt it. Dikkops like bare, open ground or very short grass. I've never observed them in stubbly, ploughed up vegetation, are you sure?'

'Yes, and it didn't break when it fell, must be a tough shell.'

'What colour, was it?'

'Cream.'

'Among the first set of bones?'

'Yes, you found the second set, sir, and Chanza the third.'

'So I did, Ncube. Now that is interesting. You may have saved Forensics some work and given me a puzzle to unravel.' Sibanda fell silent again.

Ncube didn't mind what Sibanda unravelled, he was finally communicating with his boss, although what bird's eggs had to do with Forensics he couldn't begin to imagine.

They arrived back late morning to a station in chaos. The radio in the charge office was blaring and bleating, PC Khumalo was manning the desk.

'Oh, sir, thank goodness you are here. Is there fuel in the Santana?'

'Half a tank.'

'It's enough, can I … er, borrow your phone, sir. I've got no money on mine, end of the month, I'm skint and I need to contact Detective Chanza.'

'Use the radio, he's in the new pick up isn't he?'

'The vehicle radio isn't working.'

'Already? It's brand new.'

PC Khumalo wore an alarmed expression as if to say you don't want to know.

'And what's all the drama, have they found the body?'

'No body, they've found a live girl wandering along the railway line.'

'Injured?'

'Just a bit shocked and dazed.'

'Are they bringing her in? I need to question her.'

'They can't.'

'What do you mean, can't?'

'The new car sir, it's it's … oh God, we're in for a rough time. I don't know how to say this.'

'Spit it out Zee.'

'The new vehicle has gone.'

'Gone where? Stolen?'

'No, burnt to cinders. A bushfire overran it where it was parked. Chanza and the guys were all too far away searching. So you see, sir, I need the Santana to rescue them urgently.'

'Has anyone told Cold War?'

PC Khumalo almost collapsed. 'No, not yet, I was hoping …'

'Don't worry, Zee, I'll do it, I need to speak to him anyway.' Sibanda took command, 'Sergeant, take the Santana and bring the girl in. I want her here within the hour.'

Ncube was happy to go. He could only imagine the scene in the Officer-in-Charge's office when he got the news and he didn't want to be around for the rage to follow.

Sibanda made for Mfumu's office.

'Detective Sibanda, you are back with the case wrapped up, I hope. The nail polish on my front door was an assault. If you got on to the killer sooner, then it wouldn't have happened. I don't like it.'

'Not quite. In fact most of our suspects have alibis. You've heard about the incident on the train last night. The killer again.'

'Yes, Detective Chanza is looking for the body.'

'There is no body, the girl is alive. She must have escaped. Sergeant Ncube is bringing her in.'

'Sergeant Ncube, why him, where's Chanza, isn't he out there?'

'Yes, but the new vehicle is no longer available, it's been destroyed in a fire along the edge of the park.'

The ensuing commotion was heard as far as the Blue Gnu. Mfumu's practised oratory muscles were straining and roaring. Regimented pens and pencils were leaping around the desk as his fist pumped down and down on the suffering wood.

Sibanda waited it out until exhaustion took over and the Officer-in-Charge collapsed in his chair, head in hand. 'I am cursed, I am a sparrow that does not flutter, a swallow that does not dart, an undeserved curse has come to rest. I have proved Proverbs wrong, the exception that verifies the word of God.'

Sibanda handed him a glass of water, his throat would probably be raw after all the shrieking. The detective was actually beginning to pity the man.

'It's you!' he said, pointing his finger with renewed energy and venom. 'You've cursed this station, destroyed the new vehicle and put my life in danger and you can't even catch a serial killer. He's running rings around you. You're nothing special after all.' The tirade finished him off, he collapsed again. Even his starched shirt began to crumple.

'You're right, not about the vehicle, but about the serial killer. He's clever, but I have a plan and with your approval I'll have the Sparrowhawk behind bars within a week. It's a promise.'

Mfumu looked up. Sibanda had rather taken the wind out of his sails with his generous admission of failure. As the detective detailed his plan Mfumu's eyes grew wider. You had to give it to the man, he had the arrogance and effrontery of the devil.

'Do you need medical attention, Miss Woodford?' Sibanda was sitting opposite the young woman rescued from the railway line. Despite her ordeal she was remarkably relaxed.

'Call me Michie, everyone does. Nah, bleeding tin-arsed lucky to be alive.'

'Is it okay if I ask you some questions?' Sibanda looked at her finger nails, they were painted red. She was a pretty girl.

'Grateful for your guys coming to the rescue, but I was prepared to hike to the next stop, once I got me senses back.'

'Tell me what happened from the beginning.'

'I've been camping in the park for a few days, hitched a lift from there to the station with a family going to Vic Falls, I was headed on to Bulawayo. I wandered around Gubu, not much to see, if you don't mind me saying, bit of a dump really. Found a nail bar. Can you believe it in a place like this? Not my normal look, but it passed the time. Had a bite at the diner and then headed for the station. I booked a compartment, settled meself in, opened a few tinnys,' Sibanda looked confused, 'you know, a couple of cold ones. Mate, I like Zambesi beer, it's a rare drop. Anyway, like I said, I settled in for the night.'

'And then someone broke into your coupe?'

'Yeah, bit of a light sleeper meself, even with a skin full. Bloke swung in through the window like bleeding Tarzan and the apes – shit, didn't mean anything, him being black like.'

'It's okay, Michie, no offense taken.'

'Right, well, he come in, eyes blazing and launches himself at me.'

'How did you get away?'

'I was brought up on a farm with four brothers, detective, two older, two younger. I'm smack in the middle. You learn to defend yourself quickly or you go down in a heap. There are only so many tears to be shed before you get up and fight back. Taken a few bruises, broken a few bones, skinned a few knuckles, but me brothers learned they couldn't pick on me. I gave as good as I got, bloodied a few noses, blackened a few eyes. No one takes on Michie Woodford and gets away with it.'

'So you hit him?'

'Bloody oath I hit him and screamed me lungs out fit to bust, then he come at me throat. For a minute there I thought I was brown bread, couldn't breathe, me eyes popping out their sockets, so I kneed him in the goolies – not strictly ethnical like. Me dad said he'd clobber me good and proper if any of the boys lost their manhood.'

'And then what?'

'The bastard collapsed in a screaming heap but he was up again in seconds, this time with a knife. I'd earned meself enough time to open the compartment and run. I got as far as the outside door and he was inches away when I opened it and jumped.'

'You were lucky to survive a fall from a train.'

'Nah, practised, always jumping off bailers and tractors, plus the train slowed for some reason, something on the track. I know to jump as far ahead as you can, lessen the impact. I leapt like a 'roo into the unknown. Took the wind out of me, by crickey. Me ankle is twisted and I reckon I wrenched me shoulder, but I rolled, hit soft sand. Nothing a few cold ones won't cure.'

'Did you get a good look at your assailant?'

'Jeez, detective, it was pitch black in the compartment, and he was … black too, but I can tell you one thing, he's a smoker, a real puffing

Billy. Smelt like a bushie, blasted me with a waft of the old Virginia weed, disgusting stuff.'

'I'm sorry this has happened, Michie, you've been a great help and we will catch him.' Sibanda wished he could have been more convincing.

'It's okay, detective, don't apologise, he's just a dipstick, we have 'em in Oz too.'

PC Khumalo took the young Australian down the corridor to a waiting Sergeant Ncube. Together they took her off to the clinic for a once-over with Sister Angel Better. She was staying in Bulawayo with friends and promised to keep in touch with her movements.

Sibanda remained in his office fine tuning his plan. It had to be a good one. The only clues he had to go on now were the Sparrowhawk was an African, scarf-wearing smoker, too vague and if his plan didn't work ...

A blackcollared barbet lured his thoughts away briefly, hammering his brain with a loud repetitive snye-koppe, snye-koppe call. Moments later the bird fell silent and then came into view in aggressive pursuit of another species. Even though this wasn't the breeding season, the barbet still harried his arch enemy, the lesser honeyguide, who haunted the barbet's life and parasitised the family nesting holes. Birds could teach you a lot. He needed to take that unseasonal persistence and track down the Black Sparrowhawk with as much zeal. Time for drastic measures.

Sergeant Ncube and PC Khumalo gathered in his office, having delivered Michie Woodford safely to a reputable bus service.

'We are going to trap the Sparrowhawk and I need your help. I ask for it freely and on a volunteer basis. This strategy is going to be dangerous.' PC Khumalo leant forward, eyes glowing with excitement; Ncube shrank back and felt an ominous rumbling penetrating every sphincter.

'You're going to trust me again, sir, I made such a mess last time?'

'You were brilliant, Zee, you showed initiative and courage. I couldn't ask for anything more.' Zanele Khumalo blushed from the tips of her toes to the singed ends of her expensive weave.

'Are you in?'

'Count me in,' she gushed. Ncube just nodded having been involved in Sibanda's plans before. He was sure there had to be a bigger word than 'danger' to describe the detective's complete disregard for safety. He would have to consult his dictionary.

Sibanda began to describe his plan: 'Two nights from now, Monday, we will all be in Bulawayo to catch the train back to Gubu. We'll travel on it every night from then until we trap the Sparrowhawk.'

'How do we know he won't murder again before Monday?' PC Khumalo asked. Ncube looked at her pityingly, of course the detective knew. Didn't she understand his second sight?

'The Sparrowhawk only kills in the older carriages. The overhead ventilation shaft and gutters offer him a way to manoeuvre between compartments unseen, a way to cling to the top of the train. I've asked the line controller to use the newer carriages until then.'

'What's my role, sir?' Her eagerness was childlike. Ncube stayed silent; he didn't want to know anything of his part in the plot.

'Listen carefully, Zee and then tell me if you still want to go ahead. You are the bait to flush out the killer. You'll travel in a first-class sleeper alone, window unlatched. Sergeant Ncube and I will be in the next compartment. We'll be with you at the first hint of trouble.'

Ncube couldn't stay silent, this was a stupid plan. 'But you will be recognised, sir, everyone in Gubu knows who you are and all the suspects certainly do. The Sparrowhawk will stay away from the train if he sees you on it.'

'I'll be in disguise, Ncube.'

'But what about the sergeant, sir? He is just as visible as you in this village, possibly more so.'

'Oh, I have a great disguise planned for him. Not even his own children will recognise him. We'll travel to Bulawayo separately so as not to alert anyone watching. Zee, you'll take the bus and Ncube, you can safely go by train.'

'And you, sir?'

'I'll make my own arrangements. Now go home and have a relaxing weekend. I'll meet you in Bulawayo on Monday. And Zee,' he called as she was leaving the office. 'I just have one other task for you.'

Sibanda closed up the office and walked towards the nail bar. Thula was behind the counter, face in a book, she smiled when she saw him. 'Detective, you've come back for a manicure.'

'Sadly, no, but I've come to pay for someone else. She'll be in tomorrow.'

Thula tried not to let her face drop, tried to hide the jealousy gnawing her innards. The detective had a girlfriend and why not, he was a man among men. Every girl must lust after him. Even though she knew he could never be hers she didn't like the idea of him belonging to anyone else. 'Anything special?'

'Yes, the works, give her the longest most glamorous blood red nails on offer.'

CHAPTER 27

Berry was driving, she had borrowed her dad's Hilux. She remembered something the nice sergeant had said about Jabu driving like a maniac.

'So where have you booked us in?' she asked.

'A lodge in the Matopos. It's not far from Bulawayo and I have to be in town on Monday.'

'Criminal business?'

'No, just some police procedure course. Are you sure you don't want me to drive?'

'Nope, I'm fine for now,' she smiled at him. For the first time ever they were having trouble chatting. With no spontaneous laughter, the silences grew longer. When they did talk it was both together.

'Sorry–'

'No you go–'

'It's okay.'

Sibanda felt the tension was worse than any stake-out, worse than waiting for the serial killer to strike, 'Berry, this is ridiculous, where are we going?'

'To the Matopos, of course.'

'You know that's not what I meant.'

She pulled over, off the road and into the shade. The road was deserted. It was just the two of them and the vast Matabele canvas, painted with the voices of a thousand warriors, brushed by a royal dynasty and spattered with the hard-earned dust of a million hoes furrowing the implacable land. The winter wind whispered these images as they caught each other's eyes in truth at last.

'I'm going wherever you want me to go, Jabu. I've been waiting for you forever and if now is not the moment, if there's someone else ...'

She didn't finish, he kissed her, tenderly at first, but then harder as he understood it was Berry's lips responding to his and Berry's arms holding him tight.

When they broke apart, they laughed, her blue eyes were brimming, his heart was pounding.

'Berry,' he started, 'my job is demanding, I can't promise ...'

'Shh ...' she put her fingers to his lips, 'I don't care, let's live in the now and talk about the what ifs later.'

The rest of the journey to the lodge seemed an age. Berry wished she had let him drive so she could cuddle under his armpit and gaze up at his chin and at those lips that delivered on every promise they advertised.

They barely listened to the booking-in procedures at the lodge, the meal times and the touring options. Their voyage of discovery had been long in the waiting and it didn't involve sightseeing.

'Where did you disappear to after Nottingham, Jabu?' she asked, as she lay in his arms glowing with the ache of lovemaking. They had hardly made it through their chalet door, 'I looked for you.'

He kissed her on the top of the head, and ran his fingers through the shining silver tangle of hair. 'It's complicated, I'll tell you one day.'

She hung onto the words, 'one day'. It meant there would be other days and nights like this one.

'Come,' he said, 'time to go for sundowners and dinner.'

'I'd rather stay here.' Her cheeky grin almost convinced him.

'No, let's at least take in this glorious scenery. The night will come soon enough.'

'Okay,' she conceded, 'but one last question before I race you to the shower and then I won't pester you again.' She stared hard at him, her blue eyes serious and wide. 'Why did you take so long?' She would make a good interrogator, and he wasn't sure if she would see through him, through his past kept firmly locked away and through the half-truths he was about to tell.

'You gave me no reason to pursue you and then I was tied up with work and you had Barney and I was engaged.'

'Barney Jones?'

'You never stopped talking about him in England. I thought he was the one.'

She burst out laughing. 'He was a teenage fling, you're not jealous are you?'

He wasn't completely honest with her, nor would he ever be. The race issue was one he fought to overcome. His mother would never forgive him if he came home with a white girlfriend. She was old-school Ndebele, you married someone from your own tribe. You could play away, but a serious relationship was in-house and traditional. Miscegeny was ingrained in the Sibanda family from childhood. He didn't want to mess with Berry. He respected both her and her father, but he would have to see where the relationship went and face any consequences down the line. He was already spinning lies; not a good start.

When he had booked the lodge, Sibanda had organised a bush dinner – a romantic table for two on top of the rocks, candlelit, with a campfire nearby would be wooing enough. He smiled, he hadn't needed it. The sun's final rays blessed the tumble of boulders and windswept domes and while a pair of black eagles brushed the mountains, Sibanda and Berry, alone in the vast, spiritual theatre of granite, stood arm in arm around the fire sipping wine.

'This will be my favourite spot forever,' she said. 'Thank you for this, Jabu.' She turned and kissed him, sealing the words and the promise of a night of fever.

Berry dropped him off at his brother's house in the afternoon that Sunday. 'I wish I could stay, Jabu, but I have to teach.'

'And I have work.'

They shared a long kiss before she drove away reluctantly.

'There's trouble, my boy,' his brother nodded towards the disappearing car and voiced the elephant in the room as they met on the verandah.

'Leave it Xholi, it's not up for discussion.'

The following morning the trio gathered at Central for a briefing. Zanele Khumalo with her smart hair and long nails looked every bit the vamp. Sibanda noted she was not shy to put her manicure on show, splaying her fingers on the desk, resting them coquettishly on her cheek, punctuating her conversation with hand gestures. The nails were certainly going to be noticed. He just hoped the Black Sparrowhawk got a glimpse of them.

'Make your own way to the station tonight, Zee and don't make eye contact with either Ncube or me at any stage, ignore us completely. Here's your ticket. We will be in the next compartment. Scream as loudly as you can if anyone comes near the compartment. Now go home and sleep for the rest of the day, I want you alert and awake all night.'

'Thank you, sir. I hope I don't let you down this time.' She walked away from the station having all her plans in place. She would wear her best clothes on the train to attract the killer, and get a taxi to the station. The business card for Tixi Taxis rescued from the Gubu Police Station floor would be perfect. She would ring up and get collected, that would startle her aunty with whom she was staying. No crushed and rickety commuter taxi for her, why not travel in style? She had been given the allowance to do so.

'Should I go home and sleep too, sir?' Ncube found the thought rather delicious. He could eat and sleep his way through the day in an empty house with no children to pester him. This trip could turn into a sort of holiday.

'No, Ncube. You and I are going to trawl through local mug shots to see if anyone rings a bell and then later we have an appointment at the theatre.'

The mug shots proved fruitless. The Sparrowhawk was not on any record. They got a lift down to the theatre with a crew heading for the evening shift road block duty. Sergeant Ncube had never set foot in a theatre in his life and was nervous about what to expect. 'What are we doing here sir?'

'Getting our disguises. Mrs Warner, my ex-English and drama teacher from Marula Tree School, has agreed to help us.'

'I thought we'd just put on a hat or a heavy coat or even a scarf like the Sparrowhawk?'

'Ncube, nothing that simple is going to camouflage your fine figure.'

'So what are we dressing up as?'

'I will be an old man and you, Ncube, will be my wife.'

'What! I … No, I refuse, the shame ... a woman? Never. I'm sorry sir but I withdraw my volunteering.'

'Ncube, it's the perfect disguise and no one will ever know, it will be our secret.'

'But PC Khumalo will know,' he wailed, 'and she's got a mouth as big as a barbel. She can spread gossip faster than a Ferrari.'

'Ncube get a grip. You're getting this makeover.' Sibanda grabbed him by the arm and frog marched him towards the back of the stage.

Mrs Warner certainly knew her stuff. Not only did she apply make-up and costumes but she made the pair practise their walks and mannerisms over and over again.

'Too upright, Jabulani, I see you haven't lost those muscles, bend over more, shuffle and lean on the walking stick. I always said you should have gone in for the theatre.'

Ncube watched the detective getting a telling off to which he was responding meekly. It gave him some comfort.

'Right, Ncube, legs together, shorter strides, less swinging of the arms and don't grab at things, pick them up gently. Get to it!'

'I can't, I really can't do this.'

'Yes, you can. Roll more, sergeant, that's the way,' she bellowed, in her jolly hockey sticks voice.

Ncube felt he was back in school with a very demanding teacher. The headscarf she tied, much like his wives', low on his forehead and knotted at the back was so restrictive he could hardly hear and the earrings Mrs Warner made him wear were squeezing his lobes like the pincers of a scorpion, but he had to admit the elasticated waistband of the long and voluminous skirt flapping around his ankles was more comfortable than his uniform trousers and the blouse, while colourful, was very loose. Nonetheless he felt ridiculous. If they asked him to carry a handbag, he would absolutely resist. Somehow Sibanda with white hair and wrinkles looked distinguished and gentlemanly. Trust him to come out of this almost looking better than when he went in.

After a further hour or so of repetitive coaching, she said, 'You two won't be winning any Oscars, but I daresay you'll pass muster. Your homework is to walk around the streets for a couple of hours, get used to the role and see if you can avoid discovery.'

Sibanda knew they had delivered when they hobbled past the roadblock detail that had dropped them off three hours earlier without a second glance. He checked his watch as though he was short sighted, squinting and tipping the face towards the light. 'No phone, this generation still wears watches. Time to move towards the station.'

'Are we going to walk all that way, sir?'

'No more, "sir", Ncube. Call me Joseph and try and speak in a higher voice.'

'And I suppose that makes me Mary,' Ncube rarely attempted a joke but he was beyond caring, walking brazenly down the streets of Bulawayo in a skirt and a headscarf, swinging a large brown handbag and twittering like a woman was going to be humiliating. He expected sniggers at every corner.

'What about Precious as a name for you? And yes we'll walk. We'll work up a nice sheen of authenticity on the way.'

Joseph and Precious made their way to the station without a second glance from the people they passed. Mrs Warner knew her art well. The station was already crowded with travellers when they arrived. Joseph and Precious blended in perfectly as a bewildered rural couple on their way home from a city they barely comprehended.

Zanele Khumalo flounced out of the taxi, flashing the nails she was so proud of as she paid the driver.

Richard Ngulube watched her walk away. He lit a cigarette and took a long and considered drag. The urge was becoming irresistible; it was building again, pulsing around his body and itching like a thousand maggots wriggling through his blood. The urge to scratch viciously, to tear the skin from his own body was insatiable; he craved the long nails that would give him relief. Two of the last bloodsuckers got away by kneeing him, the bitches, but he had that covered now. He hadn't played cricket for nothing. In his bag of tricks was a new addition, an abdominal protector, a box, in cricket parlance. It sat next to the skinning knife, sharp as a razor, his pliers and wire and the rolled-up plastic sheeting to keep all the mess contained until it could be salted and prepared for his own personal trophy room. He took the bag from the boot and slammed it shut.

What would she think of him now, the woman who brought him up in a brothel, made him watch her tricks, rented him out when the men wanted something new and fresh? He watched her raking her talons along the backs of men, faking her passion, belonging to no one.

'I want a baba, why don't I have a father, can't you choose just one of the men?' he once asked, and she scorned him, dug her nails into his arms and slapped him, screaming in his face, 'No man will own me and when your time comes, you will own no woman. Who will stay with you, you snivelling little shitbag?' But he owned them all, married them. They didn't all agree to begin with but in the end they were begging him for commitment, promising themselves to him forever with tears of joy. What would she think if she were alive? He was almost sorry she had been his first killing. She could have witnessed his triumph. He was sorry, too, he hadn't taken all her skin to caress on dark days and to talk to when the urges came and were satisfied. He only had a small patch from the inside of her thigh. And soon there would be another trophy to hang in his wardrobe.

Are you proud of your son, mama dearest?

PC Khumalo mingled with the waiting travellers and sauntered along the platform as instructed. She expected to see Detective Sibanda and Sergeant Ncube and it would have been comforting to catch a glimpse of them. What if something had happened and there had been a change of plans, or they missed the train? She glanced again at her phone for messages. It was worryingly empty. She used her long red nails to access an itchy patch on her scalp caused by the pulling of the tight weave and the healing of her cut; the only thing they were practical for, she mused. Her focus otherwise was absolute, no mentally wandering off this time. She might get more than a brick over the head.

Joseph and Precious sat tucked away on a bench, nibbling from packages they had bought on their way to the station. Precious produced them from her handbag from time to time. They appeared to chat together amicably. Precious spent much of the waiting looking downwards or eating while Joseph looked up from time to time to scan the faces of the passengers, showing little interest. Sibanda hoped to recognise someone. The Sparrowhawk was vaguely familiar, the scarf and the smoking swirled in his head.

'Off again, are you, didn't I see you here last week?' The ticket seller asked.

Richard Ngulube hesitated for a moment, taken aback, and then replied, 'Yes, my mother is sick, taken a turn for the worse. Gubu is home.'

'Gubu? Never been there myself. What's it like?'

'It's okay if you like elephants.'

The man laughed and he gave Ngulube his third class ticket. 'Not for me then.'

He supposed Gubu was 'home' if anywhere was. He had even worked there for a while in the safari industry as a labourer. He watched the skinners closely. His mother used to drag him back to Gubu once a year to stay with her gogo. Her own mother disappeared to South Africa years ago. No one heard from her again, gogo brought her up. Did the old woman ever know what a whore her granddaughter was?

He loved his gogo, she was the only one who showed him any affection. After he killed his own mother, he went home to her. It seemed natural. She comforted him. Little did she know the elation and release that swept over him. Gogo didn't last long after the shock find of the body, the mutilation and the diagnosis of murder. He was sad she went to her grave in mourning.

Some years ago when he first started to haunt the trains, Richard discovered a spot on the platform at the very end that shielded him from the masses but gave him a view of those catching the train. There was a perfect hidden position in Gubu too. From there he could pick out his next wife for their brief but very exciting marriage. He didn't need to spot a candidate this time, because she had phoned and ordered his cab. He could see her now on the platform, her silver jacket made her stand out like the whore she was. Soon those arrogant, confident eyes would be professing eternal love for him. He watched as the train pulled in; the carriages were the ones he preferred. Sometimes, if the carriages were the wrong sort, he had to abandon his marriages and then the itch and the pounding drove him to distraction, even the whores on Samuel Parinenyatwa Street gave him no satisfaction. But tonight, perfect conditions had collided, tonight was written in the stars. His target made towards the first- and second-class sleepers as he knew she would, third-class passengers walked or took *tshovas*.

'Come on, Precious, remember to roll now and take my arm; pretend you like me at least.'

Ncube wanted to explode or run away and hide but he swallowed his indignation and made a fair imitation of an old lady walk, muttering as the pair hobbled to their carriage.

PC Khumalo had already boarded. She entered the compartment, stowed her bags and realised for the first time since she left Gubu the seriousness of the situation. There was no sign of Sibanda and Ncube, despite a few surreptitious glances to look for them. Ncube would be impossible to miss. She was on her own, but never considered abandoning her mission. PC Zanele Khumalo was made of sterner stuff; hadn't the detective called her brave and resourceful? Well, she would show everyone just how quick-witted she was, and anyway, the Sparrowhawk was probably not on the train. It might take several days to lure him out of hiding.

What she hadn't taken into account was the animal cunning and strength of her stalker, nor was she aware she had already met him and sealed her fate.

Chapter 28

The sidings slid by one by one, the train dropped off passengers on its way north and picked up a few extras. The night grew colder, flirted with freezing. The old carriages were draughty and Zanele Khumalo pulled a blanket from the made-up bed and wrapped herself up. She hadn't slept all day as the detective suggested, but had gone to town with her cousins whom she hadn't caught up with for ages. Once home, they chatted, and when she did try and sleep the family news bubbled in her brain like a caffeine fix.

In the adjoining compartment, Joseph and Precious exchanged speculation on the killer while listening intently for any disturbance from next door. After an hour, Sibanda walked down the corridor, stretching to ease the muscle cramps of the aged, halting briefly outside Zanele's door. At Sawmills siding, he stepped out again, feigning interest in the comings and goings of the passengers on the platform. If the killer was on board he would have to act soon. Murder, rape and skinning were a couple of hours' work. The bodies had been thrown from the train between the Ingwe and Isilwana sidings, between the leopard and the lion, some irony. This meant the killer had to make his move in the next two hours.

PC Khumalo put down the magazine she had been flicking through and closed her eyes, just for a moment, she promised herself. Sergeant Ncube, bored with the detective's conversation and speculation, let his head drop onto his comfortable, cushioning jowls; Richard Ngulube shifted from his hard bench in third class and walked towards the toilets at the end of the carriage, his bag slung over his shoulder. He watched the waddling madam get into compartment number 5. He knew it well, that's where he'd caught the stupid nun. Of course she wasn't a nun, she was a whore in disguise. What nun painted her finger nails? A particularly satisfying marriage, she prayed for him on her knees. He liked the white skins for the startling contrast they made against the black ones, all hanging together in his wardrobe like beautiful gowns.

The taxi driver made his way to the exit door. At the next siding, a small one, he slipped out and onto the roof, unseen in the dark and the turmoil of the station. Within ten minutes his adventure would begin. He took deep breaths to calm himself, the excitement was taking over, a steady hand and cool head were essential to negotiate the carriage roof and break in through the window.

Sibanda stared at the passing bush. The moon was high, half full and sprightly. Visibility was fair and the night was as sharp as an icicle.

Ncube was asleep, breathing deeply. The detective kicked him in the shins. 'What's happening?' the sergeant mumbled through a mouth sticky with drool.

'Nothing, but stay awake. If the Black Sparrowhawk is on the train, then his time is coming.' Ncube sat up and began a regimen of pinching himself through his skirt; staying awake in the swaying carriage was a torment beyond imagining. When the door rattled, he was gratified to note the detective jumped nearly as high as he did.

'Tickets, open up please.'

'I'll do the talking, Ncube.'

'Sorry to disturb, I missed you earlier. You haven't had the beds made up yet, do you want me to send for the attendant?' Isaac Manhombo asked.

'No, we can manage and it's only …' Joseph examined his watch with myopic artistry in the dark carriage, '… 9:30. Oh goodness, it is late. Precious, dear, it's time to sleep.'

Precious just nodded. Joseph fumbled with his tickets, searching his pockets and slapping the empty ones. 'Here they are,' he sounded relieved, as though his memory failed him, or he had misplaced the vouchers.

Manhombo clipped the tickets. 'Better get the blankets out. It's going to be a freezing night.'

'We will, thank you.'

Ncube was amazed, the detective truly was a chameleon. He had fooled Isaac Manhombo completely. If he could fool him then the Black Sparrowhawk would never recognise them.

'Did you hear anything, Ncube? Manhombo was talking loudly. I heard a sound next door.'

'No, nothing. Isn't PC Khumalo going to scream if the killer comes?'

Sibanda put his ear to the panel separating the compartments.

Richard Ngulube swung in through PC Khumalo's window with consummate ease. She hadn't even locked it, the stupid bitch, which meant he could slide the window down and use the inside rail to grip on. She didn't even wake. He had the duct tape out of his pocket and around her mouth before she could open her eyes. He did fumble for a brief moment. His fingers, despite the tight gloves, were freezing. It had been a difficult crawl into the knifing wind. After this one he would wait for the warmer weather. The whore managed a moan, but he sealed the gap tightly before any more noise escaped.

Now that her wrists were taped, the ceremony could begin. Once the wedding ring was on he would take the customary patch of skin from her inside thigh. That's when the real fun began, when they started their pleading. He could hear them even through the tape, it was amazing what sounds the human nose could produce. He liked tradition. The excitement all started with the square of thigh skin. Over the years, he'd sewn the patches together, hoping for a full chessboard one day, right now he only had one row. He sighed, picked up the pliers and wire and looked into the terrified round eyes of the next castle square. 'Do you, whore, bitch, *amawuli* agree to be my wife? Just nod, no, no, don't shake your head,' he whispered, producing his knife. 'Now, I'm asking you nicely to be my wife, you agree, don't you?'

PC Khumalo nodded, trying to erase the terror. How was she going to attract anyone's attention? Why had the detective and the sergeant missed the train? Why had she gone to sleep? The questions buzzed as he took her hand and kissed her red nails one by one. He wrapped wire tightly around the ring finger on her left hand and then took the pliers to tighten the band, 'you can't take this off and throw it away; you are mine forever, sealed to me only. I own you,' he purred with menace. The pain in PC Khumalo's finger was excruciating as the blood pooled at the end, unable to escape and circulate. With the pain came tears. The killer kissed them away and placed a sheet of plastic on the floor. 'Don't cry, this is a wonderful, happy time for us. Now we start the honeymoon. Open your legs, my darling whore. I just need a little sample of the wares. He pushed her knees and held them apart with his. But no man sampled PC Khumalo's wares without PC Khumalo's consent. The pain gave way to anger.

'Ncube, I can hear whispering next door,' Sibanda was alert.

'Probably PC Khumalo talking to herself, she does it all the time.'

'Listen, can you hear something?' Sibanda didn't want to blow the operation by exposing his position too soon and scaring off the killer, but he was becoming increasingly tense.

PC Khumalo strained to close her legs, wriggled on the seat to get rid of the Sparrowhawk and then she kicked out. Her legs flailed in the air, she tried again, this time the pliers resting on the killer's thigh flew off and struck the window. The Sparrowhawk ignored her struggles, continuing with his torture. The knife went into her thigh. He began to slice.

When the plans had been formulated, it was agreed PC Khumalo would leave her door unlocked. When the detective never got on the train, she locked it.

Sibanda, ear to the panel, heard the chinking noise of metal on glass. He flew towards the door, shouting at Ncube, 'There's someone in Zanele's compartment. He's here.' He cursed when he found the next door compartment locked. 'Open up,' he shouted and shouldered the heavy door, but it didn't budge.

'Here, sir, let me.' Sergeant Ncube didn't have a run up, but he didn't need it. With the first hit, the door splintered, it gave more on the second and the lock broke away on the third. Ncube fell into the sleeper and sprawled on the floor. Sibanda hard on his heels, took in the scene, PC Khumalo, trussed and bleeding, the Sparrowhawk disappearing through the window.

'Look after Zanele, Ncube,' Sibanda shouted, as he used the sergeant's back to springboard himself onto the safety bar and through the window. The icy air hit him like a pounding blow from a mattock and took the wind from his lungs. He grappled up onto the roof, swinging himself up using the guttering. In the moonlight he could see the killer ahead of him making progress towards the back of the train. No one could have gone forward against the force of the wind. The Sparrowhawk was well ahead and had home ground advantage. Each inch of progress for Sibanda was trial and error as he felt for finger holds, but the roof was smooth. If the Sparrowhawk reached the guard's van ahead of him, it would be game over. A ladder ran down the back of the van and the Sparrowhawk could slip down onto the rails and into the bush. He'd get away with some gravel burn at worst. The only way for Sibanda to catch the fleeing killer was to stand up on the roof and hope his balance held. The train was running on the Gwaai straight, 116 kilometres of dead straight track that once held the world record, at least there would be no surprises. The Sparrowhawk was looking over his shoulder and Sibanda could almost read his features and sense the killer's relief as he saw the detective was not gaining. Sibanda had to stand soon, his fingers lost all feeling and his grip was weakening. He hauled himself onto his knees but the blast from behind pushed him forward onto all fours. He crawled for a few metres but crawling was never going to get him closer to the snake ahead. The murderer was slithering along like a commando. Slowly, Sibanda was beginning to get a feel for the pressures acting on his body, for the wobble of the train and the gait and stance he needed to adopt and then the Sparrowhawk disappeared at the end of the carriage.

For a moment Sibanda thought his foe had ducked back inside the train, but he had climbed down, inched across the coupling and up again onto the next carriage. The detective staggered along like a drunk, each foot placed with exaggeration, arms wide for balance, silhouette crouched to minimise the impact of the following wind. Suddenly, he saw a way to make significant progress. Some metres before the gap, he ran and leaped across the break in carriages, hoping his schoolboy long-jump skills hadn't rusted, making the distance easily because of the speed of the train passing underneath him, but he misjudged the impact of the landing, slipped, tried to grip the roof lights, failed and slid over the side of the carriage.

The Sparrowhawk glancing back, saw his pursuer disappear over the edge and laughed. But Sibanda had not fallen. In desperation, his fingers lunged at the guttering running along the edge of carriage, the very guttering that had alerted him to the Sparrowhawk's escape route. He held on by his bloodless, freezing fingertips. His body swayed and bounced against the side of the train as the wind forced him almost horizontal, clawing at his grip, sucking every ounce of strength. Beads of sweat broke out on Sibanda's forehead as he struggled to maintain his hold. Trees flashed by in the moonlight; if he were flung off the train then he would break his back on impact.

Slowly, using every arm and wrist muscle he could muster, he clawed his way back until he had enough purchase to swing himself back onto the roof. The killer made more progress, slow and steady, but Sibanda knew the crawling method was no longer an option for him. He had to make up the distance lost. Standing again, he jumped over the next coupling, bent his knees and landed as though he lived his life as a gymnast. He was gaining on the Sparrowhawk and when the killer slithered down the space between the last carriage and the guard's van, Sibanda knew he had him. As the Sparrowhawk emerged from the well and climbed up to the next carriage roof, Sibanda leapt on him and delivered a punch that carried the weight of disgust, of retribution for the death of so many girls, for the trouble the killer put him to and for his own failure to catch the Sparrowhawk sooner. He never felt the impact, his hand was already numb. The killer retaliated with a punch of equal venom and somehow managed to roll and pin the detective under him, putting practised hands around Sibanda's throat, thumbs exerting lethal pressure on his larynx.

'You won't catch me, you're done for, detective,' the killer gloated.

Sibanda's lungs were screaming. Deprived of air, he gasped, but with one swift outward thrust of his arms he broke the strangler's hold. The Sparrowhawk darted away; Sibanda grabbed him by the ankle but the killer kicked accurately and hard in the detective's face. For a moment, blood streaming from his nose, tears of pain clouding his eyes, Sibanda feared he would roll off the roof again.

It was touch and go before he managed to stop himself near the edge, this time by hooking his left leg and left arm against the guttering. The Sparrowhawk was upright and making for the back of the guard's van. Sibanda caught him before he reached the ladder. The two men wrestled on the train roof. Sibanda manoeuvred the killer into the face of the wind where breath was hard to draw and the driving wind was an ally. They clung to one another for balance, swinging from side to side in a deadly waltz until Sibanda deftly tripped the killer with a wrestler's swipe to his ankle and landed on top of him. He punched again and again. When his rage subsided, a brightly coloured knitted scarf came into focus and he finally recognised the features that had been staring him in the face for some days.

'Richard Ngulube, the taxi driver, you bastard!' he shouted above the howling wind, and pummelled the killer harder. But Richard wasn't giving up yet, his powerful, murderous hands dug into Sibanda's biceps and, with the aid of his foot, he rolled the detective over his head so their positions were reversed. Sibanda fell hard on his back, winded. The Sparrowhawk added to the pain by planting his feet on the detective's solar plexus and heading off for the back of the guard's van.

In seconds, Sibanda was up after him, struggling to breath. Sprinting across the roof was foolhardy and risky as the train sped through the night, but he had no option. Richard Ngulube reached the ladder. Sibanda leant over as he climbed down and grabbed him by the wrists. The train began to stop, screeching hard on the rails, exploding sparks into the night sky.

'Give up, Ngulube, you can't get away now.'

'You'll never get me, Sibanda. I'm the Black Sparrowhawk and I've got nothing to lose.' And he launched himself upward, still gripping the rungs, and head butted his captor, catching him across the bridge of his already damaged nose.

Sibanda's head snapped backwards and blood spattered from his nostrils like the sparks from the rails. He let go of the killer's wrists. The Sparrowhawk jumped the rest of the way, landed on the track and headed for the bush.

Sibanda could barely see through watering eyes and the pain shafting up through his head. He swiped the blood mixed with grease paint from his nose and set off after the killer, sliding down the ladder. Now, he was in his comfort zone; the bush was as familiar as the back of his hand. He was already picking up scents, signs and tracks as he ran. There were buffalo in the area; he could smell their acrid sweat and the grassy smell of their dung. It was important to keep Richard Ngulube running and panicked. If he stopped and hid under a bush or behind a tree, the odds of Sibanda finding him were remote. Right now the sounds of the Sparrowhawk crashing through the bush made him easy to follow, the moonlight allowing glimpses of him in open patches.

A whistle to his right alerted him to the presence of Sergeant Ncube and he caught a flash of flowing skirts. Given the sergeant's terror of the bush during the day, he appreciated the bravery of his following him at night. The sergeant could never keep up, but he may come in handy. Sibanda was hurdling fallen logs, running past thorn bushes and whipping branches but he was gaining.

And then he heard the buffalo, close, a mix of low moaning, grunts and clicking horns and hooves. Richard Ngulube was going to spook them unless he could shepherd him away from the back of the herd and move him around to the front so that he was running towards them, so they had his wind. He might trap him, leave him nowhere to run but back.

He began by picking up logs, anything he could find and throwing them off to his left. As predicted, Ngulube, hearing the sounds, began to veer right. Not too far right because Sergeant Ncube was crashing through the bush, like an elephant in full flight, his skirts flying. Sibanda called to him. 'Keep coming Ncube, stay on the track you're on.'

'I'm not far behind you, sir,' he gasped.

'Perfect, we'll have him soon.' The shouted conversation was entirely for the benefit of the killer so he would know which way to flee. As predicted he was now running parallel with the herd, completely oblivious to their presence. Sibanda sprinted, ran behind the Sparrowhawk and took over his right flank. Soon the herd was behind them and the detective was herding the killer back towards the front phalanx of the buffalo, calling continuously to Ncube and a band of fictitious chasers. He expected Richard Ngulube to stop and turn when he understood what was ahead but the Sparrowhawk was panicked and tiring. He knew little of the bush or the behaviour of animals. He fled headlong into the herd. The moonlight glinted off the horns in flashes of golden fire, highlighting the lethal points and sturdy shafts of the most treacherous of adversaries.

'Stop where you are, Ngulube. A buffalo herd is ahead, you're in danger.'

'I'm not scared,' the killer called over his shoulder, 'you won't fool me with tricks.'

'Don't risk it, don't be a fool.'

'You're the fool, Sibanda.'

The buffalo agreed with the detective, they had been harried all the previous night by a pride of lions, one of the cows had been raked down her flanks and a bull had his tail tugged off, a strange creature hurtling into their midst was the last thing they would tolerate. When danger presented, bulls filtered to the front of the herd. It was their tried and developed defense strategy. A large and particularly cantankerous specimen already in the vanguard charged the incoming threat head on.

Richard Ngulube finally turned and tried to escape, but he was too slow and the bull hooked him through the groin, tossing him high in the air like a winter leaf on an updraught. He screamed, a high-pitched, piercing shriek of pain and terror.

Sibanda cursed and swore. The Sparrowhawk didn't deserve the risk he was about to take but he had to try and get to him or distract the herd. The detective moved forward but a young bull looking for swank and status came at him, head down, snorting nostrils shining in the moonlight. Sibanda leaped aside at the last minute, arching his back, a matador without the cape. The young and steely horn missed him by a whisker. The detective found cover behind a large acacia. An older bull took an interest and came at the tree, veering before he struck the bole. Sibanda dodged to the other side. Several other buffalo looked in his direction; he would have to make a strategic retreat before they all stampeded. He edged back, never taking his focus off the restless herd, moving from tree to tree with an eye to low branches in case he had to climb out of danger.

'What's happening, sir?' Ncube finally arrived, puffing and gasping. His race was run. He was bent double with his hands on his hips, sucking in huge breaths, his skirt in shreds.

'Buffalo, Ncube, the Sparrowhawk has flown straight into the herd.'

'Is there nothing we can do?'

The Sparrowhawk was tossed again, the horn piercing and ripping his stomach. The herd milled and bellowed in triumph. The Sparrowhawk lay silent and winded, spilling his intestines over the ancient sands.

'No, Ncube, Richard Ngulube has made his choices. We can't get to him, not without a weapon.'

'Did he make choices, sir?'

Sibanda looked sharply at his sergeant. Was he becoming philosophical?

'We all make our beds, Ncube.'

Ncube glanced at the detective. There were depths to this man he would never plumb and an unknowable past, but he witnessed bravery tonight of a sort he could only observe and never participate in. Detective Sibanda fought the serial killer on the top of a speeding train and then plunged into the centre of a rampaging buffalo herd to rescue a murderer of no worth. The Ndebele said it best when celebrating courage and strength: *uyindoda*, he is a man.

'Come on, nothing more we can do here, let's get back to the train.'

'I'm sorry, sir.'

'For what?'

'Not stopping the train sooner, the communication cord wasn't working. Once I'd checked on PC Khumalo, I found Manhombo and he ran to the engine and the driver stopped as quickly as he could.'

'How is PC Khumalo?'

'She's fine, she'll need a few stitches, but she has come through okay. She was angry when I left her, always a good sign.'

They walked back towards the track. 'We'll collect the body in the morning ...' the detective was interrupted by a shrill scream that rent the night.

'Sir?' Ncube shuddered, glad the detective was close.

'Just a barn owl, Ncube,' he said, but no barn owl every made that call. Despite his murdering ways and the torture he inflicted, Sibanda hoped death came soon for the Black Sparrowhawk.

Epilogue – Sibanda

Barely from the train, Sibanda drove off before first light in the Santana. He wanted to pin point Richard Ngulube's body and phone it in so a squad with a body box could come from Detaba. He had to be the first one to find the killer to see if there was anything he could have done. The Sparrowhawk was better off dead. His survival and a court case might have helped Lois's and Kerry's family and friends with closure, but he had seen both the tosses, watched as Richard Ngulube was speared and gored and his intestines spilled mid-air, witnessed the glistening fascia in the moonlight.

He left Ncube back at Gubu catching up on sleep, trying to overcome the scarring female impersonation would leave him with, and later to mop up the details of the case. Although he suspected at the first opportunity he would be under Miss Daisy, rejoicing in her reprieve at the expense of the new vehicle. It seemed like the station was stuck for eternity with the old wreck.

But they would all bear the scars of this investigation. PC Khumalo was in hospital. Her wound wasn't serious and the square of skin Ngulube had tried to remove had been stitched back, but she needed complete rest, and time to come to terms with her near-death experience.

A couple of hours into his journey, as the sun cracked through the ice on the horizon, he spotted the vultures, parked the vehicle and followed his own tracks in. The Sparrowhawk lay on his side, one hand holding in his intestines, either ineffectively or else they had burst onto the earth after death, the other stretched into the sand. Richard Ngulube had been alive for a while at least, the evidence being in the copious amounts he bled, the thick, black swarms of flies buzzing and feasting on the dark wet patches. There were marks in the sand as though he tried to write something, impossible to decipher, was it an 'S' for sorry or for Sparrowhawk? Mfumu and his interview told him of his nickname. He loved the notoriety.

Sibanda checked around the corpse. The buffalo had milled for a while and jackals had tried to approach but Richard Ngulube had kept them at bay. Maybe they had reached his intestines, eaten some before he died, impossible to tell. It couldn't have been an easy or painless death, and given the severity of the injuries, he couldn't have survived longer than an hour or two at best. Medical help would never have got to him in time. Sibanda took a tarpaulin from the Santana, wrapped the body and flagged the spot.

He drove slowly back towards Gubu, stopping at the site of the first set of bones. Bits of yellow tape still clung to the sticks. Forensics hadn't bothered to clean up. He did it for them and then fossicked around for a time until he found what he was looking for. As he bumped along the dirt track running alongside the railway, another storm awaited in Gubu.

When he turned his phone back on a message came though from PC Tshuma, Forensics confirmed Lovemore Moyo died from peritonitis and septicemia caused by a punctured bowel, not torn or ripped from trauma but caused by a sharp implement and exacerbated by blows to the stomach probably with an *umgigo*, the traditional pounding stick with the distinctive rounded end. It was looking like the crime of a woman. They were the ones skilled with the *umgigo*, developing the power from young womanhood to bash down hard, pulping stubborn mealies to powder. The bruises and the peritonitis were all the hallmarks of a traditional crime, a sharpened bicycle spoke the usual implement, inserted via the anus to pierce the intestines while the victim was in a drunken stupor since the anus didn't have the sensitivity to register the fine caliber of wire. The *umgigo* blows ensured distribution of the poisons and speeded up the results.

Paul Johnson had recorded several instances of the crime. He called it 'a rural favourite to rival poison'. Lovemore's wife Gloria had to be the prime suspect; poor Lovemore was right to call her a witch, proof domestic violence wasn't always male against female. Exhumation of her two previous husbands may well show similar details. How many serial killers could Gubu come up with in a week? The paperwork was looking horrendous.

Back in Gubu he made straight for his house and Sister Martha's box. He looked at the photos again that he had so casually dismissed as family sentimentality, pocketed one of them and headed off to the convent of St Monica.

'Ah, the handsome policeman come to bewitch us all. How are you Detective Sibanda?' Sister Emmerentia was in good form.

'A lot has happened since we last spoke.' Sibanda handed the ivory egg containing the rosary beads to the nun.

She looked at the weathered piece in her hand, 'Sister Martha?'

'Yes, we have found her remains by the track.'

'What happened to her?'

'She was raped and murdered. This was found in her hand. She kept it close to her throughout her ordeal. She fell victim to a serial killer.'

The old nun bowed her head, clasping the cross around her neck. 'Poor, poor child,' she muttered some prayers. She shrank in her chair.

'Are you alright, Sister Emmerentia?'

'I'm asking for forgiveness, for the wrong I did Sister Martha. I thought she abandoned us all, her parents, the convent, but she was true to her faith until the end.'

Sibanda gave her a moment for reflection before handing her the photograph. 'You knew didn't you?'

The nun looked at the well-worn image of a baby, the photo curling at the corners, black and white and fading.

'Yes, I did. Arghyro gave birth at our mother house in Bulawayo some time before she came to us. The child was adopted.'

'Because the baby was of mixed race?'

'To be sure, the family felt it would bring shame that she slept with an African man, even ten years has made a difference to those views, but she was so young, too young, only fifteen. Don't you see, she wouldn't have had a life.'

Sibanda didn't comment on the obvious. What sort of a life did a nun have? 'We could have identified the bones as someone else's, a prostitute's. It would have helped if we'd had this information to begin with.'

'I'm sorry, detective. She was unsettled and I thought she had gone back to try and find her son. She talked about him to me sometimes, he was on her mind. When can we have the funeral?'

'It might take a while. We have some bones but there could be other body parts, her skin, elsewhere.'

Sister Emmerentia blanched, the walnut tan draining from her face. 'The murderer must have been a troubled soul, we'll pray for him, and a prostitute, you say?'

'Yes, but we haven't yet been able to trace her relatives.'

'Then she too will have our prayers and a place of rest here when you release her remains.'

'Thank you sister, and one last request. I take it you'll put the baby photo in the coffin when you bury Sister Martha?'

'Yes, I will, and these rosary beads that must have given her solace.' She glanced at the egg still in her hands.

'Can you add this as well,' he passed her the letter, 'it's from Nokhuthula Nxumalo.'

'The disabled girl?'

'Read it, Sister Martha was her saviour.'

'Then she goes to her grave a saint.'

Sister Emmerentia walked Sibanda to the door. 'If you ever need us, detective, we are here.'

As he drove away, his last view was of the old nun summoning the ever-gardening Sister Mary Bernadette to her office, his second last thought was of the unwanted, mixed-race child, neither Arthur nor Martha as the saying went, and then his attention turned to Berry. His heart did the usual flip whenever she came to mind but it was the issues and complications the future would bring and the baggage of his past that plagued him. Did they have enough love to sustain them through the cultural maze? That thought hounded him as he drove off to see Nokhuthula Nxumalo.

Epilogue – Wilhelmina Bawtry

The petite and pert young lady, in a very fashionable dress and carrying a carpet bag, stepped off the train into the blazing sunlight of Victoria Falls. A pretty hat enhanced her golden curls and kept the brutal sun from her flawless skin. Wilhelmina Bawtry, just seventeen, was still quivering inside but externally she had all the poise of wealth and class. After all, she'd seen it up close and could mimic it like a parrot. A porter took her bag and led her along with the other passengers to the hotel sitting within sight of the spray of the world's largest waterfall. There would be time in the next few days to fine-tune her story and to decide her future, a future that only a few hours ago seemed impossible. But with the wealth of jewels tucked away in the carpet bag and Monty out of her life, there would be no stopping her. It was strange how things turned out.

The blade came down hard and she would indeed bear a bruise for a week or two but the handle of the toilet chain saved her life. The blade stabbed downwards with murderous power, glanced off the blue and white porcelain and into Monty's thigh. He let go of her and gripped his leg in agony, the elephant head still planted in his flesh swaying to the motion of the train. Billy unravelled the chain from her waist in a flash and had it wrapped around Monty's throat. She blessed her life on Boggy Fen Farm and the chores that developed muscles and strength in her hands. She pulled so hard on the chain, long after Monty asphyxiated, that she nearly severed his head from his neck. Her hay-bale-hauling back made easy work of lifting Monty and dragging him through the open carriage door. She flung him into the wilderness. The sleeping passengers heard nothing. The last sight was of the elephant head dagger in his thigh, glimmering in the moonlight.

She washed carefully in the basin, pinned up her hair and changed into the dress Monty bought for her with the promise one day she could go back to being Wilhelmina, but for now, he said, he needed a son. It would make it easier for them both.

Wilhemina looked around at the remote surrounds of Victoria Falls, at the spray that rose into the air like billows of white fairy dust, at the pounding noise that echoed in her chest like the drums of excitement, and smelt possibility in the air. Bleak and deserted as it was she saw promise here, tourism was a new and untried industry but she was prepared to give it a go. Perhaps she would settle in this wild land where sun bleached the cares of the world from weary bones and gentle spray washed away memory. Yes, she would stay, take stock, reinvent herself and become a toff. Wilhelmina Bawtry would become Lady Montague Bingley, widow of the beloved late baron.